Dorinda's blue-green eyes glittered. "I have no call to go to Williamsburg, much less to visit you!"

"Ah, but you do, Dorinda." For a moment his steely gaze upon the golden-haired girl crouched in the big bed was wistful. "For 'tis really I who must give your hand in marriage, isn't it? Suppose I told him—"

"Oh, you wouldn't!" she gasped.

"Would I not?" His mocking smile flashed.

Dorinda's hands clenched the chemise she was holding up to hide her nakedness. Suddenly the delicate fabric seemed no protection at all from that bold gaze. "You are a blackmailer, sir!" she whispered.

"Call it what you will," he shrugged. "Tomorrow then at the White Hart?"

She would keep her appointment at the White Hart tomorrow, they both knew. For her, there was no way out...

Novels by
VALERIE SHERWOOD

THIS LOVING TORMENT

THESE GOLDEN PLEASURES

THIS TOWERING PASSION

HER SHINING SPLENDOR

BOLD BREATHLESS LOVE

RASH RECKLESS LOVE

WILD WILLFUL LOVE

RICH RADIANT LOVE

LOVELY LYING LIPS

BORN TO LOVE

Published by
WARNER BOOKS

Born To Love

Valerie Sherwood

WARNER BOOKS

A Warner Communications Company

WARNING

The reader is hereby specifically warned against using any of the unusual foods, cosmetics or medications mentioned herein. They are included only to give the authentic flavor of the times and readers are implored to seek the advice of a doctor before undertaking any "experiments" in their use. For example, the popular seventeenth-century cosmetic ceruse contained white lead, which is lethal; other concoctions of the day were often as bad and the "cures" used for illness were sometimes worse than the disease itself.

WARNER BOOKS EDITION

Copyright © 1984 by Valerie Sherwood
All rights reserved.

Cover design by Gene Light
Cover art by Elaine Duillo

Warner Books, Inc.
666 Fifth Avenue
New York, N.Y. 10103

 A Warner Communications Company

Printed in the United States of America

First Printing: July, 1984

10 9 8 7 6 5 4 3 2 1

Dedication

To that dazzling pair of ladies, Mopsy and Chow, our beautiful silky-furred calico cats, green-eyed, white-whiskered and elegant. Daughters of Fancy and Spice, they were born on my lap in the car near Fredericksburg, Virginia, on a hot summer day and hand fed by us when Spicy, their beautiful mother, was internally injured during the birth of her six kittens and could not feed them herself. Dainty fluffy feminine Lady Mops with her endearing ways and her big jewellike eyes and her endlessly expressive ears that she wears cocked or turned down or riding high like a hat to express her changing moods. Mopsy with her trim figure and her ready purr, always eager to rest her soft white chin on my arm and doze. Sleek exuberant Lady Chow, dancing with fairylike grace and astonishing all the cats with her remarkable leaps and twirls. Flirtatious Lady Chow with her beautiful face and luxurious soft markings and the glamorous dark-outlined eyes of a soubrette. Dear cats—Mopsy with your winning but temperamental ways and Chow, so sparkling yet so shy and afraid to give your heart, yet both of you as enchanting as any of my heroines—to you this book is affectionately dedicated.

Author's Note

The period from 1666 to 1717 was a magical time for England and its raw new American Colonies, a time of turbulence and change when armies marched, when fashion reached extravagant peaks, when fortunes were made and lost. This single novel encompasses four generations of dashing and courageous women who passed down—mother to daughter—the name "Dorinda." And although all the characters and events herein are entirely of my own invention, the story of the first Dorinda is actually based on fact. Although the real life lovers met quietly in the rustic beauty of the English countryside and not (as in my story) dramatically during the Great Fire of London, and the elegant country seat of which the real life impoverished (and astonished!) bride suddenly became mistress was on a scale even more lavish than the "Grantlands" of my story, the true story of these long ago lovers so touched my heart that I bring it to you so that you may live again with me this bittersweet fairy-tale romance of an English lord and a beautiful chambermaid.

Although for brevity's sake, I have somewhat hurried the pace of the terrible aftermath of the Monmouth Rebellion, glorious red-haired Rinda's story could indeed have happened in those tumultuous times when England's West Country rose in a desperate effort to place the handsome young

Stuart Duke of Monmouth upon the English throne. Like Civil Wars everywhere, it was a time when star-crossed lovers met and loved for a season, ever to be remembered out of time.

For my readers who love old houses as I do, let me say that I grew up among the old Colonial mansions of West Virginia's fabled South Branch Valley and Northern Virginia's famed Shenandoah Valley, some of the most notable of the former's mansions having been built by my own ancestors, and I often spent summer vacations at my Aunt Kitty's home near Winchester before whose gray limestone walls stands a bronze marker commemorating the "oldest house in Northern Virginia." Colonial times seem very real to me—after all I spent my youth surrounded by places and things my own pre-Revolutionary ancestors had known and loved. It is therefore with loving care that I have described real Virginia houses:

"Haverleigh Plantation," the Ramsay seat with its majestic banks of chimneys and its lovely rooftop promenade, is of course beautiful "Stratford Hall," magically transported in my story from the Rappahannock to the James—although I could not resist surrounding "Haverleigh" with the enchanting gardens of famous "Brandon" on the James.

"Riddlewood," where mysterious events take place in my tale, recalls ancient "Toddsbury," which I have borrowed from the Chesapeake country's Gloucester County and swept from the North River to the banks of the James—although regrettably in my story the house is partially destroyed by fire!

And the Claridge home where my heroine attends her first ball in Virginia and dances with the fictitious "Governor Newbold" will be recognized by my readers as being outwardly the Ludwell-Paradise house of Williamsburg, although I have changed the interior to suit my story. (And I might add that amorous Lucy Claridge, who occupies the house in my story, is not nearly so colorful as the Lucy Paradise who lived in it some hundred years later—that same Lucy Paradise who scandalized London society by splashing an annoying gentleman with boiling water from her tea urn! Back in Williamsburg she had her coach taken apart and reassembled indoors and there regally entertained her visitors, being rolled up and down the hall by servants! Poor Lucy was an original, but it must have been somewhat of a relief to her neighbors when she was eventually committed to the state asylum. The house remains.)

As for "Merryvale Manor," which my heroine tries so desperately to inherit, it is really "River Edge" on the Old Indian Trail Road in Charles City County, whose original ten thousand acres once stretched along the James from Gunn's Run to Herring Creek. Although the early records were burned in the Civil War, the house is believed to have been standing at the time of my story. Both house and setting are portrayed as accurately as possible and although I cannot vouch for the color of its interior paint in that long ago day (I have used typical Williamsburg colors), or for the musk roses in its gardens, it is logical to believe that this bit of old England, brought over as roots so lovingly by the early settlers, should have been firmly rooted and blooming when the fourth Dorinda picked them.

And although Colonial Williamsburg was roughly as I have described it, the White Hart, where the fourth Dorinda came to grief but later triumphed, is a blend of two famous Williamsburg landmarks—Marot's Ordinary and the fabled Raleigh Tavern. (Even so I could not resist taking the reader to dinner at the actual Raleigh Tavern, for my hero—like a later patron, George Washington—chose to stay elsewhere but preferred to dine at the Raleigh.)

And I must tell the reader that most of this novel is occupied by the wild saga of Dorinda the Fourth, who lived out the last line of an old maxim I so often heard chanted in my childhood:

> *It takes one generation to make it,*
> *One generation to lose it,*
> *One generation to talk about it—*
> *And one to make it again!*

But it was too tempting to recount as well the lives and tumultuous love stories of those three brave and lovely women who had gone before and whose sterling graces and human frailties shaped the destiny of that fourth Dorinda. And so this novel will sweep you from the Great Fire of London to storied Dorset and the wild times of the Monmouth Rebellion—and in the story of my main heroine, lovely Dorinda the Fourth, across the seas to Colonial Williamsburg and Philadelphia.

I invite my readers to ride with me down the lanes and along the cliffs of Dorset where the seas will ever break and murmur over the legend of Dorinda the First and her predestined lover. Sail with me the wine-dark seas to the raw young American Colonies and into the world of romance and adventure that awaits you as beautiful young Dorinda the Fourth clasps her dangerous lover and defies the world!

Perhaps I can best sum it up in verse:

While the restless moments pass,
Let us pause and drain a glass
That is lifted to the loves of yesterday!
Lovers old and lovers new, lovers faithless, lovers
*   true*
Will live again their reckless lives today!

Valerie Sherwood

Contents

It takes one generation to make it,
One generation to lose it,
One generation to talk about it—
And one to make it again!

One Generation to Make It!

BOOK I

Angel Face

Life seems a shining ribbon
Leading on to joy—and more
When first you kiss your lover
On youth's sweet golden shore!

PART ONE

Angel from the Ashes

The Night of the Great Fire
LONDON, ENGLAND
September 1666

Chapter 1

In her attic room Dorinda Wynne, tired out from
polishing all of the household's knives and spoons—
even the pewter ones—under the fierce supervision of
Barnes the housekeeper, had fallen asleep exhausted
and was dreaming her usual impossible (but highly
satisfying) dream of finding a lover with a coach and
six. As noise drifted into her consciousness, she moaned
softly in protest and with a sleepy gesture pushed away
a lock of the fine shimmering pale hair that silvered out
in a great plume over her straw-filled pillow. And then
her handsome dream lover and his gilded coach were
snatched abruptly away as the howls from downstairs
fought their way into her dream world and woke her
with a start.

"Fire!" someone from downstairs was screaming. The
word reached Dorinda thinly through the rafters from
below. "Fire!"

That galvanized young Dorinda into action. "Binnie!"
she cried as she started to her feet, for she must alert
the other chambermaid who shared these cramped
cubbyholes at the top of the house. "Binnie, wake up!"

When there was no answer, she plunged for her

4

clothes, finding them without benefit of candle. Her thin white linen chemise she had worn modestly to bed, even though it was a hot night when most (including the master and mistress, Binnie had reported, giggling) slept naked. Now she groped for her worn gray linen kirtle and got it around her, fastened it at the waist. In panic, she realized that the murkiness at the tiny window wasn't just the greasy smear left by sea coal and pea soup fogs, but new smoke curling in around the panes. Terrified at the thought of being trapped up here and burned alive, Dorinda dived into her shoes. With one more sharp bleat of "Binnie!" she snatched up her thin black linen corselet-type bodice that emphasized rather than hid her rounded young breasts. She was trying frantically to lace it as she ran down the wooden staircase.

At the second floor landing she was jostled by Banks the footman and for the first time at close quarters he failed to give her a surreptitious pinch—which showed the extent of his fright. At the bottom of the stairs she almost collided with Barnes the housekeeper, burdened by a heavy rosewood chest which Dorinda knew contained most of the cutlery she had spent the long hours before bedtime polishing. Around her the large low-ceilinged room was a beehive of activity and Binnie, rather fetchingly dressed with her hair laced with bright ribands (she must have sneaked out again for a tryst with the bootmaker's apprentice across the street), caught sight of her and called out cheerfully, "Did you know London Bridge has burned down and all the wharves are aflame?"

Before Dorinda could fully take that in, Barnes thrust the rosewood chest into her arms. "Here, wench, be careful of this!"

"Where do I take it?" gasped Dorinda, her slight frame almost sagging beneath the weight.

"I know not," was the distracted answer. "All London's burning!" Barnes turned away as her employer gave a shriek, giving Dorinda a view of Mistress Watley in a hastily donned gown. Mistress Watley had just peeled off the chicken-skin gloves she wore at night to make her hands soft and now she shrieked again as a second expensive delftware plate slipped from her greasy fingers and shattered upon the flagstone floor.

"Oh, Barnes, get that up!" she cried, her voice thin and high from hysteria. "It will cut our feet!"

"Never mind cutting our feet!" roared her excited husband from behind her. "We've got to save what furnishings we can! Yates, see about getting that wagon from the Willises down the street!" And an unintelligible yelp from Yates outside.

Dorinda stood helplessly clutching the rosewood chest. Around her fragile form swirled snatches of shouted conversation: Binnie's excited, "They do say the waterwheel by the bridge has burned and there won't be no water to fight the fire!" And Mistress Watley's moan of "My petticoats! Oh, we must save my petticoats!" (For petticoats were made of the richest stuffs and were very valuable.) And her husband, his wig on sideways and his shirt on backwards—he who never so much as lifted a stick of kindling to make a fire—groaning and straining as he and Banks tried to drag a great cupboard into the street and instead knocked it over with a great crashing of cups and plates from within.

"My china! You've broken my china!" wailed Mistress Watley. And Dorinda, aware that she must not just stand there, picked her way over broken glass and crockery, edged by the fallen cupboard which was half-blocking the door, and made her way into the narrow street.

There was an acrid smell of smoke everywhere and from the direction of the waterfront a murky red glow lit up the sky. People were running wildly past her in every direction, dragging furniture, children, framed pictures, pets—and even one old lady in a nightcap clawed at a mattress that she was hauling painfully over the cobbles. Looking up, Dorinda realized where those tendrils of smoke she had seen at her attic window had come from. An errant spark, catapulted by one of the long tongues of flame rising now ominously from the direction of the waterfront, had landed on the roof shingles and, fanned by the strong east wind, had set the house alight. It was the only house on fire on either side of the narrow street so far as she could see, but the searing heat the wind was bringing and the roar of the flames which could be heard even from here, promised that there would soon be more.

Dorinda, with no idea where to go, stumbled forward with her burden, glad for once that this outgrown skirt was short enough not to trip her. She plunged down the street away from the waterfront and its licking flames. Candles were burning in the overhanging half-timbered houses, some of which had stood since medieval times. Doors and windows stood open and people were rushing about, dragging their goods and chattels into the street. A few carts were being loaded but it seemed unlikely that the Watleys on such a night would be able to borrow a wagon from anyone, not even their best friends the Willises, who would be needing their cart to rescue their own goods.

"Them flames is leaping over the houses!" shouted a thin lad to someone in an upstairs window as he charged past her. "Best look to yourself, Sudie!"

His answer was a hysterical, "Lud, ha' mercy!" and a crash as the stocky woman in the upstairs window dropped a washbowl upon the cobbles.

Dorinda ran on.

Unfamiliar with London—she had only been here a week—Dorinda had no idea where to go to elude the onrushing flames. At a cross street she paused and looked about her in fright. From both right and left came a warning red glow. (How the Watleys, who had congratulated themselves on being so conveniently near the fish markets, must be regretting their nearness to the burning Thames waterfront!) Up ahead the street writhed and turned, Dorinda could not see what lay ahead. Could it be that she was running directly into the fire?

As she stood poised in panic, she heard the unmistakable sounds of men fighting and turned to see three men in the mouth of a nearby alley trying to wrestle a fourth to the ground.

"Get his purse!" cried one burly fellow whose back was to her, and there was a gasp of pain as someone struck the victim—who looked, as best she could see in this light, to be a gentleman—in the midsection.

Dorinda took in the scene in an instant. She did not hesitate. Old Nurse, when she was alive, had warned her of London footpads and not to go out at night alone if ever she visited London. Now Old Nurse was dead and Dorinda had come down from the North Country looking for Old Nurse's sister whose name Old Nurse had gasped out on her deathbed—and found her dead too of the Great Plague which had ravaged the city only last year and emptied so many of the houses, some of which around her were still dark and unoccupied. But the gentleman's broken-plumed hat lay almost at her feet where it had fallen when he was attacked and Dorinda's lightsome dreams of a lover with a coach and six gave wings to what must always seem to be in retrospect sheer madness.

"Here's aid, sir!" she cried recklessly and on the instant charged with the heavy chest in her arms at that burly back, sending the fallen gentleman's most immediate attacker sideways to the cobbles with the combined weight. Her own momentum carried her forward, the chest catapulted from her arms, and she tumbled in a wild tangle of dainty bare legs and white ruffled petticoat atop the fallen gentleman.

There was an angry howl from the man she had sent sprawling and Dorinda felt a moment of stabbing fear that they would all be on her instantly, pummeling the life out of her for daring to interrupt their wicked design. But the heavy rosewood chest proved a godsend. It broke open, raining spoons and knives with careless abandon about the cobbles. At the sight of so much silver the three footpads with yelps of joy abandoned their gasping victim, still doubled up from a blow that had knocked the wind out of him, and turned their attention to scooping up the loot.

The fallen gentleman, who seemed to have a great wealth of dark russet hair that spilled down over a gold-braided brocade coat that looked to be wine red in this uncertain light, made a convulsive movement toward his sword and a look of chagrin spread over his features as he found he had none. His swift glance took in the clawing cutthroats, snatching at the silver cutlery with dirty hands—and then the bright red glow just above the houses at each end of the alley.

Dorinda, just gaining her knees and with her heart thumping in her chest, guessed it was a hard decision for him to make—for he gave the scene a last look of wild regret as he regained his feet, seeming to tower over her. She felt a bitter disappointment that he had no sword—undoubtedly having lost it in the unequal battle when he was surprised in the alley—but at least he had presence.

He did not waste words which would alert the rapt trio that their prey was escaping. His strong fingers lifted Dorinda to her feet. Clutching her hand, he led her on a mad dash away from the three men scrabbling on their knees as they snatched up silver cutlery from the cobbles.

There was a time to fight and a time to run, Dorinda knew, but she still felt responsible for the silver. "The chest!" she cried, looking back.

"—will not matter," he finished for her, and now she could see that behind them the red glow that she had observed from both ends of the street had suddenly joined in an overarching flame as the wind-driven fire swept through the narrow alley. There were hoarse shrieks that could have come from the clawing footpads and then one of them ran from the alley with his clothes on fire and plunged through an open doorway into blackness.

Dorinda, who had never seen violent death before, felt sick for a moment and wavered on her feet.

"Don't faint," grated the man beside her. He seemed very cool, she thought, in this mad world London had turned into. She looked up and found comfort in his strong determined face with its hard cheekbones and flat planes, in the grim narrow line of his mouth. He looked like a man who could get you through it—if anybody could!

"But 'tis not my silver," she wailed. "I was entrusted with it—"

"'Twill be nobody's silver soon," snapped the man she had just rescued and who was now rescuing her. "We must hurry or we'll be trapped!" This as she paused and hopped on one foot as she shook an errant pebble from her shoe. "This whole end of town's going up like tinder and we'll be lucky if we're not cut off by these confounded overlapping houses!"

In horror Dorinda wondered if the Watleys, lingering to pile up their possessions in the street, had been cut off—then she decided they had not. They knew the area like the back of their hands—they were not like her, a North Country lass who, Binnie often taunted, got lost every time she was out of sight of the house!

At least the determined gentleman dragging her along seemed to know where he was going. Breathless, Dorinda was aware even through her fright that he cut a striking figure in his wine red coat and dark gray trousers. A man ran by carrying a torch to light the way for a careening coach and she realized suddenly that his gold braid was tarnished and that the wine red coat that fit those broad shoulders so well was not only dirty from tumbling in the street but looked well worn—as did the trousers that encased his long striding legs. A very striking gentleman he was indeed with his wealth of luxuriant russet hair bared to the night, for he had snatched up his plumed hat with his free hand and was carrying it as he strode along. A down-at-the-heel gentleman, one who had fallen upon hard times, she surmised, for all his air of command. A rover probably, who had acquired his polish in gaming halls. Old Nurse had warned her about *them* too.

Dorinda, studying him covertly as she panted along beside him, was most attracted.

Her gaze fell away as the gentleman, whose clear gray eyes had been studying every alley intently as his big head swung about, gave her a preoccupied look. She felt suddenly shy that he should look down and find her studying him so boldly.

"Are you a Londoner, sir?" she gasped, her breath sobbing in her throat from running so hard. She was hoping he would tell her he'd grown up here.

"Arrived last night," was his cryptic answer. "And woke to find my inn and the whole street on fire. Here, the way looks clearer in this direction." He was dragging her along by the hand as he spoke and Dorinda, with her heart pounding, was finding it hard to keep up with him. But his instinct was sure and the smoke which drifted over the city seemed thinner here. He slowed his pace. "I thank you for saving my life, mistress," he said with a keen look down at her. "Those three would have done for me—once they'd taken my purse."

"Oh, did they get it, sir?" gasped Dorinda, forgetting the loss of the silver in this new concern for her rescuer.

"No, they didn't, thanks to you. You risked your life for me. Why?"

The question, suddenly shot at her, caused her confusion to peak. How could she tell him it was all part of a quixotic mix-up with dream lovers and coaches and

six and plumed hats that had caused her rash intervention? "It was—only what I should have done, sir," she
said shyly.

His voice softened and some of the bitterness left his
face. "I shouldn't think so," he said gently. "Frail young
girls aren't supposed to protect full grown men. It's
usually the other way around. What's your name?"

"Dorinda Wynne, sir."

"I'm Grantland Meredith." He smiled down at her
with a fine flash of white teeth. It occurred to her that
Grantland Meredith had a face made for smiling but
that most of the time his mouth had an ironic expression verging on bitterness. She looked quickly away lest
he note that she was studying him.

"Well, Mistress Dorinda," he said cheerfully. "We'll
take ourselves to some safer place than this. 'Tis like
being inside the chimney when the fire's being kindled
below!" He nodded at the sparks which were even now
pursuing them and falling on the rooftops nearby. Two
of those sparks set fire as they watched to the tinder-
dry wood for it had been a summer of drought. Those
flames, she knew, would soon consume the roofs.

With a frightened look at the igniting houses and the
red glow that seemed to be following them vindictively,
Dorinda stumbled along beside Grantland Meredith,
thankful for a guide—newcomer though he might be—
through the tangled maze of London's streets.

Now they were in a densely populated area and had
to take shelter from the careening wagons, the rearing
horses, the people running this way and that carrying
their possessions in their arms with their families streaming behind them. "'Tis war, the Frenchies did it!"
someone bawled. "'Tis the French who've fired the
city!" And beside them a sensible-looking man, soberly
garbed, brushed by, crying, "For God's sake, let me
through. The nation's archives are in the White Tower
with ammunition packed solidly above it. 'Twill blow up
half London if it ignites!"

In the distance Dorinda could see the White Tower and she cowered against her tall companion, who had paused a moment in the din to ask directions from this sensible fellow who, even as he struggled to get through the crowd, shouted a reply.

"It would seem St. Paul's is considered the safest place," Grantland reported. "Come, let's see if we can reach St. Paul's."

They found St. Paul's Cathedral a beehive of activity. It seemed that all the booksellers in London were rushing distractedly in and out, storing their precious and flammable volumes inside the huge stone building with its heavy leaden roof. St. Paul's had long been a London landmark, its mighty bulk dwarfing the buildings around it just as the mighty wooden Guildhall dwarfed everything on the waterfront.

Dragged along, Dorinda took an uneven step. She was flagging now. She had had a hard day and an even harder night. Sensing that, her companion slowed to a halt.

"Ye must rest," he observed. And when she would have protested, he cut off her protests with, "If you collapse, I'll have to carry you."

Dorinda was suitably silenced. She almost fell against the wall of a nearby building in her fatigue and gave him a grateful smile. She found that her legs were trembling and her heart fluttering in a warning way.

Grantland, aware of her distress and the exceeding pallor of her lovely face, frowned. "We'll stay here till you're rested," he said shortly and found her a doorway where she could sit down.

They managed to buy some food from a vendor who had set up cheerfully in the street, as if he had been ready all along for just such an emergency, and was hawking his hot cross buns as serenely as if the milling crowd about him were revelers at some picnic instead of panicked citizens struggling to rescue their goods. Some of Dorinda's color came back and she felt a little better, but Grantland still did not like the way she looked—as if she might faint, he thought. So his father had looked the night he died.

Getting any kind of conveyance was hopeless. Accommodations were nowhere to be found and Meredith knew the dark alleys would be full of footpads and cutpurses and looters roaming the helpless city and pouncing on anyone they could catch. The girl still looked too ill to run if they were attacked.

"I wish you had your sword," she said wistfully and Grantland gave a start.

"How do you know I own one?" he demanded.

"Because I saw you reach for it back there."

"Ah—so you saw that?"

She nodded tiredly. "And now I see you've no scabbard. I suppose you lost them both back there?"

"Not in the alley—at the inn where I was staying," he sighed. "I woke with the inn ablaze, the place full of black smoke. I was hard put to help the people in the next room to get out. When I realized I'd left my sword, the fire was too hot to go back!"

Dorinda nodded solemnly. Such were the ways of fires. For a moment her small hand rested comfortingly on his brocade sleeve. It was like a bird's wing, he thought, feather light.

"We'll rest here a bit longer." Grantland let his long frame down beside her in the doorway. Dorinda gave him a sweet exhausted smile and fell instantly asleep, her slight body slumping against him. He put a protective arm about her and she stirred slightly and murmured in her sleep, then cuddled up against him as trustingly as a child.

The last woman he had cradled so in his arms—raven-haired, fiery Lady Polly Edgecombe—had sighed from boredom. She had been eager to get back to the dancing despite the fact that it was his last night in Dorset. Little she cared!

He thought suddenly of the betrothal ring he had

given Lady Polly and automatically studied the hands of the girl whose soft body fitted so well against his own hard form. They were innocent of any rings.

Lady Polly's hand had sported not only *his* betrothal ring but at various times before that several others, and her ivory throat and shell-like ears glittered with brilliants no harder than her gold-green eyes that seemed to be perpetually measuring her latest betrothed—and finding him wanting.

They had quarreled in Dorset when he had caught her kissing Charles. She had flung his ring into his face and he had stalked off cursing the day he'd met her and headed for London. But all the way here that ring—like Lady Polly's mocking smile—had haunted him. For it was the third time in six months that she had thrown her betrothal ring at him. And every time before he had proffered it again—and every time before Lady Polly's gold-green eyes had flashed in triumph and she had bestowed on him a wanton's kiss that heated him to sizzling and slipped the ring contentedly back on her finger.

Not this time! This time he had left his raven-haired lady in Dorset and set out for London intending to study law at Gray's Inn at the Inns of Court and to forget all about the woman who had set his heart afire every time he looked at her.

Now, brooding about it, he looked down at the limp feminine burden leaning against his chest, a servant girl by her clothes, who had been entrusted with the family silver and come to grief. His gaze on the tumbled flaxen head was perplexed. All his life he had been assured that he would find nothing but perfidy in London and that no London wench was to be trusted, they were all full of guile. But it seemed that it was a West Country lady with slim swaying hips and a mocking smile who had betrayed him while this pale chance-found waif was certainly guileless. Moreover, she had saved his life at great danger to her own and asked nothing at all in return! How defenseless she looked in her worn gray kirtle... One sleeve of her chemise had been ripped half off by a passing cart as they struggled through the crowded streets. Her great mass of fair hair tumbled over a slim bare shoulder and her face was smudged with soot from the smoky debris-filled air. He supposed he looked as bad himself. Certainly his trousers were in sad shape, grimy with soot and dirt from the cobbles where he had fallen when the footpads surrounded him.

He must get this tired child out of here, he told himself, goaded by the sweet warm pressure of her body in the crook of his arm. She was looking to him for help, and he would take her wherever she wanted to go. He owed her that much.

Sitting there crouched in the doorway during a night lit with the evil orange-red glow of the fire and punctuated by the frightened neighing of horses, the creaking of overloaded carts, the swearing of their drivers, the frantic barking of dogs, the shouts of people running hither and thither in wild confusion, he realized there was no hope of finding the girl's people, wherever they were. The city was completely disorganized. No one seemed to know where anyone else was. He could hear mothers frantically calling their children, wives wailing for their husbands, husbands bawling their wives' names as families sought each other.

His jaw hardened as he heard from passersby how the irresolute Lord Mayor had made light of the fire, insisting scathingly that "a woman could piss it out!" And that amid reports of how the docks were burning, the Thames a sea of small boats filled with refugees, the fire spreading unchecked!

"This madness will surely cease," Grantland Meredith told Dorinda when, about to drop off in spite of himself and only too well aware that his purse contained gold, he reluctantly waked her. "Keep watch for me for half an hour and don't worry. They'll surely get the fire under control—even in a city as mismanaged as this one, someone will rise up and take command and keep the city from burning down!"

But by the time Dorinda waked him—and she let him sleep out of compassion for she could see the lines of fatigue etched into his strong face—they were deep into Monday, the Second Day of the Great Fire.

Grantland Meredith awoke to a sky brilliant with leaping flames and learned from Dorinda that the Poultry and all of Cornhill were afire and that the flames were even now licking at the entrance of Cheapside. "'Tis said a mile of riverfront has been consumed," she told him excitedly.

They drifted here and there through the day, vainly seeking shelter, not sure where to go next. That night was as bright as day as a halo of flame rose above the doomed city.

But Monday night did offer some respite to the exhausted pair. That night they commandeered quarters in a house abandoned by its terrified owners who had left, forgetting to lock it, and Dorinda slept in a bed that had been abandoned downstairs because there was no room for it on the departing cart, while Grantland slept fitfully, guarding the door with the length of his long body.

Tuesday morning found the mighty Guildhall burning. The Custom House and the Royal Exchange fell victim to the flames as well. And that night the magnificent Gothic cathedral of St. Paul's, in whose shadow they had first sought shelter, caught fire and burned so hot that its huge stones exploded like cannon balls, sending out projectiles in all directions, and a river of molten lead from its enormous roof poured down the street like a stream of lava from some volcano. The booksellers of London had chosen the wrong spot to store their volumes.

Word reached Dorinda and Grantland that the Duke of York on orders from the King had taken over from the Lord Mayor and had ordered out demolition squads. From here and there came the sound of deafening explosions as buildings were demolished by gunpowder to make firebreaks to halt the march of the steadily advancing flames.

" 'Tis a vision of hell," muttered Grantland Meredith, looking at the blackened waterfront with its backdrop of roaring flames, led by those two great landmarks of St. Paul's and the ancient Guildhall, both of them fiery pyres that seemed to reach up to heaven. By now they were drifting on the Thames in a small boat, along with many others of the population, all of whom seemed to have taken to the water in an effort to avoid the searing heat from the fire. Before them the evil black pall of smoke ruptured by sullen red flashes did indeed lend a demonic splendor to the scene.

He looked down at the girl, saw that her blue eyes, turned tawny by the fire's reflection, were fixed in horror on the sight of London burning.

"Dorinda," he said gently. "We can't stay here. Where would you like to go?"

"I don't know," she faltered, giving him an anxious look. Indeed her thoughts had been occupied with staying alive another minute, another hour, ever since she had met him.

"Are ye betrothed?" he asked suddenly, for even without a ring she could already have pledged her troth. He wondered if somewhere there was a sturdy fellow to whom he should turn her over.

She flushed, unseen against the fiery backdrop that turned both their faces coppery red and her pale hair a brilliant orange.

"No," she said shyly.

"And have ye any family?" he pursued.

"No, there's no one."

Another boat barked up against theirs and the boatman cried out sharply, "Careful there!" But the contact had thrown Dorinda against Grantland and her soft breasts were crushed momentarily against his hard chest as she tried to steady herself.

In that moment Grantland Meredith decided not to study law, as had been his intention, in this scorched charred city, nor indeed to stay in London at all.

That decision made him feel abruptly lighthearted. He would guide this girl to his native West Country where fires—even consuming ones—were on a smaller scale.

"Dorinda," he said firmly. "We're going to get ourselves out of this. Do you feel up to a long walk?"

And when she nodded, he began to row, to row with determination, making his way somehow through the floating parties of aimless watchers, their boats dark spots on the river's broad breast which reflected the demonic redness of the flames.

And as he rowed, he felt better. He was going home!

THE ROAD TO THE WEST COUNTRY, ENGLAND
September 1666

Chapter 2

For four days London burned, but the fourth day was a dwindling day and by the fifth only isolated fires were burning. The mighty conflagration had consumed over thirteen thousand houses and left half the city homeless. In all, nearly three hundred and forty acres had been charred to ashes, burned over by the fire.

London would pick itself up, of course. It did, in fact, and a city of brick and stone rose from the ashes of the noble old wooden structures, but neither Dorinda Wynne nor Grantland Meredith were there to see it. They had left their boat by the waterside and had begun their long walk through a smoke-filled countryside, wondering if the stench of burning would ever leave their nostrils.

They found the countryside full of refugees who jammed the roads with their horses, their carts, and their baggage. They marched among them, heading west. When they crossed a stream they left the road and followed it up to a little waterfall. There they took off their outer clothing and washed it in the stream. Then they hung that clothing on the overhanging branches of the trees to dry and splashed happily in the water—Grantland in his small clothes and Dorinda in her torn chemise.

"Br-r-r, it's cold," muttered Grantland, who was used to the warmer waters of Lyme.

"Not too cold," said Dorinda critically, for she was used to the icy streams of Yorkshire, running down out of the snow.

"Indeed?" Playfully he ducked her under and she retaliated by striking at the back of his knees and pulling him under with her.

They surfaced laughing, and he realized, with her now clean face, her blue eyes shining and water dripping from her perfect nose and chin and running in rivulets down her peachbloom cheeks, how very lovely she was. And the picture of Lady Polly dimmed slightly in his mind.

"You have a lovely name—Dorinda." He was lifting her wet hair from her shoulders as he spoke. "I hereby christen you Queen of the Forest Glade!" He scooped up a handful of water and let it trickle over her laughing face.

For a moment, looking at his water sprite with her long wet fair hair, Grantland felt she was his very own creation. It would have been tempting to linger in that pool through the long afternoon.

"Come on," he sighed. "We've bathed long enough if we're to find an inn before dusk."

Dorinda followed him out of the water, bewailing the fact that they had no soap. If he had not noticed before, he would have been struck then with what a dainty figure she had with her small-boned delicacy, for the thin wet fabric of her chemise stuck to her as she emerged dripping from the water, as if she were naked. He watched her, smiling, as she slipped her bare feet into her shoes.

"And a pretty sight ye are," drawled a coarse voice from behind them. "Now if ye'll just oblige us by taking off that chemise, ye'll be prettier yet!"

Meredith whirled to see a pair of hulking bullies standing there grinning at them. And the nearest had a knife stuck in his belt.

It was a bad moment, but Meredith did not wait to discover how bad it could get. He swung on the nearest one and Dorinda, who had a way of rising to the occasion, rose to the occasion now.

Without warning, she seized her wet kirtle, which dangled invitingly from the nearest branch, and threw it over the other one's head. It met him like a slap in the face. Before he could fight free of the wet clinging material, she did what Binnie had always told her she should do if she was out late and someone leaped from an alley and tried to grab her—she kicked him violently in the groin. He doubled up and buckled to his knees with a howl just as Meredith, who had caught a blow on the jaw, landed rolling at her feet. His assailant made a dive for Dorinda, who had turned to run, and caught her by the ankle, but the fallen Meredith lifted a foot and tripped him up neatly, sending him with a yell headfirst into the stream. He came up with a knife glittering in his right hand and Meredith grabbed Dorinda with one hand and his boots and wet clothing with the other.

"Let's get out of here," he muttered and led the plunge into the wild undergrowth, holding out a long arm to keep the branches from snapping back into her face. Dorinda, tearing along breathlessly behind him, found that it was a real maze in there and was glad to have him taking the brunt of the stubborn underbrush that blocked their way, resisting passage. He paused only to tug on his boots and then rushed on.

At the entrance to a little clearing he checked and held up a hand. Dorinda tried to quiet her sobbing gasps and cocked her head as he did to listen. Around them were only the sounds of the woodland, above them an untroubled sky and shimmering leaves.

"We can rest here," he said, pulling her down beside

him. He laughed ruefully. "Faith, we look worse than we did when we started!" For now they had countless scrapes and scratches from the thorns and tree branches they had pushed through.

They lay stretched out on the grass, panting, under the rustling September leaves that patterned the sky above them with the shadowed colors of early fall.

After a time when the silence was broken only by the lazy buzzing of bees and the chirping of crickets and the scurrying sound of a pair of squirrels chasing each other through the branches overhead, Meredith rose on an elbow. He looked down at her anxiously for she was very pale again.

Dorinda lay on her back, determined to ignore that familiar flutter in her chest. Her head was pillowed on one arm and she smiled up at him in the heat of the waning afternoon. She had never been so happy. London where she had slaved, and Yorkshire where she was scorned, had vanished, retreated into the past on the arrival of this masterful stranger.

She had very trusting eyes, he thought. Dusty blue, the color of distant hills, endlessly beckoning.

"I'm glad you didn't have to kill him," she said softly.

Grantland had sorely doubted his ability to dispose of the brute with the knife. The shock of the fellow's fist had knocked him pretty well endwise. Had he had his sword, that would have been another matter, for he was skillful with the blade. But Dorinda's calm belief that he would have won out even against overwhelming odds made his spirits abruptly soar. His inner self, badly shaken by Lady Polly's defection, arose and dusted itself off. He began to feel himself a man of some worth. At that moment he noticed a tiny scratch on the inviting bare shoulder that rose through her long drifting fair hair—and of a sudden he felt a great and encompassing tenderness toward this chance-met maid with whom he had been through so much, shared so much.

Impulsively he bent his head and his lips brushed the

small scratch caressingly. "I'm the cause of that," he sighed. "I should have kept better watch."

"Nonsense," she said sensibly. "How could you? I had just pulled you under and you still had water in your ears! You couldn't be expected to hear every leaf crunch in the forest!"

She was making excuses for him! It felt wonderfully good. Lady Polly had never made excuses for him. Besotted with love for her as he had been, he had not realized that. Polly was at all times critical of him: *Grantland, you near tripped me up in the dance—can't you do something about your feet?* Or, about a new coat of which he was vastly proud, *Grantland, that coat is far too out of style—couldn't you send it back to your tailor and have the sleeves changed?* Or, when he had felt himself to have carried off an evening rather well, *You must have noticed, Grantland, that nobody was laughing at your jokes. Charles didn't laugh. Charles knows all the latest jokes from London— everything the Court is laughing at.* Polly Edgecombe had always cut him down. He could never quite please her. Charles, Lord Chell, who had spent two seasons in London, was the mirror to which she held him up— and always Grantland Meredith came in second.

Well, he had left the field to Charles!

He smiled down now at this pretty waif he had snatched from the burning city. She was blushing and her soft lips were parted. She obviously expected him to kiss those lips.

A vision of Lady Polly, beautiful, imperious, with a tone of command that froze footmen and suitors alike, rose up to haunt him. It seemed to Grantland in that moment that Lady Polly in the flesh had somehow stepped between them.

"Well, I suppose we'd best be on our way," he said, springing up in dutiful response to that angry-faced vision. He removed his boots and began to pull his still damp trousers over his smallclothes. It was a difficult task.

He looked up to see consternation on Dorinda's pretty face.

"I've left my kirtle behind!" she wailed. "And my blue bodice! I can't go about like this!" She indicated her thin chemise which the sun and wind had dried and which billowed prettily about her, its plain cotton ruffle seeming to foam around her delicate ankles.

It was Grantland Meredith's opinion that she could hardly look better—not unless she took it off, but he saw at once the gravity of the situation.

"We must go back for them," she insisted.

Grantland was of the opinion that to go back might be to invite far worse than the loss of a kirtle and bodice. Both those oversize renegades back there would undoubtedly be raging over having been overcome by a lighter fellow and a slip of a wench. They might well be waiting, assuming she'd come back for her clothes. And he, without a sword to defend her, might very well come off second best! And what would happen to her then?

"We'll get you other clothes," he promised her gravely.

Only slightly mollified, Dorinda followed him through these unknown woods. It was one thing to flee for one's life in wet undergarments but quite another to wander around in dry ones! She was half of a mind to go back and get her clothing.

Grantland sensed that and prudently kept hold of her hand as he led the way beneath oak and willow into the dusk.

The moon was up when they found a tiny cottage nestled between a small hayfield and a pasture. Here there were no refugees from charred and smouldering London, here was only a rotund farmer and his pink-cheeked wife and a round half dozen children of stairstep sizes who peered bright-eyed at this pair of rovers arrived with the dark.

"We were set upon by brigands," explained Grantland cheerfully. "And the lady needs a kirtle and bodice. We could also do with supper and a night's lodging." He smiled his winning smile. "I'll pay in gold."

The farmer's wife straightened up at that and exchanged glances with her husband. "I've an old black linen bodice I wore when my waist was as small as hers," she exclaimed. "And I've been making myself a new kirtle. I could cut it down to fit her."

She held up a coarse home-dyed linen garment of a soft shade of pumpkin and Dorinda pounced on it with relief. "See how splendid I am?" she laughed when, after a reviving dinner of pigeon pie and parsnips and turnips, washed down by good country cider, she pirouetted before him in the loft above the small barn, where they were to spend the night.

Grantland was lying at his ease in the hay, thinking how trim her tiny waist was in the "old black bodice" that had once fit the farmer's wife, how slim and white were her bare legs in the moonlight as her skirts swirled. "Very splendid," he agreed.

"Save that mine is plain," she added honestly. "While you have all that gold braid."

"Tarnished gold braid," he amended, looking ruefully at the wine red coat flung onto the hay beside him. That braid had survived several thundershowers on the way here, a fall into a river when a wooden bridge gave way, the London fire and innumerable brambles during their run through the woods, but it was still there. It even glittered in spots.

"'Tis beautiful," she said wistfully, kneeling down to stroke the braid. "A pity 'tis tarnished."

It was on the tip of Grantland's tongue to say that braid was easily replaced. But the sight of her bending down in the moonlight with her fair hair flowing down like a waterfall of pale silk over her slender white forearms made him catch his breath.

"Dorinda," he said, and the shadow of Lady Polly no longer wavered between them. "Dorinda." Huskily. He reached out and touched her arm, felt the tremor as his fingers made contact. "Dorinda," he murmured, drawing her to him gently. She seemed to drift toward him, unresisting. There was a wistful yearning in his low voice. "Do you think you could learn to love me?"

Her soft body was pressed against him now and he could feel the moisture on her cheeks, the lashes that brushed him were wet with unshed tears.

"I already do," she whispered. And it seemed to her suddenly that all her life she had waited for this moment.

It was enough for Grantland. His muscles tensed spasmodically. Lovely wench, she was his for the taking! But still he hesitated, even as his hands wandered eagerly down the lines of her sweet young body. "Dorinda—you're sure?"

For answer she wriggled closer, embarrassed that he should see her tearstained face. After all, Binnie was older and wiser and Binnie had told her that it was important to giggle a lot if you decided to "do it" because men liked a merry wench and were sure to come back for more—and sometimes, only *sometimes*, mind you, they'd bring baubles!

Dorinda had lost all interest in baubles. Gone was her vision of the coach and six. All she wanted was the man in the tarnished gold braid she had snatched from the footpads and who had returned the favor this day beside a lonely stream outside London. She wanted to lie in his arms and dream there. She wanted to take care of him and iron that fine white shirt that he had just shed, and cook him fine suppers and bear his children. A little sob broke from Dorinda at the very intensity of her wanting him. It was all too splendid a dream to come true, of course. This night in the barn loft was probably all she'd get, but she'd make the most of it and have something splendid to remember—always.

And then her tears dried on her cheeks and her lips parted softly as new and rapturous sensations began coursing through her. He was sensuously enjoying her body, stroking her smooth skin gently as he might a cat to hear it purr. And then his fingers grew bolder, bolder—teasing, tweaking, caressing—until she closed her eyes in embarrassment and delight.

But the touch of her spurred him too and his grip on her tightened. She could feel the tension rising in him and her own senses seemed wild and released. Pinioned in his arms, she had never felt so free. His every touch was magic.

Now, lying beneath him with the sweet smelling hay for a mattress, she felt breathlessly the swift motion of his thighs, of his masculine hardness pressed against her. She stiffened and forced back the cry of pain that rose to her throat as he entered her and heard, with swimming head, his muttered apology. And then they were past that and flying through a strange new world of tindery emotions that sparked and flared and ebbed and flowed and sent her winging on a voyage of discovery through unknown fields. Dorinda clung to him, moaning, for she was riding a sensation of splendid joy and she wanted it to go on—endlessly.

They had found more than a farmer's cot that night— they had found each other.

Softly, softly they spun down from the heights and Grantland's hands were gently caressing a body that seemed to her new and strange in some exalted way. Her breath caught and she felt a small sob of desire escape her as those hands trailed lightly along her torso, touching areas no man before him had ever caressed. She was still lost in a blaze of glory and newfound delight and her dream of a lover with a coach and six was forever fled. She knew she would be content forever with a lover in a worn coat with tarnished gold braid, a rakish gentleman who had seen better days for all he had gold in his purse.

Which brought up the worrying thought, *How had he got it?*

"The gold you paid for my kirtle," she blurted, tensing suddenly. "How came you by it?"

Grantland, his fingers poised over a tender pink nipple, felt his russet brows lift in astonishment. But the worry on her sweet young face could not be misunderstood—worry for him.

"I won it," he told her lightly. "Dicing with some fellows I met at an inn on the road to London."

So he was a gambler! At least he was not a highwayman! She could be thankful for that. Binnie's advice about highwaymen had been specific—for she claimed she'd once had a highwayman for a lover. "Don't never take up with no highwayman," she'd warned. "They don't last. They get themselves hanged!"

" 'Twas not your last goldpiece?" she worried.

A sudden chill came over Meredith. All and sundry had warned him about London wenches who would speak you fair and play you false. And this one seemed now to be concentrating on his gold. Her next words made him feel ashamed.

"For if it was, I should not have let you spend it on a kirtle and bodice for me," she said earnestly. "But I want you to know I have three gold pieces in my shoe, which I have had ever since I left York—in case things turned out badly in London, and so I can repay you."

Grantland Meredith swallowed. And he had thought her mercenary to be asking about gold at such a time!

His head bent and he let his lips rove lovingly down her smooth face, along the delicate skin of her neck and her pulsing bosom, to glide over the soft sheen of her breasts and down the quivering flesh of her white stomach and hips.

Dorinda shivered in his arms, responding to him with all the gentle giving of her nature. He had never known such trust and sweetness in a woman—certainly not in Lady Polly, whose fierce exciting lovemaking had scorched him with its heat, but like a storm had raged and was gone. This girl was . . . different. He touched her reverently—and then his own lusty body heated up and together they climbed to the top of the world again.

"I care not," Dorinda told him seriously, after they had slept fitfully for a while and waked to rediscover each other, "that you are a gambler."

"I did not say I was a gambler," he protested. "I said I had won the gold."

"You did not have to *say* you were a gambler," she chided him. " 'Tis obvious that a man with his clothes in such condition as yours is not well off, and if the gold in your purse came from gaming, why, then, a gambler you must more than likely be!"

He grinned at this feminine logic, and thought how delicately the moonlight silvered her fair young body and how her nakedness became her. Next she would be asking him to win her a fortune!

When Dorinda spoke again, it was to address that flash of white teeth that smiled at her. "I have been lying here thinking about this," she told him seriously. "And I wanted to say that I know a gambler's life is a chancy one and for all that I lost the silver at my last post and can expect no recommendation there, I believe that I would be able to find work in most towns and make enough to tide you over when you are down on your luck."

She waited anxiously and there was indeed a silence for on the face that was abruptly turned away from her sudden unwonted tears glimmered on lashes unused to tears. The little wench had lain awake while he slept trying to arrange his future! She was a kind of woman, he felt, entirely foreign to him, exalted, pure—and he was not good enough for her.

"You would go with me?" His voice reached her huskily. "From town to town, finding work as you could to help support us through the bad times?"

"Yes," she said with surprising energy—and with much joy, for she felt she had been throwing herself at

him and had not been sure how he would react. "You
will take me with you?" she asked in a small voice.

For answer Grantland, who could not speak, so overcome with emotion was he, turned and let his russet
head fall to her breast—where he heard an alarmingly
irregular heartbeat.

He sat up, concern lighting his strong features. "But
you're ill!" he protested. He peered down into her face
in alarm.

"It's nothing," protested Dorinda. "In Yorkshire the
doctor told me I had a weak heart and that I mustn't
overstrain it. And tonight..." Her faint smile in the
moonlight told him what tonight had been.

Grantland Meredith, who had been about to embark
on another wild bout of lovemaking, abruptly changed
his mind. "We will rest here another day," he said.

She shook her head tiredly. "That would only use up
more of your little store of gold."

"At least I'll find you transportation," he muttered. "I
won't have you walking in the heat!" And cradled her
comfortingly in his arm to sleep the night away.

The next morning they bought the farmer's mule—
he had no horse—and with Dorinda riding and Grantland
striding along beside, they made it blissfully to the
ancient cloth town of Guildford in Surrey, said to have
been the home of Elaine, the Lily Maid of Astolat. A
sheep and cattle fair was being held there when they
arrived and Grantland deposited his lady at an inn, and
told her he was off to find some gaming at the fair. He
came back with enough gold that they left Guildford
riding horses and Dorinda now had six pieces of gold
in her shoe!

She considered that he had won a fortune and was all
for hoarding it. She counseled him earnestly all the way
to Winchester.

But long before they reached Winchester, Grantland
Meredith's mind was made up. Lady Polly, who blew
hot and blew cold, would have to find some other man

to badger. He would offer lovely Dorinda, who had given herself so freely, so trustingly to him, nothing less than marriage!

It was in storied Winchester, lost in legend, earlier than Rome, a city of hills where six Roman roads converged and the Saxon kings lay buried, that the banns were cried and Grantland married Dorinda—she in her homespun kirtle, he in his wine red coat with its tarnished braid. They made a charming couple and none who saw them could help but smile, for the bride's dusty blue eyes glowed like blue flame in her joyous face and the tall bridegroom looked proud and possessive as he took her to wife.

Afterward they spent a cozy night at an inn in the High Street. Although Dorinda was doubtful they should be spending so much money, Grantland lightly brushed off her demurrals, saying with a grin that he'd "no doubt be lucky again before he died!"

In the morning Dorinda, sitting by the small paned window and looking out into a sky of endless blue, turned to watch the chambermaid smoothing the big feather bed with a wooden bed patter which looked remarkably like a butter paddle except that the handle slanted to the side. She thought of how many beds she had patted smooth herself with a paddle like this one and felt guiltily that she should offer to help.

But Grantland would have none of that. She must get all the rest she could—he was firm about that. And riding might not be the best thing for her either, he decided, once they reached Southampton, twelve miles distant. There he traded the horses for passage on a tall masted ship which would take them to Lyme, for Grantland was becoming familiar now with Dorinda's sudden pallor, the blueness that came over her lips, and he feared that to ride such a distance would overtax her.

"I'm taking you home to Lyme," he told her simply and shrugged off all questions of his life there. "'Tis well enough there," he would say, but there was always a slight tightness to his lips as he said it for he was wondering how Lady Polly would take this.

There was something mysterious in Grantland's past, Dorinda decided, watching him. Something that must be kept hidden. She speculated on what it was—and never guessed the truth. She finally decided, reluctantly, that although he had acquired polish in his wanderings, he might be ashamed to have her know his lowly beginnings. Perhaps, she reasoned, he was some cottager's son who had learnt fine town ways and now he was uneasy to be bringing home a bride who expected more to plain country folk! She hastened to set his mind at rest.

"I was orphaned early," she volunteered. "And never rightly had a home at all."

They were leaning on the taffrail as she spoke. Above them white sails billowed as the ship made its majestic way down the Solent. On one side lay the Isle of Wight and on the other side stretched far away the New Forest where William the Conqueror had hunted.

The tall man at her side gave her a surprised look. "You were brought up in an orphanage?"

She shook her head and the sun gleamed on her fair hair. "My mother died young—six months after I was born."

"And your father?"

"I never had a father. The old Marquess of Tonby shook my mother till her teeth rattled, so I've been told, but she refused to name him. They kept her on anyway though—she was a chambermaid there the same as I was later—but she pined away. Old Nurse said she died of a broken heart."

Grantland digested that. "Who brought you up?"

"Old Nurse. 'Tis no disrespect to call her that— everyone called her that. I slept at the foot of her bed in the attic of Colemere House where she took care of the Marquess's younger children. He had an older son at Oxford and a second son who left in some kind of disgrace, they said."

Grantland's smile was bittersweet as he looked out at the coast of Hampshire rushing by. Dorinda was innocently perhaps telling him the real story of her conception and birth—a son who had erred with a chambermaid and been cast out of the house, a chambermaid who had loyally refused to name him and been kept on, an old nurse who brought up all the children of the family—even one who did not know she was a part of that family. "Your mother must have been very beautiful," he said gravely.

"Oh, she was. Glowing. Old Nurse said so. I don't remember her, of course."

"And the second son?" he asked gently. "The one who disappeared?"

"Died at sea, so they say. There was a great storm the week I was born and it battered the whole east coast and piled up ships all the way down from Newcastle on Tyne. His ship was but an hour out of the Humber when the storm struck. Old Nurse told me all about it—several times."

And she had her reasons, no doubt!

"And your mother, when she heard the news?"

She stared at him. "I don't know what you mean. They said that after I was born she wept a lot. You can't mean—?"

"Very likely," he said quietly. "Didn't you ever ask Old Nurse who your father was?"

"Yes," she whispered. "I used to beg her to tell me and she always said, 'I know, but I won't tell you till the day you marry—or go off to seek your fortune.' She called me to her the night she was so ill. She knew she was dying and she told me in a weak voice to go to her sister in London—she'd take me in. And then she said, 'You're his grandchild, 'tis right you should know. Your father—' I leant forward to hear but the words rattled in her throat and I couldn't make them out. She tried to speak again but she was gone. I never dreamed—I thought my father must have been some married man who never meant to marry my mother!"

His voice was melancholy and his strong hand closed over hers. "You were granddaughter to the marquess but he did not choose to claim you." He rebelled inwardly that she should have been treated so, this brave lovely girl who had come so readily to his defense in a dying city, who had given herself to him so proudly. "He drove his son to his death and he probably blamed your mother for that. We should call you 'Lady Dorinda,'" he added softly.

"Oh, no." She blushed. "It would be like sailing under false colors because I don't really know—I'll never know."

His arm went round her protectively. "You have my name now, Dorinda." His voice was husky.

Above them the wild gulls screamed and England's scenic south coast went flying by.

LYME REGIS, ENGLAND
Autumn 1666

Chapter 3

Their approach to Lyme was made ominous by a red glow that lit the sky and billows of black smoke. Dorinda felt nervously that she had somehow come full circle and that she was back on the Thames watching London burn. She cowered back against Grantland's broad chest, for it seemed to her that the whole world was ablaze.

"'Tis nothing," he soothed her, for he guessed that the bituminous shale of the fossil-rich cliffs had been ignited by a fisherman's fire. "It happens now and then but 'twill soon be out." He nodded toward the west where thunder rolled as regularly as the throb of some great drum.

Rain was pouring down in torrents and the fire on the cliffs had been extinguished amid clouds of black smoke before they dropped anchor in Lyme Bay. Dorinda and Grantland spent their last night aboard ship listening to the sound of raindrops pattering down on the wooden deck. A lovely night, close in each other's arms with the future far away. Dorinda found joy and happiness but a touch away in Grantland's lean body.

But the uneasy feeling that red glow had brought her came back to her the next day when they landed at the curving stone wall known as the Cobb and walked on foot through the narrow bluestone alleys with Dorinda anxiously asking, "Is your house far away?"

"In the countryside," he answered noncommittally. He nodded briefly to people as they passed and they scrupulously returned his greeting, some of them doffing their hats and bowing quite low, but she was too excited to take any notice of that.

He procured for them a pair of horses, leaving her waiting outside the livery stable as he did so, and she was silent as they headed out of town into the beautiful Dorset countryside.

Dorinda had apprehensions of being ill-received by his family but Grantland dispelled her fears by explaining that he too was an orphan with no relatives save an uncle in Axminster who came down on occasion to tell him the error of his ways. He let her believe she was on her way to a country cot, and that the dusty traveling clothes he had worn when he met her were the best he owned.

He was whistling as they rode together down a lane that was hardly better than a cowpath (Lady Polly had constantly railed at him for not keeping it clipped). But he liked it as it was—and so did Dorinda, looking about her in delight and asking eagerly about every cottage they approached, "Is this your home?"

Always Grantland shook his head and she fell silent, afraid she might give the impression of expecting better housing than he might be able to provide.

Carefully, for effect, Grantland approached the house from the east front and it burst upon her suddenly: the stone wall, the dovecote, and beyond that the massive stone house with its oriel windows glittering gold in the afternoon sun.

She caught her breath. "Oh, this couldn't be—?" she began in a shaky voice.

"You're home at last." Grantland dismounted and lifted her down with a flourish. It was a proud moment for him. Lady Polly, who considered Grantland Manor shockingly old-fashioned and had threatened to redo it down to the last chip of plaster, would not even have understood.

"But I thought you were a gamester!" faltered Dorinda.

"And so I let you believe." Grantland brushed a kiss lightly across her furrowed forehead. "I must confess, Dorinda, that the gold I came by in Winchester was not the result of gaming but from the sale of some cattle to be delivered shipside at Southampton harbor."

A groom came running up. "Your lordship," he panted, beaming broadly. "We didn't know you were home, sir." He gave Dorinda a curious look.

"Glad to see you looking so well, Garth." Grantland made a dismissive gesture. "Return those horses to the livery stable in Lyme after they've been fed and watered."

"Your *lordship?*" murmured Dorinda, overcome, as the grinning groom led the horses away.

"Yes. Allow me to present myself anew. I'm Grantland Meredith, Earl of Ravensay."

"Which means that I'm—"

"A countess," he finished for her. "Lady Dorinda Meredith, Countess of Ravensay."

A countess! Dorinda was rendered speechless. She had expected an up-and-down life as wife to a gamester—and now this!

"Perhaps you'd like to view the gardens first? My mother set them out, had trees and shrubs imported from all over. She was very proud of them."

With her hand clutched in his, the new Countess of Ravensay let her bridegroom lead her, dazed, down a stone-paved path edged with cushions of old clipped yew. She gazed with wonder at the elegant boxwood maze and the bowers of fragrant roses, the lattices and trellises and evergreens—and a whole wealth of shrubs that were completely new to her. She breathed deep of this new wonder-world and turned to Grantland with childish gratitude for this great gift. And kissed him as reward for bringing her here.

Grantland's lean face glowed. For him it was a spectacular homecoming.

But his bride's face paled at sight of the enormous hall built in Tudor times with its high-flung arch-braced roof and elaborate carved timber cornice. "I could never keep all this clean!" she whispered in panic at sight of the paneled great parlor with its Ionic pilasters.

"You won't have to," Grantland told her. "You'll have servants to do that. Ah, I see Mawkers has found us," as a tall gaunt woman with an ageless young-old face and an extremely light walk came into the room. She swept them a deep curtsy which trailed her black skirts across the floor. "Dorinda, this is Mawkers the housekeeper. My new Countess will be counting on you, Mawkers, to show her round all the nooks and crannies I overlook."

At the words "my new Countess," Mawkers froze in her curtsy and when she rose—slowly—there was wild mirth in her eyes, instantly controlled as she said with suitable gravity, "Allow me to wish you both every happiness." And to Dorinda, "Your ladyship has only to command me."

Mawkers looked as if she meant it and Dorinda was overcome—both by being called "your ladyship" for the first time and by realizing she now had a housekeeper of her own—she who had been ordered about by housekeepers so often in the past.

"I am sure we will get along very well together, Mawkers," she heard herself say.

Grantland looked down at her proudly, but he directed his words to Mawkers. "We'll make do with my room tonight, but tomorrow I want you to prepare my mother's bedchamber for the Countess."

Mawkers turned to Dorinda with kindling eyes. "It has great casements that look out over the gardens. You'll like it, my lady. Especially in summer when the climbing pink roses under your windows are at their best. Would you like to see it now?"

"Oh, yes, I would, Mawkers!" said Dorinda impulsively. She was losing her shyness, for it was obvious the tall housekeeper liked her. Along with Grantland she followed Mawkers up the broad Jacobean stairway to the room that was to be her own. She looked around her with delight at the pretty, feminine furnishings, the lofty ceilings, and the tall casements that filled the room with light when Mawkers pulled back the drapes.

"Of course you can redecorate it if you like," murmured Grantland behind her.

"Redecorate?" His bride gave him an astonished look. "But it's perfect as it is! Oh, I love that shade of blue!" She was gazing raptly at the "Turkey carpet" as she spoke, then up at the delicate French wallpaper. "And what a wonderful bed! Ah, there's the step-stair that leads up to it—I didn't see that at first and I thought we'd have to vault in!"

Over Dorinda's head Grantland's eyes met Mawkers's in perfect contentment. He had always loved this room—as had Mawkers, who had been in attendance the night his mother died here. They had shared a mutual anxiety that Lady Polly might change it.

Which brought him squarely back to Lady Polly.

"Mawkers," he asked suddenly, "has there been any message for me?"

Mawkers guessed what he meant. "None," she said calmly. "It's been most peaceful here since your lordship left."

Which, Grantland surmised, meant that Lady Polly—always a disruptive force in Mawkers's opinion—had not visited Grantland Manor since his departure.

"Oh, Grantland, I can't believe it!" Dorinda hugged him after Mawkers strode out with a swish of black skirts. "I feel I must be living in a dream! Here you let me badger you all across England about saving your money so we'd not end up in the poorhouse or debtors' prison and all the time you had *this!*"

But her worried admonitions had been pleasant to his ears. They had proved she loved him....

"Tell me, Grantland," she asked him roguishly, for she was fast recovering her aplomb. "Do you have a coach and six?"

His brows shot up at this unlikely question. "We have two coaches," he admitted. "And more than enough horses to draw them both with six each."

His countess collapsed with laughter. "And to think," she gasped, "the night I met you I was dreaming of a coach and six and hated to wake up!" She stopped laughing suddenly. "And I came here dressed like this!" she gasped, looking down at her shabby clothes. For Grantland, hoping to keep his wealth a surprise, had carefully refrained from buying her a new gown. "What will the servants think?"

"It's not what they think of *us* but what we think of *them* that counts," he replied coolly. But he frowned. This was a problem he had overlooked, knowing there would be a whole wardrobe waiting to replace the wine red coat gone shabby on his journey. "You're about my mother's size," he murmured. "Let's see what we can find in her press." He moved to the big sturdy wardrobe that dominated the room, pulled out a lavish gown of dusky blue silk iced with tiny brilliants that gave it a shimmering effect.

The dress was hopelessly out of fashion with its long pointed stomacher and out-of-date lines, but Dorinda drew in her breath at the sight of it. Those full romantic slashed sleeves lined in satin garnished with lace that bared the forearm, that breathlessly deep décolletage, that long pointed waist over the wide skirts—and underneath a silver encrusted petticoat! "Oh, Grantland, I'd love to wear it!" she breathed.

"Good," he said contentedly. "It was my mother's wedding gown. And her mother's before that. I'm sure

they'd both approve your wearing it on your first night
here!"

He changed clothes himself to a French gray velvet
coat trimmed in silver that contrasted with pearl gray
satin trousers. His new countess thought he looked very
elegant when he came for her, although she inwardly
mourned the loss of the wine red coat with tarnished
gold braid that had made him look so rakish. She had
tied up her fair hair with some blue satin ribands she
had found by rummaging.

"I have something for you." He slipped around her
neck a necklace of pearls and sapphires.

Completely overcome, Dorinda trailed beside him
down the wide Jacobean stairway into the great hall
below with its enormous fireplace and massive oaken
furniture.

They dined that night on pheasant in the oriel room
which adjoined the hall and Dorinda could hardly eat
for excitement.

Mawkers, passing through the room, stopped, riveted
by the sight of the ancient wedding gown being worn
casually to dinner. She flashed Grantland an accusing
look.

"All the Countess's things were burned in the Great
Fire of London, Mawkers," Grantland told her expansively, realizing the servants were listening and knowing how gossip flew about the servants' hall. "Also her
London house." He grinned at his new Countess, who
gazed back at him dazed. "We barely escaped with our
lives, and so ruined was her clothing that we bought
what we could from a farmer on the road. I was
running out of coin, so I've waited till I brought her
home to outfit her."

"I came to tell you what I forgot before," said Mawkers.
"Which is that the Lyddons' ball is a fortnight hence
and his lordship rode over last week especially to invite
you." She kept staring at the wedding gown. "He said
he'd hoped you'd abandoned your 'mad scheme' of

studying law in London and would be back as you'd originally planned."

Grantland laughed. "I did indeed abandon it. Well, I'm sorry I missed Tom Lyddon." He paused. "Perhaps we'd best wait for the French fashion dolls to arrive and have the Countess properly dressed when she meets the entire county."

"Indeed I'll have enough to do taking charge of so large a household," said Dorinda, hoping she'd be able to learn the new dance steps fast enough not to disgrace him.

"Yes, I suppose it is bigger than your London house," agreed Grantland. "Although probably not so large as your grandfather's."

So she was to assume a whole new background. . . . Dorinda's hand tightened convulsively on her glass.

Grantland turned to the housekeeper with studied casualness. "My wife's health has been poor for some years and her mother chose not to instruct her in running a household, so it will be up to you, Mawkers, to help the Countess learn what she needs to know."

Mawkers was looking at "the Countess" keenly. Something was amiss here. This girl, for all her ethereal beauty, had none of the easy aristocratic ways of Lady Polly, none of that hauteur born of always knowing just where you stood. But Mawkers had always liked Grantland and her heart went out to some mute appeal in his glance. "I'll take my lady in hand, sir," she promised warmly. "And Smithers might help as well," she added diffidently.

Smithers had once been a lady's maid at Court. Although she had been dismissed after she developed gout and had trouble hobbling around and had come back to her native Dorset to find work as a chambermaid, she would be a tower of strength in arranging hair fashionably, in selecting the right clothes and assisting "my lady" in the social graces.

Grantland gave the housekeeper a look of gratitude. "Couldn't get along without you, Mawkers," he grinned.

"I'm aware of that, your lordship," agreed Mawkers tartly. She gave him a fond smile. She had been his nurse before she had become his housekeeper and if Grantland chose to elevate some servant girl out of London to mistress of Grantland Manor (for she had already guessed his secret) Mawkers was going to help him!

He hears a distant wailing on the wind
And he shudders that it's vengeance for his sin
But the whirlwind in the skies cannot match her dazzling eyes—
Torn and buffeted, he knows she's bound to win!

PART TWO

The Devil Mistress

Autumn 1666

Chapter 4

"Who is Lady Polly?" asked Dorinda as she pulled off her shoes in the green bedchamber Grantland had occupied since boyhood.

Grantland, who was just in the act of removing his French gray velvet coat, felt his shoulder muscles jerk.

"Where did you hear of her?" he asked.

Dorinda stood up barefoot. Her lovely face was guileless, he noted. "I just heard her name muttered by two of the servants and I wondered who she was."

Grantland took a deep breath. Explanations, he knew, had to be made—she would hear things. "Lady Polly Edgecombe," he said, amazed that he could sound so casual. "We were betrothed on and off. She broke it off just before I went to London."

"Oh," said Dorinda. She looked troubled. "Did you love her?"

"No," said Grantland harshly. *But he had—oh, he had!*

Lady Polly herself came storming over in the morning. From an upstairs window Grantland saw her galloping down the drive and hastened downstairs to meet her. He was glad that Dorinda was at the back of the house "getting to know the kitchens," as Mawkers put it, for Lady Polly Edgecombe had never been known for either her tact or her reticence.

She flung off her horse just as he closed the outer door behind him.

For a moment they stood at gaze and he was struck as always by how very beautiful she was. Her abundant hair was a midnight cloud with blue-black highlights, her eyes long and gold-green—and at the moment savage. Shadowed by her wide-brim hat aflutter with lime-green plumes, those eyes were fixed on him, glittering—and for a moment in the sunlight they gave off the iridescent reflection of cats' eyes in the dark. Beneath her tailored olive broadcloth riding habit, with its wide-cuffed sleeves trimmed in black braid and spilling a wealth of lace, her sleek body seemed to undulate with feline grace. The tight fabric of her bodice rose and fell in a way that drew the eye and Grantland felt a familiar stirring as he looked into that arresting face. She was a magnificent woman—he could not help but admire her.

"Well?" she cried, planting her booted feet and throwing back her dark head so that her thick raven curls cascaded back over her shoulders. "What have you to say for yourself, Grantland?" Those accusing gold-green eyes pinned him and before he could frame a reply she added in her slurred, slightly rasping voice that always sent shivers down his spine, "Do not think you are fooling me, Grantland! You were *seen* bringing a woman off a ship in Lyme harbor yesterday and you took two horses from the livery stable in Lyme—horses which have since been returned by one of your grooms!"

"I do not deny it," said Grantland in an easy voice. He looked very fit and calm for all that his gray eyes held a desperate light, for he had dreaded this meeting with his formidable former fiancée.

"You do not—?" For a moment the reed-slender woman before him was speechless. "You *admit* you have brought some woman to your house? That you are keeping her here? By heaven, I will have words with her!" She would have rushed past him but that Grantland blocked her way.

"Polly, you broke off our engagement yourself."

"Yes, but I didn't mean it! I was angry. *You knew I didn't mean it!* Oh, do get out of the way. I will view her for myself!"

She tried to thrust him aside and Grantland caught her by the shoulders to keep her from passing him. Her touch could still stir him, he noted uneasily, for the soft flesh he held seemed to send wild ripples of desire through his fingers. Polly had always affected him so, he was wrong to think that he had changed. She looked up as they tussled there and the sudden mockery in her iridescent eyes told him she *knew* how holding her affected him. *Knew and was amused!*

His face lost some of its color and his strong fingers bit into her shoulders as she struggled to free herself. If he was hurting her, she was too proud to admit it. He tried reason.

"Polly, I will not let you see Dorinda while you are in this state! The sight of you thus would dismay any bride!"

Her near shriek sent a shiver through him. "Any *what?*"

"Bride. I have married her."

Lady Polly shook free of his loosened hold and stepped back from him. Her beautiful face was momentarily devoid of all expression. "But you are still betrothed to *me!*" she cried.

"You flung my betrothal ring in my face once too often," Grantland reminded her with irony. "Dorinda and I were married in Winchester."

Those words wrought a sudden change in Lady Polly, terrifying to behold. Her unusual eyes seemed to darken murkily until they were all pupil, black spots in her white accusing face. A pair of angry red spots lit up her cheeks and her widow's peak hairline seemed to draw upward.

"You are lying!" she gasped, and she sounded as if she could not get her breath.

"No, I am not," Grantland assured her, grateful that he could keep his voice level over the tumult in his heart for he was wondrously attracted to her. He had forgot, in his bitterness in London, how wild she was and how beguiling—he had remembered only her wilfulness, her wanton ways. "I have brought home a bride."

She surged forward. "I will see her for myself!" she cried in a passion. "I will tell her what manner of man she has married—*a betrayer*!"

Grantland had had enough time to think over Lady Polly on the road to London and back. He had told himself bitterly that his defection would not cut her deeply—at least it would not penetrate to her heart, if she had one. Again he blocked her way.

"You'll not see her in your present temper," he said stubbornly. "In time you two may become friends but for now—"

"*Friends!*" She made the word sound like an epithet. "Oh, that you could do this to me! That you could make me a laughingstock before the whole county!" Grantland had no time to remind her how nonchalant she had been about her own rejected suitors. Her hand, clutching her riding crop, was upraised. "*But you will not make a fool of me, Grantland!*" Her voice caught in a sob. "I will not allow it!"

He ducked as her riding crop slashed at his face and it landed instead on his velvet shoulder. With a sob of fury and a billow of olive broadcloth skirts, Lady Polly leaped into the saddle and vented her spleen on her horse. She wheeled the terrified beast around so fast that he reared up and nearly lost his footing. Heedless of the danger, she dug her spurs in so painfully that the big chestnut fairly catapulted back down the drive.

More shaken than he cared to admit, Grantland watched her go. It had come to him with sickening force that had Polly Edgecombe been within range of his vision he would never have married the girl who waited inside the house. He shook his big head to clear it. What was done was done. Seeing Polly again... It had been worse than he thought but at least it was over.

He looked behind him at the sound of the door opening and saw that Dorinda had come out and was standing beside him.

"How much did you hear?" he demanded.

"Enough to know she will give us trouble."

He nodded soberly and put a protective arm around Dorinda. Lady Polly would find a way to vent her spite, no doubt, but he would see she did not harm this innocent creature who had been fool enough to love him!

Neither of them could guess the direction Lady Polly's "spite" would take.

Grantland realized how deep was Lady Polly's rage when two days later his friend and neighbor Tom Lyddon stopped by with a bit of news—and got some himself when he met Grantland's bride.

"Why, I'd no idea," cried Tom, who was a bluff ruddy man built like a young Boston bull and with gentle manners. "So ye've brought home a bride, Grant? And a beauty to boot! Ah, Grant, ye do not deserve her!" He bent gracefully over Dorinda's hand and she dimpled and acknowledged the compliment with a curtsy and a little laugh. "Indeed," he continued. "I'd thought to be the bearer of bad tidings and not the recipient of joyful ones!"

"How's that, Tom?" Grantland was leading his friend into the drawing room as he spoke.

"Why, that Lady Polly Edgecombe announced last night at a party over Bridport way—you mean she didn't *tell* you?" His friend was incredulous. "Why, I assumed that was how you came to bring home a wife! I mean—" His honest face reddened.

"Perhaps you'd best tell us what you mean, Tom."

Grantland busied himself pouring liquor into glasses from a crystal decanter while Dorinda urged their visitor into a chair.

"Well." Tom Lyddon seated himself with a flip of his coat skirts and gazed at them both, bright-eyed. " 'Twill come as no surprise to you, Grant, that Lady Polly's always fancied Charles."

Polly's predilection for Charles had always been all too apparent, but somehow hearing it from Tom seemed to turn a knife in Grantland's chest. "You mean she's betrothed herself to Charles now?" He managed to keep his voice steady as he held out the glass to Tom.

"More than that! She claims to have been married to him for all of three months! Says she was just toying with you while Charles was in Bristol and tossed you aside the moment he came back! Did you ever hear the like? Lady Willowford said such behavior should strike Lady Polly from all the guest lists. *I* thought Polly was just making it up."

The glass stilled in Grantland's hand. Tom's words had struck him as solidly as a blow. Polly . . . *his* Polly!. . .married. . . .For a terrible moment he envisioned her going to bed with Charles, saw the white chemise slip elegantly over her dark head as it had once done for him, saw it flung away to drift lightly down upon the coverlet, saw that beautiful pale ivory body emerge and sway languorously toward Charles. Each scene was jagged and etched raggedly as if on shards of broken glass in his mind as he imagined Charles reaching out his spatulate fingers to caress those tempting breasts— breasts the very sight of which had left Grantland shaken with desire. In mounting horror he envisioned Charles's coarse fingers roving at will down Polly's slim sinuous body, slipping along the silken hollow of her waist, clutching the satin of her buttocks until the pale flesh turned pink with the imprint of his eager fingers. In his tortured mind he could hear Polly moan, could see her press her slim white thighs against Charles's heavy muscled ones. In agony, he saw her throw back her head with its wealth of raven hair, arch her long neck and crush her soft breasts against the buttons of Charles's coat—as she had in the past crushed them against *his* coat. His breath came hard as he envisioned that beautiful naked body writhing in Charles's heavy arms, saw her slender white back curving toward Charles in passionate desire. He passed a hand over his face to dispell the visions of hell he had conjured up. The world came slowly back into focus and he realized that Tom was watching him brightly—it reminded him that Tom had been one of Polly's rejected suitors. No sympathy there!

Of a sudden Grantland wondered if Charles really had married Polly. A cold sweat broke out on his face. She was so eager to seem to have bested him, his tempestuous girl—for he still in his heart thought of her as his—she might have run away with Charles without benefit of matrimony, meaning somehow to make it all come right later. His heart ached for her.

He tried to put it out of his mind, to tell himself that Polly, whatever her troubles, was no longer his responsibility and that Dorinda was looking pale and worried.

Tom was smiling. "As for you, Grant, you've come out the winner. You could never have stood it. Poor Charles saddled with a wife who changes her mind with the weather! First she must have all gray horses, then nothing but chestnut will do! D'you think she'll insist on redecorating all of Hawkings Castle? Or just the major rooms?" He smote his knee and roared merrily. Grantland tried to join in but his own laughter sounded hollow to his ears.

"I know naught of any marriage," he said slowly. "Nor can I credit it that she was already married when she broke off our betrothal."

"But it *would* be a reason for doing so, wouldn't it?" put in Dorinda anxiously. For some reason that spitting

cat of a woman on the doorstep had frightened her—
for Grantland.

"I suppose it would." Tom laughed. "Anyway Charles
bore her away and I'm told this morning that she's
moved out of Edgecombe Hall and into Charles's place
at Hawkings."

But along with the pain, the news Tom had brought
had made Grantland thoughtful. It occurred to him
that tempestuous Lady Polly might make life very difficult for his new bride.

"I'm sorry we can't attend your ball a fortnight hence,"
he told Tom Lyddon frankly. "But all of Dorinda's
finery was burnt to a crisp in London and we must
send to Paris for fashion dolls and then seek out the
drapers for suitable fabrics and put the sempstresses to
work—afraid our coming is out of the question, Tom."

"Nonsense," said Tom. "Our house abounds in fashion dolls. My wife is forever sending for new ones!
She'll send you over a brace of dolls. And there's a ship
just arrived in Lyme harbor this morning with a load of
silks and damasks from Italy. If you hurry down to
Lyme, you should be able to take your pick before she's
unloaded."

"My thanks to you, Tom," said Grantland, cheered
because he had seen Dorinda's blue eyes sparkle at the
mention of fashion dolls and silks. He told himself he
loved Dorinda no less because he had not quite got over
Lady Polly. "We'll take your advice and you can count
on us at your ball."

The fashion dolls arrived, a full half dozen of them,
with Mary Lyddon's compliments. And that afternoon
they rode into Lyme and went aboard the stout wooden
ship that had made the voyage from the Mediterra-
nean. Grantland was lavish in his selection (perhaps as
penance for his mixed loyalties) and before the afternoon was out, a breathless Dorinda was the proud
possessor of a myriad collection of delicately hued silks,
rich damasks and brocades, some gossamer sheers that

the captain said vaguely came from "some heathen place called China" and as rich a selection of garnishings as any lady in Lyme.

They brought it all home and Dorinda, with the help of a chambermaid, draped long lengths of material on the bed and from the overhead canopy and on all the chairs and tables in her bedchamber. Grantland, coming in in the midst of this exercise, stood and laughed. And then he bade the chambermaid find work elsewhere and locked the door and still laughing gently carried Dorinda over to a long length of midnight blue velvet she had spread upon the bed. He laid her down upon it and set himself to undressing her.

"Oh, no, we'll ruin the velvet," she protested.

"'Tis the fate of velvet to be crushed!"

Grantland neatly pulled her chemise from her body, and tossed it aside. He looked, Dorinda thought, very determined.

She made a half-hearted grab for the flying chemise and then snuggled down into the soft velvet, her lovely fragile body ethereally pale against the midnight blue. The feather bed brought the velvet up around her so that her nakedness seemed framed by its deep blue shimmer.

Grantland told himself with force that he had never seen anything lovelier than Dorinda at that moment. A veritable angel! Hastily he divested himself of his clothing and joined her on the feather bed, sinking deeper into it as his weight pressed her down farther into the fluffy mattress.

"I think we'll suffocate!" gasped Dorinda, as his busy teasing fingers traced intricate designs upon her breasts and tweaked her pink crested nipples to hardness. "And this velvet tickles!"

"Then away with it!" said Grantland merrily. He lifted her up and flicked away the velvet. It drifted into a luxurious gleaming pile on the rug. His naked lady

was sighing now and looking at him seductively through
her long lashes.

"Grantland," she murmured. "I do believe you love
me."

"Wicked wench!" he laughed, and brought her body
to him in a single effortless gesture so that every pulsing inch of her seemed fitted to his long lean frame.
Tenderly, delicately, he stroked her body, her squirming
legs, the silky flesh between her thighs. Chuckling at
her aroused ardor, he lifted her buttocks lightly in his
cupped hands and entered her blithely—a lighthearted
lover, playful, teasing.

She felt the difference in him, and told herself it was
the easing of his tensions now that Lady Polly was well
and truly married.

That little flutter in her heart nagged at her as her
passions crested to match his own but she chose to
ignore it, for she was sublimely happy and when we are
happy it is hard to see the future clear. And if she felt a
moment of "goneness" in her chest, as if life had
suddenly departed, it was over instantly and she was
smiling up into her lover's face and reaching up with
gentle fingers to trace the smile on his eager lips.

"Do I make you happy, Dorinda?" he murmured.

She nodded, her heart too full to speak but the
sudden tears that dusted her lashes telling him all he
cared to know.

"I am so glad." He buried his face between her
breasts and Dorinda thought desperately, *Oh, let it last. . . .
please, please, let it last. Let me linger forever in his arms.*

So, delightfully, afternoon fled into evening, shadows
replaced the shafts of sunshine, and dinner beckoned.
Clad again in borrowed but glittering blue and silver
bridal finery, Dorinda and her lover strolled down to
dinner and were never sure afterward just what they
ate.

There are moments when the gods are kind, and
Dorinda and Grantland were experiencing one of those

moments. With his newfound angel beside him, Grantland found a brief forgetfulness. That week was laced with golden moments for which he would be forever grateful—but with the nights he would remember Lady Polly again and feel a raging jealousy of Charles who was at this moment taking her splendid body in his arms and ravishing all her delights.

To his credit, Grantland never let Dorinda know by word or look how he really felt.

Autumn 1666

Chapter 5

To the ball at Lyddon House went Grantland and his bride. And this time Dorinda, dressed in a faithful copy of a French fashion doll's finery, was clad in whispering Italian silk that changed from sea-green to softest violet blue and brought out amethyst lights in her dusty blue eyes. Her paleness was heightened with alabaster powder and her cheeks rouged delicately by Smithers with Spanish paper. At the elbows her big full sleeves spilled silver lace and at the focal point of the low-cut neckline she wore a brooch of sapphires to match her necklace and earbobs. Her hair was elaborately done and shone like palest gold, for Smithers had not forgot her touch. "As good as any Court lady's, I'll be bound," she remarked to Mawkers when she had finished. And Dorinda's blue-green satin toes peeked out from under a petticoat that was a miracle of silver embroidery over rustling midnight blue taffeta.

It seemed that everyone at Grantland Manor had contributed some bit of aid to the mistress's costume and they were all beaming at her as she climbed into the coach to leave—as if she were their protégée and not their employer.

Grantland was enormously proud of her.

"But I don't know any of the dance steps," she worried as the coach jolted along the short way to Lyddon House.

"Fall back upon your delicate health which kept you from learning," advised Grantland, who considered himself the world's worst dancer and had refused to teach her. "Every man there will yearn to teach you the latest steps—you'll see!"

"But I don't know anybody!"

"Nonsense, you know your host and hostess." For Mary Lyddon, a charming—and always somewhat disheveled—caricature of a French fashion doll herself, had ridden over to Grantland Manor to deliver the dolls and been as charmed by Dorinda's innocuous grace and ingenuous manner as her husband had been.

"But will people like me?" wondered Dorinda doubtfully. "Oh, I'm sure to do something dreadful and disgrace you!"

"Couldn't help liking you! Stop worrying." Grantland pressed a kiss on her nose and brushed off the dusting of crushed white alabaster his lips had received as a reward. "Must you wear so much of that stuff?" he sputtered.

"Smithers powdered me," said Dorinda nervously. "And she gave me this little pot of powder." She patted her blue silk purse that exactly matched her lavish blue silk fan. "She said I should refresh my powder when I arrive so that my nose will be very white—but I'll wash it all off before I go to bed, I promise!"

Grantland grinned. That couldn't come too soon for him. In bed his world always straightened out. He was already thinking up excuses to leave early when they arrived.

Dorinda was tired out from the endless fittings of her ballgown which had gone on endlessly, and bewildered by the number of people she met on every side and whose names she must somehow remember.

Grantland carried her through it all with aplomb; he was a tower of strength in dusty rose brocade. Around her thousands of candles seemed to be shining, the mirrored ballroom of Lyddon House gave back a reflection of the great chandeliers and of the banks of yellow roses that Mary Lyddon so favored. Dorinda hardly had time to take it all in before she was dancing, her Italian silk skirts whirling among other lavish skirts upon the shining floor. First she danced with Grantland, and then with Lord someone—she really couldn't have told you who—who delighted in showing her the latest steps and seemed almost touchingly pleased when she rewarded him by treading on his toe.

"Oh, I'm sorry!" She blushed, feeling contrite.

"Never you mind," said Lord What's-his-name, beaming on the pastel vision before him. "Just allow me the next dance and you can tread on me eternally!"

By now Dorinda was beginning to recognize "party gallantry" when she saw it. She dimpled up at him and was about to make a carefree rejoinder when he said, looking over her shoulder, "Aha, I see that another new bride has entered the room!"

And Dorinda turned her fair head to see Lady Polly and a hulking, rather soft-looking fellow, wearing his own startling saffron-colored hair, and splendidly garbed in puce satin, whom she was sure must be "Charles," enter the room. She was thankful when the dance was over—and even more thankful that by the time Lady Polly, moving circuitously through the crowd, reached her side, Grantland had turned up to buttress her.

Grantland felt dazzled anew by Polly Edgecombe's beauty and vaguely resentful that he should be so moved by it, but he made the introductions as calmly as if he felt nothing.

But Dorinda, standing beside him, echoed none of his aplomb. She could feel her palms grow damp in

their white kidskin gloves and her throat constrict
from tension as the glorious brunette beauty stared
down her classic nose at her—from the bastion of the
most cleverly constructed apricot satin gown Dorinda
had ever seen. Its rippling skirts seemed to spill a
cascade of rosettes in shades of palest to deepest
apricot and the peach-bloom bodice managed to reveal
not only a supple waist but an elegant expanse of
ivory skin.

Above that glamorous gown the long gold-green eyes
were remorseless, however, and they pinned Dorinda
as a collector might pin a butterfly. Several of the guests
had gathered, whispering behind their fans, to witness
this first confrontation of the new brides.

"What a lovely gown," drawled Lady Polly in a clear
carrying voice of thinly veiled contempt. "Did you make
it yourself, Lady Meredith?" She swept Dorinda with a
scathing gaze that caused the onlookers to nudge each
other into attention.

Beside her, Dorinda felt Grantland stiffen. He might
never be able to get Lady Polly out of his blood but he
would not stand by and see his wife scorned.

Before he could answer for her, Dorinda spoke up.
"No, 'tis a copy of a recent fashion doll from France. I
am beholden to our hostess, Mary Lyddon, for the doll
and to Italy for the silks and—" she turned with a sweet
laugh to her husband—"of course to Grantland, who
swept me into Lyme and near bought out the cargo of
the *Albatross!*"

It was a good answer and from nearby Mary Lyddon,
who had always resented having people say she had
married one of Lady Polly's cast-off suitors, found her
lips curving in an amused smile.

Grantland smiled too—and if it was a rather fixed
smile, no one noticed.

"Tit for tat," someone muttered behind a fan.

Lady Polly heard that. Her graceful white shoulders

moved sinuously as if to shake off something—convention perhaps—and her lips tightened into a straight line.

"I am told your entire wardrobe was roasted in the Great London Fire, Lady Meredith," she observed. "Are you from London then?"

"No, I'm from Yorkshire originally," said Dorinda hastily, for she supposed elegant Lady Polly must know London and she had no desire to be publicly caught up in all the many things she did *not* know about London society.

"Ah-h-h . . . Yorkshire." Lady Polly digested that and gave Dorinda a satisfied Cheshire smile. "I have a cousin in Yorkshire," she purred.

Grantland felt his heart sinking to his boots. He had forgotten that Lady Polly had a cousin in the North Country. "'Tis the largest county in England," he said easily. "Who does *not* have a cousin there?"

There was a little ripple of laughter from the onlookers at this sally. Lady Polly frowned. "Where in Yorkshire, may I ask?"

"Colemere House," said Dorinda promptly. "'Tis on the River Swale in the North Riding."

"Really?" Lady Polly pounced on that. "My cousin lives in the North Riding, somewhere near Middleham. Algernon Palmer. Do you know him?"

Before Dorinda could make some slip that would be impossible to mend, Grantland cut in.

"To save us dozens of fatiguing questions, Lady Polly," he said recklessly, "let me say that my bride is a granddaughter of the late Marquess of Tonby—the title has now passed, I believe, to his nephew who is unfortunately bedridden. Dorinda was frail as a child and spent most of her time quietly at home. She had just arrived at the London house her father left her on his death when the Great Fire broke out and destroyed everything. It would be kind of you not to insist that my wife talk about either Yorkshire or

London, Lady Polly, as both bring up sad memories which I am anxious to dispel."

With a quelling nod he swished Dorinda on by, leaving Lady Polly fuming in his wake.

"Oh, Grantland!" breathed Dorinda when they had run the gauntlet of the staring room and reached at last the shelter and solitude of a small anteroom where Grantland could shut the door. "Why ever did you tell her that I'm the Marquess of Tonby's granddaughter? I may be but I can never *prove* it!"

Grantland, now that his anger was cooling, realized bitterly the folly of what he had done, but there was now no alternative but to brazen it out. "I said it because Lady Polly is the daughter of an earl—and I was determined that you should take precedence over her," he muttered, unaware that he was using exactly the same logic that Lady Polly had in proclaiming her earlier marriage to Charles. "For that matter," he added bitterly, voicing gossip he had heard but always before discounted, "there are some who say Lady Polly isn't the daughter of a Viscount at all but the daughter of an exceptionally personable groom who lorded it over the Viscount's stables and proved irresistible to the Viscountess!"

"She was furious at you for besting her there with everybody looking," warned Dorinda. "She will call *me* to account for it," she added gloomily.

It was Grantland's firm intention to stand between dangerous Lady Polly and this frail child he had brought into a mess that was none of her making. "Nonsense," he said sharply. "I'll not allow it!" He threw open the door, prepared to meet the fray, and his gaze grew wintry. It passed with distaste over Charles, Lord Chell, just leading his new bride, Lady Polly, out upon the floor. "In any event," he muttered, "before the evening is out, I will make it known that any who cast aspersions on my wife cast aspersions on

me and that I will be limbering my sword in anticipation of such an affront!"

Dorinda gave him an unhappy look. She had been so
delighted to attend this, her very first, ball. Now she
wanted nothing so much as to say good-night to her
hostess!

"Perhaps we should make our excuses and leave," she
murmured.

But Grantland, who had announced himself so eager
to return home to taste the delights of the bedchamber,
was now in no haste to leave. His smouldering gaze
followed Lady Polly about the room and of a sudden he
left Dorinda, advanced upon the dark beauty and claimed
her for a dance.

The whole room watched as Grantland swung the
elegant lady in apricot out upon the floor. Dorinda was
standing now beside a sympathetic Mary Lyddon, who
had once watched Lady Polly snatch Tom away from
her—and even though she had got him back, she knew
what Dorinda must be going through. Dorinda, feeling
forlorn, was totally unaware of Mary's presence. She
was thinking wistfully what a handsome couple they
made, how lithe Lady Polly seemed to know instinctively
every move Grantland would make and to match him,
heartbeat for heartbeat. She could see them gazing
angrily into each other's eyes as if held by invisible
bonds—bonds that chafed but yet held firm. Lady Polly
was giving off almost visible sparks from those remarkable eyes and at one point Dorinda saw Grantland's
face whiten and she thought for a wild moment that he
was going to strike Lady Polly.

It came about when Lady Polly said in a purring
undertone, "I have discovered that Charles is a much
better lover than you, Grantland. It was a most delightful discovery!"

Grantland felt the blood rush to his head and then
retreat from it, leaving him colder than ice.

"I am sure you have a wealth of experience to guide you," he said roughly.

Lady Polly, moving with feline grace across the floor, missed a step. "How dare you?" she gasped. "That night with you was the *only*—"

"Quiet," he told her bitterly. "The perfect lover might hear!"

They danced several steps in angry silence. Then:

"How could you actually *marry?*" she shot at him. "When you knew—you *must* have known—that I would come back to you?"

"I am not a mind reader," Grantland said heavily. "I found you in Charles's arms and when I taxed you with it, you threw your betrothal ring in my face."

Her shrug was a light gesture of dismissal. "Oh, that was shabby of me, I admit it, but *you*, Grantland—you should have *known*. . . ." She sighed and gave him a fond sad look that wrenched his heartstrings, a look that reminded him he had planned to marry this tempestuous wench ever since he was a boy. No other girl had ever crossed his mind. Until Dorinda. Lady Polly's smile flashed suddenly, a brilliant smile that took his breath away. "We haven't lost each other, Grantland—we'll be back together again," she said confidently.

The floor seemed to rock under Grantland's feet. He missed a step—and that too was noted by the onlookers who could not hear their low-voiced conversation, but wished they could!

"Polly's too much for him," muttered a gentleman in purple satin and there was a titter among those who heard his remark.

Mary Lyddon heard it and her distressed glance flew to Dorinda, whose expression was quite set and who was gripping her fan rather hard.

On the dance floor, Grantland was responding to Lady Polly's audacious suggestion.

"You seem to have forgotten something, Polly," he

said hoarsely. "We're married now—and not to each other."

She gave him a defiant look. "Need that stop us?" she challenged.

"Being betrothed to me didn't stop you with Charles, did it?" he asked bitterly. "So it follows as the night the day that being married to Charles won't stop you with me, is that the way you see it?" He did not wait for her to state how she saw it, but rushed on while his blood was up. "Well, you may dishonor your marriage vows with half the county if you like, but I intend to honor mine!"

For a moment he thought she was going to slap him and would have been almost glad if she had. He was dying to lay violent hands upon her; at the moment it would have been a joy to throttle this woman who attracted him more than any other ever had—or ever would.

But Lady Polly resisted—surely with an effort—her impulse to strike his words from his lips. Her gold-green eyes glowed more brightly than leaping embers on a hearth, but she kept her aplomb.

And then the dance mercifully ended and he returned her, flouncing a bit but otherwise with her composure fully recovered, to a smiling Charles who as usual had noticed nothing. Lady Polly was promptly swung away by someone else into the dancers but Grantland remained. His jaw jutted out truculently and he gave Charles every opportunity to nettle him—but nimbly Charles avoided every opening for an affront.

"Faith, we should both be happy tonight!" The saffron-haired young lord clapped Grantland familiarly on the shoulder, as became old friends. "Both of us bride-grooms, both of us with bonny brides. A toast to their eyebrows, I say!"

Somewhat mollified, Grantland drank, but over the rim of his glass his smouldering gaze sought out the maddening wanton beauty who was just now outrageously flirting with every man in sight.

Tom was right, he told himself grimly. *I am well out of it. Charles can have her!* But he knew himself for a liar.... Abruptly remembering Dorinda, who stood forlornly by Mary Lyddon, he went over and devoted the rest of the evening to her exclusively. It gladdened him to see how his paying court to her brought a tremulous smile to her anxious features, and then at last the kind of truly happy look a bride should have.

She was indeed a bride, he told himself, and happiness was her right. He would not let Polly—for all he could not forget her—steal that happiness away!

But he stayed close to home for some weeks, for to wander about might bring him into contact with Lady Polly—and now he did not trust himself in her company.

Dorinda was delighted to stay home, believing it meant that Grantland had no wish to leave her side. The ball—and those twinges of fright she had felt, seeing them together—had faded from her mind. She was Grantland's wife. Who could ask for more?

The next time Grantland and Dorinda saw Lady Polly was a different kettle of fish altogether.

They were driving out in their carriage in the crisp morning air. The horses were prancing, but Grantland held them to a sedate pace for he had not of late liked Dorinda's pallor. The mists that had haunted the night had fled before the sun which now struck golden on Dorinda's amber velvet gown and fashionable red fox muff, and glinted on Grantland's wine-red velvet coat trimmed in gold braid (Dorinda had coaxed him to buy it in memory of that other much loved wine red coat with the tarnished braid that he had since thrown away). Most of the trees had lost their leaves, but some of the ancient oaks still sported rust-colored leaves almost as bright as Grantland's russet hair.

They looked the picture of rural contentment and they were on their way to Lyddon House to pay an early morning call when Lady Polly, on a big chestnut horse, came thundering down the road toward them. She was riding hard in the direction of their front gates and Dorinda had a sinking feeling at the sight of her. Above her dark green velvet riding habit, with its spill of white lace at the throat, Lady Polly's face was flushed and her blue-black curls and the emerald plumes in her hat were flying straight back in the wind. Almost upon them, she brought her horse to such a violent halt that he reared up, skidding on his hind legs and terrifying Dorinda, who thought for a moment those uplifted front hooves were going to crash into her face.

Grantland, who knew of old Lady Polly's skill with her mount, had sat unmoved by her dramatic arrival. "That's Charles's best hunter you have there," he warned her as a greeting. "If you lame him, Charles will have your hide for it!"

But the scornful-faced woman who confronted him was not to be distracted by talk of horses.

"I've made inquiries and the Marquess of Tonby *has no granddaughter*!" she cried. "You found this wench in some London gaming hall and have made her your doxy! You are not married to her—you but said that to make me suffer! Admit it!" And before Grantland, who had risen to his feet in the carriage, could form a proper rejoinder to this amazing speech, she threw at him something that she carried and Dorinda saw with horror as its folds spread over Grantland's head that it was a hideous gown, torn and stained, of striped black-and-orange satin trimmed in frayed magenta and yellow ribands. "This is what your London trollop should be wearing!" shouted Lady Polly, and before Grantland could extricate himself from the enveloping folds of material, she had whirled and was pounding off down the road to Hawkings Castle.

With an oath he wrenched himself free and threw the distasteful garment to the roadside. His face was white, his teeth clenched as he seized the reins again.

"No! Don't follow her!" cried Dorinda, flinging the weight of her whole body onto his arm. "Don't you see, that's what she wants? A confrontation between you! She wants a scandal that will involve us. Oh, Grantland—" her voice rose to a wail—"don't let that awful woman ruin our lives!"

At the pain in her voice, Grantland checked himself. He was trembling with rage as he gently extricated her arm from his.

"Very well, I will not pursue her—*this time*," he said in as reasonable a voice as he could manage at the moment. *"But if there is a next time—!"* His menacing tone left no doubt as to what the outcome of any "next time" would be.

"She can know nothing about me," babbled Dorinda. "Don't you see, she is trying to bring me out, to startle me into admissions, to wreck us both! Oh, Grantland!" She flung herself into his arms. "Grantland, what disaster have I brought down on you?"

"No disaster," he muttered, glaring down the road in the direction Lady Polly had gone. "You've brought me naught but happiness, Dorinda, and yon harpy scurrying down the road has no power to wreck us."

"Oh, but she has, she has," moaned Dorinda. "I am new here, conventions are strict, if my lowly beginnings should become known, I would not be received. And then, if I had a child, that child would not be received either and—"

"Hush." He put a finger to her lips. "There is no question of not being received. I will run through with this blade—" he patted the sword at his hip—"any gentleman who closes his doors to you."

Dorinda shivered and of a sudden she could not get her breath and her world spun.

"Dorinda!" cried Grantland sharply and caught her as she sagged toward him.

To Grantland Manor came a doctor, summoned in haste by the young lord of the manor who was pacing back and forth frantically by his pale young wife's bedside. By now Dorinda had come to, and her blue lips were murmuring, trying to comfort him. There was pity in her dusty blue eyes and the keen-eyed doctor noted that pity as he bustled into the room carrying a black bag.

He left a little less jauntily and conferred with Grantland in the corridor outside.

"Her heart is weak," he said, frowning. "She needs rest—and no excitement. No excitement at all. I have seen cases like hers before. They usually seem to follow on some fever contracted as a child—a mysterious ailment."

"Are you saying she will not recover?" Grantland was seriously alarmed.

"No, I am not saying that. I am saying merely that she needs the kind of life—" the doctor's gaze on the worried young man was apologetic for he knew that Grantland was a recent bridegroom—"the kind of life an invalid might have. I am saying that it would be very dangerous for her to attempt to bear a child."

Rocked back on his heels by this unexpected blow, Grantland stared at the doctor. He moistened his dry lips with his tongue. "Do you mean—" he began carefully.

The doctor held up his hand. "I am not saying that you must not sleep with her," he said hastily. "Only that you should be very careful. I cannot answer for her life if she attempts to bear a child."

Grantland digested that. "I will be careful," he told the doctor slowly. *More careful than you know, for I would give my life for that slip of a girl we just left on the bed.*

"I have a nostrum that might be of help," said the doctor unhappily, for he had hated to bring that haggard expression to the young lord's face. "Wait, I will leave it with you."

But Dorinda took one whiff of the doctor's "nostrum" and wrinkled her nose. She pretended to take it but actually she managed to throw it all away. It was just as well. That particular nostrum was not only ineffectual, it had contributed to carrying away two elderly patients in Bridport but a fortnight ago.

After that, Grantland was suddenly very careful in bed.

"I am not made of fragile delftware." Dorinda chuckled, noting his new caution, for a week had passed and she felt quite recovered. "So do not treat me as if I am!"

Grantland gave her an uncertain look. Feel well she might, but he had been frightened to death by her sudden lapse into unconsciousness. He felt she could not stand another such attack. And as for the doctor's warning, he felt he must take it seriously.

And so his lovemaking assumed a new dimension. She was so fragile, he feared his very lustiness endangered her. His lovemaking was tenderness itself, but he held her oh, so delicately. And always remembered to spill himself harmlessly upon the bedcovers—he was determined not to make her pregnant.

Dorinda objected. "If we are to have a child, Grantland," she said unhappily, "you must not do that!"

"Time enough for children later," he told her with a light kiss. "For now, just the two of us is enough."

Dorinda was a little depressed over that, but she soon recovered her aplomb. Grantland would relent, she told herself confidently, and she would bear him an heir. Meanwhile the days passed pleasantly, time spun out at Grantland Manor as if being unrolled into some luxurious skein. Neighbors came to call, nobody pressed her about her antecedents and—best of all—Charles, perhaps alarmed at his young wife's recent behavior, took Lady Polly abroad.

The thought that vindictive Lady Polly was too far away to reach them was a great relief to Dorinda. She never connected Grantland's new moroseness or the fact that he sometimes stared into space for long hours with Lady Polly's absence.

Lord Chell and his tempestuous lady were reported to be touring the Continent. Some—among them Tom—ventured the opinion that they would never come home.

Dorinda thought that would be wonderful.

The weeks slid into months and a whole year had passed when Grantland made one of his brief cattle-buying trips. He had promised to be home early on Thursday and when the shadows began to lengthen, Dorinda, impatient, had set out on foot to meet him, for she was a notably poor horsewoman and never quite felt right ordering out the carriage for minor errands.

She walked determinedly in the direction of Hawkings Castle, for that was the way Grantland would come. An evening mist was creeping in from the sea and in the fading light Dorinda began to feel vaguely uneasy. For a moment she wished she had ordered out the carriage after all. Around her in the fog the big trees began to assume strange unreal shapes, like half-seen monsters.

She had half-turned to go back when from up ahead came the sound of thudding hooves coming fast toward her. Her heart leaped—that would be Grantland hurrying home to her! He would take her up before him on his saddle and tell her about his trip and the shrouding mists that seemed threatening now would become a romantic backdrop to his homecoming.

She stepped eagerly out into the center of the road to hail him and suddenly out of the mist broke a horse and rider, thundering down upon her.

"Grantland!" she called—and the words froze on her lips.

Charging straight at her—and showing no sign of checking her big chestnut hunter's breakneck pace— was a woman whose distinctive silhouette there was no mistaking.

Lady Polly.

Even as Dorinda, too startled to run, froze in place, she thought she saw a look of gleeful triumph on that fast approaching face. Horse and rider were almost upon her.

Dorinda closed her eyes.

GRANTLAND MANOR, DORSET
1667

Chapter 6

So loud she thought the scream must have been torn from her own throat, Dorinda heard a horse's terrified whinny. There was a sudden rush of wind past her face. Her eyes snapped open to the terrifying sight of the big chestnut towering above her, for he'd been pulled up so sharply that his front feet pawed the air. As Dorinda flinched back, those hooves came crashing down to earth, striking the road beside her with force.

And completely in control, staring down at her with amusement, was Lady Polly—looking astonishingly beautiful in a black broadcloth riding habit.

"Tell me, Lady Meredith," she inquired politely. "Are you tired of living that you leap out in front of passing travelers?"

Dorinda was trembling as violently as the big chestnut horse that rolled its eyes and stamped beside her. But now the slightly contemptuous edge to Lady Polly's voice stiffened her spine and steadied her voice. "I thought it was my husband coming down the road."

"And you thought to greet him thus?" Lady Polly laughed. "Faith, what a life Grantland must lead with you!"

Dorinda was about to make a hot answer about reckless riders when she realized that the woman before her was wearing not only a black riding habit and black gloves, but a black plumed hat as well and from that hat, pinned well back, a flowing black veil—something must have happened. Certainly there was no trace of sorrow in the hard gold-green gaze that bored down at her.

"You are—in mourning?"

"Certainly. I am widowed," came the calm answer.

Dorinda's anger evaporated. "Oh, I am sorry to hear it." And then impulsively. "I am *truly* sorry."

"Are you? I can't imagine why. You hardly knew Charles." The gaze of the woman in black had a taunting quality. "True, I have lost Charles, but I have a fine son to show for our marriage. And you have been married—is it a year now? And yet I hear there is no patter of little feet at Grantland Manor and none expected!"

Dorinda felt suffocated, for Lady Polly's jab had struck a raw spot. Above the turmoil of her feelings she tried to answer but there was a pounding in her head—like hooves growing louder. And suddenly her world went dark and she toppled to the road.

At that moment Grantland rode out of the mist and spurred his horse forward at the astonishing sight of his young wife lying in the center of the road and above her on horseback, looking dauntingly beautiful, the woman whose face he had seen reflected in his hearthfire night after night.

"What has happened?" he demanded hoarsely, as he leaped from his horse and bent over Dorinda.

"She dashed into the road almost under the hooves of my mount. I was hard put to miss her! She babbled something about coming to meet you and collapsed—from fright, I think."

"She is alive," he murmured thankfully as a soft moan escaped Dorinda's lips.

"Of course she is alive! Let me help you, Grantland."

Polly was off her horse and leaning over him. He could smell the faint citrusy scent that was so typical of her. He glanced up and for a moment met her smiling eyes. Even in this moment of stress, they had the power to shake him.

"I must get her back to the house," he said.

"Good. I'll help you."

When Dorinda came to, she was in her own bed looking up into Grantland's haggard face.

"I thought you were done for, Dorinda," he told her huskily. He put his face in his big hands and for the first time in her life Dorinda saw a grown man cry. And how could she know that his tears were partly from frustration that Polly could still sway him when he wanted so desperately to be true to this girl lying pale and limp before him?

"Don't," she murmured in alarm and compassion. "Oh, Grantland, don't."

She squeezed his hand and closed her eyes as hot tears stung her eyelids. Grantland loved her so much and now she was certain of what she had so long suspected: she wasn't going to live to the happy old age he had promised her. She knew that now. Indeed, she'd be lucky if she saw five more Christmases. The shortness of breath, the nagging pains, the sudden weakness, the light-headedness—all these things were worse now. Worse in spite of all the tender care she was receiving.

Grantland would one day soon be a widower. And looking at him now with compassion she felt he wouldn't be able to stand it. He might—do something foolish.

Unless he had someone to give his heart to, someone to get him through it—and not that cruel-faced woman in black who seemed not to care that her young husband was dead!

If only she could give him a child . . . like Lady Polly's "fine son."

Which brought her back to where Lady Polly was now. She asked him.

"Gone home," he muttered. He had got control of himself and now he lifted his big russet head. "She helped me get you up before me. I was afraid I'd hurt you."

Dorinda would have endured any number of bruises rather than accept Lady Polly's aid! "Her widow's weeds must have been tailored in Paris," she said bitterly. "They certainly become her."

"Yes, she was looking very fit," he agreed.

But then Polly Edgecombe had always looked very fit, and black had always become her. He remembered a masked ball at Hawkings Castle one Allhallows Eve when Polly had been seventeen and he but a couple of years older. Polly had worn rustling black silk highlighted with jet and a narrow black satin mask that had turned her startling iridescent eyes into cat's eyes. With her dark hair piled up and alight with orange brilliants she had looked, Charles's mother had remarked spitefully, like a black candle, burning. *A witch, casting her spells about!* She had looked like that today, he thought. And she was still casting her spells about; she had enchanted him, hadn't she?

And now here he was, caught between two women, between a devil and an angel—and just learning that his wild girl was back was tearing him apart. For he had loved Dorinda since he had met her—but he had loved Polly Edgecombe all his life. He could not shake off the spell of the gorgeous witch who flamed like a black candle in his heart.

But the gorgeous witch had worked her spell on Dorinda as well. From that day, Dorinda schemed to become pregnant. When she broached the subject, she found Grantland adamant. Her health was too fragile to risk motherhood.

Dorinda turned away from that conversation, her soft mouth very set, her blue eyes rebellious. No matter what Grantland said, she would work her own ways. . . .

Strong drink, that was it! She almost crowed when she

thought of it. She was looking into her dressing table mirror of fine Venetian glass at the time and Smithers, who was combing out her long fair hair and dawdling over the pleasant task, later remarked complacently in the servants' hall that the mistress was much better— you should have seen her eyes sparkle just now!

Having decided on her course of action, Dorinda could hardly wait to put it into effect. She chose a night when Tom Lyddon had come to call (alone, for Mary Lyddon was too far advanced in her own pregnancy to be "carted about the county," as he put it) and stayed to dine. By pleading every time Tom rose to go that he stay "to drain just one more glass" she managed to get both men solidly drunk. Tom was carried away to bed by the servants while a message was hastily dispatched to Mary Lyddon telling her Tom would not be home tonight. But Grantland, swaying on his feet, made it upstairs to bed under his own power although Dorinda had a couple of bad minutes when she felt his long legs might buckle and send him plunging down the entire flight.

She ordered Cleves, his valet, to undress him and put him to bed and when Cleves had left, she took off all her clothes and slid in beside Grantland, feeling excitement thump in her chest.

"Grantland." He had turned over and was lying on his face in his nightshirt, snoring. She struggled to turn him over but he lay there, a massive inert weight, too heavy for her to move. She frowned, considered calling Cleves back to turn the master over, but rejected the notion. Cleves would think it distinctly strange and might remark on it to Grantland tomorrow. And Grantland would wonder about it—and perhaps come up with the right answer. She would not want that, it would make him doubly careful in future!

"Grantland." She tried again to move him but Grantland was deep in sleep and only grunted.

Not sure how best to proceed, she edged close and

managed to worm one arm beneath him in the soft feather bed. She could feel his sinewy thighs, satiny to her fingertips, a tangle of curly hair and then the smooth silk of sleeping masculinity. Her arm felt deadened by his weight as she tried to tickle him to life and of a sudden she had done it.

Still asleep, but responding to a call as ageless as time, the man beside her shifted his position and threw an arm over her tingling body. A moment later he had thrown a leg over her and she melted into his arms with a satisfied sigh as instinctively Grantland claimed her as his own.

He seemed to come to himself groggily as he entered her, and his voice was blurred as he muttered something that sounded vaguely like "Polly" but Dorinda forgave him that for he was not himself. She shivered against him and felt his arms tighten about her as, responding only to his own pleasure and with no slow delightful playful buildup as was his usual way with her, he brought the whole thing to a quick decisive culmination and shrugged his body off of hers and sank back into a dreamless sleep.

Dorinda, lying naked and pulsing beside him, pulled the coverlet up and went to sleep with tears of thankfulness trembling on her lashes.

The next morning Grantland woke with a hangover and considered her anxiously. "Did I make love to you last night?" he asked bluntly. "For I was well into my cups and knew not what I was about." He sat up and winced as a pain seemed to split his head apart.

"What would it matter?" she countered blithely. "I am not likely to be 'caught' by one time, even if you lost your head and forgot to be careful." With studied casualness she let the coverlet slip down so that it revealed the naked roundness of her delicate breasts.

But Grantland ignored the invitation. "I have promised myself to be careful," he muttered, groaning as he got up. "What did we do with Tom?"

"Put him in the yellow bedchamber to sleep it off," she laughed. "And sent a note to his wife not to worry!"

"Good girl," he said, running a hand through his russet hair. "Remind me not to drink so much!"

Dorinda sighed. She had rather hoped he would feel like making love to her again this morning, but she supposed he would prefer not to with a splitting head. "Anyway," she said rebelliously, "what would be so terrible about my becoming pregnant? Lady Polly is back, bringing with her a fine son!"

So that was it! Grantland turned a bemused look upon her. She wanted to emulate Polly! But Polly had an iron strength.... His lips closed in a firm straight line.

"I will not need to be reminded not to drink so much," he said dryly. "I will remember it all by myself!"

Dorinda, just tugging her silk stockings onto her slim legs, made a slight irritable movement with her shoulders that rippled the flesh of her pale bare back gently. She was a lovely sight and his gray gaze softened.

"I *must* remember, Dorinda," he told her gently. "For both our sakes."

"Not for mine!" she flashed, getting up and turning to look for her chemise. "*I* would *like* to have a baby!"

How frail she looked, standing there challenging him, with her delicate bones and her pale sweet flesh! How innocent and how charming in her nakedness, dewy fresh. Grantland felt a lump rising in his throat. He was not good enough for her—he would never be good enough for this sweet creature who had come to him like a gift from a flaming city—but at least he could safeguard her against her own folly. In that moment he resolved to be twice as careful.

Two months later a shining-eyed Dorinda announced that she was pregnant.

Grantland took the news as if he had been dealt a blow. He looked shocked. "You are sure?" he asked at last.

Dorinda nodded happily. "I have skipped two periods. And this morning I was ill before breakfast. Oh, Grantland, I am *certain*! We are going to have a baby!" Impetuously she threw her arms around his neck and felt his long drawn out sigh.

"I tried to be so careful," he muttered.

"And look what God has given you!" she mocked him joyously.

He gave her a tender look. "I am glad you are so happy, Dorinda."

"But—are you not happy?" she asked uneasily. "Don't you *want* our child, Grantland?"

"Of course I do," was his hasty response. But she could see the shadows clouding his gray eyes. He was afraid for her....

The next months were the happiest of Dorinda's life for Grantland tried to spend every waking moment with her. He showered her with gifts and seldom left her side. She had never felt so cherished.

They would have been peaceful months save for the scandal that had broken over Lady Polly's head. Charles's cousin, intent on inheriting the title, insisted that Charles had never legally married her and that even though she had borne him a son, that son was a bastard and could not inherit. The courts, which had been so ready to turn over everything to the new little Lord Chell, were brought up short by the fact that there was no record of the English wedding ceremony Lady Polly had at first claimed. Could there have been in fact a "common law" marriage? Had the requirements been met?

Grantland, hearing it, shook his head and there was pity for Lady Polly in his eyes. He had not seen Polly since the day she had nearly ridden Dorinda down.

It was in early spring, a day of scudding clouds and sudden patches of blue, that unavoidable business took him again on the road past Hawkings Castle. Halfway there his head came up in surprise as he saw before him, saddled and bridled and grazing by the roadside, the big chestnut hunter that Polly favored. The rider was nowhere in sight.

Frowning, Grantland dismounted and searched nearby. "Polly," he called. No answer came back through the chill damp of the springtime woods. Polly took chances, he knew. She could have been thrown, knocked unconscious. She could be lying somewhere bleeding to death right now in these woods. Grantland seized the big hunter's reins and headed his own mount toward Hawkings Castle. If Polly was lost somewhere in the woods, he would institute a search.

Almost as he mounted, the heavens opened up and rain poured down, soaking him as he turned down the familiar drive to Hawkings. Suddenly, among the old gnarled oaks and locusts the castle loomed up before him. It was made of ancient stones but it had been remodeled many times. On its other side—the side that looked out from the cliffs to the sea—was a library with big glazed casements that opened out onto a stone terrace. But from this side the house presented a formidable medieval front with a doorway of intricately carved stone that arched around a thick oaken door studded with nails against attack by arrows. Charles had been proud of that door, he remembered.

On that oaken door he pounded with the big iron boar's head knocker and when a servant let him out of the downpour and into the ancient great hall with its flagstone flooring and enormous yawning fireplace and high-arched beamed ceiling, he said tersely, "I've brought back Lady Polly's chestnut hunter. Is she at home?"

"She is," said Polly's voice from the library door, which lay some distance away to the right. "Come in, Grantland."

The servant disappeared and reluctantly—for he had hoped to postpone this meeting as long as possible—Grantland strode toward the open library door.

The sight within was a startling one.

The high-ceilinged familiar room where Charles's father had stored his cherished leather-bound volumes was unchanged. The room still smelled faintly of leather from the old bound books, and of the mustiness of age from dusty vellum. Across from him on the stone hearth burned a welcome fire, warding off the damp.

He saw that Lady Polly, now that the legality of her marriage to Charles had been challenged, had abandoned her widow's weeds. But then Polly had never cared a whit for convention! Her fashionable burnt orange riding habit, soaking wet, lay tossed over a tall carved chair. An orange hat with sodden plumes formed its own pool on the long trestle table. A pair of dainty boots reflected the glow of the leaping red-orange flames and Lady Polly herself, down to a sheer wet chemise through which the dusty rose of her nipples and the silky black triangle of hair at the base of her hips were plainly visible, tossed aside her wet stockings and turned to greet him.

"Come in, Grantland," she said, composure itself. "Would you mind handing me that comb? My hair feels plastered to my skin!"

Grantland picked up the silver comb that lay on the table. Warily he advanced toward her. "You have moved downstairs?" he hazarded, looking around him for a bed.

She laughed and took the comb from him. He was uncomfortably aware of her sinuous body in fabric so revealing it might as well have been gauze. " 'Tis the only fire that's been lit and I thought to dry me off before going upstairs to change clothes. So you found my hunter? We parted company when we ran into a beehive! I went out of the saddle and we ran in opposite directions. Rather than pursue him and perhaps meet the bees again, I decided to walk home and send a groom back to fetch him." She was combing her long wet raven hair with the silver comb as she spoke. To Grantland that shining surface looked like undulating black satin against her damp ivory skin. "But halfway here," she added, "it began pouring. I see you were caught in it too. Take off your coat and shirt, Grantland. You can dry them over these chairbacks which we will pull up before the hearth." Her speculative gold-green gaze seemed to see right through him, as if she knew the effect she was having on him.

Grantland felt he was losing himself in the depths of those iridescent eyes. He divested himself of his sodden coat, hesitated, then at Polly's shrugging, "Oh, *do* take off your shirt, Grantland. We are neither of us unduly modest!" addressed his fingers to his wet shirt. She was coiling up her hair as she turned about before the fire. That turning not only served to dry her off, it presented her tempting body, aglow in the firelight, at changing angles to Grantland's fascinated gaze. His shirt came off and he draped it over a chairback. "I have been worried about you, Polly."

That imperious dark head went up, and as her chin lifted Lady Polly's expression turned noticeably chilly. "I cannot imagine why anyone should worry about me!" she said waspishly. "As you can see—" she waved her arm about her, the gesture encompassing all of this clifftop castle—"I want for nothing."

But all of that could soon be snatched away. Grantland felt suddenly terribly sorry for the defensive beauty, who had spent all her life as the belle of the ball and now was deserted by all—even by him. And with her marriage challenged....

"Charles should have married you before he left England," he growled. "It was shabby of him not to do so."

She gave him an uncertain look but when she spoke it was with the frankness he had always found so endearing. "Yes, well—I was unwilling to wait for the crying of the banns. I was angry with you and I wanted to make the announcement immediately that we were already wed. And then we actually did have a ceremony on shipboard but the captain has since perished along with his ship's log and there is the matter of securing the testimony of witnesses, for Charles's cousin has declared the papers to be a forgery."

Grantland was not sure whether the papers were forgeries or not. The handsome minx before him was quite capable of forging any papers she felt she needed—or having it done.

"If there is anything you need," he said slowly, remembering all the years that he had loved her, "call upon me."

"We will drink to that," she said, going over to a small cabinet. Silently she poured them both glasses of port and he was very aware of her. Each supple movement of her splendid body reminded him—he who was so anxiously practicing abstinence at home, worried as he was about his young wife—of what it had been like to clasp tempestuous Polly Edgecombe in his arms and roar with her to passion's close.

She gave him a sweetly mocking look through her lashes as she waved him to a chair and handed him a glass of the rich red wine. Grantland, who had sunk down onto a tall-backed chair of carved oak with velvet pillows thrown upon it for comfort, felt somehow trapped—as if he had followed a strolling tigress into her lair and now she had turned on him.

He lifted his glass. "To other, better days, Polly."

"To us." She touched her glass to his.

Grantland felt the strong wine heating his throat as it went down. Faith, he needed it. Just being this near his old love was strong wine in itself.

"For myself, I shall drink mine as I used to do when we were alone, Grantland." She sank gracefully down on his lap.

Beneath his rain-wet trousers, Grantland felt the muscles in his groin contract. She had taken him by surprise but it was hardly civil to leap up and unseat one's hostess. Or to seem to reject her at a time when she was in such deep trouble. He would let her drink her wine, he told himself firmly, and then dive into his coat and shirt—wet or dry—and depart.

But Lady Polly was in no hurry. She slowly sipped the deep red liquid and smiled up into his face. "I have missed you, Grantland," she murmured in that voice so laced with intimacy that always wore across his senses. She reached out and tenderly pushed back a lock of damp russet hair that had fallen forward over his eyes. As she moved, her seat shifted upon his knees and both the pressure of her rounded buttocks and the light touch of her questing fingers went through him like a bolt of lightning leaping from hill to hill.

"Polly," he said thickly, and it was the voice of a man who had held himself in check too long.

And then it happened. Of a sudden she had flung herself against him, and there was nothing between his naked chest and her soft rose-crested breasts but a gauzy layer of wet chemise. Through that layer he could feel the pressure of her breasts, crushed against him, burning into his chest like twin points of fire. He heard without heeding the small crash as she tossed her wine glass carelessly toward the hearth where it broke and spattered wine to hiss in the flames. Theirs was a shared madness, and his own empty glass dropped from his fingers to roll across the deep blue Turkey carpet.

Her hot moist lips were pressed against his own, her tongue was probing ardently into his mouth, he could hear her gasping sighing breath explode in his throat as her eager fingers massaged the back of his neck and slid downward, grazing his back with her nails.

Grantland had been a long time continent. Too long. Memory and desire—a mad desire for her flesh that had never really left him—overwhelmed him at that moment. He had found her again, she was in his arms and he was in no mood to let her go. His sinewy arms seemed to go round her of their own volition, his lean body fitted itself to hers as if he had never held another woman.

Her breath was sobbing in her throat as they slipped to the floor and then she was beneath him, lying upon the thick deep blue pile of the carpet. Outside rain beat down, slamming against the big casement windows in gusts, seeming to close them into a private world of their own. The servants were all occupied elsewhere, above the crackling of the fire his blood roared in his ears, he was too overheated to stop.

Grantland was vanquished. With emotions too strong to gainsay driving him, he tore at his trousers—and she was helping him, their eager hands collided. Now in gorgeous dishabille, she seemed to purr beneath him, her slender body writhing, arching to his lightest touch. The supple length of her was fitted to his arms with a tenderness that was something new for her—for she had never been tender before, only passionate. Now she touched him lovingly, she murmured little lost endearments that flickered away even as they were spoken. She had managed to shrug out of her chemise and now the silky still damp smoothness of her woman's body slid along his own wet skin. Her fingernails clawed lightly, vibrantly, at his back and her lithe torso seemed to plunge upward to meet his downward thrust.

These were moments of madness when they both held a wild belief that they had ventured into some unreal world where conventions were suspended and only desire held sway. Knowing at heart that these were perhaps the *only* moments clasped in ecstasy that they would ever share, they held onto them by main strength. Fiercely passionate now, they savored the violence of their own feelings, touching, turning, twisting, embracing, finding new ways to excite, new delights to savor, wringing the last drops of sweetness from every moment until inexorably they were lifted on a great broad river of untamed desire and swept like leaves toward the sound of distant falls murmuring enticingly up ahead. Swiftly, inexorably, they were carried forward, the murmur became a thunder, the thunder became all there was, and in a last great burst they sparkled down in a waterfall of wonder, back to the soft deep blue pile of the Turkey carpet and the sound of rain driving in gusts against the windowpanes.

It came to Grantland, as to someone emerging from a dream, that they had not locked the door.

His big head lifted—and sure enough, a shocked chambermaid stood there.

"Close the door!" screamed Lady Polly. "And if you tell what you have seen, I will have you whipped!"

The sight of the open-mouthed girl staring at them, rooted, before she slammed the door and ran, the sound of Polly's raging voice, brought the real world back to Grantland in a rush. Still shaken by the fury of passions so recently sustained, he pulled away from Polly's clinging arms.

"Don't go," she whispered brokenly, reaching out her hands in mute appeal. "The girl will say nothing, Grantland."

In a kind of mortal agony, he looked down at her. Desire was writ across her face, and an expression that had in it elements of heartbreak. So Polly—Polly, that he had thought so heartless—had suffered too.... She had never stirred him so, and in his heart he knew that he must go now—or he might never leave her at all.

"I am sorry," he muttered. He ran a distracted hand through his hair and readjusted his trousers to present a decent appearance.

Lady Polly did not rise from the floor. She lay there in tempting ivory nakedness with her long dark hair still wet and glistening—and she looked surprisingly fragile, lying there, for all her lithe strength. It was a fragility that tore at his heart. Around her, tumbled, lay the damp white chemise, and its billowing torn lace ruffles against the deep blue carpet gave her the look of rising from a frothing midnight sea. He would always remember her thus—he knew it just as he knew the sun would rise tomorrow.

"Why are you sorry?" she whispered. "I am not."

He frowned down at her, trying to erase his desire for her from his mind—and could not. "I lost my head," he said. "It was too much, having you sitting on my lap again."

She looked mistily up at him and he marveled that those were real tears on her sooty lashes—she who never cried, not when her favorite horse broke its neck, not when she burned her hand in the fire, a scar she still bore. "I have dreamed of having you back," she said simply. "And now here we are. Together again."

"Not back together," he demurred, giving her a haggard look. "We must forget this ever happened." He was tucking in his shirttail as he spoke and telling himself that he should look in some other direction than toward this entrancing woman. But he could not tear himself away, not just yet. He wanted to fill his eyes with the sight of her, for it would have to last him a lifetime. He had wronged Dorinda but—he swore a great inward oath—it would not happen again.

"Oh, Grantland, why fight it?" Lying on her back, Polly stretched luxuriously and her gold-green eyes were smiling for she could see the effect she was having on him reflected in his tormented gaze. "We were meant for each other—we've known that all our lives."

Grantland never doubted the truth of that statement. She had always been for him the One Woman. But it was too late for devilish Lady Polly and her wiles; there was an angel at home to be thought of.

"Whatever might have been is over," he said roughly, and seized his coat. "We have made our beds."

"And now we must lie in them?" she mocked. "Oh, Grantland, it is that granite heart of yours that I have always fought! That is why I left you again and again— it was that immovable rock-hewn beast in you that I

couldn't budge! And yet—" her misty smile glimmered—
"I always took you back, didn't I?"

Grantland's jaw hardened for it was true. Polly, wily
wench that she was, had wanted to bend him this way
and that according to her latest whim, and his straight
back had never taken to such bending. The taste of her
kisses was still warm on his mouth, the remembered
touch of her still excited his loins in a way he had
hoped to forget, but he knew that at last it was over
between them.

It had to be. For Dorinda's sake.

Lady Polly saw that hardening of his face. She scrambled up from that tangle of white chemise and ran
naked ahead of him and blocked the door just as he
reached it.

"Do you want me to go out the window?" he asked
politely.

"I don't want you to go at all," she whispered vibrantly.
"I want you to stay and share another glass of wine with
me—for old times' sake."

"We have shared enough wine," he said with irony.
"And rather more than wine!"

She was looking up at him, her entreating iridescent
gaze seeming to pull him downward toward the silken
trap of her soft lips and softer breasts. He steadied
himself against the pressures of his own desire and
reached behind her to open the door.

"Oh, don't go," she whispered, sinking to the floor
and throwing both arms around one of his legs. "Don't
leave me, Grantland!"

"Polly," he said hoarsely. "Let me go. I cannot stride
out of here with you hanging onto me and entreating
me not to leave you. What will the servants say? That I
was dragging you naked about the hall? You will become a scandal!"

"I am already a scandal," she said wistfully. But she
rose and stepped back from him. One last light touch
she gave his cheek before she let him go—and it took

all his willpower not to respond to that touch by bearing her to the floor again. "Grantland, Grantland..." she murmured with a sigh.

And then he was through the door and striding out of the castle into the rain to flay himself with abuse for betraying Dorinda.

HAWKINGS CASTLE, DORSET
1667

Chapter 7

But the woman Grantland left behind in the library of Hawkings Castle—and in whose arms he had found such brief and bitter bliss—had watched him go with a mixture of emotions so violent they threatened to tear her apart. For the first time in her heedless life she had wept bitter tears. And hated from her soul the woman who stood between them—that frail young wife who was bearing Grantland's child.

Lady Polly's personal maid, Tress, who had been sent on an errand into Lyme, came back to find that Lady Polly had made a shambles of her bedroom and ripped several ballgowns to shreds. When Tress, who had been with Lady Polly before she went to Europe, had timidly asked what was the matter, Lady Polly had screamed, "Get out!" and had leaped up and thrown the bed pillows and a bottle of scent at her.

Tress had fled in fright to the kitchens and there found Cook bullying the cowering chambermaid into confiding the truth. Tress had listened and then nodded her head in complete understanding.

"She loves him right enough," she told Cook wisely. "I always knew it. Oh, she enjoyed having Lord Charles and all the others chasing after her and driving them wild, but it was Lord Grantland she always meant to take to her bed in the end—and now he's gone and got him a wife, and even though she's had a child and lost a husband, my poor lady still can't get over him."

"How do you know that?" demanded Cook scornfully. "She didn't take you to Europe with her, she left you at Edgecombe Hall!"

"And came to get me the moment she got back!" Tress bridled. She heaved a deep sigh, wandered from the kitchens and moped about looking tragic for the rest of the day. For it had always been Tress's habit to fantasize that she herself was Lady Polly and to envision her own white arms held out enticingly to a variety of men, and giving herself to each with reckless abandon. Since Tress was "as homely as a mud fence" according to Cook, this was never likely to happen except in her dreams.

But by nightfall Lady Polly, who had a tendency to rise above adversity, told Tress tartly to "give up this long face" she was wearing and to "buck up," whatever her trouble was.

For Grantland, Polly told herself—with all the assurance of a beautiful woman who has tested the power of that beauty many times—would soon return. Did he not have a pregnant wife with a weak heart? God's teeth, he would fear to make love to the wench! Lady Polly's smile flashed at the thought. Seated at her dressing table, she looked into the Venetian glass mirror with its ornate frame and studied her reflection narrowly.

The mirror gave her back the face of a schemer. It was a face of wicked beauty, lit by those long, soot-fringed gold-green eyes. Her slightly pointed chin was lifted at the triumph she foresaw in the not too distant future—for Grantland was a young, strong, virile male. He would chafe at being without a woman (and Lady Polly scornfully discounted his pregnant wife!) and he would remember that Hawkings Castle was but a short ride away.

Ah, he would be back! For a moment her curving lips trembled and the gold-green eyes held honest pain for Lady Polly—bent on the pursuit of pleasure and completely amoral—had learned too late that she truly loved Grantland. How her heart had writhed at the thought of him holding some other woman in his arms! She had moaned in her bed at night, imagining every kiss, every silken embrace—and waking to the bitter realization that it could all have been hers, that Grantland had been very patient with her but that even a lover's patience can wear itself out.

And so she had lost him.

And the shock of that loss had driven her irrevocably into Charles's waiting arms.

But even Hawkings Castle had been too close to her former lover. She had been waspish with Charles—some nights she had denied him her bed and had gone for long dangerous walks on the cliffs overlooking the sea where the white surf boomed. Once, on a foggy night, she had missed her footing and nearly plunged down to the wet black rocks below.

Charles had had an answer for it all—he had taken her to Europe. And Lady Polly, with her emotions torn and lacerated, had been glad to go.

But Charles had died and that had changed everything. Now she was back and she wanted all that had been hers before she went away. She wanted Grantland. And she was determined to have him.

Lady Polly had judged her man correctly. Before the week was out Grantland was back, a pale unhappy Grantland who had been warring with himself, who had taken even more tender care than usual of Dorinda all week, restraining himself manfully from making love to her even though she had given him wistful looks. And every night he had tossed and turned, remembering what it had been like to hold his Polly in his arms again.

From one of the oriel windows Lady Polly saw him ride up and she rushed downstairs to open the door herself. Grantland was marching toward the door, frowning as darkly as if he were on his way to the gibbet, and Lady Polly drew a long shuddering sigh. In her heart she had been terribly afraid he would not come. . . .

He broke stride for a moment at the sight of the arrogant dark beauty, elegance itself in a gold-green gown that matched her shining eyes—and then he increased his pace almost to a run.

"Grantland," Polly murmured. "How nice of you to come. . . ." And went, as if she belonged there, directly into his arms.

With silent crushing force, Grantland embraced her. They stood for a moment thus, rapt, swaying in the doorway. Then Grantland carried his lifelong love up the broad stairway—that stairway up which Charles had once carried her on what they had playfully termed their "wedding night." But tonight the heavy carved four-poster in the ivory bedchamber overlooking the sea knew for her an ecstasy that she had never known with Charles.

Grantland sent back word to Dorinda that his horse had gone lame and he would be late. He stayed until the moon was high and even then it was hard to wrest himself from the raven-haired woman on the big feather bed. She had always bewitched him and now her enchantment had assumed a clandestine flavor, hard to deny.

"Polly," he murmured, ruffling the dark hair that shimmered silver in the moonlight round her head. And then more hoarsely, "Oh, Poll, Poll, why did you break our betrothal? Didn't you know my temper was like to snap?"

It was then, on that wistful note, that Polly knew she

had him. He would come back to her now, she never doubted.

"I was a fool, Grantland," she said softly, her iridescent eyes glowing as she spoke.

A groan choked in his throat as he took her again, took her with all the yearning of a man for his boyhood love.

And then at last he rose.

"Must you go?" she asked wistfully. "Could you not say that you feared for the horse's leg and you had spent the night at Tom Lyddon's? You know he would back you up—and you could be home early in the morning."

Grantland shook his head to clear it of this entrancing wench, disporting herself naked on the bed. "No," he said firmly, and he was pulling on his boots as he spoke. "I must get me home. Dorinda must not worry that something may have happened to me."

His wicked lady cocked an eye at him. "I know Dorinda must have no excitement." (For Dorinda's delicate health was common knowledge.) She yawned and stretched gracefully. The stretch made her ivory stomach muscles ripple and her rose-tipped breasts moved slightly. It was as if she were a willow, he thought achingly, and the wind had rippled her leaves.

By main strength, Grantland tore his gaze away from her.

"When will I see you again?" she called to him as he reached the door.

"Never," said Grantland and stalked off down the hall.

Behind him he heard Lady Polly's mocking laughter.

Two days later he was back. In the daytime and for a short time only. Haggard, worn out with fighting it, he told her how it would have to be with them. He would get away when he could, make what excuses were necessary. Tom Lyddon would back him up if need be.

Lady Polly threw her arms about him in delight. "Oh, Grantland," she breathed. "I have got you back at last!"

The servants, all sworn to silence under pain of dismissal or worse, shook their heads and wondered where it would all end.

Grantland was living these days in a private hell. The arms of Lady Polly and her passionate caresses were irresistible to him. Like a bee drawn by a single exotic flower, he could not stay away. But every time he returned to Grantland Manor and saw his young wife, growing big with child, penitence overcame him. He felt so guilty that he went to ridiculous lengths to please her, he showered her with gifts, he neglected the affairs of the manor to sit with her for long sunny hours watching her exclaim over the lovely baby clothes that the women of the household were busy stitching.

"If 'tis a boy, we will name him Grantland," she cried merrily.

"If 'tis a girl, we will name her Dorinda," he countered.

"Oh, but it *must* be a boy." She frowned. "You will want a son to carry on your name, and—" She stopped suddenly for she had almost said, *And one child may be all that I will ever have.*

Grantland, miserable, did not know what he wanted. "All I ask," he said hoarsely, running a hand through his russet hair, "is that you come through it all with flying colors."

She gave him a smile of such sweetness it broke his heart. "This baby means so much to me, Grantland," she murmured. "I have always wanted a child, something of my very own."

Grantland swallowed and looked out, past the sundial in the garden, in the direction of Hawkings. *He* was supposed to be something of her very own, he told himself, but he had given her a heart divided.

Only Tom Lyddon knew the truth and he kept his own counsel.

"Go slow," he warned Grantland. "Lady Polly's got

the bit in her teeth and is like to run with it. She'll bring you to grief if you don't take charge!"

But Grantland was past warnings. He was embarked on a voyage upon a dark sea that could lead him over the edge of the world as he knew it. He was in love with two women: an angel and a devil—and he would be forever torn between.

Of nights when he saw Dorinda's sweet face on the pillow framed by an aura of pale hair in the moonlight, his heart was near to bursting with love of her. And at these moments he promised himself that he would never bring her sorrow, that Hawkings Castle had seen the last of him.

And yet his blood raced at the very thought of wild Lady Polly and he could hardly concentrate on the food on his trencher for thinking about what kind of excuse he could make this time to get to Hawkings Castle. And once there, it was as if he and Polly—the Polly he had loved since boyhood—had never been separated. They flung themselves into each other's arms with all the abandon of lovers who know they are soon to part—and made love with a desperation that heightened everything, and brought a bittersweet tang to their days—and a wild splendor to their nights.

Two women—and only his one bursting heart to contain them both.

"He'll come to a bad end," Tom Lyddon muttered, watching Grantland ride by. He passed the front gates of Lyddon House without seeing either Tom or Mary Lyddon, who were walking their horses down the drive, and there was such an expression of raw anticipation on his lean face that Tom was glad that Mary was staring down at a clump of roses at the side of the drive and had not seen him.

"What was that you said, Tom?" Mary Lyddon, who was out riding for the first time since the birth of her child, inquired.

"Nothing," said Tom hastily, glad that Grantland had

passed on by. "I think you've had enough exercise for the first time out, Mary." He turned his horse's head back toward the house. Mary followed him without protest, never dreaming that Tom's reason for shortening the ride was not her health but that he did not want her to see Grantland taking the road that led to Hawkings Castle—and perhaps remark on it to Dorinda.

Sometimes Grantland met Lady Polly in the woods. Fearing he might be observed taking this winding road too often, he found a little deserted woodcutter's hut and they made it their own. There the lovers sighed and kissed and found forgetfulness—until it was time to go back, he to his life, she to hers.

Although they sometimes discussed Lady Polly's situation (her parents had disowned her, Charles's cousin was pressing his case in the courts), neither of them ever mentioned divorce. Lady Polly knew instinctively that Grantland would never divorce Dorinda. Not that divorce was even possible—it could only be had by Act of Parliament and Parliament was not likely to act on behalf of a besotted West Country gentleman to rid him of his blameless—and pregnant—young wife. But both of them felt, as they embraced in that woodsman's hut, that their lives had been somehow blighted by Grantland's trip to London.

Lady Polly sensed something else too. She sensed that Grantland truly loved Dorinda, although in a different way from the way he loved her, which was deep and old and tangled along with his boyhood dreams in a web of broken betrothals and rich reunions. She sensed, with a flicker of fear, that Grantland loved Dorinda in an almost religious way, for her purity, for her goodness.

It was a hard thing to fight but Lady Polly had ever been a fighter.

"I want you all to myself, Grantland," she mumbled one late September day when there was a sudden nip in the air. "When all this interference in Charles's affairs is over"—for she always called the aspersions cast by Charles's cousin upon the legality of her marriage "interference"—"couldn't we go away together?" And then in a pleading tone, "Oh, Grantland, these past months, haven't I been as true to you as you could ever have asked?"

"Indeed you have, Polly." Grantland stared down at her soberly. Wistfulness was new to her and she was very appealing there in the early morning chill in the woodsman's hut, uncomplaining that the soft flesh of her breasts that she had bared to him had turned to gooseflesh. "I'll make a fire," he said abruptly.

"No, the smoke would only attract notice—and we wouldn't want that." She snuggled down among the woolen blankets with which they had furnished their trysting place.

This thoughtfulness was a new side to Polly. He gazed down on her with vast tenderness. "I wish we could go away together," he said—and meant every word.

Those big iridescent eyes gazed up at him and that lovely mouth, so wistful before, curved into a smile. "Oh, Grantland, we can—*we can!* Once the child is born, once Dorinda is out of danger—*then* you can tell her about us." And at his startled expression, she added hastily, "There would be no need to disturb her. She and the child could continue to live comfortably at the Manor. But you and I, Grantland, we could go abroad! Oh, there is so much of the world that I would show you, places that Charles and I—" Her voice cut off and she immediately regretted that she had mentioned Charles's name for it was obvious that she had upset Grantland.

"Tell her?" he repeated, amazement and anger blending in his voice. *"Tell her?* You must be mad! The shock would kill her!"

"No, it would not!" Cold and irritable and tired of creeping out of her house in the darkness and making her way to an uncomfortable hut to meet her lover, Lady Polly gave him an indignant look. "We cannot go on like this, Grantland!" Her voice sharpened. "I want all of you," she cried desperately. "Not just Dorinda's leftovers!"

He was straightening his clothing, pulling on his boots. "You are right," he muttered. "We cannot go on like this. We must end it."

"Oh, no!" Polly came up out of the covers, ignoring the cold. Her body was white and lovely and she clasped her arms around his boottops. "I cannot give you up, Grantland," she wailed.

He gave her a bleak look and rose to shake her off. "After the child is born," he began, "we—"

A look of terror washed over her beautiful face. *So he meant to break off with her after the child was born!* She could see it writ clear on his frowning face. "Oh, no," she gasped. "Do not say it." She put her hands to her ears and her cloud of dark hair fell over her face, shielding it. "I will not hear it!" she cried desperately.

"I will see you tomorrow," muttered Grantland, moving toward the door.

"At Hawkings—it is too cold here," she insisted.

He paused in the doorway and her heart nearly stopped for she sensed he was on the verge of saying good-bye to her. Then: "At Hawkings," he agreed with a frown. "But only briefly, for Dorinda's time is very near."

Which meant the time that he would leave his lightsome mistress was very near as well. All that day Lady Polly paced the heavy black oak floors of Hawkings Castle. Her face was very set, her hands twisting together. By nightfall she had made her plans. And that night, when Grantland came, riding up in the moonlight (for once he had looked in on Dorinda in her separate bedroom and assured himself she was sleeping, he could get away—if she woke and did not find him, he could always tell her later that he had been investigating some noise downstairs, or gone out to see about a foaling mare in the stables); that night Polly was at her most charming.

She met him dressed regally, as though for some great ball. She was wearing the narrow-waisted, low-cut, black silk dress trimmed in sparkling jet that she had worn that Allhallows Eve when first she had let him make love to her. Her wide skirts billowed over a rustling petticoat and her big full sleeves, caught at the elbows with flashing jet, spilled black lace over her slender white forearms. Even her dark hair was the same as it had been that night, alight with orange brilliants, when Charles's mother had said she looked like a black candle, burning. She glided toward him as he entered, carrying with her two glasses of wine, one of which she held out to him.

Grantland, who had been thinking about her all day and had finally convinced himself that he must say good-bye and say it now, for Dorinda's child was due at any moment, was caught up by the sight of her, by the memories her gown evoked.

"That dress," he said. "Weren't you wearing it when—?"

"Yes." She laughed. "I was wearing it that first time. You tore the bodice in your eagerness, but it has been cleverly mended." She whirled about that he might view the magnificence of her trim bustline, the gleam of her pale ivory shoulders, the slenderness of her waist. "I wore it tonight—as a reaffirmation!"

His sober face told her reaffirmation was not what he had in mind.

"Come," she mocked. "Why such a long face?" She held out the glass, insistently. "Drink with me, Grantland—a toast to us!"

He shook his head but he took the glass.

"Very well, then drink to all that has been!"

"To that I'll drink. But we must end it, Polly—we both know it."

"Then let us end it on a note of joy, Grantland! Drink to the joys we've know together. Come, drain your glass!"

Her voice was high and excited. Grantland knew he was going to have trouble with her this night and wondered desperately how he could avoid it. For he must get back to Dorinda, whose labor pains, he had been warned, might start at any time. Polly knew that, he had told her this morning! And Dorinda did not deserve the blow of discovering that her husband had been with another woman while her child was being born! This was going to be difficult, for Polly was in a rebellious mood, but he must get on with it. He lifted his russet head and drained his glass.

"Another!" cried Lady Polly, beckoning him toward the stairway. "Come upstairs and we will share a bottle of wine together."

He shook his head. "Not tonight or any other. That is what I came to tell you, Polly. I must have been mad to begin with you again." He looked at her morosely. Just the sight of her had always heated his blood—the sight of her heated it now. Especially in that dress, with its memories.

"Ah, Grantland," she sighed, but there was a sudden change in her, a remoteness. He could sense it. "Come into the library at least. Do not let us end it here in the hall." She was moving toward the library as she spoke.

Reluctantly, Grantland followed her through the massive library door. He would not shame her by ending up in a shouting match with her in the hall. He would hear her out—and then he would go. Back to a blameless wife with whom he belonged and whom he loved deeply—with half a divided heart.

A single candle guttered on the library table beside a bottle of wine. Polly, he decided, had expected this and had prepared the library in advance. The room had a gloom by night that even the vast echoing hall with its high-beamed ceiling did not have. Restlessly, Grantland crossed the large room and turned to stand with his back to the windows which the heavy dark green damask draperies now concealed.

"So we are doomed lovers?" Lady Polly mocked.

"Not doomed, Polly," he said tiredly. "It is just that our ways must part."

"And you have come to tell me this?"

"Yes." Bluntness, he now felt, was the only course.

"Pour yourself a glass of wine, Grantland—and some for me, I think I need it."

Sighing, he did so. And when he looked up, he saw that she had managed to slip her bodice down so that her naked breasts were piquantly displayed. To his startled gaze, with the candlelight sparkling on the jet and the watered effect of the black silk, she seemed to have risen from sea-wet black rocks. And as he stared, she shook her head back and forth, shaking out the pins that held her high fashionable hairdo, so that her gleaming blue-black hair spilled down scattering orange brilliants over the midnight blue rug, creating more than ever the illusion of a lustrous dark siren rising from the foam to lie upon the wet rocks and sing her siren song.

He left his wine untouched—and so did she.

"Polly," he said in a tired voice, "this can avail us nothing. We long ago set our feet upon the road that we must travel."

"Did we, Grantland? *I* did not!"

Of a sudden she turned and darted back through the door, slamming it behind her. He heard the turning of the big key in the lock. Her ringing cry reached him from the other side of the heavy door. "You will stay with me, Grantland, whether you like it or not!"

Sighing, Grantland crossed to the door. This was going to be worse than he had thought. "Polly," he said. "Polly, be sensible. You are a proud woman. Do you want your servants to know that we have ended up at odds like this? For you seem to have forgotten that this room is on the ground floor. If you do not let me out the door, I will only go out through the casements onto the terrace."

"Try it!" she jeered.

Irritated, Grantland strode across the room and threw wide the drapes. An astonishing sight met his gaze. Stout boards had been nailed across the casements, making a solid impenetrable barrier which did not even let in the moonlight.

"This room is full of heavy furniture," he ground out. "Do you think that I will not batter down this door?"

"Oh, in time I think you will," she mocked. "But in the meantime a messenger has been sent to your dear Dorinda, to tell her that her darling Grantland has suffered an accident, that he is dying, that he has been carried to Hawkings and she must get herself here at once if she is to speak to him again in this life!"

Grantland felt cold sweat break out on his forehead. This was no idle threat; the woman on the other side of the door would do it! And Dorinda, frail and pregnant, her time already upon her, jolting along—!

"Polly," he pleaded desperately, for his wild terror for Dorinda brooked any compromise. "Call back your messenger. Do not do this thing and I promise I will spend the night with you."

"No, no, Grantland," she corrected. "You are going to spend *many* nights with me. For the wine you have just drunk contained a strong sleeping potion. Even now you must be feeling drowsy—are you not?"

With an oath, Grantland looked around him. He seized a chair. It was an armchair, of heavy carved black oak, and it looked as strong as a battering ram. He swung it against the door and heard the stout timbers of the door protest. Again he swung it. This time there was a rending sound. He was panting now for he must be quick about this, before the drug took effect. He could dash from the castle and throw himself upon his horse—perhaps even lash himself to his horse if he felt his senses reeling—and pray that somehow the horse would carry him home.

His mind raced ahead. If the servants at Grantland Manor had any sense, they would not tell Dorinda that he had arrived in that condition—and please, God, let him arrive before Polly's messenger!

His straining shoulder muscles burst the seams of his coat as he swung the big chair again—a mighty swing.

The door, unaccustomed to this kind of assault, burst open.

He saw Lady Polly, standing well back, her gold-green eyes sparkling. She had rehooked her black bodice and except that her black hair was streaming down, she was once again the lady of fashion she had been when she had received him.

"Ah, Grantland," she murmured. "What a masterful performance! We will be able to tell our grandchildren about it!"

He was halfway across the room and she was following him when the drug brought him down. He reeled and collapsed at her feet.

Lady Polly stood regarding him thoughtfully with her head at a slight angle. "You were always mine," she said ruefully, nudging his fallen body gently with the toe of a black satin slipper. "Didn't you know that? Nothing—not even death—can ever sever us."

She stood musing, looking down at him, remembering the many times that he had looked at her with love in his gray eyes.

And then she called the servants to put him to bed in her bedroom.

"Ought we not send word to Grantland Manor of what has happened?" asked a shocked Tress, who had been visiting relatives in Lyme and had returned with the dawn to find the servants milling about uneasily, and the mistress standing by the feather bed in her ivory bedroom looking down at an apparently sleeping

Grantland. "Cook told me you'd locked him in and he broke out and was taken by a fit and fell down!"

"That's not the story we'll send to the Manor," a composed Lady Polly told her. "And you will carry the message yourself, Tress, for I want it done right. You'll say the Earl of Ravensay is badly hurt and is calling for his wife and that's all you know about it." She smiled, a wicked smile. "By the time Dorinda arrives he'll be waking—and I'll be here in bed beside him!"

Tress's pale eyes widened. This, she felt, was a new low even for her reckless mistress. To send for a pregnant woman about to give birth so that she might view her husband lying in another woman's bed! Her heart revolted.

"I won't do it!" she cried indignantly.

Lady Polly turned the full strength of that gold-green gaze upon her. "Do you remember when your brother was about to be hauled off to debtors' prison, Tress? I helped you then and you said you'd do anything for me—anything."

Tress swallowed. It was true, she owed her mistress a debt—and her mistress was calling that debt now. But what she was about to do stuck in her throat. "I'll go," she said tartly. "And then I'll be giving you my notice—for none will speak to me hereabout when they find out what I helped you do!"

"Very well, Tress," said Lady Polly silkily. "You may seek another position if you like, but jobs are not easy to come by. And remember, there's your old mother—you wouldn't like to see her go to the poor house, would you? And you told me she's too poorly to work and has seizures.... You'll be needing my help again, won't you, Tress?"

Tress's thin shoulders sagged. The mistress had her hooks into her, right enough. "I'll go now to Grantland Manor," she said in a defeated voice.

That lovely wicked smile played over Tress. "There's no hurry," purred the woman in black. "Let's let the lady of Grantland Manor rise and discover her husband's not breakfasting with her, that he's gone off somewhere, no one knows where. She's overdue for the baby, I hear—let's give her time to worry a bit."

Pale and shaken, Tress nodded, biting back the words that sprang to her lips. *God will punish you!* she thought bitterly. *He may have overlooked a lot of things in the past but He won't overlook this!*

"Don't breathe so hard, Tress," said Lady Polly gently. "I can almost hear your thoughts screaming at me. I'll call you when it's time to go."

Tress stumbled out. She told herself that what Cook sometimes muttered was true: Lady Polly was indeed a witch. She had cast her spell over everyone—including Tress. Including the gentleman lying so peacefully in the bed. *He* had tried to break out, to get away—as *she* had just now, but the lady with the long gold-green eyes and the dazzling magnetic smile had proved too much for them both. In her doubt-filled heart, Tress almost feared that Lady Polly would prove too much for God!

Chapter 8

Not till after it was over did Grantland hear what had happened. He had sat up in Lady Polly's bed, still groggy with sleep. He had shaken his big head to clear it—and remembered:

Polly had locked him in. Polly had some scheme afoot to harm Dorinda, momentarily expecting his child!

He came off the bed in a bound, waking Lady Polly, who had sent Tress off to convey her message and—just as she had promised—had gone to bed beside Grantland clad in her laciest black chemise. Lady Polly, rising now on an elbow, watched him charge through the door, almost hitting the door jamb, for the drug was still on him. For a moment her expression was regretful, for she had hoped for a dramatic scene when they would be confronted in bed by a shocked and wavering Dorinda. Then she shrugged fatalistically. What would be would be.

She stretched, yawned, and fell asleep again as carelessly as if she had not set into motion that day a train of events that would overset her world.

Grantland arrived at the Manor at a gallop, tossed his horse's reins over a hitching post and hit the ground running. The wind and motion had cleared his head and he was agonized with fear for Dorinda. All those hours he had been at Hawkings—what would she think, deserted when her child was expected momentarily?

At the stairway he collided with a weeping Mawkers, who was holding a lace-trimmed apron to her face. The apron came away as he jostled her and she gave him a wild look. "You're alive!" she gasped. "We thought—"

"Never mind about me!" He seized her arm. "What has happened? I saw the doctor's horse outside. Is Dorinda all right?"

Mawkers was gulping down sobs as she answered, her bony shoulders shaking with grief. "When we got word your lordship was hurt and like to die and calling for her, Lady Dorinda refused to wait for the carriage to be brought round. She had a horse saddled and tried to ride to Hawkings Castle—and me riding alongside her for I wouldn't let her go alone. But her time did come upon her before she was halfway there and I saw what was happening and I managed to catch her as she fell off her horse—"

Oh, God! he thought, and sweat broke out upon his forehead. "What then?" he demanded hoarsely. "Is she all right?"

"Cleves was with us and I sent him back for the coach and we got her back home."

All that jolting way . . . in labor. Cold fear held him. "And then?"

" 'Twas I delivered the child—in the coach."

"It's over?" cried Grantland, joy and fear mingling in his gray eyes.

Mawkers nodded dolefully. "Ye've a daughter," she said. "But the doctor came later and he says my lady won't live."

Grantland's face went white. Abruptly he released his grip on Mawkers and dashed up the stairs. At Dorinda's door he stopped and got a grip on himself. He didn't want to frighten her by plummeting in, wild-eyed and disheveled. He smoothed back his russet hair with impatient fingers and squared his shoulders, afraid of what would meet him when he opened that door.

And then he opened it.

From the big bed a very pale Dorinda was smiling tremulously at him. Her long fair hair was tangled and damp upon the pillow and nearby hovered the doctor, looking grim, and a couple of scared-looking chambermaids.

Grantland moved forward and they fell away to let him pass.

"Oh, Grantland." Her voice was weak as he bent over her. "You're alive. I was so afraid...." Her voice dwindled away tiredly and Grantland said, "I'm not hurt, Dorinda. 'Twas a mistake—a garbled message. 'Twas my horse was in trouble and I wanted my head groom to ride over since he knows about such things."

"Oh." She was regarding him mistily from her dusty blue eyes, as if she wasn't quite taking that in. "We have a daughter, a beautiful daughter."

Grantland's gaze left her for a moment to contemplate a tiny bundle held in one of the chambermaid's arms. Then he looked at the doctor, who nodded toward the corridor.

Grantland bent to kiss his wife. Her eyes seemed to be closing.

"I've done all I could—I've given her a sleeping potion," the doctor told him earnestly when they were outside in the corridor with the bedchamber door closed. "You will remember," he added impressively, "I warned you the Countess should not bear children."

"Yes, yes," said Grantland impatiently. "But the deed is done. The child has been born. What now?"

"I am afraid there is nothing more I can do," sighed the doctor.

"But 'twas a quick birth. Shouldn't that—"

"Aye, her hip bones moved well. But despite the quickness of the birth, she is very weak. Frankly, I had not expected her to survive the birth—and in a jolting coach on the road!"

Grantland winced. He was glowering at the doctor, who moved his shoulders irritably, then answered that look with resentment in his voice. "She may linger for a day or two," he said testily, "but I have little hope for a recovery. I had a patient like this in Lyme and *she* did not last the day. If only her ladyship had not gone riding and then been jolted about in a coach. I am afraid she has been injured internally."

All that day Grantland sat with his head bowed by Dorinda's bedside. She did not stir, but lay pale and wan in exhausted sleep. The doctor was taken downstairs and fed lunch alone in the big deserted dining room. He came back up to remonstrate with Grantland, who had refused food but was drinking brandy.

"Ye do her no good here, your lordship," the doctor protested.

But Grantland thought differently. He gave the doctor a curt answer and resumed his drinking as he sat by the bed. Hour upon hour he silently flayed himself for all that he had done wrong. Had it not been for that witch at Hawkings Castle—!

Suppertime came and went. The sun went down and the moon came up. Still he sat there, hunched over, waiting for that fragile life before him to flicker out.

He started at the doctor's pitying voice. "She seems stable, surely nothing will happen before morning. I beg you, your lordship, to get some rest. I'm sure she'll last till morning."

Grantland looked up at him with red-rimmed eyes. The doctor privately considered it a face from hell. He stepped back warily. He had seen men look like this before and it was as well to stay out of their way!

Time, was there? Disjointed phrases came and went in Grantland's disordered brain: *Gone riding...jolted about...injured internally...last till morning*— and all of that he laid at Lady Polly's door! Tense and half-drunk, overwhelmed by powerful emotions, something snapped within him. *This was all Polly's fault! She had killed Dorinda, the only really good thing that had ever come into his life. By all that was holy, that raven-haired sorceress should not survive her!*

He rose violently to his feet, nearly oversetting the doctor, who stood agape as Grantland rushed from the room. Downstairs he charged outside toward the stables, threw a saddle over his horse's back, and rode for Hawkings Castle as if seven devils pursued him. It was a dangerous ride for there was a heavy fog now. Through that fog the moon was only a distant pale glow and tree branches and gnarled trunks loomed up suddenly and were gone in the mist.

Grantland thundered on the door of Hawkings Castle and a sleepy servant opened it and peered out. Grantland brushed by him, his booted feet pounding on the stairs.

The noise of his arrival awakened Tress, who slept in a tiny anteroom off Lady Polly's spacious ivory bedchamber. She peered out in time to see Lady Polly just coming out of her sleep. Aroused by the sound of the door being flung violently open, she was sitting up, her dark hair and white body silvered by moonlight as Grantland crossed the room like an arrow shot from a bow and seized her.

Tress heard Lady Polly's bewildered, "Grantland!" as he swept her up unceremoniously, and then at sight of his furious face her voice changed, grew level. "Where are you taking me?"

When he did not immediately answer, she tried to break free and he seized her long dark hair in a cruel grip and held her firm, facing him. "I am going to throw you over the cliffs," he muttered, and his words carried to a cringing Tress. "Then at last I'll be free of you!"

"What is my crime?" cried Lady Polly, twisting her head painfully so that she might view his dark vengeful face the better. "All that I have done was done only for love of you!"

"Love?" His harsh laughter chilled the listening Tress. "You are incapable of love, Polly—you do not know the meaning of the word!" By now they had reached the door and Tress, sensing that they were oblivious to all but each other, melted like a shadow into the bedroom, afraid to speak.

Lady Polly had courage; she proved that now. "How can you say I do not love you, Grantland?" she cried. "I have endured much to meet you in the woods these damp nights! And how can you want to harm me—a woman you have held in your arms?"

"A devil I have held in my arms!" They had reached the top of the stairs now with Tress trailing along behind them in horror. "But I will free myself of you this night!"

Lady Polly seized a carved spoke of the wide Jacobean stairway and stubbornly refused to let go. "Granted I was a little carried away when I locked you in," she wailed. "But that was only because I could not bear to lose you! *But what else?* With what do you charge me, Grantland?"

"You have killed Dorinda," he accused her hoarsely, glaring down at her there on the stairs. "And by God, you shall pay for it!"

"I have killed—!" Of a sudden, hysterical laughter welled from Lady Polly's throat. "I have not even *seen* Dorinda these months past!"

"No, but your message did its evil work!" Grantland gave her a sudden violent jerk that tore her clutching fingers from the baluster.

Frozen at the head of the stairs, Tress watched her mistress flying down it in the strong arms of the master of Grantland Manor. Lady Polly's long dark hair was brushing the stair treads and her white arms were twined around Grantland's neck now. She was running her fingers through his disheveled russet hair and her voice had taken on a sweet beguiling quality—although Tress could not hear the words. Her black silk chemise floated out around his trouser legs and her bare white legs dangled over one of his arms.

Lady Polly had always won out in her dealings with men. Tress expected her to win out now. Lady Polly's voice was hypnotic, her nearness a goad to the senses. Hers was a siren song that dragged men away from virtue, away from hope. Yes, surely her captor would slow the pace that even now was carrying them fast across the flagstone flooring of the great hall!

When they reached the door, Tress was again galvanized into action. She ran down the stairs, raced across the great hall, and was in time to see Lady Polly taken up before Grantland on his big black horse, in time to see the dark gleam of Lady Polly's long hair flying back and mingling with Grantland's own russet mane as they thundered away, disappearing into the fog.

Gone, thought Tress, leaning shakily against the doorjamb. *Gone!*

She wondered if she should tell someone. For Grantland had threatened Lady Polly and from the sound of his hoofbeats, fast disappearing into the distance, she knew that he was heading his horse for the cliffs.

But the servant who had let Grantland in had gone off to bed and Tress abruptly remembered the evil bargain Lady Polly had exacted of her. Her face went stony. Whatever happened, she would give Grantland time. . . .

No one ever saw them again.

Tress always stoutly maintained that as she stood there, wondering what to do, she heard a distant scream— that would have been Lady Polly's scream as the horse slipped and carried them over the cliff edge, down and down and down to those wet black rocks and the wild white-capped waves below.

It could have been like that. Or a maddened Grantland

could have spurred his horse in the fog directly toward the cliffs—and over them, into the sea in a wide wild arc to death. But it was possible too that Lady Polly had screamed as the horse slipped, but that Grantland had got the horse's head up and they had dashed on in safety. It was possible that Grantland, lured once again by his illicit love now that she lay purring again in his arms, had ridden on to some far place where he could hold her against the world.

In any event, no one ever knew the truth, for neither horse nor riders were ever found. They were presumed to be lost somewhere in the treacherous depths and swirling currents off the Dorset coast.

Tress was never certain in her romantic heart that Lady Polly had not prevailed at last, that Grantland had not ridden with her to some secret cove and there made love to her, and later taken her with him on some smuggler's ship to France, where they could forget all that they had left behind them, ignore the shambles they had made of their lives, and live only for each other. Years later Tress would sometimes pause at her work and imagine them there, golden lovers, meant for each other, and secretly hope that it was true.

While all these events took place, while Grantland stormed away with Lady Polly and Tress trembled and waited, back at Grantland Manor, Dorinda rallied. The doctor, sitting patiently by her bedside waiting for her to die, could hardly believe his eyes.

"She is stronger," he told Mawkers at last. "I cannot account for it, but I think that she will live."

Mawkers accounted for it. "There is a God up in heaven, after all," she muttered, and wiped away thankful tears.

The doctor, a most religious man, gave her a reproving look.

Cook accounted for it in somewhat more colorful fashion. Cook was superstitious and she told everyone solemnly that she had seen a hawk fly thrice past her window that night and then she had heard one of the panes break. That hawk was his lordship, she insisted, for had he not been bewitched at Hawkings Castle? Turned into a hawk by that witch, Lady Polly, he was! But he'd come back to make amends and his spirit had entered into the dying woman on the bed and had given her life again.

Nobody believed Cook—but then nobody could really refute her explanation of what had happened. And since the heart was at the time a most misunderstood organ, the nature of palpitations not understood, and Dorinda's problems could neither be properly diagnosed nor treated, her recovery seemed a miracle.

A Puckish fate had gone round full circle.

The strong had died; the weak had survived.

Dorinda never believed any of the gossip surrounding Grantland's death. She believed the story a sympathetic Mawkers made up to cheer her—that the doctor who waited on her had left, that she had seemed to take a turn for the worse, that Grantland had been spurring his horse down a shortcut along the cliffs to overtake the doctor.

The world knew better.

But because the widowed countess who was bringing up a small daughter at Grantland Manor was frail and charming and fair, because Grantland had been popular, because Tom and Mary Lyddon stood beside Dorinda (and too, because so many had hated Lady Polly!), those who might have told her the truth did not.

But as time went by, reasons for Lady Polly's last desperate moves began to show up and heads nodded wisely. For Lady Polly's "marriage" to Charles was presumed never to have taken place and Charles's son was disinherited while he was still a tot. The cousin who had brought action against Lady Polly had won at last and, as the new Lord Chell, had set himself up in style at Hawkings Castle. Lady Polly had got wind of it in advance, the gossips said, and had tried to bring

Grantland Meredith to heel too soon—and that had been her undoing.

Truth is not known to flourish in circumstances such as theirs.

But the manner of their death had been too flamboyant to be allowed to be forgotten and before the year was out, the cliffs where they had perished were said to be beset by eerie screams that echoed over the rocks on foggy nights. As time went by they became known as "Screamer's Cliffs" and were avoided by the superstitious.

Of all of this, Dorinda was oblivious. From the moment of Grantland's death, she had worn motherhood like a cloak, insulating herself with it from the pain of the world around her, making life bearable (when it was not) by concentrating on that small sweet creature that she had given life, and who looked to her for everything. And so—somewhat to Mawkers' surprise— Dorinda got through it in the same sweet fashion that she had accomplished everything else. She counted the days she had known Grantland as the best days of her life and never thought to blame him for a single thing.

She was bringing up a beautiful daughter whom she had named Dorinda, but whom everyone affectionately called "Rinda."

"She will follow her heart as I have done," Dorinda told Mawkers softly.

But where it would lead her, none then could guess.

It takes one generation to make it,
One generation to lose it,
One generation to talk about it—
And one to make it again!

One Generation to Lose It!

BOOK II

The Reckless Lady

Her future's assured—his future is dim
And yet she knows she belongs to him. . . .
Is she always to love him, always to wait,
Trembling and poised at heaven's gate?

PART ONE

The Young Lovers

Years Later...

Chapter 9

Rinda Meredith first saw Rory Edgecombe when he was tussling in the roadside dust outside Lyme with two young bullies. She was six years old, riding by primly in a carriage with her pale lovely mother and the inevitable Mawkers, who clucked over Grantland's widow like a mother hen with only one chick. The housekeeper muttered to herself as they came up to where the small boys were fighting but Rinda, who saw they were but a little older than herself, nearly tumbled out of the carriage in her excitement.

Two of the boys were urchins from the town with greasy hair and shifty faces—they did not interest her. Her sparkling gray eyes (Dorinda never looked into those eyes that she was not reminded of Grantland) followed the third, a golden lad, younger and more slender than the other two, who seemed to be getting the worst of it. As she watched, he suddenly broke free from the grip of one of them, brought up his knee in a way that sent the larger boy reeling and smashed his young fist into the surprised face of the second.

They might have swarmed back over him then, save

that one of them—the largest—noticed a horseman fast catching up with the carriage filled with ladies and they both took off on the run. The winner dusted himself off and gave the little girl in the passing carriage a smile she would always remember—flashing, confident.

Then he too noticed the approaching horseman and his saffron head came up like a deer catching the scent of a hunter. For a moment the lad hesitated, on the brink of running off like his recent attackers. But the wide gray eyes of the little girl, still craning her neck from the carriage, were watching him and instead of running, he gave her a lighthearted wave. Then he squared his thin young shoulders and moved off jauntily to meet the oncoming horseman, a gentleman with rather dilapidated plumes on his hat and an expression that would have daunted the bravest.

The carriage moved on past the scene of recent battle and little Rinda plucked at her mother's elaborate taffeta skirts and asked, "Who was that boy we just passed? The one with the yellow hair?"

The Countess, who had been staring pensively at the driver's broad back, came to herself with a start and asked vaguely, "What's that, dear?"

It was Mawkers who answered. "Trash," said Mawkers gruffly. "You're not to concern yourself with such like, Mistress Rinda!" She bent to rearrange the perfectly pressed pink silk skirts that billowed over the child's short legs, dangling from the carriage seat.

Rinda sighed and looked back. The dilapidated gentleman on horseback had reached the lad now and as she watched he leaned over and gave him a smart cuff on the side of his head. That in itself was not unusual. Schoolmasters routinely thrashed erring pupils with stout sticks, masters cuffed—and sometimes whipped—apprentices. Even Rinda's own gentle faded governess had once or twice in fury at her spirited charge's inattention boxed the child's ears. What was unusual was what Rinda was not to know—the extent of the punishment meted out to the small swaggering lad for fighting.

For Rory Edgecombe had just been taken in tow by his uncle, Rolfe Edgecombe. Rolfe was Polly's dissolute older brother and the present master of Edgecombe Court. Rolfe had hated Polly who had always faced him down, he had hated Charles who had been so much wealthier, he had shaken the dust of Dorset from his boots and gone to London. In London he had ruined himself by his disastrous passion for gaming—even the fine clothes in which he had left Dorset had been lost across the gaming tables. He might have ended up in debtors' prison save for the providential death of his parents. He had returned sulkily to Dorset to find himself with a mortgaged hall and an illegitimate nephew on his hands whose saffron hair and green-gold eyes never failed to remind him of Charles and Polly. With his dark face scarred by dueling (for Rolfe was notoriously contentious), he had been unable to find a suitable heiress to rescue him financially and he regularly vented his pent-up anger on his sister's "bastard" son. The boy took these beatings stoically, with his father's courage, but his green-gold eyes sometimes flashed with the wicked leaping valor of his wild mother. On this particular occasion Rolfe Edgecombe wheeled his horse about and took Rory home merely for the pleasure of beating him near insensible with a cane.

Rinda, of course, dreaming in the carriage as children will (her dream was that the golden-haired lad was a cabin boy on some buccaneer ship), never knew about Rory's suffering.

It was two years before she saw him again.

She had come into Lyme with her mother—Mawkers for once had been left behind—to view some fabrics brought in by a ship's captain from Italy which were supposed to be ideal for new draperies to cover the great mullioned windows of Grantland Manor. But the fabrics had proved disappointingly delicate and Dorinda, paler now and easily tired from any exertion, had paused to consider the offerings of a little flower girl and had engaged the shy child in conversation.

Adventurous Rinda, more interested in the narrow rag-stone alleys of Lyme than in bunches of flowers held in a child's grubby hands, had detached herself from them and wandered on ahead. She had paused at the sound of a flock of screaming gulls just then wheeling overhead. She whirled around, looking up at the white flutter of wings against the high clear blue of the sky—and it was then that she had heard the clatter of hooves behind her. Aware of the narrowness of the stone walls on either side, she had stepped quickly into a doorway.

The boy who had dashed by on a borrowed horse would have seemed unremarkable to many with his shabby tattered clothes and his strong young legs, too long for his ill-cut trousers, emerging to be lost into a pair of battered boots two sizes too large for him. But to Rinda he seemed to emerge suddenly into the sunlight like a golden vision with his unkempt saffron yellow hair seemingly ablaze. He had looked so wild and exciting as he had flashed by that Rinda had caught her breath. As the sound of his pounding hoofbeats disappeared down the maze of alleys, she had run to ask her mother who he was.

The gentle Countess, bent over the flowers and unaware that Rinda had even left her side, looked up absently from her inspection of the roses. "I didn't see anyone, Rinda. I heard the hooves but I didn't look up."

Rinda had sighed impatiently. She was eight years old.

"It was Rory Edgecombe," volunteered the alert little rose seller importantly and Rinda thought she saw her mother's back stiffen a little. "He lives at Edgecombe Court."

Rinda had never been to Edgecombe Court although twice they had driven by in a carriage with her mother's back very stiff and straight and her mother's dusty blue eyes holding steadily to the road and giving not so much as a glance as they passed by the mellow pile of stone that had been home to generations of Edgecombes.

"Have you ever been there?" Rinda had asked, gazing down the long drive at those mullioned and transomed windows catching the sunlight. And her mother, with compressed lips, had answered with complete truth, "Never." And had not explained.

Now Rinda was thinking about that. There were so many places hereabout that she had never been: Edgecombe Court and its neighboring manse, Wildwood, where another Edgecombe held sway. Hawkings Castle, which lay just past the small estate of Lyddon House by road, although so near to Grantland Manor (part of its lands adjoined), was not on her itinerary of places to visit either. There were "new people" at Hawkings, the servants said uneasily when she asked, and they "weren't receiving." Which meant, she learnt later, that the new Lord Chell's heavy debts had had to be settled by the sale of most of the estate's livestock and furnishings. He was living there in genteel poverty with his invalid second wife and his two young sons. They seldom went out and never entertained. Rinda had sometimes seen the sons riding by the gates of Grantland Manor and the older one, a tall dark boy, had given her a speculative look but she had never spoken to either of them— Mawkers, who was Rinda's constant shadow whenever the Countess was not there to guard her, had always quickly jerked her away.

Now her curiosity surfaced. "Mother, why don't we ever call on the people at Edgecombe Court or Wildwood or Hawkings Castle?" Rinda asked her mother meditatively, after the purchase of the roses had been completed, the urchin departed, and they were strolling down toward that pier of unhewn stones men called the Cobb.

The Countess's shoulders jerked. She bit her lip and looked down at the small daughter who had inherited her own angelic loveliness of face and her father's clear gray eyes and a wealth of flaming red-gold hair that was a combination of both of them. She had dreaded that question for so long and now at last it had been asked. She looked out at the wild blue waters of the English Channel stretching out toward the shores of France where Lady Polly had once sought refuge.

Through stiff lips she began, "A long time ago—" And suddenly she thought, *Why tell the child anything? Why not let her grow up not knowing that her father and Lady Polly Edgecombe were ever betrothed? That there had been bad blood and wild rumors?* "The Edgecombes have never been friendly," she hedged. "And as for the new people at Hawkings Castle, I've never actually met them. They keep to themselves—I suppose because they want to." *Or perhaps they did not call upon the Countess of Ravensay because they had heard the rumor that she was but a scullery maid from London "upped" to wife of a peer of the realm! Dorinda shrugged. Grantland Manor did not need Charles's landed but penniless kin!*

"Oh," said Rinda, frowning. She decided secretly and at once that she'd stroll over and make their acquaintance, for it seemed to her childish mind that there was something beautifully mysterious about them.

She was almost nine before she managed to get away from Mawkers's supervision long enough to attempt the long walk to Hawkings Castle—and even then she never made it. She was skimming like a sunbeam through the woods when she came to a sudden halt.

There before her, etched like an ink drawing between two trees dark against the sun, was a bent-up old hag. She was clawing about, looking for wild parsnips and edible roots. When the old woman looked up,

Rinda saw that for all her dirty rags of clothing and straggly gray hair, a pair of very bright eyes looked out from among the wrinkles.

"You there, child," she called peremptorily to Rinda, who had come to an uncertain halt in the shadow of a large oak. "Come out into the light where I can see you."

Reluctantly, for there was something vaguely frightening about the creature whose clawlike hand beckoned, Rinda moved out into the sunlight and the old eyes viewing her widened.

"I know you," cackled the old woman. "You're the chambermaid's daughter!"

Rinda's head jerked. "I am the daughter of the Countess of Ravensay!" she cried indignantly.

"That's right, that's right." The gray head was nodding in agreement, but the burning eyes never left her. There was something malevolent in them. "Did ye know I can tell fortunes, child? And tell them to ye in verse? Did ye know that?"

Rinda shook her head. She felt pinned by the old woman's gaze, unable to move.

"Well, I can!" Triumphantly. "Come closer, child, and I'll tell you *your* fortune."

"I don't want my fortune told," whispered Rinda, for the thought of approaching that dirty figure, perhaps being snatched at by those long clawlike hands, was somehow frightening.

An ugly expression passed over the wrinkled face before her. "Then I'll tell ye a fortune that holds for *all* the Meredith women—and you're a Meredith daughter so that includes you!

> *"Their futures will wither, their fortunes lie waste*
> *And all their lives long only scorn will they taste—"*

Panic suddenly overcame Rinda—and with it a sense of doom. "I don't want to hear any more!" she cried and turned to run. Her foot caught in a long trailing vine and she was thrown to the ground. Before she could get up she heard a cackle of laughter behind her and a voice gone suddenly from singsong to mocking:

> *"Till in the far future, some reckless young maid*
> *Will forfeit her heart to a dangerous blade!"*

Rinda scrambled up, shaken, and ran for home. She was panting when she got there and Mawkers, who had been looking for her everywhere, shook her until her teeth rattled.

"Where've you been?" she cried. "Your mother was near worried sick for fear you'd fallen over the cliffs!"

"I went for a walk in the woods," gasped Rinda.

"And something happened," guessed Mawkers, seeing the child's white face and frightened eyes.

"I met an old woman who said she told fortunes, and I didn't want her to tell mine but she did anyway. She said terrible things about us all."

"Oh, you've found her, Mawkers!" cried a relieved voice, and Rinda looked up to see her mother hurrying toward them in a blue silk dress.

"Don't say anything to worry her," cautioned Mawkers, shoving Rinda in the direction of the oncoming Countess. "That old woman was only Old Gert, and if you have sense enough to stay out of the woods you won't be seeing her again." She didn't add that Gert had been a scullery maid at Edgecombe Court in the old days and had worshiped the ground Lady Polly walked on—no need to fill the child's head full of old troubles. "Mistress Rinda took a wrong turn and got lost in the woods," Mawkers told Dorinda. "She won't be doing that again." She gave the child a significant look.

So Rinda never told her mother of Gert's dire prediction for their line, and although she temporarily abandoned her plans of seeing Hawkings Castle, in time she forgot about it and began to take short walks along the cliffs whenever she could get away.

It was on one of those forbidden walks, when she was ten years old, that she saw Rory Edgecombe again. Always before she had gone but a short way, but today she was more venturesome and decided to go at least within sight of Hawkings Castle. She was well aware that the ban on strolling in that direction was still in force because the way was reputed to be treacherous, but the lure of the wild seabirds calling above her, wheeling in an ocean of blue, and the tangy salt air, was too great.

And besides, she told herself blithely, they would never miss her. Her fragile mother was "resting," as she so often did these days, and Mawkers was fussing over her—and that had given sparkling-eyed Rinda her chance to slip away.

Although to reach Hawkings Castle by the road one must needs pass Lyddon House, on the seaside the lands of Hawkings and Grantland Manor adjoined, stretching around Lyddon House's smaller acres which did not reach to the coast. The woodlands grew almost to the cliffs, but the salt air and gales had stunted those trees nearest the sea so that the broken cliffs here were topped by blowing grasses.

Why did they say these cliffs were so dangerous? wondered the child scoffingly as she walked, sure-footed, along the grassy top, edging around upthrust boulders and looking down with interest at the steep drop to the narrow strip of white beach below. *On a clear day like this, there'd be no reason to miss one's footing!*

She was concentrating on the panorama below, almost blinded by the sun's bright glitter on the blue-green water when of a sudden a voice "hallooed" her and she jumped at the sound, so startled she almost tumbled down the sheer rock face.

She looked up indignantly. A saffron-haired lad in a

tattered white shirt and worn trousers was bounding toward her.

"I say, I didn't mean to make you fall," he apologized as he got close. "I've been watching you walk along and I wanted to warn you there's been a rockfall and there's a break just there—" he pointed up ahead—"and you could fall straight down to the beach if you didn't know it was there. I'm Rory Edgecombe."

Rinda shuddered at her narrow escape and warmed suddenly to this stranger. "I'm Rinda Meredith," she said.

"I know," he said. "I've seen you before. In Lyme."

And Rinda was reminded suddenly of the golden-haired lad on the flying horse who had given her a fleeting smile as he dashed by through a rag-stone alley. That same smile was flashing now. She dimpled for it was flattering to be remembered.

"They told me you lived at Edgecombe Court," she said. "I've only seen it from the outside."

"You wouldn't want to see the part where I live," he scoffed. "Little hole in one of the attics—freeze in winter, roast in summer."

Rinda frowned. "But your name is the same as theirs," she protested, leaving unspoken the thought that people's blood relations didn't usually sleep in the attic.

"Same indeed," he said morosely.

"Then are you—?"

"Nephew to the present earl," he said, and his voice roughened. "Not that I'm treated like a nephew!" And Rinda was suddenly aware of a blue bruise just beneath his left eye. He saw her studying it. "A lovepat from my Uncle Rolfe," he said bitterly. "He can do better when he's a mind to!" And as she digested the dark possibilities he had conjured up, he said more cheerfully, "Would you like to see Hawkings Castle? If we go through those trees, we'll come out into the park."

Exploring was something ten-year-old Rinda dearly loved, and this lad, who couldn't be more than a year or two older than herself, seemed a competent guide. Soon she found herself looking up at majestic Hawkings, rising like the sentinel stronghold it once had been, near the cliffs.

"It doesn't look friendly like Grantland Manor," she said critically, studying those almost windowless walls.

"It's better on the other side," he told her. "The garden side. Would you like to go down to the beach? There's a way down just over there—some steps have been cut into the stone."

For Rinda that was an enchanted afternoon. There in the frowning shadow of Hawkings, they raced each other along the narrow beach which would be covered when the tide came in, they searched for shells, they took off their shoes and stockings and laughed and frolicked barefoot in the edge of the surf.

At last, breathless, Rinda sank down on the sand and let her light calico skirts billow out around her. There with the sea wind blowing her bright hair she listened as he described the rooms of Hawkings for her—the lofty great hall, the musty library, the spacious bedrooms above stairs.

"Do you visit there often?" she asked, impressed by his detailed knowledge.

He looked astonished. "Oh, they'd never receive me!"

"Then how do you know so much about it?" she asked, puzzled.

"I made friends with some of the servants and they let me wander through the place sometimes when the family is at church."

"Why would they do that?"

He drew himself up a little and there was pride—and arrogance too, inherited from Lady Polly—reflected now in his young face. "Because Hawkings is my rightful heritage and they all know it. And someday—" his green-gold eyes flashed and he looked suddenly hard and older—"*someday* I mean to get it back."

How he would manage that hung breathless on the air between them.

Rinda, bewildered, would have asked him more but he jumped up, looking over his shoulder toward the sea. "We'd best go," he said hurriedly, reaching out a hand to her. "I'll tell you all about it some other time. But now the tide's coming in and the path leading up the cliffs will be underwater in a couple of minutes."

He started off on the run and Rinda, who was never allowed near the sea, for her North Country mother feared it as a monster that had swallowed up Grantland one foggy night, made haste to follow. He helped her up the cliff path and she climbed with sand in her shoes and the sea wind blowing through her red-gold hair.

"Come back tomorrow and I'll build you a sandcastle," he offered once they were atop the cliff.

"I'll try," Rinda told him breathlessly.

But she did not come back that day, nor the next, nor for many days thereafter. She reached home worried that she had been gone so long and found that no one had even noticed her absence. A doctor had been sent for from Lyme and there was another on the way from Charmouth.

"Your mother's been taken bad," Cook told her as Rinda came in through the kitchens. " 'Tis her heart again, poor lady." Cook's eyes looked weepy and Rinda felt terribly frightened as she ran up the stairs, no longer aware of the scratchy sand in her shoes.

It was but the first of many attacks that two years later claimed the lovely Countess who had once been a London chambermaid.

The entire household grieved. But especially Rinda—and Mawkers. Mawkers, who had promised Dorinda on her deathbed that she would "take care of the child" and who clasped young Rinda to her as if she would build her future by main strength.

They were not to be let alone, of course. The youthful Countess—for Rinda was by right of descent now Countess of Ravensay—required a guardian and one was duly found in the person of Lord Mellowby. Lord Mellowby was a bachelor cousin of Grantland's on his mother's side and he came from "the wet end of Somerset," that remote but fertile region south of Taunton.

"What is he like?" asked Rory the first day that Rinda was "out" after the funeral. He thought Rinda looked smashing in her thin black silk mourning dress with her flaming hair floating about a pensive face. They had become fast friends, these two, flying like the sea birds for the cliffs whenever they could and trysting there companionably.

Rinda was seated by the cliff's sheer edge with her legs curled up beneath her and her black silk skirts billowing. Below her green swelling waves were crashing in over dark shining rocks. As she answered she looked out over the sea. "Oh, he's—very correct, I suppose," she sighed. "He's going to move in. Into father's room, I think. When I met him he told me not to worry, he'd get me married all right—which I think was meant to cheer me up!" She turned an indignant face toward Rory. "I told him I wasn't ready to think about marriage and he laughed! He said I'd change my mind soon enough!"

And so you will, thought Rory wistfully, for he was passionately aware of her budding beauty. But well he knew that a girl in silks—and a countess to boot—was not for a lad with patches on his trousers and nary a cent to his name! *Yet was he not rightful heir to Hawkings Castle? Was he not Charles's son?*

"*I'll* offer for you, Rinda," he said on a derisive note.

Rinda recognized that derision for what it was—the wincing of an old wound rubbed raw. But at his words her heart seemed to still suddenly. *Rory would offer for her!* She stared in front of her, seeing not the blue-green waters of the Channel, but herself in bridal finery trailing down the long stairway of Grantland Manor, saying her vows beside Rory before the fireplace in the drawing room. With newfound gravity, she turned to the tall lad lounging beside her and looked directly at him. "I would accept you, Rory," she said steadily.

Across from her, with the salt wind blowing his tangled saffron hair, Rory caught his breath. The gray eyes looking into his were level and honest. She meant it. "You couldn't consider marrying me," he said almost roughly. "How would I take care of you?"

"You wouldn't need to," said Rinda, who had spent much time considering this problem and had it all worked out. "*I'd* take care of *you*. I'm a wealthy woman—or going to be. Lord Mellowby says so."

"I don't choose to be taken care of!" said Rory icily. His bronzed young cheeks flushed dark beneath their tan. Did Rinda think he'd be willing to be a kept man, dancing attendance on her every whim? He was going to support the woman he married!

Rinda, who had some inkling of what Rory must be feeling at that moment, gave him a tormentingly lovely smile. "Lord Mellowby says I'm a catch," she murmured.

"Lord Mellowby be damned!" Rory jumped up and suddenly picked up a rock and threw it with great force out into the sea.

By now Rinda knew the story of Rory's birth. Rory himself had told her about it, adding resentfully that when he was old enough he was going to locate some of the passengers from that lost ship and somehow get proof that his mother's marriage had been legal. But Rinda did not know the story of that wild night of her own birth when Grantland Meredith and Lady Polly had disappeared into the fog.

"I wonder if she could still be alive somewhere," Rory muttered, sinking back down again beside Rinda.

"Who?" asked Rinda.

"My mother. There are some who say she and your father ran off together the night you were born."

Rinda paled. "Who says that?" she demanded truculently.

"Some of the servants at Hawkings." Rory shrugged. "Most of them think they plunged into the sea and drowned."

"You mean they were *together*?" gasped Rinda. "On the very night my mother was having a baby?"

Rory nodded. His gaze, looking out to sea, was morose. "They'd been betrothed before he married—and they were lovers after." His somber gaze returned to her. "'Tis said the Edgecombes and the Merediths are always attracted to each other." And it could be true, for the pull was there whenever he looked at Rinda's enchantingly lovely face.

And he could never have her! Not unless . . .

"I'm going to find those witnesses," he said bitterly. "They're out there somewhere and I'll find them."

Rinda had heard that before. Her troubled look turned into a witching smile. "And then what will you do? Come back and take Hawkings Castle away from the present owners? I don't think they'll stand for it!"

Rory's mouth had formed a grim line. "They'll have no choice for it's rightfully mine—the land, the castle, everything there belongs to me!" His voice rang out purposefully.

Dorinda sighed. She loved Rory with all her heart—and he was so bitterly set on having his rightful heritage restored. Grantland Manor, she felt, would never be enough for him, he would always go wandering off trying to get back the place his careless parents had contrived to lose for him.

"When are you going?" she asked, idly plucking at a grass blade.

"Tomorrow morning," he said curtly.

Rinda gave him a stricken look. "But you're only a boy," she protested. "Can't you wait?"

"I'm a man," he said softly. "And nothing can wait." For the loveliness of her still slight immature figure was not going to wait, it would be in full bloom in another year or two. He was only too aware that many girls married at thirteen, fourteen—even twelve, and although Rinda might hold off her guardian for a while, she could not hold off forever. He would betroth her to someone, whether against her will or no. And she would be married...and lost to him. He could hear those distant wedding bells ringing now in his ears and every peal sounded a death knell to his hopes. To a lad as intense and single-minded as Rory, moves must be taken now, now while there was still time. "Nothing can wait," he repeated, and added with a deepening look, "Will you wait for me, Rinda?"

Twelve-year-old Rinda, who had already so desperately given her heart, caught her breath. She would wait for him always, *always*. But some deep feminine wisdom told her it would give Rory too much power over her were he to know that.

"Perhaps," she said airily. "If you aren't gone too long!"

He kissed her then, a swift sweet kiss. It was the first time a boy had ever kissed her and the pressure of his hard young mouth woke her soft lips to sensuous desire. New feelings, strange and sweet, taunted and beckoned. Rory's very presence drew her—it always had. And now he had drawn her to him with a tender boyish kiss. For a glorious moment, her well-ordered world seemed to waver and sway. Eager for the unknown, her lithe young body strained toward him and then—more shaken than she cared to admit—she pulled away.

Rory was watching her and she saw the unmasked desire in his eyes, saw his arms drop abruptly to his sides. For all that he was thirteen, Rory was a man—and holding her in his arms had waked in him a man's ardent desires. He had felt the sweet surrender in her kiss and for a treacherous moment he thought to take her, here and now, to leave his imprint before he went away.

But he knew that he had nothing now to offer her. Were they to run away together, to marry somewhere, her guardian would follow hot on her heels and annul the marriage, snatch her back. Were he to get her pregnant now—and there was always that chance if he had his way with her—her guardian would rise to that occasion as well—by swiftly betrothing her to some aristocratic young wastrel who cared more for fortune than honor. In either case, she would be lost to him forever. And something deep inside—perhaps inherited from Charles, for Lady Polly would instantly have taken whatever was offered and gone her way—told him to remember how young she was, how innocent, and to respect that innocence. It was a wrench to draw away from her, but he did it—and he knew that he would carry her bright face like a flag in his heart.

"Things aren't right for us, Rinda," he whispered hoarsely. "Not yet. And I guess you're too young to understand that. But I'll make them right. I'll make you mistress of Hawkings Castle! Depend upon it, I will."

Brave words! And insubstantial as mist. . . .

Rinda nodded through a glaze of tears and told herself that by tomorrow Rory would have reconsidered. Oh, surely he would!

But he did not. Instead she heard through Cook that Rory had gone, run away somewhere. "And no surprise it is, considering the way they treated the lad over at Edgecombe Court—and he of the same blood as they!"

Rory was gone and Rinda, deserted, forlorn, mourning her mother, licked her wounds in private. But as the weeks turned into months and the months flew by without ever a word from him, she sometimes escaped into wild dreams of a lover—and waked in shame for the ardent masculine face in those dreams was not always Rory's.

Were dream lovers ever to be her lot?

She was growing up now, beginning to bloom, and she asked herself: *What was she going to do if Rory Edgecombe never returned to Dorset?*

September 11, 1684

Chapter 10

At Hawkings Castle the great masquerade ball was going as well as could be expected (for indeed it was the first ball the "new people" had ever given at Hawkings and it had been approached with trepidation by one and all). Things were entirely out of kilter in the servants' quarter, what with Cook swearing at the temporary help even as she perspired in the hot kitchens. And if the venison was underdone and the huge pastry near burned to a crisp, the sweating cook ardently prayed that the guests, fortified by Lord Chell's wine, would be too drunk to rightly notice.

In the great hall of the castle things were proceeding more smoothly, for the September night was unusually warm and a soft wind was blowing in from the sea. The masked guests, warmed both by Lord Chell's liquor and their exertions in dancing, to the tinkling music of the harpsichord, over the flagstone floor of the great hall, were reaching a mellow mood when few of them whispered behind their gloved hands about the sparseness of the furniture (for it was well known that the present Lord Chell had brought with him debts so heavy that most of the furnishings and livestock had been stripped from Hawkings to stave off his creditors).

And among the masquers, clad in a coral and ivory silk gown encrusted with tiny seed pearls, the dashing young Countess of Ravensay, now a dazzling sixteen, was on the brink of making a momentous decision.

She had arrived at the ball cloaked not only in a coral silk mask that hid her lovely regular features and matched her wide rustling skirts, but in an enveloping sense of desperation.

When her mask for the ball was being fitted, Mawkers had fixed her with a knowing look. "They're really giving this ball for *you*, Rinda. Although they don't say so, they're hoping this will be the night that Elfred snares you. You could do worse, you know, than marry the heir to Hawkings Castle!"

A masked ball with masked intentions, thought Rinda and felt inclined to laugh.

She had so far resisted all efforts to betroth her, and Lord Mellowby, so badly afflicted with gout that he spent most of his time groaning, with his right leg propped up on a pillow, had let her have her way, but Mawkers's mention of Elfred made her wince.

Oh, dear, she thought. *Elfred is going to go stiffly down on his knees again and plead for my hand!* As the catch of the county, Rinda was getting rather used to that kind of behavior from lovesick swains, but Elfred was sure to make a mess of it—he always did! Once he had got tangled up in the words and become so embarrassed that he choked and she had to thump him on the back. Another time his knee garter had broken at the crucial moment, and allowed his stocking to slip down, depriving him of his dignity as he clawed at it. And the last most horrific experience had been at Lyddon House during a party when Elfred had managed to dance her into the empty stone-flagged servants' hall. With enormous gravity he had spread out his kerchief on stones he considered too dusty for his puce silk knee. She had been half-expecting the butler and a brace of scullery maids to dash through carrying huge chargers and overset them—but nothing like that had happened. Instead, just as Elfred knelt upon the lace-trimmed kerchief and assumed the soulful look he considered appropriate for a proposal, a terrible ripping sound had announced that the thin worn silk of his knee breeches had given way under the strain of Elfred's not inconsiderable bulk. Rinda had almost choked in her effort not to laugh. Now at the ball she tried to lose herself in amused imaginings of what new calamity would fall upon Elfred if he took it upon himself to propose again—but she didn't quite make it.

For back at Grantland Manor, her guardian's gout was improving and with every lessening of the pain in his leg, he put more pressure on his ward to marry. Even though Lord Mellowby had not seen fit to accompany her to Hawkings Castle this night, his last words as she stepped into her carriage to depart still rang in her ears: "Ye must make a decision—*and soon*. I care not which lad ye choose, so long as he be a gentleman and presentable—though ye'd be a fool to choose less than an earl—but I'll not have ye languish here at Grantland Manor and become an old maid!"

Soon, he had said, and she had known with a sinking heart that this time Lord Mellowby meant it. She was but trying to stave off the inevitable because she was in love with none of the young bucks who clustered around her. She supposed that was Rory's fault—although Mawkers attributed it to pure stubbornness!

The masked crowd of merrymakers in the vaulted great hall of Hawkings Castle swirled around her, but at the thought of Rory her lovely face had gone melancholy. Four long years had passed since Rory Edgecombe had left Dorset determined to find proof of his parents' marriage—four years without a word, but still she could not quite forget him. Those days on the cliffs seemed forever ago. Even the wild sweet dreams of him that had haunted her nights were fading: *Those visions of a wedding gown and a circlet of seed pearls around her long unbound red-gold hair. The flashing images that made her blush of a shimmering wedding night when she would no longer fend Rory off with a slanted witch-smile, but would stand trembling as he removed her wedding circlet, and then her stiff handsome ivory wedding gown with snippets of riband wedding favors still left upon it here and there.... The dress would come off slowly for Rory would have reverence for its meaning and she would stand there clad only in the sheerest of chemises and a pair of silk stockings that had by now slipped down around her ivory satin slippers—for the wedding guests, by ancient custom, would have merrily snatched off her bride's garters and left the blushing bride alone with her bridegroom and now would be toasting the happy couple's health downstairs along with a smiling Lord Mellowby.*

And then Rory's questing hands would be fumbling with the ribands that held her chemise and her heart would pound near to bursting. The ribands would come free and the delicate lawn fabric would come floating down and she would step out of her slippers and Rory would pick her up and carry her to the big square wedding bed with its beautiful new ivory hangings that would close them about, making the world seem far away. She would sink down shivering into the endless softness of the big goose-down mattress, and Rory, who had magically lost his clothing just as she had magically lost her stockings—never mind how—would be pressing his long body against hers and together they would begin a long long road of sampling forbidden delights and—

"Rinda!" It was Elfred, Lord Chell's eldest son, masked and perspiring in a fur-trimmed cape, but unmistakable both by his bulk and by his loping walk, bearing down on her.

The young countess came back to the present and laughed. "You are not supposed to see through my disguise, Elfred," she chided, and added, "The castle looks beautiful alight with so many candles—and how packed the room is, you must have invited half the county!"

Behind his narrow mask, Elfred's broad face flushed with the excitement of the chase—for this night the girl in coral silks was the quarry. Besides, his father was counting on him. Marriage to the young Countess of Ravensay would mend the ailing family fortunes. "Could anyone miss a figure like yours, Rinda?" he demanded roguishly. "After all, 'tis one I'd make mine—as well you know."

Rinda struck him a light chiding tap with her ivory fan. "Not tonight, Elfred," she pleaded. "Indeed if you protest you love me once more, I'll think you daft!"

Somewhat taken aback by these cool words (for his father had assured him that the lure of ancient Hawkings Castle ablaze with candlelight and sparkling with revelry would be too much even for the elusive Rinda), Elfred looked about him for aid and found none. While he was pondering how to proceed, a black and purple domino in a black mask and a wide-brimmed black hat claimed his beloved and she went whirling away from him with a laugh.

Elfred glared at the domino. He could not recall having seen the fellow earlier—he must be one of the newly arrived group from Lyme, some of whom had brought with them houseguests from distant parts. It was all a part of the new restless pattern of living, he decided, with the King reputed to be ill in London. His father said so and his father was always right.

But was he right about Rinda? Morosely Elfred studied her flying coral skirts and her up-tilted laughing face as she challenged the masked domino, no doubt, to reveal his identity.

On the flagstone floor among the dancers that was exactly what Rinda was doing.

"Who are you, sir?" she demanded merrily. "To pounce upon me thus, just when I was engaged in conversation with Elfred? Do I know you? Speak and let me guess who you are from your voice!"

But the domino, whose mask was a black scarf with

holes cut in it that completely covered his face and tied behind his head underneath his thick dark hair, refused to speak.

Yet when the dance was over he did not convey her back to the wall to yield her to another partner. Instead he kept a tight grip on her hand and whirled her about the floor again, while Elfred scowled and grew restive.

"You'll have Elfred in a rage," laughed Rinda, who found dancing with the tall domino exhilarating and was amused by possessive Elfred's chagrin. "And I warn you he has threatened to call out anyone who takes too much notice of me!"

From the concealed mouth of the domino emerged a sound that could best be classified as a growl and Rinda, delighted, said, "Ah, you have a voice of sorts! Well, if you won't tell me who you are and we *must* play guessing games, give me some sign that I may guess your identity!"

For answer she was whirled across the room and through the library door—that same library where her father had found himself locked in by a vengeful Lady Polly—and suddenly let go while the domino turned and locked the door behind him.

Rinda watched this bit of byplay in amusement, but in spite of herself she felt a little thrill of anticipation rush through her. She was locked in with a stranger and all she knew about him was that he danced like an angel.

"You were about to give me a sign?" she suggested with an impish smile.

The domino gave her a sign. Of a sudden he tore off the scarf that covered his face and along with it his hat and the dark wig he wore over his own saffron-yellow hair.

But even had he only unveiled his lips and pressed them against her own, she would have known him. For nobody ever had—and she was sure nobody ever would—kiss her with such conviction as Rory did now.

All the likely lads who had sued for her hand—all those that on the way over to Hawkings in the carriage she had been seriously considering—were sent scurrying away on the instant. Her whole body seemed to flame up at his embrace. All the tormenting yearnings which had been nagging her of late flared up and were set ablaze.

"Rinda, Rinda, I've missed you." He sighed as he let her go.

And Rinda looked up into that well-known, well-loved face, and saw that this was not the Rory Edgecombe she had known. She had loved a boy—this was a man and there were grim lines now around a mouth made for smiling.

"Rory," she breathed. "I thought you must be dead—you never wrote! Oh, Rory, why did you stay away so long? What happened to you?"

He laughed exultantly. "I swore I'd not return until I could tell you I'd be Lord Chell of Hawkings!"

Her heart leaped—and then common sense took over. "Oh, Rory, don't tease me!" she entreated.

"Oh, I'm not Lord Chell yet," he admitted. "But I will be, as sure as the sun sets in the west, Rinda. I near killed my horse getting here."

"You've found your witnesses!" she cried, overjoyed. "You can prove your parents' marriage was valid!"

He shook his head. "No, all the witnesses are dead—or vanished. But Lord Chell I'll be yet, for the King's health is worse than they're admitting. He can't last long!"

Rory was off pursuing wild dreams again. "How could the King's death possibly benefit you?" she asked, for he must have a plan—even if it was a harebrained one.

"Not the King's death," he corrected her sharply. "But the ascent of his true son, the Duke of Monmouth, to the throne when the King dies."

"You have met this Duke?" she challenged.

"I do not need to. He'll need supporters and he's finding them. You should know that here in the West Country."

Yes, she knew that. All the West Country hoped to have the King's brother James barred from the succession, all hoped for Monmouth, admittedly son of the King's own body—but that hope was fragile at best.

Rory was leaning toward her earnestly. "The present Lord Chell favors James—'tis a known fact." She knew that too, but Lord Chell was not alone, her own guardian favored James! "And should Monmouth invade—and invade he will!—Lord Chell must needs declare on the side of James. And when Monmouth wins the day," he added blithely, "as he is sure to do, then the lands of those who fought against him will be confiscated by the Crown and bestowed upon his supporters. *Of whom I will be one.*"

She saw his scheme clearly now. He would join Monmouth, try to distinguish himself in the Duke's cause, and then claim as his reward Hawkings Castle and the title his father had borne.

He could die in this dangerous endeavor.

He was looking deep into her eyes with that compelling green-gold gaze and she felt her breath coming unevenly. The stays of her coral gown seemed suddenly too tight and she yearned for air.

Whatever he did, whatever his folly, she knew that she would aid him! For he was the lover of her heart, he was the reason she had refused so many suitors, toyed with so many hearts, and left them all baffled and rejected. She had always loved him, she knew that now, since that first day when she had seen him overmatched, fighting overwhelming odds, and he had flashed that confident smile at her.

And now he was once again overmatched—and smiling again, and lifting up her chin with a tender finger.

"I came here only to see you," he said. "I ride for Lyme and my passage to Holland is already arranged

by powerful friends. I will join the Duke of Monmouth
in Amsterdam."

She felt her throat go dry. "When do you sail?"

"At dawn. On the morning tide."

*So much could happen to him. Ships sank, street brawls were
common, jealous men surrounded mighty dukes, duels were
frequent. And if the Duke did invade when the King died, Rory
would be storming the beach alongside him....* So she
envisioned it. And she had been so happy when first
she had seen him standing there! She had imagined—
oh, God, she had imagined that he felt as she did, that
he had come home to her!

"Rory," she whispered. "Don't go."

That iridescent green-gold gaze—so like Lady Polly's
had she but known it—held her in a vise, just as her
father had once been held. She could not have moved
had she wanted to. She felt trapped, like some small
animal caught in a snare.

"I must," he said simply. And then he added in a
voice gone deep with yearning, "But I would give all
that I possess to stay with you this night."

A surge like the sea wind coming in wild by night
swept through Rinda. *He was asking...what she most
desired.* To spend a night in her arms.

"I know that I ask a great deal," he said quickly,
leaning close so that his hot breath seemed to sear her
face. "I know I have no right. Yet I swear to you that
not a day, not a night has gone by that I have not
thought of you."

"And yet you never wrote," she reminded him wistfully.

He hesitated, and there was a tormented look on his
face. When he spoke, she knew she was hearing the
truth. "Sometimes I was so downhearted that I thought
I could not go on. Once I even decided to take my own
life."

"Oh, no!" Her warm heart, so attuned to him, so
entwined with his destiny, reacted violently to that. She

threw herself against him as if she would shield him with her body from a cruel fate.

"Then I was taken into the household of a Monmouth supporter. As a footman. When he had learnt my story, that I was a gentleman born, even though disinherited, he enlisted me into the Duke's Cause. 'Tis he who has given me these clothes and my horse outside and the gold in my pocket. Along with letters for the Duke to be delivered in Amsterdam."

Treasonous letters! They would mean death to the courier who bore them if they were discovered! She felt a thrill of fright go through her for even now someone was pounding on the door and she could hear, above the noise of the music drifting in, Elfred's voice saying, "Rinda? Are you in there?"

"We must let him in," she said desperately. "Or they will break down the door and take you!"

He shrugged. "They do not know who I am—an anonymous domino at a masquerade ball. They'll assume I am some guest of one of their neighbors." He was reaching for his masklike scarf as he spoke.

"Not if they break down the door! *Then* there'll be an unmasking!"

For a moment his wicked smile looked as if he might enjoy that. Then the concealing black scarf came down again over his face and was tied behind his head. Wig and hat followed. "We could go out those casements," he suggested. "I could take you up behind me and we could ride for an inn in Lyme?"

And be caught, for there'd be pursuit and the devil to pay!

"No," she said rapidly. "Let me handle this, Rory. Just melt into the crowd the moment I open the door and come to me later at Grantland Manor. I'll leave the garden door unlocked."

Behind the mask his iridescent eyes gleamed in triumph. *Come to me....* Those were the words he most wished to hear.

Rinda crossed the room, unlocked and threw open the heavy door.

"Oh, Elfred." She collapsed forward into his arms, the sudden weight of her body almost sending him off balance. His arms went around her automatically and the domino slipped by them and melted into the crowd of dancers, working his way toward the door. "I felt faint," Rinda told Elfred weakly. "And I asked the gentleman with whom I was dancing to take me into the library where I could throw open the windows."

Elfred looked past his semi-limp coral silk burden into the library. "Yet the windows are not open and I found the door locked," he said sharply.

"The poor fellow I was with is quite deaf—and of course I did not know that. He did not understand—he thought I was asking him to lock the door instead of opening the windows!"

It was a poor subterfuge but it satisfied slow-witted Elfred. He had an uncle on his mother's side who had inserted a large horn into his ear and was forever shouting, "Speak up, boy! I can't hear you!"

"But are you really ill?" he asked, all solicitude.

"I think it is just the heat and the excitement." She batted her lashes at him and had the satisfaction of seeing him look dazzled. "If you would bring me a glass of wine?"

Elfred brought the wine readily enough and by now the domino had disappeared. Rinda breathed easier. At least they would not catch him this night!

"I still feel faint," she complained, hardly touching the wine, but dropping her fan.

"Perhaps you should go upstairs and lie down," suggested Elfred, restoring the fan. He was delighted to be fussing over the heiress to Grantland Manor.

"No—no, I may be coming down with something." She gave him an appealing look. "I had best go home, Elfred."

Elfred looked upset. A whole ball gone to waste—

and it had cost a mint! "I will escort you," he declared stoutly.

"You should not leave your guests," she reminded him. "Your father is relying on you."

So she had noticed that! She must find him of some account after all! Elfred brightened.

"If you would just have my carriage brought round, I'll slip out without spoiling your party, Elfred," she told him wistfully.

"You could never spoil any party!" Gallantry was speaking.

Rinda sighed. "I shall sleep all day tomorrow," she announced. "And perhaps the day after as well, and so shake off whatever is plaguing me."

"Yes, do that," he urged. "And I shall be over three days hence to take you out riding."

Her plan was working! Rinda gave Elfred a bright smile, but she managed a weak exit, leaning heavily upon his arm, as he escorted her out to her carriage.

And so a masked lady rode home by moonlight, taking the evening air. Her gray eyes were sparkling and she quite mystified Elsie, her maid, who rode with her in the carriage, for she constantly started up, listening. It was the sound of hooves she was listening for and twice she thought she heard them, pounding softly in the darkness toward a tryst at Grantland Manor. She would listen alertly for a moment—and then sink back with her heart beating so loudly she thought surely Elsie must hear.

For she was about to give herself to a lover long gone, one she'd thought had forgotten her. A lover magically returned and beating at the door of her heart.

A lover about to leave for Holland.

That thought made her catch her breath, for in the heat of the moment with the stars winking overhead and the salt air blowing fresh in her face as they rode sedately beneath the tall overhanging trees, she had pushed aside the thought that Rory was leaving on the morrow.

Now her soft mouth tightened, and a wicked light played like summer lightning in her wide gray eyes.

Innocent of the way of a man with a maid she might be, but she promised herself she would learn fast. And she would lead Rory into such a wild world of swirling emotions that come morning he would have neither will nor wish to leave her!

The Same Night...

Chapter 11

"Don't tell Mawkers I felt ill—she'll fuss over me and I'm quite recovered now." For one who had had to be helped into her carriage, Rinda bounded out of it with surprising strength and both the driver and her maid exchanged surprised glances as she picked up her coral skirts and ran into the house.

Was he here? she asked herself excitedly. He must find the garden door unlocked else he might leave, thinking she was only toying with him. Such a thought was not to be borne! She flew down the hall and into the servants' corridor in panic toward the garden door.

Once she had unlocked it, she meant to dash upstairs and change from this rustling ball gown into something more sinuous—a light silk robe over a chemise perhaps. In any event she must change her chemise before he arrived because right in the front of the bodice was a hastily mended tear, got when her maid lost her footing reaching up into the tall press while Rinda was dressing. The girl had been near tears until Rinda had soothed her by saying it was no matter, stitch it up and she would wear it anyway. But the shaken maid (her last mistress would have boxed her ears for less) had sewn it awkwardly with big stitches—easily concealed by the ballgown but now soon to be seen!

Even as she ran toward the garden door, Rinda found herself blushing at the thought that she was actually planning to greet a man in her underthings!

She threw open the latch—and the door opened instantly. Rory stood there, a tall dark shape against the moonlight. The light silk domino costume he had worn over his clothes was gone, no doubt stuffed into his saddlebags, along with the mask and wig. It was the Rory she had known—a little older, a little harder, his hot eyes kindling—who stood there surveying her. Rinda felt her breath leave her and for a moment lost her jauntiness. Confronted by him so suddenly, she could think of nothing to say.

Rory at least was in complete command of the situation. He stepped inside on booted feet, moving as silently as a shadow, and she wondered suddenly if this practiced ease came from stealing into houses on other trysts. . . .

"I—I thought you would not be here yet," she whispered, and felt a thrill go through her as he brushed against her silken breasts coming through the door.

"Did you think I would have forgotten the way to Grantland Manor?" he demanded, amused.

"No. Of course not." Trying to sort out her mixed up feelings, Rinda closed the door. Now that he was actually here and not just expected, she was tempted to escort him into the library or the drawing room and talk a bit and drink some wine to get her courage up. For it is a big step to lose one's virginity and she had not yet really faced the consequences.

"I wish I had more time," he murmured, bending over to brush her bright hair with his lips. "Tomorrow seems just a breath away. . . ."

That mention of tomorrow decided her. "I will go up the front stairs," she told him. "You wait five minutes and then go up these side stairs." She nodded at the dark flight behind her. "I will leave a candle burning in the hall outside my door. You will see its light easily around the bend of the corridor."

"I know which room you occupy," he surprised her by saying. "Many the night I have stood outside in the moonlight and watched your candles snuffed out and wished that I were older and in possession of my birthright so that I could offer for you." His hand lightly stroked her shoulder as he spoke and she jumped slightly as if he had given her a shock.

"Five minutes," she said breathlessly.

"Five minutes," he echoed, nodding.

She looked back once as she left. It was dark where he stood but she could see the gleam of his eyes and that too rattled her. She scurried away from him with a swish of coral skirts, hurrying toward the front of the house and the front stairway where she found her maid hesitating on the stairs as if not quite sure what to do.

"Go to bed, Elsie!" she snapped at the surprised girl. "Else you will be sleepy-eyed tomorrow and unable to do my hair properly. And make sure you do not disturb me in the morning until I call you for I wish to sleep late." And when the maid still hesitated, "To bed!" she cried with such energy that Elsie took off up the stairs on the run.

With a sigh Rinda followed her, forcing herself to mount the stairs at a more decorous pace than she would have liked. Then with no one watching she dashed toward her bedchamber, where Mawkers always kept a light burning for her when she was off at some party. She seized the dish-shaped candleholder and set it in the hall outside her door, for Rory could very well take a wrong turn in these corridors and it would be dreadful if he ended up in Lord Mellowby's room down the hall! She quailed at the thought of the scene that would cause—and at the danger it would put Rory in.

She meant to change her gown and realized suddenly that she had set the only candle outside. She must go out and get it and use it to light another.

She hurried to the door—and bumped into Rory.

"I could not wait," he muttered. "Anticipation drove me." And closed the door with his foot, reaching behind him to draw the latch.

The moment was upon her. She took a breathless step backward and her high heel caught in the edge of the rug. She would have fallen but that Rory stepped forward instantly and caught her in the crook of his arm. He was laughing as he bent down and brought his mouth down firmly over her own.

Any embarrassment she might have felt at stumbling so awkwardly dissolved in the magic of that kiss. Unconsciously her arms crept around his neck and she was clinging to him as if her life depended on it. Forgotten was the rustling coral silk ballgown with its intricate folds and enormous puffed sleeves. Those sleeves were leaving her anyway, for Rory was untying them even as his lips wandered away from her lips and down her hot cheeks to the white column of her throat to come to rest at last in the pulsing hollow at the base of her throat. Forgotten was her mended chemise—the mending did not show in the moonlight anyhow—and somehow that was leaving her too, like her dress which, magically unhooked, had left her body as if a strong wind had whipped it away.

She felt a sudden sense of panic as Rory's gentle hands eased down her chemise and made a soft sound of protest as he swung her away from him so that he might view her naked body, silvered by the moonlight.

"Beautiful," he breathed. "Just as I always imagined you would look." And the hot look in his eyes seemed to pour over her and turn her skin from alabaster to blushing pink.

Instinctively one arm came up to cover her breasts and the other went down in an attempt to hide the silky red-gold triangle of hair at the base of her hips. But Rory laughed low in his throat and lifted her up in his arms so that her slender bewitching body was once again bared to his sight.

"I never knew such loveliness could exist," he murmured in a voice gone dreamy. And even as she shrank back in embarrassment he swept her up and carried her—just as she had long ago imagined it—to the big square bed and laid her carefully down upon it, letting her sink softly into the depths of the feather mattress. And the only difference between reality and her long ago dreams was that she had imagined herself in bridal finery and the bed a bridal bed.

And why should it not be considered a bridal bed? she asked herself rebelliously as she lay there, breathlessly watching him undress. *What words could ever be spoken over them that would have more meaning for her than this simple act of taking forever a mate?*

She felt shy lying there, watching his shape change in the moonlight from man of fashion to a lean stranger of bone and muscle and blood, a stranger who moved toward her sinuously, towered over her for a long devouring moment, and then lowered his long form confidently upon her tingling body.

It felt strange and wondrously exciting having him there with her in the big bed. A sense of exaltation filled her as his kisses grew more demanding, as his hands moved expertly over her body, exploring all her secret places, and she felt as if she were butter and he the churn and she was whisked this way and that with no will of her own. His touch was tender and meant to delight, and he had sympathy and compassion for her innocence. She felt dizzy with new and unexpected sensations and desires and her eyelids grew heavy and her mouth sultry in the moonlight.

He seemed to know that she was ready for him to take her—and take her he did. Holding her body clasped tightly to his own, he made a sudden thrust that left her for a moment breathless with pain. A slight moan escaped her and he desisted instantly, his strong thighs relaxing as he whispered, "Am I hurting you too much?"

Afire with desires that were new and strange to her, sailing alien seas, Rinda still had the presence of mind to gasp, "No, no, 'tis all right. 'Twas but for a moment...." Her voice drifted off and he took that as a signal and thrust anew. Another gasp and a wider deeper pain—and then a soft delight began to consume her, and pain and maidenhood alike were forgotten in this new close warm wonderful world of joy.

Freely, madly, she let him carry her up and up and up, sailing beyond the treetops, above the roofs, above the drifting clouds into a magical mist that climaxed suddenly as if the sun had broken through in a blaze of glory that shimmered everything in its own splendor.

She had never known anything remotely like it.

It awed her as she drifted back to reality and realized that Rory was leaning on one elbow beside her, breathing heavily from exertion and smiling down at her.

"Did you like it?" he asked and she was suddenly crimson with embarrassment and turned her face away from him and her body too in a convulsive gesture that turned her back to him.

His hand ran tenderly down her shoulder, along her side and over her soft bare upthrust hip, making her shiver. "I didn't mean to embarrass you, Rinda," he said reflectively. "It's just that I wanted you to enjoy it too."

"Oh, I did," she said, muffled.

"Then—" he turned her lightly over toward him, his fingers cupping one of her breasts as he bent and softly planted a kiss on the quivering pink nipple—"why don't we do it again?"

Breathlessly she melted into his arms for another even more devastating exploit.

"You'll be hard to leave," he murmured ruefully,

when the magic had gone its shimmering way to wherever magic goes, and they were lying stretched out together, their bodies fitting companionably side by side, damp with effort and relaxed as never before.

His words were like a sharp knife, reminding her that he was soon to leave.

"Oh, don't go!" she cried, her words a soft low wail, and she flung her naked body over him as if to hold him there by her own slight weight.

He accepted that weight eagerly, letting his arms close round her in a fond gesture of unself-conscious elegance.

"I told you I must." He was running tender fingers through her long gleaming hair as he spoke. "But—" his voice grew hoarse with feeling—"I will carry you with me—just as you are tonight—wherever I go."

That was it! He must carry her with him—not as he meant it, but physically, in the flesh. "Let me go with you," she pleaded. "Whatever happens, we can face it together."

He shook his head. "I would not have you travel overseas and suffer hardships on my account."

But dawn would soon break, and the new day dawn without him, for he would be on a ship being carried far away perhaps never to return.

"I *will* go with you!" she cried, sitting up.

He laughed softly and pushed her back down in the bed. His detaining arm was thrown across her abdomen, pinioning her. "My wild wench," he said fondly. "I'll be back for you, never doubt it!"

"You'll have no need to come back for me," she said hotly. "For I'll be at your side!" She was struggling with him and he seemed to be enjoying it. He threw a leg over her flailing ones, holding them down.

"I'd make love to you again," he murmured. "But there's no time. That's a false dawn out there, and it means there's time for me to get to Lyme and aboard ship—but none to spare. Be a good girl and let me go." His voice was coaxing.

Of a sudden there was a pounding on the door and her guardian's voice demanding loudly, "Who's in there? I hear a man's voice. Rinda, answer me!"

Instantly Rory was on his feet. "You can say you were talking in your sleep," he muttered, thrusting a long leg into his trousers. "I'll climb out the window and slither down on the ivy." And at her terrified look, for it was a long drop, "Don't worry. I've done it before." She looked so affronted that he chuckled. "Not leaving a wench, Rinda, but escaping the King's men who had pursued me to an upstairs room outside London."

That allusion to the King's men brought back his danger afresh and Rinda's tears of fright and disappointment and frustration threatened to spill over. "We can dash past Lord Mellowby and ride for the ship," she pleaded, her gray eyes enormous with appeal.

"And how would we pay for your passage?" was his practical rejoinder.

"With the gold you carry!" she protested.

"'Tis not enough." Dressed now and ready, he planted a last lingering kiss on her trembling lips. Coolly, he ignored the clamor at the door where Lord Mellowby was thundering that he'd have the door broken down if Rinda did not open it.

Rory paused at the window, swung a long leg over the sill and gave Rinda a last look, as if he would fill his eyes with her. "Good-bye for now," he whispered against her cheek, for she had followed him forlornly to the window. And added hoarsely, "'Twill not be for long, I promise you!"

She wanted to scream, she wanted to throw her arms around his waist and physically restrain him from leaving, she wanted to call after him that he could not desert her, that she would follow him to the ship and book her own passage—but she could not.

His very life was in her hands this night. Had he not told her that the King's men had pursued him in London? And they could as easily have followed him to

Dorset. That explained his wig, the way his mask had covered his entire face instead of being a narrow thing that shielded only his eyes—he was a hunted fugitive, making his way to Holland!

And all she could do for him now, she who loved him so much, was to ensure that he made good his escape.

His head had already disappeared from view as he made his way quickly down by way of the old ropy ivy that seemed as firmly a part of the house as the stones themselves.

Rinda turned with a sob catching in her throat and cried out to her guardian in a voice of complete bewilderment, "What is the matter? I was having a terrible nightmare. It was awful—I seemed to be two people and I was talking to myself. Did I cry out?"

"Open the door!" thundered Lord Mellowby, his voice fairly crackling with rage.

"In a moment," called Rinda. "'Tis so hot I was sleeping without my—" she stopped as if embarrassed. "You must wait 'till I put something on." She gave a sudden wail. "Oh, dear, I have barked my shin on this great bed whilst I looked for a candle. It is so dark in here I can see nothing. I can't understand why you do not go back to sleep!"

"I will inspect your room!" came a roar from the other side of the door and the very timbers of the door seemed about to crash inward from the impact of the blows rained upon it. "Open up!"

Rinda ignored her guardian's bluster. He would not call the servants to break down the door while she was still stirring about, talking to him through the door—she knew him too well for that. He was not a man eager to bring down scandal upon his head. And she must give Rory time to escape, for it would be perfectly in character for Lord Mellowby to cry out at sight of an intruder and to set every man at Grantland Manor chasing after Rory.

She dawdled in lighting the candle—talking meanwhile. She dawdled in putting on her dressing gown—complaining with each reluctant gesture about being disturbed. She even made a quick search of the room to make sure Rory had left nothing behind before she opened the door a crack and said irritably, "Well, what on earth is it?"

The door was pushed inward with enough force to carry Rinda backward as her guardian burst in. He was carrying a candle that promptly went out from his forceful slamming of the door behind him. In nightshirt and tasseled nightcap he stood with his feet planted in the center of the floor, looking suspiciously about him.

"Well, produce the fellow!" he bellowed.

"Produce *who*?" Rinda stood her ground bravely. "There's no one!"

Grinding his teeth, her guardian made a thorough search of the room. He pawed through her big clothes press, scattering ball gowns helter-skelter, he peered under the bed, he even opened the lid of a heavy chest and tossed out half her underthings before he did what Rinda dreaded—he went to the open window and leaned out.

"I don't know what you are accusing me of," she said sulkily.

Lord Mellowby turned around. He was cooler now and he was studying her narrowly. "I heard laughter in here and a man's voice." When she would have protested, he raised his hand to silence her. "'Tis plain whoever was here has gone—and 'tis also clear that you are more than ripe for betrothal." His eyes glittered. "Lord Chell's son Elfred has asked for your hand," he added ironically. "Tomorrow I intend to give my consent. You have played the field long enough!" *That would smoke out her lover if there was one!* he thought with satisfaction.

Rinda thought fast. *Delay—that was the thing!*

"I do not object to Elfred," she told him carefully.

Lord Mellowby regarded her, thunderstruck. Was it

possible the man in here had been Elfred? If so, he must certainly have gone down the ivy and for the ivy to support Elfred's weight—! He regarded his ward with some fascination, for he had been certain that she would resist at all costs a betrothal to Lord Chell's less than attractive son.

"You do not?" he said at last.

"No—it is just that I have no wish to be tied down so soon. I will consent to the betrothal if the marriage can be put off for a year. Otherwise—" she gave him a rebellious look—"I will lock myself in my room and scream and cry and refuse to see Elfred and send him insulting messages and tell everyone that—"

There was no understanding wenches but Lord Mellowby knew when he had won a victory.

"Elfred will be impatient but I am sure he will accept that condition," he cut in dryly. He gave Rinda another searching look as if he would have from her the reason she had so quickly—after refusing to accept any of her suitors—changed her mind. Then he bowed to her curtly with a shake of nightcap tassels and left.

Rory's ship sailed at dawn but Rinda sat by her window, unable to sleep, until the morning sun dazzled her eyes and she turned away and threw herself back onto the great bed where she had known such wonders the night before.

She had lost her virginity and her lover and been betrothed to a man for whom she could never care—and all in a single night!

Chapter 12

Time passed with agonizing slowness for Rinda, trapped in a distasteful betrothal and unable to admit the name of her lover, for she guessed that Lord Mellowby would simply brush any protests aside and have the banns cried at once. September passed into October and the nights became cool. But not for Rinda. She tossed in a bed overheated with memories.

She was rude to Elfred, who cheerfully accepted her rudeness, and she moved about the house like a sleep-walker, looking at familiar objects as if she did not see them. Mawkers worried about her health. Lord Mellowby thought her behavior most odd, but put it down to mere "missishness."

But a terrible dread was now plaguing Rinda, a dread which in November she was no longer able to ignore.

She was pregnant. And the father of her child was somewhere in Europe and only God knew when he would be in England again.

For Rory had written her on arrival in Amsterdam—two letters, one hot on the heels of the other.

"I am speedily arrived after a fast voyage," his first letter

164

had begun. *"This is a wondrous place, full of canals, and the people—at least the poorer sort—clog about in wooden shoes. The girls here are very fresh-faced* (that *had sent a jealous pang through her*) *and the gentlemen very urbane. It is a city with hoists on the house fronts gallantly concealed by decorations, for the top floor always seems to be a warehouse and every man a merchant."* There was much more, but Rinda, impatient for personal messages, for words from the heart, skimmed through it. *"I have an audience with the Duke tomorrow,"* it ended. And almost as an afterthought, *"I miss you."*

Rinda had put the letter down with shaking fingers and stared, vexed, out into the trees. Beyond those trees lay the sparkling Channel where ships were beating every day to Europe, sometimes to Holland. . . .

The second letter, which had arrived the following week, was very exuberant. It had described in detail his audience with the Duke who was *"most optimistic"* and had sent Rory on a mission to Germany where he was hoping for support from a nobleman *"who has a beautiful wife to whom, it is said, he listens. His grace feels that I will be able to charm her!"*

Frustrated, angry, Rinda had crumpled the letter and thrown it at the fire—and then in panic lest it burn, this only link she had with her absent lover, she had followed it and almost set herself ablaze trying to retrieve it and stamp out the blackening corner. Weeping, she had smoothed the letter out and locked it away in the little chest in which she kept the first—a chest that was shortly to be filled with letters from all over Europe as the Duke of Monmouth, a man who would be King by any method, sent his handsome young henchman out as "bait" to trap restless young wives and spur their husbands into aiding his shaky Cause.

Rinda, realizing her letters were not being received, but were being stored up awaiting Rory's return to Amsterdam, wrote anyway, frequently and in some heat.

"You must come home," her first November letter

said. "For I am now certain that I am bearing your child."

That letter at least was received by Rory, back in Amsterdam for Christmas.

"*Arrived in Amsterdam exhausted,*" he wrote, "*and spent the night reading your letters which I had put in order so that I might read the oldest first and so follow your progress while I have been gone. It was dawn when I read that you are now certain you are with child and I threw open the windows and set up such a loud halloo that I must have waked all the neighbors! This is wonderful news, Rinda—to become a father!*" He went on and on, urging her to "take all care of herself" against his return, but leaving in the air when that was to be, for as he added in a footnote (obviously put there after having had another audience with the Duke) he was "*off to some of the Huguenot provinces of France*" where help for the Protestant Duke might well be forthcoming.

Rinda, sitting curled up in the broad windowseat in the drawing room, read Rory's reply with mixed feelings. In France Rory would be in real danger, she knew, for King Louis considered himself especially commissioned by God to stamp out the Protestant faith, and an emissary from the Duke of Monmouth would get short shrift if caught. Rinda shivered at the thought.

"What, moping about again?" Lord Mellowby, who had been out for a walk on this sunny day, came into the room and Rinda quickly stuffed the letter under the pillow beside her. "I would have thought that on a day so clear and bright you would be out riding with your betrothed."

"I do not feel like riding," said Rinda stiffly.

"Pish and tush! If not riding, then taking a stroll down to the cliffs with young Elfred."

"I do not feel like walking either, and I see enough of Elfred in our drawing room without wandering over the cliffs with him."

Lord Mellowby was a trifle daunted. It seemed to him that a maiden should show considerably more interest in her betrothed, and he knew for a fact that Rinda had turned Elfred away from the door on flimsy pretenses thrice this week.

"If you're ill, I will send for a doctor," he observed.

Rinda started at that and turned a shade paler. A doctor would divulge her secret to Lord Mellowby! She would be found out—and what would happen then she preferred not to imagine. " 'Tis but a momentary distemper," she said, jumping up as if to show how recovered she was and pacing around the room. "I will be well enough tomorrow."

"If you are not," her guardian warned, "I shall assuredly send for the doctor and have him examine you."

So Rinda, like it or not, found herself strolling about the grounds almost daily with Elfred, who could not understand why she would not set an earlier date for the wedding.

"But why wait?" he cried in an agonized voice (for he sensed her indifference and lived in dread that she would break the engagement and settle her fancy on some other likely lad). "What is to be gained by it?"

Time was to be gained by it, time to get Rory home—but Rinda could hardly tell her betrothed that. "Next September," she said stubbornly. "I have promised to marry you in mid-September and not till then, so do not press me, Elfred!"

She was growing more desperate every day, surreptitiously letting out the waistline of her dresses. And when in January Lord Mellowby remarked caustically as she swept in to dinner that she was gaining weight and should ride more, she answered bitterly that she had a taste for sweets—and proved it by stuffing herself with custard and little tarts.

Her letters had taken a new tack. *"You* must *come home,"* she wrote Rory. *"For I am afraid my guardian will advance the date of my marriage to Elfred. Do you want your son to be born under another man's name?"*

When she received no answer as the weeks passed,

she decided to undertake the dangerous winter voyage through the storm-lashed English Channel and the North Sea to the shores of Holland and find Rory herself. For a loveless marriage with Elfred was not to be borne—and besides, how would the groom react when he learnt that his supposedly virgin bride was well on the way to raising a family?

She had not enough gold to pay for passage for Lord Mellowby kept tight-fisted hold of her money, doling out only small sums for necessities and insisting that she "charge" the rest, all the bills to be perused and settled by him later. But she did manage, piece by piece, to get a quantity of the family plate up to her room—despite Elsie's and Mawkers's surveillance. When she learned that a ship, *Margaret's Pride,* was sailing despite the weather for Amsterdam, she stole downstairs after dinner and rode into Lyme to book passage with the ship's captain.

She found Captain Carvell at the Bell and Whistle in Lyme. He was a bluff hearty fellow seated in the common room and talking companionably with a group of local seafarers and merchants.

Rinda kept her head high, but her cheeks were pink from the curious glances shot at her—for many there knew who she was—as she sought to speak to him.

"I am sorry, young mistress," he told her indifferently, unaware that he was speaking to a member of the local aristocracy. Indeed to Captain Carvell any woman who came alone and unchaperoned into a waterfront inn by night—and especially one whose high color (which he took to be rouge) and elegant hairdo and ribands and velvet cloak were of so startlingly fashionable a cut—branded herself at once a harlot of the town. "But I'm a married man and have no interest in wenching."

Rinda gasped. Her color rose even higher and she froze to the spot in indignation.

Several members of the company heard his offhand remark and coughed deprecatingly. One of them leaned toward the captain. "'Tis not a town wench but the Countess of Ravensay who would speak with you," he hissed.

"Oh? A Countess, is it now?" The captain, who had gone back to his ale, swung around and stared at Rinda curiously. "And what would your ladyship want of me?"

"A few words—in private," Rinda got out in a suffocated voice. She was almost sorry she had come! "If the innkeeper could lend us his private dining room?"

Captain Carvell's bushy brows elevated in surprise but he came to his feet and, walking with a rolling gait, moved over to the innkeeper, who promptly came to Rinda's rescue by leading them to the tiny private dining room at the head of the stairs.

Every eye in the place watched their ascent with speculation and Rinda felt that even her ears were red as she climbed the stairs.

"And now, my lady." The captain pulled out a chair for her. "What can I do for you?"

"You can take me to Holland," said Rinda crisply. "I cannot pay you in gold, but I have enough plate to more than cover the cost of passage if you will accept silver."

Captain Carvell studied her narrowly. "For yourself only?" he asked silkily, for if this fresh-faced wench had a lover who also wished passage, he could be aiding a runaway—and that could wear out his welcome in this convenient port. Wouldn't do to rile up the gentry. Nor did he wish to be denied free access to Lyme harbor or cold-shouldered in the future by the citizenry.

"Yes, yes, for myself alone," said Rinda nervously.

"May I ask the reason for your voyage?"

Rinda had not expected this. She stiffened. "I must travel abroad for my health," she said loftily. "My physician has advised it."

"And so you come by night, knowing I sail at dawn, to make your arrangements?" he meditated.

Put thus, it had a clandestine ring to it.

"My parents are dead," snapped Rinda. "I am Countess of Ravensay in my own right."

"And yet you have not the gold for the voyage? You must rely on the family plate?" His brows shot up still higher. "At your age you must have a guardian."

"Of course I have, but he is indisposed. He suffers severely from gout."

"A painful malady," mused the captain. "Very well, your ladyship." There was a certain irony to the way he said that. "Be on the Cobb at dawn with your plate. I'll meet ye there and see that ye're rowed out to *Margaret's Pride*. And here's my hand on it." He stood up and reached out a giant paw and shook her hand firmly.

Rinda left, shaken. She was sure that every pair of eyes in the inn stared at her speculatively as she passed.

But at least she had made her arrangements! She would do what she was now convinced she should have done long ago—go abroad to seek her lover.

She had very little time. She was afraid to try to take too much with her, but she determined to wear at least three dresses, one over the other, for although she would saddle her horse herself, tiptoeing into the dark stables past a snoring stableboy, and bring a packhorse with her, the poor animal could hardly be expected to carry the plate as well as her whole wardrobe!

Feverishly she dressed, adding layer after layer of garments until she could hardly move. Oh, well, it was cold out! At the last minute she decided to leave all but the silver behind her.

She stole from the house, moving awkwardly in so many layers of fabric, half-expecting to be hailed. But everything went well. The stableboy was predictably asleep, the house windows showed no lights, she seemed alone in the world.

She rode to Lyme and reached the town as dawn was breaking, made her way through the narrow ragstone alleys to the Cobb and dismounted with a cry of disappointment.

For the captain had not waited for her. She saw him a little way out, being rowed toward his ship, her sails pink in the dawn's pale light and the sea a misty expanse behind her.

In desperation she called to him. "Come back, I can pay for my passage—I have brought the plate."

"Have you indeed?" said a chilly voice behind her and she whirled to see Lord Mellowby, his fur-trimmed cloak gathered around him against the chill, striding toward her.

She froze in her tracks, waiting as he came up to her. For now she knew that *Margaret's Pride* would sail without her.

"I have brought the carriage with me," he told her pleasantly. "You may ride beside me on the way back." And turned to frown at her packhorse, laden down with the family silver, awkwardly bundled, which stuck out at odd angles through its makeshift wrappings.

He asked no explanation as they rode back to Grantland Manor through the damp early morning air and she guessed it was the broad back of the carriage driver that kept him from asking what she was doing in Lyme. For the same reason she refrained from asking him how he had found out her plans, guessing that someone from the common room of the inn, seeking to curry favor with Lord Mellowby and thereby gain his custom, had hastened to Grantland Manor last night to tell him—or sent a messenger to do so. In either case, her plans were ruined. She slumped against the carriage seat, too tired to move, and had to be helped down from it on arrival.

Lord Mellowby seemed unimpressed by her pallor or her wavering step. When they arrived home, he ushered her directly into the drawing room and when she slumped into the nearest chair, he ordered her to stand up.

"You are grown quite thick around the middle," he remarked critically.

"I have put on three of my gowns against the cold," was her defensive answer.

"Three gowns . . . as part of your wardrobe for sailing, no doubt?"

That was so obvious that Rinda felt no need to reply. She scowled at him.

"Stand up again and turn around," he commanded.

"I will not," she said defiantly.

"You are afraid I will see what now becomes apparent," he sighed. "You are pregnant."

There was no use denying it. It would be unmistakable soon enough. "Yes," she admitted. "I am pregnant."

He looked astonished that she did not deny it. "My God, you're a cool one," he said. "Here you sit, betrothed to a lad who believes you purer than snow, and you calmly admit to me that you're about to bear a bastard child! Can it be that Elfred is deeper than I've given him credit for?"

"Elfred is not the father."

"No—I thought not. Well, let us have his name. I'll have him horsewhipped and then personally escort you both to the church!"

That last remark goaded her. "The father is Rory Edgecombe," she said between her teeth. "And he's far beyond your reach. But I can tell you he'd be delighted to marry me if he were here! I but sought to join him. And," she added tartly, "I think you had best send me to join him and soon, don't you?" She rose and stood in profile before him, her three heavy dresses making her seem nearer nine months pregnant than five.

"Oh, I don't think we'll send you away just yet," he said with more coolness than she had given him credit for. "Rory Edgecombe, you say? He'll be Polly Edgecombe's bastard son, I take it?"

"Don't call him a bastard!" she shouted. "'Tis not Rory's fault that his parents are dead and he's not been able to prove they were legally married!"

Her guardian was pacing about the room. He seemed

not to have heard her outburst. "This matter takes consideration," he muttered. "'Twould be no great catch to find yourself married to that penniless Edgecombe fellow, no matter what noble blood flows through his veins. Nor can we now ignore your condition, which I have suspected this month past."

"You should have asked me," she said bitterly. "I would have told you!"

"I believe you would." There was a reluctant admiration in his gaze. "If your father was alive, he would be filled with shame," he added, rubbing her feelings raw. "Well, you'd best go to bed now, but if you hear noises in the night, do not investigate them—there will be a guard on your door henceforth and you will not stir from your room except in the company of a manservant of my selection."

So she was to be held a prisoner! With her head very high, Rinda let Lord Mellowby—and the footman he signalled from the hall—escort her up the stairs.

She stayed in bed the whole day. Indeed she was almost afraid to go down to dinner, for she expected some grim pronouncement from Lord Mellowby. Instead she found him calm and unruffled, smiling expansively as he usually did when his gout was not plaguing him.

He waited until they had finished their meal and the dishes were cleared away and they were drinking their wine before he got up and closed the door.

"I have decided there is no longer any need for you to be so excessively polite to Lord Chell's son," he informed her surprisingly.

So he had noticed her frosty politeness to Elfred! She waited to hear more.

"Indeed," he added casually, "you have my permission to quarrel with him on any pretext you like and call off the betrothal. I will back you up in this matter."

She stared at him, not comprehending. "You are

giving your consent to my marriage to Rory?" she asked haltingly.

His look of mild amazement shook her. "Of course not," he said on a chiding note. "I am merely giving my consent to a broken betrothal. We will make other plans for you later."

"What other plans?"

"I have been considering your attributes and I feel that we have sold you rather cheaply. You have beauty, wealth, a fine old name. You are marketable elsewhere."

Rinda felt her breath leave her. "If you are suggesting that some impecunious nobleman will accept a pregnant bride—" she began in an argumentative voice.

"I am suggesting no such thing." He smiled at her directly and it occurred to her that he had a sly face. "You are not the first young lady to have slipped, nor will you be the last. The important thing is to have no scandal surrounding you when you do wed—and that will probably not be possible here in Dorset. There is no hurry now, I will make leisurely inquiries as to a suitable match for you. It is entirely possible that we can find you a fortune to match your own—especially if we send a small portrait of you to whoever I settle upon."

Rinda felt her world growing unsteady about her feet.

"In any event," he added kindly, "you are to quarrel with Elfred and break the betrothal. You should find that no great hardship." And at her rebellious expression, "After you have done that, we will discuss your future in more detail."

The next afternoon was an explosive one. Elfred arrived and told her flatly that it was being said in the town that she had been about to take ship when she was intercepted and dragged home by her guardian.

Rinda decided that was a perfect excuse.

She flew into a rage. She railed at Elfred that he did not trust her. She categorized the entire tale as a "pack of lies." She flung his betrothal ring in his face and told him never to darken her door again and ran up the stairs in a storm of tears.

Elfred rode back to Hawkings Castle and promptly struck in the face the groom who had reported to him the incident on the Cobb. He and his father had words that could be heard clear into the servants' quarters, after which they reached an agreement that they would never speak of the matter again.

Rinda came down to dinner to find her guardian frowning, for his gout was beginning to plague him again.

"I have done as you directed," she told him wanly. "And now I would have you discuss my future with me as you promised."

He got up, wincing, and made sure the dining room doors were closed to listening ears.

"We will go on as before," he told her quietly. "You will act as though nothing has happened, you will continue to dine with me—until you become noticeably large. Then you will keep to your room and only your maidservant and Mawkers will see you."

"You could send me away," she said ironically. "To Bath perhaps. There no one here would see me."

His pleasant expression had returned and she knew that the pain for the moment had left him. "And there you would find a way to slip away to Holland," he mused. "No, I owe it to your dead father to see that you do not throw your life away."

"After all, it is *my* life!" she reminded him sharply.

He shrugged as if that were of no importance. "You will bear the child here—and in secret. I will pay the doctor well not to speak of it."

But babies cried! They could hardly keep the existence of a small baby a secret in the house! Frozen in fear, Rinda waited, watching him across the long table, and what he said was what she dreaded.

"Once the child is born, we will spirit it away to some

good home in another county. You will never see it
again. True, you will no longer be a virgin and your
nipples will have changed color, but perhaps—" Lord
Mellowby gave a wry laugh as he poured his wine—
"perhaps we will be lucky and find a suitor so taken
with you that he will forgive your past mistakes." He
considered her critically over the rim of his glass. "Yes,
I rather think we will," he added with satisfaction, "for
you have lost that hoyden look that irritated me and
still kept a certain wildness that is most alluring."

Rinda didn't care how alluring he considered her.
She rose shakily from her chair. "I will not do it!" she
cried.

Lord Mellowby peered at her down the long table.
The silver glittered, the crystal goblets gathered the
light, the wine was as red as blood. "There is really
nothing you can do about it," he murmured. "The
child will assuredly be born—and it will disappear. You
will not know its whereabouts and in time you will
forget it completely. Indeed you will come to thank me
that I did not let you throw your life away!"

Rinda stared at him through a glaze of bitter tears.
She was only five months pregnant and already plans
were being made to take her child from her. She would
never hold her baby in her arms. It was all too cruel!

With a sob, she gathered up her satin skirts and fled
the room, leaving her guardian to speculate pleasantly
on what peer in Kent or Sussex or far away Northumberland might have an heir foolish enough to fall in
love with damaged goods.

But time was on Rinda's side. Guarded and watched,
she continued to dine with Lord Mellowby. She had confided in Mawkers, but Mawkers, to her horror, had taken
Lord Mellowby's side in the matter. Mawkers had always disliked Rory, seeing in him Lady Polly, who had
ruined Dorinda's life.

"Lord Mellowby's right," Mawkers told her severely.

" 'Tis hard, I know, but 'tis best ye rid yourself of this child—you'll have others."

No one, no one was on her side.

In desperation, Rinda tried again to escape.

Before dinner the next night she stuffed all the coins she owned into her shoes and threw all the candles out of her bedchamber window, where they disappeared into the massed ivy below. When Elsie, who now slept in a trundle at the foot of her bed, lit her way to bed alongside a silent noncommittal footman named Chubbs, Rinda announced that she wished to write some letters and one small candle would not be enough. She dispatched an unsuspecting Elsie for more candles.

After Elsie had disappeared down the corridor, Rinda called out, "Chubbs, there's a snake in my room. He must have crawled up the ivy and come in when the room was being aired this morning. Would you come in and kill it?"

Chubbs responded with alacrity for it would go ill with him if he allowed anything to happen to the young Countess he guarded. As he came through the door, Rinda brought the fireplace poker down onto his head and he sprawled to the carpet unconscious.

With no clear plan of action, Rinda raced down the back stairs and made it out the garden door. She only knew that she was going to save her baby at all costs. She would mount a horse, ride north. In some hamlet she would find a decent couple who would take her in and see her through the birth. After that, she would find employment until Rory could come for her....

She never reached the stables. Lord Mellowby stood there, solidly blocking her way and on either side of him the grooms were closing in on her.

"I thought you looked too sparkling at dinner," he said cynically as Rinda stopped and took a hopeless step backward. "You should not give such clear warning of your intentions."

After that both Mawkers and Elsie slept in her room.

A grumbling Mawkers, who sniffed disapprovingly that Rinda "might have killed poor Chubbs, who was only doing his duty."

"I am doing *my* duty too," cried Rinda. "My duty to my unborn child! That I may keep it with me!"

Mawkers only sighed. There was no reasoning with this raging young woman she held so dear.

But Rinda was not to be held so easily at Grantland Manor. Twice more she tried to escape—and was twice brought back. Indeed it was only fear for her unborn child that kept her from essaying a mad climb down the ivy and riding for the coast to stow away on any passing ship.

Trapped, furious, receiving no visitors for Lord Mellowby cheerfully told all and sundry that Rinda's health was now precarious and the doctor had prescribed complete rest and no excitement, Rinda passed her days dismally—days enlivened only by bitter quarrels at mealtime with her guardian in the long dining room.

She was walking heavier now and Lord Mellowby had forbidden her to write to Rory—although she still smuggled a letter out through Elsie now and then. For Elsie was young and in love with one of the grooms at Lyddon House and intended to marry him in October.

Rinda wondered dolefully where *she* would be in October when Elsie was celebrating her nuptials.

Thinking there might be help in that direction, Rinda asked Elsie to get a message to Mary Lyddon via her betrothed, but surprisingly Elsie balked at that. It was one thing to smuggle out letters via ship captains to a man overseas, but quite another to involve her betrothed in any scheme that might get him sacked—and with Mary Lyddon so ill, Tom Lyddon might be vexed enough to do just that if his wife were to be disturbed!

Rinda had not known of Mary Lyddon's illness. She abandoned that avenue.

Her friends... Well, none of the lads would help her

for most of them were still smarting from being flirted with and flung aside. As for the girls—she could imagine Meggie Lofring or Emily Tyburn laughing together over her predicament, for they had both snatched up her castoff suitors and smarted over it. Nancy Gaines and Peggy Shaw were both away visiting and would be gone for months. Pamela Redding was in mourning for her parents and would see no one and Mary Willows was so timid she would shy away in fright from any venture so desperate. No help there.

And although Rinda did not know it, Lord Mellowby was systematically intercepting Rory's letters to her, breaking them open and frowning at the treasonous information they contained, for Rory penned glowing accounts of how all Europe was lining up behind the illegitimate claimant to the English throne.

Lord Mellowby, sprawled at his ease in a velvet coat before the fire in the library, would tap the latest letter lightly with his enameled snuffbox and gaze at the walls of mellow volumes without seeing them, as he tried to sort out how much was truth and how much the youthful exuberance of the writer. Always he locked the letters into his desk and pocketed the key. Best to let Rinda think her lover had forgotten her....

They chose their path and they knew their way,
They thought—but their paths diverged
And now she must ride hard to save the day
Or sing his funeral dirge!

PART TWO

Born to Love—and Born to Lose!

Chapter 13

And then in February—a rainy February when the sky sent down chilly tears made salty by the sea air against the windowpanes, and people preferred staying home to going out in the damp—a stranger rode up dripping to the door of Grantland Manor just as Rinda and Lord Mellowby were sitting down to dinner.

Lord Mellowby came to his feet as the butler burst into the room with an unannounced stranger.

"What the devil—?" he began, frowning at the gentleman whose soaked brown woolens and drowned plumed hat were already puddling the carpet.

"This gentleman, sir, bears such tidings," began the butler in a shaky voice, "that I knew your lordship would want to see him at once."

His lordship collected himself and cast a quick look at Rinda, dressed in blue-gray velvet that seemed to turn her gray eyes blue, who sat pale and calm. What difference if she dined with a passing traveler? The fellow could not know how slim she had been before so he would hardly notice her newly thickened waistline! Lord Mellowby relaxed and became the courteous host, making introductions, and having his guest's outer garments spread before the fire to dry, then plying him with food before he would let him speak.

"I'm fresh come from London," their guest informed them over his venison. "Sent by his nephew who's studying at Grey's Inn to inform Lord Culp, who lives the other side of Lyme, I'm told, of the dire happenings there. But my horse has gone lame and I'll not reach him this night."

Both Rinda and Lord Mellowby knew that Lord Culp had a son studying law at the Inns of Court and regarded the messenger with lively curiosity.

"Dire happenings?" repeated Lord Mellowby.

"Aye. King Charles is dead."

Such a feeling of relief as she had never known went through Rinda. Rory would be coming home now! For the Duke would sail to England to claim his throne and Rory would be with him. Her baby was saved!

"When did it happen? When did the King die?" she cried on such a note of joy that her guardian frowned at her impropriety.

"On February sixth," declared the messenger importantly. "Had a stroke two days before, so they say. I'd have been here sooner but I was delayed by the muddy roads."

Rinda wondered if the news had already reached Holland. Her heart sang and her face grew radiant.

"The new King will be settling in," observed Lord Mellowby with another frown at his ward for her unseemly behavior.

"Aye. James took over the same day."

"What was the feeling in London?"

His guest reflected before he took another large bite of venison and answered almost unintelligibly with his mouth full. "Oh, he was well enough received for all he's married to Anne Hyde—and her the daughter of that infamous Clarendon." He shrugged. "London rides easier than the West Country with a new man in the saddle." He looked at them both keenly, for the West

Country was known to lean heavily to Monmouth and had tried to get James barred from the succession.

"You look feverish," her guardian told Rinda before she could launch into questions that might be considered treasonable—perhaps about what word London had of the Duke's movements. "You had best leave the table—I will have your supper sent up."

The messenger looked chagrined to be deprived of the company of the velvet-clad beauty, but to Rinda it was opportunity. She rose and curtsied.

"I will bid you good night, gentlemen." And then, boldly facing down Lord Mellowby. "I'll just go upstairs by way of the kitchen so Cook will not overload my tray."

She had the satisfaction of seeing her guardian's irritated gaze follow her as she strolled out to the kitchen, which was agog with excitement.

"Now that King Charles is dead, his son the Duke of Monmouth will be on the march," Cook was proclaiming as she waved a long wooden spoon. "He'll not let his uncle steal the throne from him."

"Monmouth's illegitimate," sighed the butler gloomily.

Cook whirled and pointed her spoon at him like a weapon. "He's his father's acknowledged eldest son, born of Lucy Walter during those dark days," (Cook loved drama), "when Charles must have almost lost hope of ever being restored to his rightful throne! And besides," she scoffed, "who's to prove he didn't marry Lucy Walter? There's many who say he did!"

"But the proof has to be on the other side," pointed out the butler bluntly. "The Duke must prove the King actually did marry his mother—and the King has denied it."

"The late King," corrected Rinda and their heads all swung around warily for none had noticed her entrance. "I'm going to finish my dinner here," she said with composure. "And I'd advise you all to be careful what you say in my guardian's presence, for he's James's man—just as we're all Monmouth's."

There was a general murmur of approval, for this was the first time the lady of the house had declared herself.

Rinda stayed in the gossipy kitchen as long as she dared, and went upstairs as excited as any of them. Now she guessed why she had not heard from Rory recently. He must have heard that the King was desperately ill and be waiting to surprise her by his arrival!

But Rinda was unaccustomed to politics and did not realize that invasions moved more ponderously than that. A letter from Rory arrived two days later (her political declaration in the kitchen had gained her one thing: the butler, who had been deflecting Rory's letters to Lord Mellowby, had an abrupt change of heart and Rinda suddenly began to receive her mail). Reading it, she was disappointed to learn that news of the King's death had not reached him. He was full of hope however and he spoke of things in his letter that would incriminate him anywhere in the land. Rinda carefully locked it away and wrote to him of the King's death, knowing full well he would have heard of it long before her letter reached him.

She told him too of her broken betrothal and of Lord Mellowby's plans and she wondered if he perhaps would have no need to wait for the main party, but could precede the Duke incognito and whirl her up and away somewhere?

His answer to that came when she was already confined to her room upstairs as being too noticeably pregnant to appear downstairs.

"Do not worry about anything," his letter counseled blithely. *"The Duke will sail soon and all England will join him—you will see! There is general rejoicing here and all of us are optimistic. Encouraging letters come from England every day...."* There was much more and Rinda pictured him tenderly, she saw him writing with wild excitement, his

quill pen racing over the paper, eager to get home, to claim Hawkings Castle and his title—and herself.

The West Country was seething with rumors, which flew about everywhere. Mawkers and Elsie brought them to her, repeating them as best they could, for both were staunch Monmouth supporters and believed in the young Duke's Cause as firmly as did Rory.

But still the months passed and Rory did not come home.

Spring came to Dorset and the fruit trees blossomed. April's muddy roads dried and crusted into May and early June flowers were bursting all about.

But in Rinda's big upstairs bedchamber in Grantland Manor there was only terror. Rory had not arrived. The baby was expected this week. She prayed it would be late, but she was agonizingly certain that it would be born on time.

And they would take it from her. And she would be too weak to stop them.

"News? Is there any news of the Duke?" she would cry the moment either Mawkers or her little maid Elsie opened the door. And every time they told her pityingly that there was none. Or else they repeated wild rumors which for a day or two buoyed her up and then let her down deeper than before.

She was very distraught these days and when she was alone she would pace the floor wringing her hands. Ah, she should have escaped when she first discovered she was pregnant, she told herself bitterly, she should not have waited to hear from Rory—she should just have gone to Holland and joined him!

But self-recriminations gained her nothing. The Duke, she told herself bitterly, was bogged down with preparations to invade and Rory was at his side, too busy to write and expecting daily to embark—at least she hoped that was the case.

Just as Rinda feared, the Duke was late but the baby was not. On the night of June 10 she was awakened by a short sickening pain in her midsection. Her cry waked Mawkers.

"I think—I think it is my time," gasped Rinda, and Mawkers shook Elsie and bade her get up and go rouse Lord Mellowby and tell him they must send for the doctor.

By the time the doctor got there—for everybody had taken time to dress all along the line, and to saddle horses and jog about—Rinda was writhing in agony.

It was an intermittent agony that was to go on ceaselessly for six hours until in a last burst of pain that began with a scream and seemed to end in hell, she came back from what she had thought must surely be death and heard from what seemed a great distance the doctor saying, "You have a fine daughter, your ladyship."

Rinda fought her way back to the world slowly, from limp exhaustion. And then of a sudden wild things began to happen, for one of the scullery maids burst into the room and cried out, "Cook's cousin just arrived from Lyme and he said His Grace the Duke of Monmouth has landed with a great force and occupied Lyme. The Duke has declared himself in possession of the town and everyone is throwing flowers for they say he's to be our new King!"

Rinda was forgotten in the commotion that followed as the doctor (who almost dropped the baby in his perturbation) and Mawkers and Elsie all crowded forward to ask the excited girl questions.

At last! thought Rinda, lying back and giving herself precious time to rest and think. "Give me my daughter," she said in a weak voice and Mawkers made haste to do so and then turned again to demand more information of the scullery maid.

Then the doctor had gone and Elsie, all atwitter, had followed the scullery maid downstairs, and Mawkers was dressing the baby in a long delicate lace-trimmed lawn gown that had been Rinda's as a baby, and there was a polite knock on the door and Lord Mellowby entered the room.

"Well, I am told all went well, despite the protracted time of delivery," he said cheerfully.

Rinda regretted that she did not have her baby in her arms. Weak or not, she would have clawed the eyes out of anyone who attempted to separate her from her child.

"I have a daughter," she said coldly.

"Yes, so I understood from the doctor—although he was more interested in Dukes from over the sea than in births at the moment."

"And well he should be!" Although there was a lancing terror in her heart, for Lord Mellowby was still in control here, Rinda managed to rise on one arm to what she hoped was a more commanding position than lying prone. "For the Duke has come to take possession of this land and Rory is beside him."

"There is an enthroned king still to be dealt with," her guardian reminded her pleasantly.

"Bah!" said Rinda. "You have heard how the people welcomed the Duke! And Rory has the Duke's promise that his parents' marriage will be recognized and Hawkings Castle and his title returned to him when the Duke ascends the throne." She gave her guardian a narrow taunting look. "Do you really want to spirit away Rory's child?" she demanded ferociously. "When Rory stands in Lyme beside the Duke?"

Her guardian surveyed her uneasily. The King would put down this rebellion in short order, he was certain. Still Monmouth was here in Lyme and James was not. And things sometimes went wrong. The vision of a malevolent James III—for that was what Monmouth would become if he succeeded the present King—was a daunting one, for Stuart justice was apt to be swift and deadly. He bit his underlip. Backing down did not come easily to him.

"I have reconsidered," he said shortly, and turned and went out.

Rinda collapsed in the bed. This last encounter had taken the rest of her strength. Silently she reached out her arms and Mawkers, who had been watching her with bittersweet sympathy, put the baby, now appropriately wearing its long dress of lawn and lace, into them.

Rinda turned her head away as she cradled the child in her arms, for she did not want either Mawkers or Elsie to see the tears that were squeezing onto her lashes.

"We have won," she whispered to the pink-faced little girl who was happily nuzzling at her breast. "Little one, we have won...."

She fell asleep exhausted and Mawkers, smiling, took the baby away. Mawkers knew what tinder and fire Rinda was made of—for had she not nearly brained poor Chubbs, the footman, who had been but doing his duty guarding her door? But now the nightmare was past. His Grace, the Duke of Monmouth, was here to put all things right and Rinda's mistake, once she was wed to a favorite of the Duke and mistress of Hawkings Castle, would be condoned. People would say she'd had no choice, with her lover a wanted man.... Mawkers smiled down at the sleeping woman whose damp red-gold hair fanned out on the pillow in a burst of glory.

Rory came with the evening—and this time he did not slip in by an unlocked garden entrance but boldly thundered the big iron knocker on the front door. This time he sauntered through the doorway with a grim smile upon his face, to be greeted by an affable Lord Mellowby who congratulated him coolly upon the birth of his firstborn, for all the world as if he had not such a short time before been intent on spiriting that child away!

"Will ye not drain a glass of port with me and toast the new arrival?" Lord Mellowby would have ushered

Rory into the drawing room, save that Rory shook his head.

"After I've seen Rinda—then I'll be happy to share a goblet with you, Lord Mellowby." There was a swash-buckling air about Rory these days and he took the stairs three at a time, leaving Lord Mellowby thinking bitterly that the cut of this upstart's suit was uncommon fine and that this reckless young Duke, if he succeeded, would sweep many such wild fellows to power and affluence. Well, he would be careful not to be netted along with their enemies, yet neither would he join them. He would walk a narrow neutral line between, he thought, as he poured the deep ruby liquid into his glass.

Upstairs Rory threw open the door and burst in upon Rinda, who was startled to wakefulness at his joyous greeting.

"Oh, Rory!" She was laughing and crying all at once as he bent tenderly to kiss her, and her fingers were running through his hair. "Oh, Rory, we have a lovely daughter!"

"Who shall be called 'Dorinda' for her mother!" Rory finished for her merrily as he smiled down at the baby Mawkers brought. The long hem of the baby's delicate dress almost dragged the floor and Mawkers frowned at him when he wanted to hold the child as if she thought his very touch might mar it.

But Rory looked down at the sweet perfection of that small face looking up at him with such blind trust and cooing in his arms, and felt a sensation totally new in his wild young life. A daughter—he had a daughter! And he would be worthy of her, he would give her Hawkings Castle to grow up in and sport through and love—not as he had done from afar, but hers to trea-sure and keep and pass on to a child of her own.

His throat was tight as he gave the child back to the watchful Mawkers, who snatched it away and retired to a far corner of the room as if those who had borne her might somehow contaminate her. And he swallowed as he turned back to Rinda, looking so beautiful there in the big bed, for the excitement of his return had brought a slight flush of color to her pale cheeks, her gray eyes were sparkling with love, her soft mouth curved in contentment.

"We will have the banns cried and be married as soon as possible," he said, giving her hand a squeeze. "Ah, you should have seen our arrival, Rinda! The Duke came ashore first and knelt and kissed the soil of England!"

It was probably sand, she thought, *considering where he had come ashore,* but she gave Rory a fond smile.

"And then we stormed through the town," he told her dramatically, "and the people came running out to greet us. They threw flowers at us, Rinda. I could not get away before for the Duke needed us all about him to make a great show of force."

"How many troops did he bring with him?" asked Rinda, envisioning a harbor that would not hold the ships and more tall sails bobbing upon the horizon than the eye could count, for Rory had written in glowing terms of the amount of backing that could be expected.

He hesitated. "Those who came with the Duke number some eighty-two men," he said, and she gave him a startled look. "But men are flocking to our side every hour," he added hastily. "I doubt not we'll have a thousand by tomorrow!"

"But those are untrained countrymen, Rory," she protested, alarmed. "And they will be going against trained soldiery!"

"The soldiery will defect to us too!" he told her merrily. "Wait and see! All England will rally to our glorious Cause!"

Dorinda hoped so. She sank back on the pillow, stunned by the small number of forces the Duke had brought with him. And she had expected thousands!

"Argyll sailed for Scotland in May with three ships,"

Rory told her importantly. "He will raise the Covenant-
ers to our Cause and sweep down from the north, while
we will advance upon London, gathering supporters as
we go."

"Do you think the King will not have his supporters
too?" she asked him wistfully, because he seemed suddenly like a little boy to her, playing with tin soldiers.

Rory shrugged and gave her a disarming smile. "We
will sweep them aside," he said in a dismissing tone.
"But I must let you rest, Rinda." Having greeted her,
having seen his child, she could see that he was eager to
be off, to seek the side of the Duke who, he hoped,
would bring him everything.

Sighing, she let him go, for she was indeed very
tired. For had she not given birth to a daughter, and
stood off the man who would have taken that daughter
from her, and regained her lover—all in the course of a
single day?

And surely, surely this mad young Duke had made
better plans than Rory had told her, surely there were
other strings to his bow, some great force from Yorkshire
or Devon or somewhere that would keep King James's
forces off balance while the Duke assembled and trained
the brave men of the West Country who, she had no
doubt, were coming in by horse, by farm cart, and on
foot, now that word of his arrival had spread.

All would be well, Rory would be with her again, her
baby would have a father at last.... These were her
thoughts as she went to sleep from sheer exhaustion
even as Rory's boots were clattering down the stairs.

But although Rory had promised an early wedding,
with himself proclaimed legitimate and heir to Hawkings Castle, the advisers who surrounded the Duke had
other plans. All that must wait until after the Duke
mounted the throne, they told Rory. To attempt to
unseat any member of this West Country nobility during these troubled times would create fear among them
all, as well as dissention through the discontent of the

present owner's servants who would naturally fear loss of their livelihood—no, the Duke had promised Rory he would become Lord Chell and that Hawkings Castle would be restored to him, but for delivery of both, he must wait.

Rory shut his teeth in anger, but he knew there was no disputing what Lord Grey and the others had decided.

"We will be married after the Duke ascends the throne," he told Rinda and her guardian airily, when several days later he dined with them in the long dining room of Grantland Manor. Hunting scenes roamed the wallpaper around them, with fallen stags and boars and great painted trees. Silver winked frostily from the long gleaming board and Rory cast a satisfied look about him. So would the dining room of Hawkings Castle look, he told himself, when he brought Rinda there as a bride—for when James Scott, Duke of Monmouth, became James III of England, he would be as generous with money and favors as his father Charles II had been, and Rory would be able to decorate Hawkings as he pleased.

"After he ascends the throne?" Lord Mellowby looked pleased.

"But surely sooner," protested Rinda. Although the doctor had insisted that she stay in bed for at least three weeks since it had been such a difficult birth, she had overruled him, and for this great occasion when Rory would dine as a guest at Grantland Manor, she had had herself carried downstairs. Dressed in a gown of light lemon yellow silk and with her pale cheeks, to which the color was only just beginning to return, rouged with Spanish paper, she sat—indeed half reclined—with her legs propped up on a straight chair on which a maroon velvet cushion had been placed. It gave her a languishing queenly look to be thus enthroned, half lying alongside the table, but now at Rory's words she sat straight up for she wanted this long-awaited marriage to take place. Now.

"Rory is right." Her guardian, Lord Mellowby, stepped into the breach. "If he marries you now, the marriage will be entered into the parish records under the name of Edgecombe. Your child will be Dorinda Edgecombe. But if he waits to get his proper name restored, his child will bear the family name of his father."

Rory frowned. In his haste to marry he had not thought of that. It was indeed wiser to wait.

Rinda threw her guardian a suspicious look, which he returned with a bland one. She wondered if this was yet another ruse of his to prevent her marriage.

"In any event, I would prefer to bring my bride directly to my ancestral seat at Hawkings Castle," said Rory grandly. "And it would be only proper to allow the present occupants a decent interval to quit the premises once title is transferred to me."

He looked so elegant saying that, thought Dorinda, her heart melting as she looked into his smiling face across a table where she had never thought to see him. His saffron-yellow hair blazed against the last rays of the afternoon sun and his eyes were that wonderful green-gold. She smiled back for she knew what Hawkings Castle meant to him—all that he had been deprived of in his childhood.

"Ah, yes," agreed Lord Mellowby. "A decent interval. Most gracious of you."

The lovers were unaware of any irony in that remark, and Lord Mellowby gave them both a contented look as Rinda agreed to wait. He congratulated himself that at least he had managed to postpone a marriage that would prove disastrous if this mad young Duke lost, and that would take place in good time with pomp and ceremony if the mad young Duke won. Either way Rinda would come out ahead.

And even though he had not been able to conceal the birth of the child, it could still be spirited away if things went wrong for Rory Edgecombe. He looked farther ahead. Grantland Manor could even be sold in that event and a London house taken in its place. Rinda would have plenty to live on, and he himself had always fancied life in London. And there he would find some impecunious gaming younger son who'd be glad enough to squire her about in the belief he was going to wed her and cancel his debts. It would give Rinda introduction to the better homes and who knew what scion of wealth and power her beauty might not enchant? Indeed, as guardian, he felt he was doing very well by his ward.

So ran the Machiavellian mind of Lord Mellowby, daintily eating his roast capon with a fork that had once made a trip to the Cobb at Lyme and back.

Chapter 14

Save for being carried down to dinner whenever Rory could escape from the Duke's busy schedule, Rinda had followed the doctor's advice and gone back to bed, for the long months of worry preceding the birth of her child had worn her down. But Rory's return rejuvenated her and she amazed even the doctor by the speed of her recovery.

A wet nurse was sent for so that Rinda might be less tied down with care of the baby. This was on Lord Mellowby's advice because he foresaw that if His Grace of Monmouth ever reached London and ascended the throne, young Rory would be lost in the crush of noblemen shoving their way forward to gain the royal favor. In that event Rinda would need to rush to London to join him, for her beauty alone might lift them from the pack. Lord Mellowby was cynical enough to know that favor with the Stuart kings could well prove fleeting (even though in his secret heart he would always believe Monmouth to be the son of Robert Sidney, whose mistress Lucy Walter had been before her liaison in Rotterdam with the then exiled and yet to be enthroned Charles II).

Rinda reveled in her new freedom for although she loved her baby, she had loved Rory first and now he was back again. He stayed overnight at Grantland Manor and she let him make love to her, although he was uneasy at first, reminding her of what the doctor had said about making love too soon after childbirth—she could become pregnant immediately and that could spell disaster.

"I care not," Rinda told him lazily, her eyes deep and lustrous in the moonlight that poured in through the mullioned windows. "All that I care about is that I have you back with me."

Rory responded vigorously and he brought a new finesse (lately learnt in Europe) to their lovemaking, while Rinda, who had been a mere girl when she had flung away her mask and let him take her in this very room, brought to their lovemaking a woman's full-blown ardor.

"I cannot bring myself to leave you," he declared hoarsely after passion had held its sway with them.

"Then don't." She was lazily nipping at his ear and letting her soft full breasts drag fierily across his chest, tickling the light furring of golden hair there.

"But His Grace of Monmouth—"

"The devil with His Grace of Monmouth. You belong here. With me."

Rory sighed. He looked very torn and Rinda regarded him fondly and with some amusement. It had come to her belatedly that he was very much the little boy, that he had never really grown up—perhaps never would. This Cause of the Duke's was for him an enchanting game in which he could be a mover and shaker of events. She could not imagine Rory buying cattle or selling hides or spending long hours over the estate accounts. That must be her part of their marriage—the practical part. Rory must needs always be there swashbuckling in the sun.

"I cannot stay, Rinda," he sighed.

"The Duke does not need you," she protested. "His troops have already swarmed into Axminster. You tell me that newcomers by the hundreds join his forces every day."

"Yes, that is true, but we are moving north. To Taunton."

"Good," said Rinda, sitting up with sparkling eyes. "I will go with you."

"There will be no accommodations," he warned her.

"I will find accommodations." Rinda was airily confident.

To Taunton she went. And there saw His Grace of Monmouth crowned King of England. She had begun keeping a journal and on that day she wrote, *"It may be that I have seen history in the making here today, for now two crowned heads claim England—we have a James in London and a James in Taunton. But what a ragtag army it is that follows the Duke! I wonder that Rory does not see it. He brags that the Duke entered Taunton at the head of five thousand men but there seems hardly to be a trained soldier among them. Rory says we will sweep across England in one long triumphal march and that the boots of those who join us will thunder so loudly that it will shake the very sceptre from King James's hand and give it to 'King Monmouth' as the troops now call him. I wish I were as sure, for there are rumors that the King is sending a large force under Lord Feversham to crush this 'rebellion.'"* She scratched through that last word and added, half whimsically, *"Rory says I must not call it a rebellion; he says it is a mighty Cause."*

In Taunton, as she had promised, Rinda found them a room with the Wyatts, whose daughter had been a school friend during the brief time Rinda had attended a school for select young ladies in Taunton. Elizabeth Wyatt—now Elizabeth Lawford—brought back to her the old days, when her mother was alive, when life had not been a struggle, when a merry and dissolute King sat on the English throne and Rinda's greatest problem was whether to wear a blue or yellow riband in her hair. . . .

"It was always so peaceful here and to think that today we find ourselves at the center of a Great Rebellion," she told her friend Elizabeth with a faint smile as they sat taking tea in the Wyatts' small drawing room and listening to the sound of marching feet as Monmouth's raw troops drilled outside.

"A great *Cause*." Elizabeth drew herself up, eyes flashing, for her husband was a Colonel in Monmouth's army and she herself a Monmouth supporter to her bones.

Rinda sighed and set down her fragile teacup. "I am weary of politics," she admitted. "Sometimes I feel I would give all I own just to retire to the country and watch the flowers bloom!"

"We will all be giving all we own if the Cause does not succeed," her hostess, Elizabeth's mother, reminded her tartly. She was a buxom woman with a newly etched worry line between her pale eyebrows, for not only was her son-in-law a Colonel in Monmouth's army but her husband was a well-known supporter of "King Monmouth"—both faced sure death if the Cause failed.

"What do you mean?" Rinda frowned.

"Why, even if we escaped with our lives—and of course we'd be hunted down and hanged—all of our property would be forfeit to the Crown. We'd be beggars!"

Rinda had not considered that. Now her gaze grew thoughtful as she stared out the window. *Grantland Manor . . . confiscated, her daughter growing up as Rory had—an outcast.* Several fresh-faced farmboys carrying wooden staves in place of guns marched past her line of vision. Not one of them could have been more than fifteen. An army ill-trained, ill-clad, ill-housed, could swiftly lose its enthusiasm, she thought. An army ill-armed was destined to defeat.

"Mother," protested Elizabeth, "don't be such a pessimist. Of course we'll win—because our cause is right!"

"All the same," muttered her mother, casting a hunted look about the blue-walled drawing room, "I wish your father would not insist on being so *conspicuous!*"

And Rory was even more conspicuous, thought Rinda suddenly. *A focal point, a target. And so,* she realized, *was she with her striking red-gold hair and her penchant for startling gowns. Hunted down . . . faith, they'd be easy to find!*

That night she was a flame that smoldered to a white-hot summer madness in Rory's arms, driving him to feats undreamed of. There was a wild sweet desperation in her lovemaking, for Feversham's troops were reported to be closing in and who knew what would happen? She embraced him with a vivid intensity that brought wonder to his eyes and joy to his heart.

"Oh, Rinda, Rinda," he whispered. "What would I do without you?"

He did not see the tears that shimmered on her lashes as she clutched him to her breast, or know that she was leaving on the morrow. . . .

Rinda did not accompany the troops that swarmed into Bridgwater—instead she rode back to Dorset and dismounted before Grantland Manor. When she came in, her manner was brisk. She ordered the servants to pack up all the plate, she was taking it into Lyme to be sold. She told the head groom to saddle up the horses, that they were taking all but her personal riding horse and Lord Mellowby's and three other mounts of her selection into Lyme to be sold.

Lord Mellowby caught her as she was cleaning out the contents of her jewel case.

"What madness is this?" he demanded, his squarish figure blocking the door.

"No madness. I will remind you that this is my house, that I am a woman grown and that I have the right to sell what is mine."

Seeing that glint in her eye, Lord Mellowby decided not to assert himself as her guardian. Instead he tried reason: "But so much is for sale in Lyme, what with families trying to outfit their sons for war, that your goods will bring no price!"

"I will negotiate with some sea captain and take what I can get."

He paled. "Is the Cause lost then? Has the Duke been defeated?" For with Rinda following along in the Duke's train, he was not sure where a defeat would leave them.

She gave him a derisive look. "Defeated? No, he has been crowned King in Taunton. Little girls dance toward him bringing him garlands of flowers and shower him with rose petals. His every step is triumphant. As I left, his troops were just surging into Bridgwater. Be good enough to unlock your desk—I would have the inventory of this estate. I would know what movable objects there are that can be sold."

"You are mad!" cried Lord Mellowby indignantly, for the furnishings of this house were much to his personal liking and through long association he had come to consider them his. "You are impoverishing yourself for this shaky Cause! I will not let you do it."

His ward's slender back straightened and her gray eyes gave him back a look of menace. "If you so much as attempt to stand in my way," she said contemptuously, "I will send word to my husband's new liege, His Majesty, King Monmouth, that you are King James's man and a traitor and have attempted to make off with my jewels. Who do you think will be believed, Rory's betrothed or you, however eloquent you may be?"

Her guardian recoiled as from a snake. "Rinda," he said hoarsely. "You would not do it?"

"I could and I would," she told him in a voice so determined it had to be believed. "But only if you stand in my way. Bring me the inventory."

White to the lips, Lord Mellowby did as he was bid. Swiftly Rinda scanned the list, checking items here and there which were readily salable.

"At least you will tell me why you are doing this?" Lord Mellowby's voice behind her was bitter.

"Because I have a daughter," she flung over her shoulder.

Her guardian went away, shaking his head. He knew others who were impoverishing themselves for Monmouth's Cause but he had not thought that madcap Rinda would be one of them.

But Rinda's troubled thoughts were not on the Cause. It took time to collect articles for sale, time to get them moved, time to get them sold and to convert into precious golden coins so much that she had treasured. And meantime word drifted down from the north that the Duke had marched west from Bridgwater and taken Glastonbury, but that Bristol—with a regiment of footguards hastily thrown in by Feversham—had proved too strong, as had Bath. On hearing that Rinda compressed her lips. Almost every man who worked on her estate—and on the neighboring estates as well—had enlisted in Monmouth's army. They would now fall back south and rumor had it that Feversham's troops were preparing for a pitched battle with the rebels. There was no word from Rory, who was with the Duke, and every fiber of Rinda's body yearned to be with him in what could well be the last days of his life. But she set her jaw and refused to think about it, and kept on working furiously.

Now that she had sold what she could, she called Mawkers to her in the garden. Mawkers came readily, her black skirts swirling about her long legs. She was as bewildered as any at all this commotion, this carting away of goods.

"Mawkers," said Rinda, who was pacing up and down before a bower of roses the same flaming color as her hair. "I know you loved my mother well and I believe you love me." ·

Mawkers' hard old face softened. A pretty sight Rinda made, she thought—and a pity she could not have fallen in love with someone other than Lady Polly's son. She waited.

"And because of the love you bear me," Rinda went on slowly, "I must ask you to perform a difficult task. It may well be the last thing that I will ever ask of you."

So serious was Rinda's demeanor that Mawkers felt alarm coursing through her. "Whatever it is, I will do it," she promised rashly for she had always felt that Rinda was the daughter she herself would never bear.

"Good. What is done must be done in secrecy. I intend to ride north where there will soon be a great battle—perhaps even waged before I can get there. You will sew into the hem of your skirts and into your pockets all the gold coins that I will give you save for a few that you will carry in a purse and say is all you own. We will leave together, with the wet nurse and the baby, and Lord Mellowby will assume that you are accompanying me to wherever Rory is quartered. But you will not." Here Mawkers's eyes widened. "Instead at the first crossroads, you and the wet nurse and the baby will ride east to Salisbury. I would have chosen Dorchester but it is too near the coast. By the time you reach there, traveling at the slow rate you must with the baby, the town may be full of fleeing men."

Mawkers gasped. "You do not believe the Duke will win?"

Rinda gave her a sad look. She had grown up in the months that she had been carrying her child, and after. She felt wiser far than her reckless Rory would ever be. "No, Mawkers, I do not think he will win."

Around them birds sang and bees buzzed lazily into the roses. The sky was a cloudless blue. Impossible to think of defeat on such a day and yet here was Rinda thrusting toward her a small box that when opened revealed a store of golden coins. And speaking of fleeing men...

"But all this gold—!" Mawkers looked down shocked at the pile of gold coins that must be sewn into her clothing. It seemed to glitter evilly at her, telling her that she would soon be weighted down with heavy responsibilities.

"If things go as I fear they will, this will not even be enough," said Rinda quietly. "Do not worry, Mawkers, I have kept plenty for myself." *Plenty for taking ship to Holland or wherever else the winds and tides will carry us.*

"But what of you, my lady?" wondered Mawkers. She did not mention Rory, for she hated him for bringing Rinda sorrow and now danger and perhaps exile. Even that beautiful child upstairs—and Mawkers had now grown fond of that child—could not make up for what Rory had put Rinda through!

"Do not worry about me." Rinda shrugged with an attempt at lightness. "For I shall follow my heart, as I always have—wherever it leads me."

Wherever he leads, thought Mawkers with a sigh. She took the box of coins and trudged back to the house, walking heavily. She was feeling her years today and the gold which must be stitched into her garments for her had lost its glitter.

The morning of July 5 dawned dismally. It was a day of sunshine and rain—unpredictable weather. In a cloudy respite between showers they set out, with Lord Mellowby standing before the house shaking his head as he watched them depart down the wet driveway. Three women and a baby, riding three horses and with a fourth horse on a lead behind them. Imperious Rinda in a red silk riding habit as flame-colored as her hair led the way on a big bay horse. She had a brace of dueling pistols stuck into a man's belt round her waist— "against highwaymen" she had said vaguely—and Lord Mellowby had no doubt that she carried in her saddle-bags all the gold she had gained from the sale of the livestock and plate. He would lay this also at Monmouth's door, he thought angrily, this beggaring of Grantland for political advantage! He imagined with glittering eyes Rinda's arrival at wherever the cursed Duke now had his headquarters, the meek handing over of that gold, and he ground his teeth.

But at the nearest crossroads, beneath dripping trees, Rinda stopped their little band. She had been riding with her baby well wrapped in her arms, looking down at the sleeping child. Now she bent and kissed that small sweet face and a lock of her bright hair fell down and tickled the child's chin. The baby's blue eyes snapped open and she looked up solemnly. To her young mother, that gaze seemed accusing.

"My little Dorinda," she murmured, and tears spilled over her lashes and ran down onto the baby's face. "Some day you will understand why I had to do this." And then she whispered almost inaudibly against her child's cheek. "Oh, Dorinda, never love a boy—find a man and love him, it will be so much easier for you!" Another lock of her bright hair loosened and fell down like a screen between herself and those two impassive onlookers who sat their horses nearby. "Oh, my little one," she breathed. "Someday I will hold *your* daughter in my arms and all of this will have been only a bad dream."

She could hardly bear to let the child go. Every inch of her screamed to keep the baby with her. But—she could not carry a baby into the fighting. And instinctively she knew that Rory, who had made so many wrong moves, would end up making the wrong move again— and unless someone stepped into the breach to save him, he would most likely die for it. He might never have loved her as much as she loved him, his might be a bright spirit that forgot easily and seldom thought of her when he was away, but hers at least was an unshakable loyalty. She had inherited that loyalty from her mother and it would be with her all of her life.

Rory needed her and she must save him.

Blinded by tears she turned and silently handed the baby to Mawkers. "Do as I have told you," she choked. *You will continue to ride east,* she had told Mawkers. *Tell whatever story is convenient—remember, your life is at stake. You have told me you have a sister in Banbury—go to her and pay her well to take care of you and my daughter.*

But, my lady, Mawkers had protested. *Banbury be forever away!*

I want my child to be forever away, Rinda had insisted. *Far from the fighting. Far from the aftermath. . . .*

Mawkers could not bear the parting. Over the baby's head, she leaned toward Rinda. "Don't go," she pleaded in a voice too low for the wet nurse, lost in her own private thoughts, to hear. "Come with us to Salisbury and on to Banbury. My sister would hide you if things went wrong."

Rinda gave her a tremulous smile but shook her head. It was very hard to part with her baby even for such a strong reason as this.

"I must go to him, Mawkers," she said huskily. "I must save him." Instinctively she touched the pistols. "It may be that I cannot, but at least I must try."

Tears were streaming down Mawkers's old cheeks. "But the Duke may yet win!" she protested.

Rinda shook her head. "Not against seasoned troops," she murmured. "The Cause is doomed." *And Rory will not face it, he will never face it—it will be all up to me.* "But if we survive, I will be back for my baby. Even if for unforeseen reasons you must move from Banbury, come back each year to the Banbury Fair and you will find me."

"There is always a great crush at the Banbury Fair," worried Mawkers. "I may miss you."

"No, for I will be very conspicuous. I will be wearing a red dress—this color, and I will ride about vivaciously, making myself noticed. Even if we must go into exile, Mawkers, I will come back—if necessary I will wear a riding mask and it will be red also. And I will sweep you both up and take you away with me. That I promise." *If I am alive to do it. . . .* The words were unspoken between them.

Their eyes met and locked in silent understanding. At that moment the sun came out and Rinda, rivulets of shining moisture running unnoticed down her face, embraced Mawkers and felt those bony shoulders shake with emotion. A little heartfelt sob escaped her lips as she pressed a swift last kiss on her baby's round pink cheek. Then quickly—lest her resolve weaken—she whirled her mount and rode away, straight-backed and armed and ready for whatever came. Around Sedgemoor a great battle was shaping up and its outcome would decide the fate of England.

And hers. And Rory's. And their child's.

A sense of doom pervaded her as she rode toward what seemed a solid wall of wet glistening trees that concealed the road ahead.

Her road ahead too was concealed from her. The mists of the future chose not to part—no more than would the mists over the dangerous marshy plain of Sedgemoor, cut by those treacherous ditches they called *rhines*. A plain over which cannon would boom soon enough, although Rinda, riding with determination toward the battle, could not know it.

She had saved her baby and now she was going to save Rory. It was a pledge she had made between herself and God. And she would keep that pledge—oh, she would keep it—if she lived.

From the crossroads, beside the downcast young wet nurse whose child had been stillborn and whose husband had been among the first to fall in one of the skirmishes between the King's troops and Monmouth's men that went on every day, Mawkers held the baby and sat her horse and watched Rinda ride away. Watched her until she was out of sight. And part of her heart went with her....

Rinda turned only once to wave—and to Mawkers's tearfully blurred vision, the straight-backed slender woman in red billowing silk skirts on the big bay horse with her bright hair shining in the sun seemed like a shimmering flame that would burn forever.

Mawkers never saw her again.

It takes one generation to make it,
One generation to lose it,
One generation to talk about it—
And one to make it again!

One Generation to Talk about It!

BOOK III

The Dispossessed

THE ROAD TO BANBURY CROSS
July 6, 1685

Chapter 15

The first remnants of a defeated army caught up with Mawkers and her little band the following day: three riders, all with hastily bandaged wounds and intent faces, riding hard for the coast. They reined up at sight of the women and one of them, the one with the bandaged arm that hung limp and useless, muttered something to the others and advanced.

"We need your horses, mistress," he said gravely. "For the King's men are close upon us."

"Are ye highwaymen then?" demanded Mawkers with asperity. "That ye'd take an old woman's horse and leave her to walk?"

The man with the bandaged arm looked shamed. "No, mistress," he sighed. "We are—"

"Enough," said one of the other men in a deep voice.

She guessed then what they were. "Is it over then?" she asked shakily, as he helped her to climb down.

The one who had first spoken nodded soberly. "'Twas a complete rout though our lads held out bravely."

And Rinda had ridden into that, thought Mawkers, and scalding tears seemed to cascade down her throat.

The next desperate group paused to eat up their

211

provisions and after that they were not only walking but hungry. *Wear comfortable shoes*, Rinda had advised. *For you may end up walking.* Mawkers was grateful now for the advice.

Over the next days as they bought and bartered for food and lodging at farmhouses and inns along their way, Mawkers pieced together the story of the battle: How Monmouth had attempted a daring night attack through the mists of Sedgemoor, that marshy waste honeycombed by *rhines*, how his army had moved stealthily through the dark until, misled, they had come up against the "Black Ditch" and there been cut to pieces by cannon fire. But their bravery could never be doubted, for those untrained West Country farmers had stood up for hours to the cream of English cavalry—and died there in their blood. The Duke and Lord Grey and some others had fled over the Mendip Hills, trying to reach the New Forest and the sea. Mawkers wondered silently if Rory had been with them. She guessed now that he had not, and understood too late what Rinda had realized well before her: Rory had been but a pawn in this Stuart game of kings. When the last card was played, he would be among those left to die.

The two women, Mawkers and the young wet nurse, were making their way, heads bent and eyes averted, down country lanes lined with limp figures dangling from the branches of trees—remnants of Monmouth's fleeing army who had been hanged summarily without trial on the spot. Since Mawkers was an old woman with a small baby in her arms that she claimed was her orphaned grandchild, with a weeping wet nurse by her side and no apparent possessions, the King's men let her through.

Behind her the West Country was dying.

Ghoulish stories reached them as Mawkers, arrived at last at Salisbury, dipped into her store of gold coins to take the coach to Banbury. And worse tales circulated among the passengers, whispered behind shocked hands, whenever the coach stopped for meals or overnight lodging.

Monmouth had been captured in Hampshire, it was reported, near Ringwood, sheltering beneath an ash tree. His hair had turned gray during his flight and he had been taken to London where he was pleading pitifully for his life.

Meantime Monmouth's followers were being rounded up and jailed—those who had not been summarily slaughtered. Anyone believed to have aided them—even old ladies—were being jailed alongside them. By the time word reached them that Monmouth had been beheaded on Tower Hill, there was other even worse news, for the King had ordered the terrible Judge Jeffreys, who had caused so many innocent men to be executed on flimsy evidence in the aftermath of the Rye House Plot, to sit in judgment on the rebels (and Jeffreys had been given a barony, created Baron Wem, it was whispered, to make him even more zealous on the King's behalf). And when word came that even the little West Country flower girls who had greeted the Duke with showers of petals were in danger of being tried for their lives, and that poor old Lady Alice Lisle, widow of a member of parliament in Cromwell's time, had been sentenced to burning by Judge Jeffreys merely for taking into her house two of the refugees and attempting to hide them, horror overcame the populace in general—a horror in no way alleviated when the little flower girls were not charged or when, by the King's "mercy," poor Lady Alice, in lieu of being burned at the stake, was allowed to have her head chopped off in Winchester marketplace.

In Dorset, in Somerset, all through the West Country, estates of those who had been party to the Rebellion were being confiscated left and right. Mawkers's thin lips tightened when she heard that Grantland Manor had been seized by the Crown and she clutched the child to her the tighter. Poor little thing, she would have no inheritance, it would be up to tired old Mawkers to take care of her, but that she would do to her dying breath!

She could learn nothing of Rinda or Rory, and she was afraid to question people because she too might be implicated as having been in the household of a woman with notorious Monmouth connections. But on the outskirts of Banbury she did chance to hear that Lord Mellowby, who had always straddled fences when it came to politics, had been seized for his "connection" with the rebels—indeed had he not entertained the notorious Monmouth supporter Rory Edgecombe in his home on more than one occasion during the insurrection? Considering the circumstances, Mawkers thought that rather amusing. But the smile left her face when she heard that Lord Mellowby had been sentenced to death by Judge Jeffreys, a sentence later commuted to transportation as slave labor in Barbados. Mawkers thought of Lord Mellowby's painful gout, how it would often hurt him just to move, and shuddered.

In Banbury, Mawkers learned to her dismay that her sister had died in the spring of a fever that was going around, and that her sister's husband had been swept away along with her. Inquiry discovered that her sister's only child, a daughter now widowed, had repaired to Maidstone in Kent.

It was a long way to Kent and Mawkers felt old and travel-worn. With the gold Rinda had given her, she took a small cottage on the outskirts of Banbury for herself and the child and the wet nurse who, as soon as she was no longer needed, found a job as tavern maid, drifted on to Coventry, and departed their lives altogether.

Mawkers was left alone with the child and her memories and her heartaches. She had loved sweet Dorinda so much and wild young Rinda had seemed her very own. Although Rinda had named her daughter Dorinda, Mawkers could not bear to call her that, for it summoned up too many memories. So she called the child simply "Dorr," which was, she felt, close enough.

Dorr was a beautiful child. She looked like Lady Polly, who was after all her grandmother as much as Dorinda—and for that reason Mawkers sometimes found it difficult to look into her face. She had inherited her father's mop of saffron hair and her eyes were the same fiery golden green of Rory's and Lady Polly's. Mawkers looked into those long lovely eyes uneasily, putting aside the thought that they were the kind of eyes men drown in. To her, they meant only trouble. It was as if a witch looked back at her out of those eyes.

Every year she took the beautiful child to Banbury Fair, and every year young Dorr, growing up straight and strong with white teeth and a slender small-boned frame and features that bespoke the beauty she would become, attracted more attention. By the time she was eleven men were beginning to turn and stare at her and Dorr would bridle and peek slanting glances at them out of the corners of her catlike golden green eyes.

Mawkers was alarmed for her. And every year more saddened. For eleven Banbury Fairs had passed and there had been no word from Rinda. And how many unnamed dead, she asked herself gloomily, had been buried after the Battle of Sedgemoor or lost forever, trampled into the mud by horses and cannon?

When, three years after Sedgemoor, England spat out King James and invited William of Orange to take the throne, much restitution to the former rebels was made and many estates restored to their former owners. Mawkers felt a great sense of excitement at this time, for exiles streamed back into the country—and Rinda could be one of them.

But time passed, and there were more Banbury Fairs and always Mawkers and Dorr trudged home alone.

At least she was not afraid to ask questions now—and she learned much. Lord Mellowby had died on shipboard before ever reaching Barbados. Most of the male servants at Grantland Manor and the surrounding estates had been killed in the fighting or hanged on country roads or sentenced to death by the terrible Judge Jeffreys. Rinda's friends were scattered. In Taunton, the Wyatts had been hanged. Lord Chell's son Elfred had been killed by mistake by the King's men when they were chasing a fugitive. Grantland Manor was under new ownership, some people from Wales.

As to Rinda—for whom she had inquired so often—there was a story Mawkers gleaned from a passing traveler of a flame-haired lady in red. He had lain wounded on a country road in the wake of the battle, so pale he had looked dead—and indeed he had lapsed from time to time into unconsciousness. He had come to himself at the sound of a shot and looked up in bewilderment to see figures hanging from nearby trees—he had recognized them as men who had fought beside him—and between the dangling legs of one of them that nearly touched his nose, a most astonishing tableau was taking place.

"I always thought afterward I must have dreamt it," he told Mawkers contemplatively. "But there was this lady on horseback with a brace of pistols."

"Flame-haired and in red silks?" cried Mawkers.

"Aye." He nodded. "She had just fired one of the pistols and the soldier who must have been left to guard the bodies lest local folk cut them down and bury them was clutching his chest as he fell across my legs dead. I lifted my head and I heard the lady call to somebody. 'Mount up!' she cried. 'We'll to the coast and take ship to France!'"

"Did she use a name?" cried Mawkers hoarsely.

"I think she did."

"Could the name have been Rory?"

He shook his head. "It could have been, but I don't remember it now. 'Tis too far back and I was sore hurt."

"Did you see him? You must have seen him mount up!"

"All I saw was his boots as he staggered past and then I swooned again from my wound, and when I woke up I was looking into an angel face. A woman from a nearby cottage had crept up to see if there was anyone alive that she could help. She dragged me back to her cottage more dead than alive. Her husband had been hurt when a tree fell on him—he was a woodsman by trade—and he had died the week before but in all the excitement with the soldiery about they'd buried him behind the house till proper burial could be had in the churchyard. But she tucked me up in his bed and she passed me off to the soldiery as him. The people about was Monmouth supporters to a man. Nobody gave us away. I married her when their majesties, William and Mary, took the throne and when she died her last wish was that I go to visit her old father in Banbury and that's why I'm here, mistress."

Mawkers, nodding her head at his words, hardly heard them.

Rinda had survived the battle, she had found Rory, when last seen she had been riding hard for the coast.... She was alive, she had to be! No...if she were alive she would surely have come to the Banbury Fair to find her child.

Later Mawkers heard another tale which for a time buoyed her up. One of the refugees who had fled England after the Battle of Sedgemoor had taken two of his servants with him. And on his return to England after years spent on the Continent, one of those servants was on his way to visit relatives in Northumberland when he stopped at Banbury Fair. A garrulous fellow, he was drawn into conversation by Mawkers, whose sharp ears had heard him mention that he had fled England via one of two sloops of refugees that had escaped the English coast near Bridport after the Battle of Sedgemoor.

"Was there a flame-haired lady on board your sloop

perchance?" she asked wistfully, for she had been disappointed so many times before. "A lady in bright red silks?"

The wayfarer gave her a strange look. "No, but I did see a lady of that description struggling toward the other sloop as we pulled away," he exclaimed. "She was half-carrying, half-dragging a yellow-haired gentleman who looked to be swooning."

Rinda! Word at last of Rinda! So overcome was Mawkers that she could hardly speak.

"And the other sloop, did it pull away too?" she cried, her voice cracking with excitement. "Or was it caught?"

"Oh, I saw it pull away all right, and none of us were caught. But our sloops were separated in a storm and we landed first and I never knew what became of the people in the other sloop."

"You never heard anything of them at all?" Mawkers looked so disappointed that he gave her a sympathetic look.

"Nothing at all," he admitted.

It was not much—and there could have been other flame-haired ladies in red dresses fleeing England that day, but it gave Mawkers hope. Hope that dimmed as she felt death circling her, riding ever nearer.

"Go to my niece," she whispered hoarsely to young Dorr, clutching the girl's slender wrist with clawlike hands, during what she knew must surely be her last illness. "Go to Kent—she'll take ye in."

"I'll go," promised young Dorr, her tears falling on that old gnarled hand. She looked down into a face that had suffered with three generations of women named Dorinda, a face true and honest with eyes glazing over now with death. "Oh, I promise you I'll go to Kent," she whispered.

"Good child," murmured Mawkers. She tried to pat Dorr's hand and did not quite make it. Her fingers slid away, just as her spirit slid away—to death.

Dorr had meant what she said. But she was young. Her young feet carried her to London.

And in London she stayed.

And there, under strange circumstances, she bore a daughter—and named her Dorinda.

June 1714

Chapter 16

In the innyard of the White Hart knelt a half-grown girl industriously polishing boots—although every now and then she raised her golden head and focused her wide blue-green eyes on Duke of Gloucester Street and the fine gentlemen who came and went through the green painted door of the inn.

The girl was Dorinda Meredith—Dorr's daughter—and close inspection would have revealed that she was going to be a beauty, given a couple of years and a dress that fit. But for now her mop of shimmering golden hair was tucked into a voluminous white cotton cap with a ruffle that hung down irritatingly over her dark-lashed eyes. That ruffle Dorinda constantly pushed back with an impatient gesture that left her dainty nose as smudged with bootblack as was her coarse gray homespun apron. Beneath her faded olive linen kirtle Dorinda's slim legs were bare (for her stockings were so shabby and so much mended that she hated for *him* to see them). And surely he would pass by soon for it was one of the great "Publick Times" in Williamsburg when the general court was in session and the town's population doubled overnight. Planters had come downriver by boat to this thriving Colonial town situated on a peninsula between the York and the James, or ridden in on horseback, plumed hatted and spurred, from the surrounding plantations. Indeed people had come from all over, for during the court sessions land titles would be fought over, criminals flogged, pilloried or sentenced to hanging, orphans' and widows' mites haggled over, civil suits brought—many of them for slander, for the Colonists were a touchy lot—and every now and then a juicy scandal aired in public.

And among those upriver planters *he* would come riding—Bainter Ramsay, tall and arrogant, a tawny aristocrat walking with measured courtly grace—and causing the heart of the girl now on her knees beside a small mountain of unpolished boots to thump so wildly that sometimes she thought it would burst her bodice.

She had seen him first—could it have been only three months ago?—when she had hurried past a forlorn looking wife beater pilloried outside the new Public Gaol to which debtors' cells had been added, and wandered with relief onto the Capitol grounds. There in front of the pink brick Capitol building he had been standing, smoking with a group of other gentlemen who had lit up their pipes outdoors, for Williamsburg went in constant dread of fire (when Jamestown was the capital, all the public buildings had gone up in flames). Therefore smoking—or even candles—were strictly prohibited in the handsome new chimneyless Capitol building which, with neither fireplaces nor artificial light, was gloomy indeed on dark rainy days.

But that particular day had been sunshiny and the sunlight had sparkled upon the shoulders of Bainter Ramsay's wide-skirted lemon satin coat and made rivulets of light dance along his wide-cuffed, gold-braided sleeves. That sunlight had reached glorious proportions when he had looked up, smiling at something someone had said, and the sun had caught his amber eyes, making them glitter for a moment like yellow diamonds in his arresting high-cheekboned face.

For a moment Bainter had seemed to be smiling directly at *her* and Dorinda had stood riveted, abruptly conscious of things she had heretofore blithely taken for granted: the ruinous state of her petticoat and stockings, her dilapidated shoes two sizes too large, the unbecoming coarse cotton cap into which her bright hair was stuffed. She had shifted her feet under that golden stare and gazed back at Bainter uncertainly. And after a moment he had gone back to talking with the other richly clad gentlemen, all of them together making a study in pastel satins.

Dorinda, whose young life had been full of violent ups and downs, had found her heart suddenly charged with new emotions and fluttering most unreliably. Overcome and blushing, she had turned abruptly and fled. Dodging past carriages and wagons, she had run panting back to the safety of her stuffy little quarters at the White Hart, there to dream of Bainter, there to imagine herself in satins and laces dropping him her deepest curtsy, being led out by him in a dance at one of the balls she had only glimpsed through the candlelit windows of the fine white clapboard houses on Duke of Gloucester Street.

Surreptitious inquiries had established who the gentleman in lemon satin was: Bainter Ramsay, recent inheritor of upriver Haverleigh Plantation, who had come out from London to settle upon his vast inherited estate. Young, they said enviously, to be the holder of such a fiefdom. And a bachelor to boot. This last had thrilled Dorinda, who had promptly imagined herself marrying Bainter—perhaps in nearby Bruton Parish Church which was even now under construction just past Market Square. She would pause a moment at whatever task she was doing—dipping candles or scrubbing floors or rending tallow or blacking boots—and with softly parted lips imagine herself a radiant bride,

lying in the crook of her bridegroom's arm as they were
rowed upriver to her new home—Haverleigh Plantation. And Bainter would be pressing surreptitious kisses
(because the rowers must not be allowed to see) onto
her blushing cheeks or nipping at an ear on which he
had just fastened a set of new earbobs while she toyed
with a golden locket inscribed *"For Dorinda with all my
love—Bainter."*

Surely it was not too much to hope for—after all, had
not her great-grandmother come through the Great
Fire of London and emerged as bride to a belted earl?
Had not her reckless grandmother, flame-haired Rinda,
been a Countess in her own right? And had not her
mother, Dorr, been the toast of London?

She knew all of this from Maud Whatton, who had
been Dorr's best friend in London and who had cared
for Dorinda since her birth. Maud, who worked in a
bakeshop and drank too much gin and was always
wandering off for a week or two at a time with some
man or other and returning penitent and muttering
that "men only cared for one thing—and they weren't
faithful even to that!" Big bountiful Maud who had fed
her and kept her and given her a motherly shoulder to
cry on all those years since Dorr had died giving birth
to Dorinda. Maud who loved to tell Dorinda stories
about her glamorous forebears, holding the child spellbound as she talked in her twangy North Country
voice.

"I first met your mother on the stagecoach coming
down to London," Maud would chuckle. "There she
was on that lurching coach trying to read that very
book there." She would point and Dorinda, who had
learned to read from a lodger Maud had taken in for a
time, would obediently turn to contemplate *The Com-
pleat Servant Maid, or the Young Maiden's Tutor.* It was the
fourth edition and it had been published the year her
grandmother Rinda had died in the aftermath of the
Battle of Sedgemoor. Dorinda had read it with awe. It

stated calmly that to achieve a good position one must write legibly not only in the Roman but in the Italian hand, be good at sums, suitably gowned, a skilled carver and preserver—the list went on and on. "I told your mother to throw the book away," scoffed Maud. "That we'd take the first job offered—and we did. In a dairy on the outskirts of London."

"Why didn't you stay there?" wondered the child.

Maud shrugged. "Your mother was too pretty," she said cryptically. And abruptly changed the subject.

"Tell me more about my grandmother—about Rinda," urged Dorinda, sensing that Maud wasn't going to talk anymore about Dorr.

"Oh, I know all about *her*." Maud laughed. "For your mother talked about her people all the time, she did." She poured herself another glass of gin and the child's eyes brightened for Maud always waxed voluble when she was in her cups. "I loved to hear her tell about her mother, Rinda—the Countess that died in the West Country Rebellion and never came to Banbury Fair to get her, and about her grandmother who lived in a castle..."

Dorinda never tired of hearing Maud recite tales of the flame-haired young Countess who had died for her lover, and the beautiful chambermaid who had saved an Earl from footpads in the midst of the Great Fire of London—and married him.

"But what of my mother?" she would sometimes interrupt. "You tell me of these others but never about her."

Maud would sigh and begin to tell her of her mother's fine clothes, of how all the men would turn to stare at Dorr when she came into a room.

"Do I look like her?"

Maud would give the lovely child a critical look. "I guess you don't," she decided at last. "Her hair was more saffron and her eyes were more of a yellow green than yours. Door looked wild—kind of dangerous like.

She was wonderful looking but—you have a sweeter face. I think you must look like your grandmother, the Countess. She had flame-red hair and gray eyes, Dorr always said."

While hers was golden—well, red-gold in some lights, and blue-green wasn't too far from gray. She *wanted* to look like Rinda, who was to her every inch a heroine.

"How did my mother die?" she asked Maud.

"In bearing you," Maud told her with a sigh. "Poor Dorr died of the childbed fever, she did."

"And was that here? Where we live now?"

"No, 'twas somewhere else," said Maud gruffly. "'Twas in London but not here." Her voice turned surly. "You ask too many questions," she told the child. "You wear me out!"

Not till Dorinda was eight years old did she learn the tarnishing truth. She learned it when a taunting street child flung at her that her mother was a thief and Jack Bridey's doxy and that she herself had been born in Newgate Gaol. Dorinda ran home crying and flung herself into Maud's arms. "It isn't true," she sobbed. "It isn't true!"

"There, there." Maud's comforting arms enfolded her. Maud always smelled like fresh-baked bread from her work at the bakery and today she had brought home a whole apron filled with little tarts. She offered one to Dorinda. "It's true—and it isn't," she said thoughtfully.

"Then—" Dorinda's world spun round—"I really *was* born in Newgate Prison?" she faltered.

"Oh, you were born in Newgate, all right." Maud nodded. "But your mother, she weren't no thief. Oh, the court *said* she was, but she weren't. *She* didn't know—no more did I—that Jack Bridey was a 'fencing cully'" (which the child knew was a receiver of stolen goods). "And she didn't know that the taffety dress he gave her was stolen. 'Twas a beautiful green-gold taffety that matched her eyes and it was trimmed in pale gold ribands. I never seen Dorr look so good as she did in that dress with her deep yellow hair alight above it and her eyes sparkling." Maud sighed, remembering. "No one could've blamed Dorr for accepting the dress, it looked so good on her."

Dorinda aged a few years as she listened. "Was my mother really Jack Bridey's doxy?" she asked faintly, for even *she* had heard of the notorious Jack Bridey.

Maud nodded.

"And was Jack Bridey my father?" she managed, and held her breath as she waited for the answer.

"No," said Maud definitely. "He was not. No matter what anyone tells you, he wasn't. Your father was a London rakehell named Jeremy Ashby. He and Dorr would quarrel and he'd leave her and then they'd make up and move back together again. Only one time she got so mad at him that she moved in with Jack Bridey just to spite him. And," she added ruefully, "Dorr was unlucky for that was the night the law come and took Jack Bridey. They caught Dorr there wearing that stolen dress she didn't know was stolen, for Jack had told her he'd bought it in Fleet Street."

"But they should have let her go!" protested Dorinda. "She was innocent!"

"They didn't believe her. After all she'd been found in Jack Bridey's house wearing the dress." *And how to explain to a heartbroken eight-year-old that her mother had had such a wild look to her* (exactly the same look Lady Polly had had so long ago) *that people would believe anything of her—except innocence?* "They sentenced Dorr to death for stealing the dress," she said soberly. "And Jack Bridey slipped a lot of money to the judges on the quiet and he got off scot-free."

"And my mother?" whispered Dorinda.

"Dorr was pregnant then by Jeremy Ashby. She didn't know it until she was in jail. She 'pleaded her belly' as they say, to save her life."

"But what about my father? My real father? Why didn't Jeremy Ashby come forward to save her?"

Maud gave the child a sad look. "He did.... When he'd quarreled with Dorr, he'd left London and gone to Lincoln. When I did finally manage to get in touch with him, it was too late. Dorr had already died of childbirth in Newgate. She was already dead when he reached London. They'd let me take you—I claimed I was a relative which I'm not."

"And my father?"

"He killed Jack Bridey for getting Dorr jailed for something she'd nothing to do with. They hanged him for it." Maud was looking at the child as she spoke, wondering how she'd take it. "They should've given him a medal instead!" she added through her teeth.

For a long moment Dorinda was silent, taking it all in. Then she swallowed and a shiver went through her small frame. "He *revenged* her," she said softly.

"That he did," agreed Maud and drew the shivering child to her. "They was both good people, Dorinda. And they loved each other—even though you'd never have known it, they fought like cats and dogs! But Dorr would have died for him and he *did* die for her. Oh, you don't never need to be ashamed of either one of them."

"I'm not ashamed of them," said the child fiercely. "I'll *never* be ashamed of them, no matter who calls things at me in the street."

But somehow her tragic young mother who had "fought like cats and dogs" with her lover had never seemed as real to Dorinda as the blazing young Countess who had thrown away everything for love. In her childish mind Rinda somehow became her real mother for she loved the story of how Rinda had gone into the Battle of Sedgemoor to claim her lover and died with him in some far lonely place.... Dorinda was hopelessly romantic. And perhaps that sense of romance was a part of her heritage from the wild young London rake who had wanted Dorr to be better than she was—and avenged his lady at the cost of his life.

Things had gotten very bad for Dorinda in London. Maud Whatton had begun to work less and drink more. Big and hearty and hospitable, the drink had not seemed to affect her much at first. A born rounder, she had opened her heart and her purse to boon companions—and found both empty. Maud was fond of rhyming couplets—especially when she was in her cups. She was very ladylike when she drank—irritatingly so. She would crook her little finger and look down over her nose and talk in a stilted fashion—and then spoil it all by hiccupping.

Then came the worst times, the times when Maud hardly worked at all, when she could get only part-time work in the bakeshops because she was unreliable. Feeling sorry for herself, Maud—who was a good worker when she was sober—began to hang around the taverns more and more. Far gone on gin and feeling bad, she would reel home in the wee hours and slump over a table, fix Dorinda with her owlish eyes in the guttering candlelight and mutter bad verse.

Other days, wincing from a bad hangover, Maud would try to straighten up and she would sing gloomily while she tried to get dressed to go out and find work, while the half-starved child, dressed in rags, huddled in a worn blanket in the corner shivering in the cold unheated room. Maud would cock an eye at Dorinda and sing derisively:

> *"From Lady to Countess to slattern,*
> *Faith, 'tis all part of a pattern!"*

And when she was very gloomy—and very tipsy:

> *"From Lady to Countess to slut!*
> *For you there is no way but up!"*

And then she would leer owlishly at Dorinda. Dorinda would frown and glare back at Maud for she didn't relish being called a slut, but then Maud would wax maudlin and cry over all the things she couldn't do for her "poor little one" and Dorinda's tender heart would melt and she would abandon the blanket and go over and throw her arms about big weeping Maud and lay her golden head against Maud's wet cheek and try to comfort her. And hope against hope that things would get better for them.

They never did.

Came the day Maud rushed in ashen-faced and told Dorinda they were leaving, they were going to America. Now—right now! Dorinda had gasped at this sudden decision because Maud always made fun of "them as went away to the Colonies and fetched themselves back no better off—just older." But when, looking back as Maud rushed her away, she saw a constable banging on the door and Maud, with a sharp muttered "Come along now—hurry!" whisked her into a nearby alley, she understood. Maud was in some kind of trouble; she was wanted by the law.

It turned out that Maud had surreptitiously laid hands on a half-full bottle of gin and been seen doing it. The tavernkeeper was in a vengeful mood and he had reported the theft to the constable.

Maud and her small charge made it out in the nick of time, on a ship bound for Virginia. Maud had wanted to go to Massachusetts but she had taken the first thing offered—and indentured herself for three years to pay for passage for herself and Dorinda.

The hard journey had brought further deprivations and midway across the ocean Maud's death by fever. A bewildered Dorinda had stumbled ashore in Williamsburg and had found herself at thirteen bound for four years to Innkeeper Buxton to pay for her own passage and the dead Maud's.

After near starvation in London, Dorinda—who had

been short for her age—suddenly began sprouting up like a beanpole. It was a thin coltish figure that knelt in the courtyard of the White Hart polishing boots—but with a heart as romantic as ever.

And because she was hopelessly romantic she had fallen in love with Bainter Ramsay in a childish dreaming way and dreamed wild improbable dreams.

Lovely dreams—but always brought sharply back to earth by the toe of Innkeeper Buxton's boot tapping warningly against her scrub bucket, or his wife's sudden box on the ear to remind Dorinda that she was not to go mooning about, there was work to be done!

Now in the sunny innyard, Dorinda Meredith, the girl with the strange heritage, was once again dreaming impossible dreams.

It takes one generation to make it,
One generation to lose it,
One generation to talk about it—
And one to make it again!

And One to Make It Again!

BOOK IV

Heiress to the Wind!

A wicked smile, it glimmers on his lips
And his cold gaze now is straying to her hips
And the dazzled way she feels makes her senses
  seem to reel
As her world's horizon soars and wheels and
  dips!

PART ONE

The Tawny Aristocrat

The White Hart
WILLIAMSBURG, VIRGINIA
June 1714

Chapter 17

Bainter Ramsay always walked into the White Hart
alone—although Dorinda *had* seen him (and stiffened
in indignation and almost tripped over her awkward
too-large shoes at the sight) strolling down Duke of
Gloucester Street with one silk- or calico-clad lady or
another, engaging them in light bantering conversation. How she had envied those women, some of them
barely older than herself—but all of them planters'
daughters or burgesses' daughters or wealthy merchants'
daughters, which put them worlds above a lowly bound
girl with three years of her indenture yet to work out.
And all of them sporting ruchings and ribands and
laces and carrying parasols or fans—not a one of them
had ever spent her entire day polishing boots!

Dorinda gave a resentful swipe at the dusty boot she
was just now polishing—and nicked her fingers on the
spur that was affixed. She gave a little cry as blood was
drawn from the scratch and in a childish gesture promptly
brought her hurt fingers to her mouth.

And so it was that her hand was pressed across her
mouth as she looked up to see Bainter Ramsay, who
had just handed his roan horse over to one of the

stableboys before he strolled toward the green door. Bainter was even more dazzling than usual, wearing a suit of bottle green silk with a frosty linen cravat carefully tied, lace edged. His wide cuffs spilled lace over his hands, one of which sported an emerald ring set in gold. A sweeping dark hat which boasted several silvery green plumes, caught likewise with an emerald, shaded a face some would have considered hard, but which the girl polishing boots considered perfect.

Dorinda watched his advance breathlessly, her hand frozen in position at her mouth. Perhaps he would notice her, even have a cheery word for her. (After all, she had seen him—regrettably out of earshot—exchange a few smiling words with one of the grooms to whom he also tossed a coin. That the coin had been a reward for finding Bainter the services of a most interesting young prostitute just over from Birmingham, and the few smiling words a review of the wench's tricky talents in bed, Dorinda was not to know.) She would have been overjoyed by any notice from the elegant Bainter, however slight.

But it was not to be. Just as Bainter Ramsay reached the kneeling Dorinda—a Dorinda who watched him through dark-lashed blue-green eyes glowing above her hurt hand, the inn's green door swung open and a gentleman in a maroon coat squiring two brightly calicoed young ladies spilled out.

"Why, 'tis Bainter Ramsay!" cried one of them with a simper—and Dorinda from the ground recognized the trilling accents of an upriver planter's daughter, Peggy Charington.

"Ah ... Bainter," said the gentleman in a voice considerably less thrilled.

"Ladies, Roger." Bainter's poise was as always impeccable. He made them an elegant leg, sweeping his hat so low the silvery green plumes nearly touched the ground. They *did* brush Dorinda's cheek, turning her face scarlet—but nobody noticed, least of all Bainter. "I take it ye're down for the general sessions?"

"Aye," said Roger Charington, drawing his sisters rather closer. For some reason he could not quite put his finger on, he mistrusted the showy Mr. Ramsay. "And how are things at Haverleigh Plantation?"

"Getting underway." Bainter shrugged. "Not so good as one would hope, but rather better than one deserves, no doubt. Mistress Peggy." He turned to the simpering girl who had not taken her eyes from his face since she had spied him. "What d'ye think of Williamsburg this trip?"

"The town seems to grow larger every time I see it," Peggy said merrily. Shs was delighted to be singled out for Bainter's attention.

"Surely ye'll all come in and share a bottle of Madeira with me?" pursued Bainter. "For I confess me I'm parched after my barge trip downriver."

"Oh, 'twould be delightful!" cried Peggy enthusiastically and jumped as her scowling younger sister Patty (who agreed with Roger as to Bainter's character) gave her a surreptitious kick in the ankle with her slipper.

"Sorry, we'd like to but we've not the time. We're overdue at the Randolphs now," Roger Charington answered smoothly. He took a firm grip on his sister Peggy, who had turned to accompany Bainter back into the inn. "Come along, Peggy. Good day, Bainter."

"Good day to you." Bainter made the group another leg as they swept past, this one a trifle ironic for he was aware in what lack of esteem the departing gentleman held him. In stepping aside to avoid Mistress Patty, who swept by with her head rather high, ignoring this newcomer who had settled to the north of them on the river, Bainter's spur caught in Dorinda's spread-out skirt.

Startled by his unexpected motion—for she had been hanging on every word they said—Dorinda gave a small exclamation and tried to extricate the spur. Too late.

Handsome Bainter glanced down, saw that it was but a mite of a scullery maid whose kirtle was pinioned by his boot and—driven perhaps by annoyance at the slight wealthy Roger Charington had just dealt him—jerked it free with deliberate and cruel force, ripping a long gash in the worn olive material of Dorinda's kirtle.

Without a word of apology he stepped free, just as one of the guests at the inn, a young French Huguenot girl staying there with her parents, strolled by from Duke of Gloucester Street. She was a little older than Dorinda with a mass of shining black curls bouncing around a pert little head. Her full mouth smiled winsomely at the corners and her black eyes were full of the exuberance of youth and a newfound female awareness that made her carry her ripe young breasts outthrust challengingly before her. As she passed Bainter he quickly stepped aside to avoid entangling his spurs in the wide ruffled pink skirts that swayed toward him and she acknowledged his courtesy with a wide dazzling smile—a smile which, as her dancing dark eyes played over Bainter's handsome face, became an invitation.

From the ground Dorinda, struck dumb with hurt, watched this humiliating difference in behavior. Bainter, her idol, had carelessly stepped on and torn her skirt— but he was all attentive care lest he brush the pink silk skirts of this wealthy young French girl (for so she seemed to Dorinda).

Big and reproachful, Dorinda's eyes followed him as he held open the inn door for the French girl. In her stunned condition she had entirely missed the open invitation of the French girl's bold smile, the coquettish toss of her head—but she had not missed the sudden quickening of interest on that hard masculine face, the alacrity with which he had leaped forward. He was sensing an easy conquest but Dorinda had missed that. All she had seen was a man she worshiped brushing her roughly aside for another.

It wasn't fair! she thought indignantly.

For the three months that she had been aware that there was a Bainter Ramsay on this earth Dorinda had dreamed of little else but that he would notice her.

"He will, you know," she would whisper confidently at night to Lady Soft Paws, the gray and white kitchen cat who had free roaming of the inn, mousing happily on the back stairs or in the capacious cellars. And Lady Soft Paws, who had adopted Dorinda just as Dorinda had adopted her, would purr an affirmation. "And we'll fall into a conversation just like he does with the planters' daughters and he'll escort me into the inn and we'll sit at the table—you'll see it all, Lady Soft Paws! You'll come and purr under the table and I'll lift you up into my lap and he'll say 'What a beautiful cat! I never noticed her before.' Just like he never noticed *me* before!" She would hug the cat to her and fall back with her upon the straw-filled mattress in her cubbyhole bedroom and the cat would wind herself contentedly around Dorinda's neck, knowing herself well loved, and two pairs of blue-green eyes would stare out at the moon through the tiny panes.

Who knew what lustrous long-whiskered tomcat Lady Soft Paws dreamed about at those moments? But Dorinda, no longer murmuring aloud, dreamed wide awake of Bainter Ramsay. She could feel her cheeks burning as she imagined him kissing her, dragging his eager lips down her chin and across her soft pulsating throat to the smooth sweep of her young bosom, and then...and then...And finally in the moon's pale light they would both drift to sleep, Dorinda exhausted from long hours of fetching and carrying tubs and pitchers and trays and being endlessly bullied by the innkeeper's wife; Lady Soft Paws tired from a long day of chasing nimble mice and sometimes the big rats that came ashore from the ships.

And now that same Bainter Ramsay had just carelessly stepped on her skirt in the courtyard. He had torn her only decent kirtle! All of Dorinda's air castles came tumbling down together and tears of indignation gathered in the blue-green eyes that followed Bainter's and the French girl's progress through the green door.

The door slammed and, fighting back angry tears, Dorinda finished polishing the boots. She rubbed them with such vicious abandon that a passing gentleman was heard to remark, "Never saw such industry. How does Buxton goad them into it?" His companion, glancing back thoughtfully at Dorinda, muttered, "Innkeeper Buxton must have an eye for beauty as well as for industry, for she's a pretty wench under those ill-fitting clothes, I'll be bound!"

His remark would vastly have cheered forlorn Dorinda had she heard it, but the gentlemen were hurrying toward meat and ale at the inn and their voices were drowned out by a planter's wife, scolding a recalcitrant velvet-clad child as she dragged it toward the inn. "Your father will spank you, he will!" she cried, giving the child a slight cuff which made it scream angrily.

Dorinda was oblivious to it all. She felt alone—alone and crushed as she had felt when Maud Whatton died. Oh, if only just for a moment she had those warm arms to fling herself into for comfort, to weep against that capacious bosom and smell the pleasant aroma of fresh-baked bread that always clung to Maud.

She was reminded of a ditty Maud had half-hummed, half-sung when she was far gone on gin:

> *"Lady Dorinda*
> *Had Rinda the Wild*
> *Who had Unlucky Dorr*
> *And her Little Lost Child...."*

Dorinda gave the last boot such a violent swipe of polish that she nearly dislocated her arm. *She didn't want to be a "little lost child!"* She wanted to be loved and cherished and made much of! And somehow she would reach that goal, despite all the Bainter Ramsays in the world!

Having finished the last boot, she dashed away a suspicious mist from her lashes, piled all the boots into her apron, and carrying her arms outstretched to hold her burden, wearily padded inside.

There the landlord's wife met her with a curt, "Put those down. You can take them up later. Mister Ramsay has ordered a tankard of ale sent up to his room and I've no one else to send. You must take it."

"But my skirt—I've torn it, I'll trip," cried Dorinda, unwilling to take *anything*, not even ale, to Bainter Ramsay.

"The kirtle can be mended later, you careless girl," scolded the innkeeper's wife. "*After* you've delivered the ale."

Reluctantly Dorinda put down the boots and took up the pewter tankard. Her heart was beating angrily as she ascended the back stairs and if any of the inn servants had happened by she would have thrust the tankard at them with some excuse.

But no one appeared.

Feeling her legs tremble beneath her worn skirts, Dorinda forced herself along the corridor toward Bainter Ramsay's bedchamber.

Bainter Ramsay had ordered up a bath. Stout Moll had arrived puffing with a metal tub and bathwater and he had told her curtly that he'd have a tankard of ale as well. That had been some minutes ago for Moll, once downstairs, had been seized onto by Cook to help lift some heavy pots in the kitchen and the innkeeper's wife had tapped her foot impatiently until Dorinda had come in with the boots, waiting for someone to send up with the ale.

Upstairs, in anticipation of his bath, Bainter Ramsay had already stripped off his coat and was in the act of removing his ruffled shirt when there was a light tap on the door.

Expecting Moll with the tankard, he had uttered a careless "Come in," and turned in surprise to see young Rochelle Leroux, the French girl who had flirted with him lightheartedly as he entered the inn, standing there in her pink ruffled dress. He might have expected a maiden so young to turn tail and run away at the sight of a man down to shirt and satin breeches, whose hairy chest was already exposed to view, but although Rochelle looked momentarily abashed, she came quickly into the room and closed the door behind her.

"Oh, Monsieur Ramsay," she said in a rush. "I must speak to you!"

Bainter Ramsay's tawny brows elevated a trifle but he stepped forward with alacrity for the situation looked promising. He measured her keenly with his amber eyes. No, he had not been mistaken, there was a roundness to that lissome young body that would fit a man's hands very well, and if there was a certain merry blankness to those black eyes, who cared? It was not a woman's wit that attracted Bainter and indeed he had often wished the waspish little monsters would all keep their mouths tight shut—except when kissing and making love, of course.

"I am at your service, mademoiselle," he said quickly.

"I am in the most terrible trouble, monsieur." Rochelle batted her inky lashes at him.

A coquette! He had judged her aright. Bainter thought he might be able to assuage her "terrible trouble" right here in the big bed behind him. He itched to try. "And what is this 'most terrible trouble,' mademoiselle?" he asked gravely.

Rochelle's words came out in a dimpling rush—just as she had rehearsed them. "There is a young gentleman pursuing me about the halls who insists he will steal a kiss and—oh, I *do* beg of you that I may hide from him here in your room but a moment. He would *never* think to look for me here!"

Bainter grinned inwardly. On his last trip down to Williamsburg, which had been only last week, he had observed that most of the eligible gentlemen at the inn considered this sparkling French baggage too young to be worthy of their attentions, and those who might have sought her out had been driven off by the sight of her rapacious mother, who had the look of a dedicated matchmaker about her. Obviously Rochelle had decided to heighten her chances by going hunting on her own! He was entirely agreeable to that. An afternoon spent discovering what was under all those pink silk ruffles might be highly diverting!

"Indeed you may remain here as long as you like, mademoiselle." He smiled benignly at Rochelle. "I am expecting a bath at any moment and would be delighted to have you share it with me."

"Oh, monsieur," giggled Rochelle. "You are making the sport with me, no?" Her black eyes had gone wary, but she did not back away.

I was right, he thought. *She is ripe and ready for the plucking, and has slipped away from her mamma in hopes she can make a conquest!*

He smiled lazily. "But you would find bathing here delightful, mademoiselle. See, I have the finest of French soap and a silken washing cloth that would turn your entire body pink if you would but let me essay to use it!"

Rochelle caught her breath and backed away a step as Ramsay advanced, grinning. She had not really considered the consequences of being alone in a bedchamber with a man like Ramsay. His bold tawny gaze was roving over her body and he looked as if he would at any moment tear off her clothes and fling her naked upon that big square bed that seemed suddenly the only piece of furniture in the room. "Monsieur!" she stammered and would have fled had not Ramsay adroitly stepped between her and the door.

Rochelle watched him, every nerve alive. She had expected to be the huntress in this game, she had expected him to make pretty speeches and court her favor, not physically stand between her and escape! She began to feel hunted.

"Ah, you are shy, mademoiselle," he said softly, and as he spoke there was a knock on the door. "What is it?" he demanded harshly.

"I have brought your ale," came Dorinda's rebellious voice on the other side of the door.

"A moment," he answered irritably. He advanced on Rochelle. "You fly from a lad who would steal a kiss, mademoiselle," he murmured. "I will show you how easily *I* steal a kiss!"

Rochelle gasped and retreated another step. "I can't be found here!" she whispered. "If that servant girl should tell my mamma where I am—!"

Bainter had the answer to that. He flicked open the curtain that made a rude closet out of a corner where clothes could be hung conveniently on nails driven into the wall. Rochelle took his meaning and, catching up her wide pink skirts, silently slipped behind the curtain.

"You may enter," called Ramsay in a bored voice and Dorinda opened the door and edged through it. She had to hold her skirt up with one hand for the rent in the hem threatened to trip her, and she held the large tankard very primly straight out before her.

The wench from the innyard. . . . Bainter scowled at her. "Well, close the door," he said testily, annoyed at this interruption and afraid his quarry might take flight and fly through that open door and be lost to him.

Dorinda hesitated and held out the tankard.

"Close the door," he repeated irritably, tugging at his cuffs. "You can see that I'm about to take a bath and its draughty in here."

To Dorinda the room seemed not drafty but stifling. But perhaps that suffocated feeling was only anger.

Bainter, she saw, was too occupied with his cuffs to take the tankard from her. She moved forward to set it down upon the bedtable, a path which led around the metal tub that would take her directly past Bainter.

She had almost reached him when the sound of a woman's shrill voice came piercingly through the door. The slightly nasal snarl of her high-pitched tones was unmistakable even if her French accent had not marked it—and both Dorinda and Bainter recognized it. "Rochelle!" she was calling. "Rochelle, come to me at once, do you hear?"

Good God, it was the mother! thought Bainter with resignation. *Roaming the corridors looking for her errant daughter!* Ah, well, in a moment she would go away and so would this sullen scullery maid and he would have that luscious French pastry all to himself.

It was not to be.

"Do not think I do not know where you are, Rochelle!" shrilled that strident voice from the corridor. "Or that I do not know what you are doing!"

Abruptly the door behind Dorinda, who had just circled the metal tub and was about to brush by Bainter on her way to the night table, sprang open and Rochelle's mother stood framed there. She seemed an indignant mass of magenta ruffles as she cast her gaze dramatically around the room.

Bainter Ramsay's reflexes were excellent. They had gotten him out of many a tight spot in the past and they stood him in good stead this day. He seemed to anticipate that opening door and suddenly he seized a startled Dorinda around the waist and pulled her irresistibly to him.

The ale splashed over them both as their bodies collided, the tankard fell sideways with a clatter, drenching her skirt and his trousers—but his end was achieved. He had Dorinda's head bent backward and was already

kissing her when the door was flung wide. Madame
Leroux was treated to the sight of an inn guest romanc-
ing a chambermaid as Bainter Ramsay's tawny head
lifted slightly to fix her with a pair of cold quizzical
eyes.

Realizing she had stumbled upon a tryst, Madame
Leroux had the grace to blush. "Oh, monsieur, I am
sorry, I have made a mistake!" she gasped.

"I think, madame, you have." Bainter's arm tightened
about Dorinda in a manner that threatened to shut off
her breath and her mouth, opened to protest, was, as
he hunched forward, suddenly stuffed with the ruffles
of his shirt front.

Flustered because she was sure she had actually *seen*
Rochelle's pink silk skirts disappearing through this
very door a few moments ago, and had been considering what to do about it ever since, Madame Leroux
departed, closing the door hastily behind her. She was
frowning as she hurried down the hall toward her own
room. Now that she thought about it, she was really
very disappointed at not finding Rochelle in Bainter
Ramsay's arms. After all no very great harm could have
been done in such a brief period of time, and on
discovering them together she would have had hysterics
and made such a great outcry that Bainter would have
felt obligated to marry the girl. And it would have been
such a *suitable* match for Rochelle, for Madame Leroux
had heard downstairs that Bainter Ramsay was both
wealthy and single. She was "Tch-tching" with her
tongue as she irritably went into her own room.

Ramsay gave her time to get there. He kept his grip
on Dorinda, who was struggling in his grasp. Confused
thoughts swirled through her head. In the courtyard
just now Bainter Ramsay had been deliberately rude to
her and now—now he was kissing her, trying to force
her protesting mouth open with his tongue. She could
feel the coarse hairs of his chest through the worn
fabric of her bodice and as he bent her backwards one

of his legs had somehow become inserted between her own. She could feel the pressure of that hard thigh even as she fought to maintain her balance, drumming on his back and shoulders with her fists.

Confusion and—unwillingly, for she was still angry—hot desire coursed through her as her racing young blood responded to the sudden onslaught of his lips. Reluctantly and with a sense of panic she felt her body abruptly melt against his, felt a mad tremor go through her slight frame as his tongue found its way between her parted lips.

And this was the man who had just publicly humiliated her!

In a sudden violent reaction against her own weakness—and with the strength that indignation brought her—she tore herself away from him and staggered backward, her face accusing.

"In the courtyard just now you stepped on my kirtle and ripped it with your spurs!" She shook the torn hem at him to emphasize the point. "And now you think to make me kiss you?"

So angry was she that she did not at first notice the faint movement behind the curtains. Her gaze was fixed with fierce intensity on his face—a face that had suddenly kindled at the latent fire he had felt in her.

Bainter laughed. Legs spread apart, he stood viewing her through narrowed amber eyes. "Oh, did I ruin your kirtle?" he said idly. "I must not have noticed."

"Indeed you did not care!" she flung at him. "You were too busy ogling that French girl!"

There was a sudden scurry from the curtained "closet," a rustle of silk, and Ramsay said, amused, "You are going, mademoiselle? But the danger is past. Your mother has arrived, found me pleasantly occupied—and departed. She will not be back. Indeed she has gone to look for you elsewhere."

Dorinda whirled as Rochelle, her face flaming, ran by her with a muttered, "I must go, monsieur! My mother may indeed be back! You do not know her as I do!"

Dorinda turned back in mute accusation to Bainter Ramsay, who was regarding her from amused narrowed eyes. The reason he had seized her and kissed her was now glaringly obvious and that reason struck her like a bucket of cold water. He had had that French girl in his room all the time! He had only seized Dorinda in his arms as a decoy to deceive the girl's mother so she would go away and leave him safe to toy with the daughter! And that the girl had been Rochelle was an added humiliation, for the young French girl had lost no opportunity to lord it over the younger servants at the inn and Dorinda had been her special target.

"Oh, you are despicable!" she spat at him.

His brows shot up. His interest was kindled by this thin little wench who dared to judge him.

"Hardly that," he said easily. "Indeed you would find me an excellent lover—a cut above the stableboys and ploughboys you're accustomed to." His bold grin invited her to come closer and find out.

"I do not have a lover!" sputtered Dorinda. "But if I did, it would surely not be a stableboy or a ploughboy!"

"Ah, you seek a gentleman then? Well, seek no further, wench. I am here!" Lightning fast, he stepped forward and seized her again, laughing.

But Dorinda was not to be caught out a second time. She twisted wildly in his grasp and felt behind her for the door. As she touched the wood there was a light knock and the door was immediately flung open.

"Are ye ready for supper, Bainter—" began a voice Dorinda recognized as one of the more dissolute regular patrons of the inn, a young man who had come out from England to buy land and instead gambled his fortune away. At the interruption Bainter's grasp momentarily relaxed and Dorinda jerked free and dashed past the mildly astonished visitor. "I say, Bainter, choos-

ing them young these days, aren't ye?" she heard him
say as she ran down the hall.

Oh, he was an awful man, abominable! She hated
him! she told herself as she ran. But she could still feel
the fiery touch of his lips upon her mouth and every
part of her body that had touched him felt more alive
than it ever had before. She was shaking as she ran
down the stairs and she was sick with disappointment
too because, for a brief romantic moment, she had
thought Bainter cared for her . . . as she cared for him.

Chapter 18

Mistress Buxton met Dorinda at the base of the back stairs. The innkeeper's wife glanced suspiciously at the girl's high color but other matters occupied her just now. A ship from England, the *Cynthia Ann,* bound for Philadelphia and blown off course in a gale, had limped into harbor downriver and many of the passengers had elected to have their goods removed and to take a later coastwise vessel. They were streaming into the common room right now and Innkeeper Buxton, crowded already during the "Publick Times," was trying with cot and trundle and turning the common room into a late barracks to provide sleeping quarters for the gentlemen, to take care of them all. Dorinda might be into mischief, but supper would soon be served, food was running short, and it was too busy a time to inquire into the caprices of the servants—and besides, the guests upstairs would be demanding their boots!

"Get those boots upstairs now." Mistress Buxton nudged Dorinda with a sharp elbow. "And mind ye keep no tips for the bootblacking is being charged on the gentlemen's bills. And as soon as you've done that, hurry back, for Nan has just burned her arm on the turnspit and is wailing in the kitchen and will be no good to me at all tonight—I'll need you to help serve."

Half-suffocated by rage and by something very like grief, Dorinda nodded. She was glad she had not been called upon to speak for her voice would surely have betrayed her. She kept her eyes cast down so that they too might not betray her feelings as she began collecting the boots. Once upstairs again, she piled them in a heap onto the floor and began knocking on doors, trying to deliver them in person for that was what the wily innkeeper had told her she must always do. Innkeeper Buxton was mindful of Dorinda's youth and thought that the sight of her smiling face would bring in trade. Innkeeper Buxton's wife held the same opinion but she felt—serving girls in her view being no better than they should be—that Dorinda might garner another kind of trade as well and gain the inn a bad reputation, and lose them the custom of the wives and daughters of the upriver planters. So she kept Dorinda defensively attired in shapeless clothes two sizes too large for her and made sure a flounced cap completely covered her shining hair at all times. She constantly badgered Dorinda about keeping her eyes cast down and glared at Buxton whenever he spoke a kind word to the girl (for along with her other shortcomings, the innkeeper's wife was consumed with jealousy and considered her heavyset lumbering husband an irresistible magnet that drew all women).

One of the pairs of boots to be delivered belonged to Rochelle Leroux's father. When Dorinda knocked, the door was jerked open by Madame Leroux, who stood for a cold moment surveying Dorinda up and down, then reached out and snatched the black boots from the girl's hands with a sniff and slammed the door in her face. Biting her lips, Dorinda continued on down the corridor, knocking on doors. She was grateful from her heart that at least she did not have to deliver boots to Bainter Ramsay!

One of the guests, whose husband's boots were the last Dorinda delivered, was a very plump· lady from upriver. When the unlatched door swayed inward with Dorinda's knock, her back was turned and she was panting with the exertion of trying to tie her corset strings. "Oh, is that you, Reginald?" she bleated. "Do come and lace me!"

"No, 'tis only me. With the boots," said Dorinda and the lady turned to her almost with joy. "Then do lace me up, child! Hurry, I'm expected downstairs for supper with the Jarvises and I can't go down half-dressed!"

Dorinda did her best, pulling the laces so tightly she was afraid she might cut the plump lady in two. It took some doing to get her laced up and the lady's groans could be heard clear out in the corridor as she kept gasping, "Tighter, child, tighter!" And in between, moaning, "Oh, if only I did not love gravy and pastries so much!"

Dorinda tugged with all her strength and left the plump lady reeling but happy as she clutched the bedpost and fanned her damp brow with a lace kerchief. As she came out of the room she met Jeddie hurrying by with a tray.

"You'd better get yourself downstairs," muttered Jeddie. "We're swamped down there. Mistress Buxton has been asking where you were once a minute—and you know her temper!"

Dorinda knew Mistress Buxton's temper all too well. She had run afoul of it numerous times to her sorrow. Mistress Buxton would not have approved of the time she had spent corset lacing! Mindful of that, she hurried down the front stairs because that was the shortest path to the tankards that she should already be filling with ale.

It turned out to be a mistake.

In that crowd below, seated with a group of recently arrived French Huguenots, Dorinda could see Madame Leroux and her husband—and his boots, which he had

ostentatiously crossed, now had a conspicuous sheen.
There was a vacant space at the table for Rochelle, sent
upstairs by her mother to collect her fan (actually
Madame Leroux only wanted to show off her vivacious
daughter to the company, for did not Rochelle look
truly elegant in her new coral silk?), was just now
reaching the stairs, swaggering between the diners.

Dorinda met the ascending Rochelle when she was
halfway down the stairs. Rochelle, posturing for the
benefit of the audience below (all of whom she was
certain had their gaze fixed upon her), gave the hurrying Dorinda a spiteful look and managed to jostle her.
Thrown off balance, Dorinda's toe caught in her torn
skirt. She was too far from the stair rail to clutch it for
support as Rochelle swished by.

And then she was falling.

She gave a despairing cry as she saw the wooden stair
treads coming up to meet her. Flailing at the air, she
tumbled to the bottom head over heels and landed in a
heap with a flash of bare legs as her torn skirts rode up
halfway to her hips.

More embarrassed than hurt, Dorinda picked herself
up at the bottom of the stairs and as she struggled to
her feet she found that all conversation in the common
room had ceased. Every eye in the room was fixed
upon her, including—to her chagrin—those of Innkeeper Buxton, his wife, and Bainter Ramsay, whose
tankard had been arrested in midair at the sight of
Dorinda's sudden wild descent down the wooden stairway. Covered with blushes, Dorinda quickly pulled her
skirts down. She was trembling as she wobbled toward
the tankards, making her way carefully between the
staring guests.

Halfway there the innkeeper's wife met her. She was
perspiring profusely for—shorthanded and with a crowd
like this—she was having to work instead of supervise.

"What do you mean, making a spectacle of yourself?"
she hissed. "I've told you time and again to use the back

stairs!" To emphasize her point, her palm cracked across Dorinda's face with a force that snapped her head back.

And Bainter Ramsay had seen that!

Overcome by mixed emotions, Dorinda threw her apron over her face and ran sobbing from the room.

Innkeeper Buxton gave his wife a reproving look. "Ye were too hard on the girl, Martha," he said. "I'll go bring her back."

"Ye'll do no such thing!" His wife moved to block him. Red spots of color appeared in her sallow cheeks, for she was Buxton's second wife and divided her wild jealousy between his first wife, now sleeping under the sod, and every scullery maid by turns—lately it was Dorinda, whose good looks were every day harder to hide. "She'll go without supper for this day's work," she declared waspishly. "Showing off her legs before everyone—the little hussy!"

The innkeeper shrugged and turned his attention elsewhere, but when his wife's back was turned he went quietly back to the kitchen where Dorinda was doubled up over a ladderback chair, sobbing her heart out.

"There, there, wench," he said, not unkindly. "'Tis no great matter. The wife's a bit hot tempered, she flies off the handle, but she means no great harm. Use the back stairs like she tells you and all will be well." He patted her back, liked the feel of it, and let his hand wander caressingly down her spine.

Beneath that caress, Dorinda stiffened and her head came up warily. She turned and gave the innkeeper a level look through her tears.

Buxton withdrew his hand.

"Well." He coughed. "Cook here will see you get something to eat, won't you, Cook?" He essayed a jovial laugh. "And when you've got some food in you—say some of that broth there, something you can eat quick (for he was ever mindful of his wife's tindery temper) —why, come on out and fill the tankards up, that's a good wench." He would have patted her again but that

Dorinda drew sharply away. She had felt the lechery in his wandering hand and she did not want him to touch her again. The very thought that he might want to touch her opened up a whole new round of horrifying possibilities. For she was bound here by articles of indenture for three years more.

It would be a long time to try to elude him. . . .

She dried her eyes and gratefully swallowed the broth Cook set down with a bang in front of her on the rude kitchen table. It was too thick and greasy for this hot day but to Dorinda, who had had nothing to eat since morning, it was heartening.

She got up and moved with foreboding into the hubbub of the common room, hoping nothing else terrible would happen.

She was filling the pewter tankards when she looked up from under the overhanging ruffle of her cap and caught Bainter Ramsay's eye. He was looking at her speculatively—and with an expression that made her redden and turn quickly away. Men looked at street women like that—appraisingly. She had seen that look in London often enough. Less frequently here.

Had she been able to read his mind she would have known that Bainter was thinking, *The wench has likely legs. Who would have thought it under that shapeless dress? Buxton's wife must be keeping her under wraps because old Buxton has a wandering eye.*

He began to laugh as he quaffed his wine. Those legs would merit his attention—and soon!

Laden with a tray piled high with tankards to be washed, Dorinda staggered out to the kitchen, which was a madhouse as Cook hastily tried to bake more pigeon pies and at the same time carve a haunch of venison. Dorinda slipped on a pool of grease and nearly dropped the tray. One tankard clattered to the floor.

Cook turned and gave Dorinda an impatient look. She snatched the tray from her before more damage could be done. "Don't try to carry so much at one time," she recommended.

Since it was the innkeeper's wife who had piled the tankards high on that tray, Dorinda had had little choice of her burden. She gave Cook a sad look. "I'll try not to."

Cook was shaking her head as she watched the girl go. It was her personal opinion that Dorinda was far too frail to be of any real help in the kitchen. Big strong girls like Nan or Jeddie were what was needed. Dorinda had not the strength to pick up the big iron kettles full of hot stew as they did. Her hands were not large enough or strong enough for so many tasks. 'Twas not for helping out in the kitchen that Buxton kept her on, Cook thought sardonically. He fancied the pretty wench to warm his bed on cold nights, and what would his wife say about *that*? She called to Nan to put more lard on her burned arm and come back and baste the brace of wild turkeys turning on a spit above the fire. The clash between Buxton and his jealous second wife, she told herself, shaking her head, would come soon enough.

It came the following night—and it involved, oddly enough, Bainter Ramsay.

Bainter had ordered a bath sent up and Mistress Buxton—shorthanded, short-tempered, and with another big crowd waiting for supper—told Dorinda to go fetch his bathwater, Jeddie was too busy to do it.

With her heart thumping in anguish that she should have to face him again Dorinda struggled up the stairs with the metal tub and a big pitcher of water, and knocked on Ramsay's door. She kept her head down as she went in, determined not to look at him, and set the metal tub down with a thump.

As she was about to set the pitcher down, a low laugh reached her. "Wait, wench—you can pour the water over me. 'Twill feel good on a hot day like this!"

Dorinda's head snapped up in astonishment. Nobody

had ever asked anything like that of her! Her face crimsoned as she saw that Bainter had removed his boots and coat and shirt and was just now unfastening his breeches, preparatory to removing those too.

"I won't!" she cried, shocked, and turned to run from the room.

But Ramsay was too quick for her. With a single leap he had blocked the entrance, his back was to the closed door, and his amused gaze raked her up and down.

"Why not?" he drawled. "Don't tell me you've never seen a naked man before?"

Dorinda hadn't but she wouldn't have admitted it for worlds. Not to this tall arrogant fellow who had been her idol and was now a fallen idol to be wept over but never put back on his pedestal again. "I said I won't pour the water over you," she said through her teeth.

"And I say you will." His voice was steely, inflexible. He crossed his arms and leant against the closed door.

Dorinda was painfully aware of his physical attraction, of the tawny length of him, of his rippling muscles, of the way he looked at her, stripping her in his mind.

"Besides," he added cajolingly, "I have something for you. Look over there." He jerked his head in the direction of the bed.

Dorinda was afraid to look around. She kept her scared gaze upon him.

He chuckled. "Well, turn your head and look. It's a kirtle to replace the one I tore."

Fascinated, Dorinda's head swung slowly around. There, spread upon the bed, was indeed a new red kirtle. The fabric had rippled as it was spread out and it winked at her invitingly. She tore her gaze away from it. She was not to be bought for the price of a kirtle!

"Well?" he asked brightly and moved toward her ever so slightly.

Dorinda jerked violently at his slight advance. She swallowed. "I thank you for replacing my kirtle," she managed.

"Oh, surely I'm to get a better 'thank you' than that," he remonstrated and took a swaggering step toward her. "Try it on and see if it fits."

"Stay back," she gasped.

Bainter's tawny eyes were very bright. He was obviously enjoying himself. "Or you'll do what?" he asked lazily.

"Or I'll scream for help," she warned, backing away.

"You do that," he countered. "And I'll say you offered yourself to me for a coin and when I wouldn't take you up on it, you made good your threat to rouse the house."

This was spoken with such bland indifference that Dorinda shrank back, trembling. He was indeed a handsome animal standing there with his bare chest and bare calves. And his lemon satin trousers fitted him so that there was little doubt as to what the rest of him looked like. She hated him for being so damnably attractive.

Abruptly she picked up the pitcher and emptied it into the tub.

"I'll have to go get another," she said with a challenging look from her blue-green eyes. *And once clear of the door she'd run downstairs and whisper to Cook what had happened and big taciturn Moll would be sent up with the next pitcher!*

Bainter guessed her plan of action. He laughed. A bar of soap had been dropped upon the floor near his foot and now with a negligent gesture of his bare toe he kicked the soap under the bed.

"Get the soap first," he ordered coldly. "And bring it to me so I can start my bath."

"I won't!" cried Dorinda. "I saw you kick it under there. Get it yourself!"

"If you don't get the soap and at once," he said, still in that cold reasonable voice, "I'll call your mistress and

tell her you refused to get the soap that you accidentally kicked under my bed."

"And *I'll* tell her what really happened."

"And she'll believe *me*," he countered.

She would too! thought Dorinda in rising panic. For
reasons she did not yet comprehend, Buxton's wife
seemed willing to believe anything bad of her! In an
agony of indecision she turned and took a step toward
the bed. It was the moment Bainter had been waiting
for. He leaped forward and by sheer momentum carried her beneath him deep into the smothering feather
mattress.

Chapter 19

As the soft enveloping mattress closed around her like a wall, Dorinda opened her mouth to scream—and found Bainter's mouth clamped down over it like a lid. His lips were warm, insidious, his tongue roved impudently. Struggling, half-suffocated, she felt her tense stiff body quiver beneath his touch. His long-fingered hands were pushing down the neck of her bodice and she could feel her lungs near to bursting as she fought for air, her breasts crushed beneath his hard chest straining for—for what? In the turmoil of the moment she did not inquire into the lethargy that was stealing over her limbs, the sultry somnolence of the senses that had nothing to do with the heat of the sweltering day but only with the heat generated by his magical touch.

For it *was* magical. It was as she had imagined it—exhilarating, unnerving. She managed to get her hand up and claw desperately at his face. Almost negligently he brushed her hand away and threw the weight of one arm across it, pinioning it as effectively as if it were the whirring wing of a bird.

"No," she cried from deep in her throat as she felt his hand move down inside her bodice, heard the material rip. But the sound seemed to disappear into his mouth and almost from inside her head came back the answer of his low laugh.

Strange unbidden feelings surged through Dorinda, murmurs from the back of her mind—perhaps echoing the street wisdom Jeddie and others like Jeddie had taught her—whispered, *You can make him yours—you have only to submit... and conquer.*

But some other wisdom, perhaps gleaned from a shrewder view of life that was distinctly her own, told her that Bainter Ramsay had had many women—and had thrown them all away. *That* was why he was a bachelor, for there was hardly a plantation owner's daughter who did not cast him surreptitious glances when he came striding down Duke of Gloucester street in the sun!

Near to surrender beneath this hot assault, Dorinda felt a sudden wave of revulsion—revulsion against what she might become—as she felt those long strong fingers tug her skirts upward over her knees, felt him massage her thighs in a way that was not gentle but urgent.

She would not be taken like any street girl, his for the price of a kirtle! By heaven, the man who took her would first have her permission!

A watchful stillness came over her mind in which she saw herself and Bainter with a dreadful clarity. To him she was a mere plaything, to be enjoyed, flung away and forgotten. To bear a child in shame, perhaps. Or to become some other man's doxy, passed from hand to hand.

Well, she would not let it happen!

She forced herself to relax and Bainter felt that relaxation, took it for submission. He eased on his side the better to pull up her skirts from her delectable legs, and for the space of a moment his mouth left hers.

Dorinda gathered what wind she had left and gave a choked but piercing scream.

Innkeeper Buxton's wife chanced to be walking down

the upstairs hallway at just that moment. Instantly she threw open the unlatched door to Ramsay's room from whence the scream had come. She was treated to the sight of a wild flailing of arms and legs as Dorinda tried to fight free of her assailant, for Bainter had promptly clapped his mouth over hers again and was struggling to subdue her.

"Dorinda!" thundered Mistress Buxton.

Bainter Ramsay looked up quickly and saw who stood there. With a grin he eased his long body off of Dorinda's and stood up. "We were just having a bit of fun," he told Dorinda's employer deprecatingly. "Weren't we, wench? No harm done."

"We weren't!" Sick at heart that she could so nearly have succumbed to him, ashamed that for a treacherous moment she had actually *wanted* to, Dorinda struggled up from the feather mattress. She was clutching at her bodice and trying to pull back up over her bare shoulder as she did so a sleeve that had been wrenched down in the struggle. "He leaped on top of me and—"

"I'll hear none of your lies," flashed her employer. "I saw with my own eyes what you were doing."

"Ah, well, lass." Bainter favored Dorinda with a deprecating smile and a pat on the rump that she found infuriating. She struck his hand away. "We can't fool Mistress Buxton." He sighed. "She's onto us, it would seem!"

"Indeed I am," rejoined the innkeeper's wife tartly. "And I'll thank you not to be seducing the help, Mr. Ramsay," she added tartly. "You'll be giving our house a bad name!"

Bainter chuckled. "Now *that* I'd hate to be guilty of," he agreed, but his tawny gaze on Dorinda was regretful. She had fired his blood, the wench had—first with that surprisingly lovely display of bare legs when she fell down the stairs yesterday, today by having a body that seemed made of silk. And she was looking at him

with sobbing hatred. A way to placate her and save the
situation at the same time occurred to him suddenly.

"The wench was but thanking me," he explained to
her angry employer. "It seems that yesterday in the
innyard I inadvertently tore her skirt. When I showed
her the new kirtle I had bought to replace it, she gave
me a kiss and—" he added blandly—"I was carried
away by it."

Mistress Buxton's eyes flew to the new red kirtle
which had slipped from the bed to the floor. Kirtles
were expensive and she had no mind to replace Dorinda's
torn one if another were offered. "That's very good of
you, Mr. Ramsay," she admitted grudgingly, accepting
the kirtle he scooped up and handed her as a peace
offering.

But Dorinda heard his words through a blur of rage.
"It's a lie!" she screamed. "I never kissed him for the
kirtle! He's a liar!"

Buxton's wife turned upon her. "Be quiet!" She seized
Dorinda's arm and almost jerked her off her feet as she
hustled her down the back stairs. "I'll teach you not to
tumble into gentlemen's beds, you hussy!"

"No, it wasn't that way!" cried Dorinda. "He—"

"He was kind enough to buy you a new kirtle! Go put
it on!"

"I won't!" Dorinda shrank back from the kirtle. "I'll
never wear it—you can't make me!"

Having reached the kitchen as these rebellious words
were uttered, Buxton's wife seized a whip from the wall
and began to flay Dorinda with it. The girl threw up
her arms to protect her face and whirled about, making
blindly for the nearest exit. But her way was blocked by
a heavy wooden table, by frightened scullery maids
running about, and finally by Innkeeper Buxton himself, attracted from the common room by Dorinda's
screams and the crack of the whip.

"What, are ye mad?" he thundered at his wife and

leaped past Dorinda, seizing the whip. "What's the girl done?"

"I found her in bed with one of the guests, that's what!" His wife struggled to regain the whip.

The innkeeper's face was thoughtful as he considered the cowering girl with the back of her bodice and chemise cut through by the whip and angry red weals showing on the smooth pale skin of her back. The next lash would have drawn blood. "Did ye now?" he said softly.

"It's not true!" wailed Dorinda. "He jumped on me from behind after I brought up his bathwater and I screamed—"

"He didn't hurt you, did he?" Buxton cut in quickly.

"No," quavered Dorinda uncertainly. He had not actually *hurt* her but he had certainly caused her to be hurt, as those welts on her back would testify!

"All right then," said Buxton in a quelling voice. "Some guest had too much to drink and made a fool of himself. Let it rest there, Martha. D'you want to create a scandal?" For indeed the commotion could be heard plainly in the common room.

Mistress Buxton's eyes narrowed. She was determined to regain the upper hand. "Take off your kirtle!" she cried, and when Dorinda shrank back and Buxton began to remonstrate, she threw the new red kirtle at Dorinda. "And put this on, so you'll look respectable."

Buxton shrugged. "Do as she says," he ordered. "'Tis a better kirtle than the one you've got." He stood at gaze, watching the novel sight of a scullery maid partially disrobing in the kitchen. The kitchen help stood around, staring. Reluctantly, Dorinda unfastened the kirtle and stepped out of it. Her coarse cotton petticoat was decent enough but she could feel Buxton's eyes kindle as they roved over the outline of her slim hips and legs. Hastily—for he looked about to lick his lips—Dorinda drew on the new red kirtle, but her gaze was mutinous. She meant to change back as soon as they were gone.

Mistress Buxton guessed that. Triumphantly she reached down and seized Dorinda's old olive kirtle and tossed it with a contemptuous gesture into the fire.

"No!" Dorinda would have sprung forward but that Buxton stopped her roughly.

"The wife wants ye to have a new kirtle!" he roared, mystified, for he understood none of what was going on between the two women. "And wear it ye will!"

Defeated, Dorinda stood and watched the olive kirtle burn.

After Buxton had removed his wife, and the kitchen had gone back to its usual bustle, she looked down at the new red kirtle and tears sprang to her eyes.

Forever after Dorinda would consider that red kirtle a badge of shame.

Tired as she was, worn out in mind and body, sleep was still hard to come by that night. In her tiny attic cubbyhole atop the inn Dorinda tossed and turned. Lady Soft Paws, tired of being constantly shifted just as she reached a comfortable position, jumped from the mattress and went off prowling somewhere. Miserable and wide-eyed, Dorinda hardly noticed her going. Lying there bathed in perspiration, she faced a terrible future.

She was growing up. Already her young breasts were thrusting forward in the shapeless gowns the innkeeper's wife thrust upon her. Soon there would be no denying that she was a woman grown—and what then? She had seen the look in Buxton's eyes, felt already the lustful touch of his hand—and she knew too well the almost insane jealousy of his wife.

The one would rape her, the other would kill her, she told herself fatalistically. She got up out of bed, determined to slip away this very minute, no matter what happened later.

And then it came to her that it was very near morning, that if she did not appear in the kitchen at sunrise she would be sent for, searched for, and that she would be without food and without funds and with no very long time to make her escape. She would do it tomorrow. She would filch enough food from the kitchen to keep herself from starving for a couple of days. She would find a rowboat and tomorrow night after dark she would row upriver, well provisioned, and try to find work with one of the new farm families that were settling in ever increasing numbers in the countryside along the upper James.

That decision gave her a kind of peace and she fell asleep and slept steadily until dawn.

But fate had other plans for Dorinda.

She was up early and no sooner had she reached the kitchen than she was being ordered about by all and sundry for the great crush of guests had worn out all the help and made them surly and touchy—even Cook, who normally was pleasant to her. But with Mistress Buxton wrangling with big stolid Moll in the common room, Dorinda managed in midmorning to escape into the innyard. Her pockets were filled with apples, and she was just wondering where in the innyard to secrete them when Jeddie, the scullery maid with whom Dorinda was friendliest, came up behind her.

"Never seen the Buxtons so mad at each other," said Jeddie blithely. Her deep blue eyes sparkled. "They was yelling at each other fit to kill."

"Were they?" What with the clattering of pots and pans in the kitchen, Dorinda hadn't heard them.

Jeddie nodded her auburn head. "And then he stalked off some place, muttering."

Dorinda's indifferent expression said she couldn't care less.

"I heard your name mentioned more than once. Couldn't rightly make out what it was about though. Mixtress Buxton was raving something about she couldn't stand it any longer and Buxton was shouting her down."

"She can't stand *me*," said Dorinda tersely. She was

looking about her for a good place to store the apples prior to her escape.

"It's your face," offered Jeddie. "She hates anyone with a pretty face." She felt her friend needed cheering up. "Don't feel bad about Bainter Ramsay," she said with a confidential smirk. "He tries out all the girls."

Dorinda turned to give her an astonished look. "You mean *you*—?"

"Poured bathwater over him when he was naked— I'll wager that's what he asked you to do!" Jeddie laughed. "Anyway, 'tis what he asked *me* and the next thing I knew I was in the tub with him with my clothes off! He don't give you no time to consider, Bainter Ramsay don't!"

Dorinda's opinion of Bainter, which had already fallen low, sank still further.

"I resisted his advances," she said stiffly.

"Ho, ho!" crowed Jeddie. "I'll bet that's the first time a wench has said no to *him* in some time! Gets them all, he does, sooner or later!"

"Well, he won't get *me*!"

"What're you saving yourself for? A wedding ring?" Jeddie laughed and slapped her strong thighs. "You'll get tired of that, you will, in four more years—"

"Three," corrected Dorinda mechanically.

"Three then." Jeddie gave her an impatient look. "The life here wouldn't be so bad if you'd warm up to the gentlemen once in a while, Dorinda. They'll give you tips the innkeeper's wife won't know about. How d'you think I got me this yellow petticoat?" She whirled about ostentatiously, showing off the yellow petticoat to best advantage and batting her eyes roguishly at a passing gentleman who looked at her without interest and passed on to enter the green door. "'Twas a gift, Dorinda—same as yours."

"No, mine was to replace one he'd stepped on and torn," Dorinda corrected her harshly. "Yours was bargained for. You gave up something for it, don't pretend you didn't."

"Nothing I'd miss," said Jeddie airily. "And you'll come round to my way of thinking, you will. Look out, here comes your friend!"

Dorinda turned to see that Bainter Ramsay in his lemon coat was striding across the innyard. On his way to the general sessions, no doubt. She lifted her chin and turned her head pointedly away from him, keeping it averted even when she heard his step coming dangerously near. Her heart began to thump.

And then, abruptly she felt her bottom painfully pinched. She gave a choked indignant cry, heard Bainter laugh and turned to hear him say, "I see you're wearing my kirtle, wench!"

Dorinda jerked away and he laughed again, striding carelessly past her into Duke of Gloucester Street. Had it not been the only kirtle she owned, Dorinda was certain she would have torn it off and flung it after his retreating figure. As it was, she stood there trembling, watching him go.

"You're getting him interested," observed Jeddie. "A little more holding him off and he'll be ready to give you a brace of petticoats! Well, I see Buxton's back—I'd best get back too."

She skipped off toward the inn leaving Dorinda sick with rage and wishing wildly that she was a man so she could pursue Bainter and horsewhip him.

After a while Dorinda hid the apples beneath some horseblankets in the back of a wagon she knew would not be moving on today and went back into the inn. In a defiant gesture, instead of going around and entering through the kitchen, she flung open the green door and walked, head high, into the common room.

Both Buxtons were standing there and as Dorinda entered, Buxton's wife gave him a significant push and he cleared his throat.

"Come along, Dorinda," he said gruffly, and now

Dorinda saw Jeddie, looking distressed and holding out a neatly wrapped bundle.

"Take it, Dorinda," sniffled Jeddie.

"What is it?" demanded Dorinda.

"Your things," said Mistress Buxton heavily, and turned to Jeddie. "Get on with cleaning those tables, Jeddie." Her broad back dismissed Dorinda.

With a last glare at his wife, Buxton jerked his head toward the door and Dorinda, wishing she'd run away last night, tagged along after him carrying the bundle containing her clothes. He looked so glum she was afraid to ask him where they were going.

He led her the short distance to the Raleigh Tavern, which was even more crowded during the "Publick Days" than the White Hart. Outside the many-dormered white frame building he paused. "I've sold your articles of indenture," he told Dorinda. "To an English couple that arrived aboard the *Cynthia Ann*." He looked sheepish. "I wouldn't do this, you understand, except that—"

"Except that your wife insisted," said Dorinda crisply.

He shrugged. "They're nice people, Dorinda. You can learn elegant ways from them.

Dorinda flushed. So he had guessed she yearned for "elegant ways!"

"And," he added, "they'll be taking you to Philadelphia with them. You'll be leaving this afternoon, on the *Swallow*."

Feeling very forlorn and friendless, Dorinda followed Buxton's broad form into the inn to meet her new masters.

In the Blores' tiny cabin aboard the coastwise vessel *Swallow*, crowded with items Elissa Blore had insisted were "necessaries," Dorinda had just been told by her new mistress to change into something "less loud" than her red kirtle. Dorinda wished for nothing so much as to be rid of it but she had to admit to having no other.

And now at Elissa's direction she was rummaging through one of the trunks.

The meeting with John and Elissa Blore had been swiftly accomplished in the common room of the Raleigh as John Blore settled up for his lodgings. Dorinda had curtsied and mumbled answers to their perfunctory questions as to her age and health. Elissa Blore's pale watery blue eyes had brightened when Dorinda had volunteered that she could read and write—a rare qualification in a bound girl. Buxton frowned at that and Dorinda guessed he was thinking he had parted with her services too cheaply.

Dorinda had had little time to size up her new employers. John Blore (who had preferred to remain on deck as the *Swallow* began her stately progression down the James) had struck her as an impatient man with a weak mouth and a rather vacant look on a face moderately handsome but overshadowed by a huge full-bottomed wig. His wife was a frothy dithering woman who seemed to have no will of her own, but was swept this way and that by her husband's moods. Both Blores' present mood was one of crisis for Elissa Blore informed her dramatically that they had brought with them three servants, but all upon arrival had announced their intention not to proceed to Philadelphia but to seek their fortune upriver and had departed on the spot. The Blores were in sore need of any help offered— and Innkeeper Buxton had offered Dorinda. The implication was plain: a bound girl would be in no position to leave.

Now as she rummaged about for something "more suitable" to wear, Dorinda wondered what her duties would be. Ladies' maid perhaps?

She was rather relieved when Elissa Blore settled on a plain gray linen kirtle and bodice—standard fare for a chambermaid. For she had recognized the Blores as not quite the gentry Innkeeper Buxton had claimed them to be. And they were got up in so much satin and so many ribands and flounces and such billows of lace that Dorinda had wondered for a quaking moment if they might not be the proprietor and proprietress of a gaming house or even worse a brothel (for Jeddie, who had a taste for the lurid, was forever telling her—with more imagination than fact—about such things back in her native Bristol).

"That's better," said Elissa Blore, eyeing the gray garments. "I can't have you going about looking like some gypsy. Here, put them on." She stepped back and her elbow collided painfully with the wall. "Oh, this tiny cabin! First that terrible voyage on the *Cynthia Ann*— and then that overcrowded inn. *I slept on a trundle!* I who never have had less than an entire household to command!"

Dorinda stole a look at Elissa as she obediently stripped off her red kirtle. Elissa wore a powdered wig even by daylight (most in Williamsburg had been reserved for balls) and she looked to Dorinda very much like the stiff little French fashion dolls with their vapid painted faces which were imported from Paris and that Dorinda had sometimes glimpsed through sempstresses' windows. There was something about that statement of commanding an entire household that jarred Dorinda too, but she couldn't quite put her finger on it.

She was still puzzling about it as, her back turned, she stripped off bodice and skirt preparatory to changing into the gray when the cabin door was flung open and John Blore entered. Dorinda's back was to that door and although she promptly flung the red kirtle over her shoulders he had caught sight of the stripes on her back.

"Look at the girl's back, Elissa," he said with a sigh of disgust. "It seems we've bought us an incorrigible. No wonder that innkeeper in Williamsburg was so hot to sell her to us!"

The last two days had been very hard on Dorinda. Her nerves were jangled. At Blore's unfair comment she threw caution to the winds and swung about. "I am not an incorrigible," she cried and added, in an attempt to establish her gentle birth, "I'm granddaughter to a countess!"

If she had hoped to gain their attention, she certainly did so. The exquisitely groomed couple exchanged blank glances. "And where is your father now, my dear?" inquired Elissa nervously.

"He was hanged," said Dorinda before she thought. "He killed the man who got my mother in trouble with the law."

"And your mother?" asked Elissa faintly.

"She died in Newgate Prison," flashed Dorinda.

From the mounting horror on both their faces she half-expected to be escorted to the deck, thrown overboard and told to swim back to Williamsburg, but Elissa said with a quaver, "I—I'm sure they both had their reasons for what they did!" and slumped to the floor in a faint.

"Get the smelling salts," roared her husband. "She's fainted again!"

Dorinda's anger had left her now but she made no move to get the salts. Instead she advanced on the fallen woman. "It isn't smelling salts she needs," she told him in a practical voice. "I've seen it lots of times before at the inn. It's terribly hot in here and her stays are too tight. Here, let me loosen them and we won't have any more trouble."

Blore began to bluster but when Elissa came to, took a couple of deep breaths, sat up and announced she was feeling much better, he gave Dorinda a look of grudging approval and Dorinda smiled back. "Oh, well, perhaps heredity isn't everything," she heard him mutter, as if trying to convince himself, as he left the cabin.

Leaving Mistress Blore to rest and fan herself, Dorinda, now inconspicuously garbed in gray, went out on deck carrying her red kirtle in her arms.

Events had moved so fast this day that Dorinda had

had time neither for regret nor homesickness, but there was one thing she desperately wanted to do. She leaned far out over the taffrail above the water scudding by and flung the red kirtle overboard and watched it float away. Eventually it became waterlogged and disappeared from view. Gone—like her life here. A life where she had watched from close hand the pleasures of plantation gentry come to town—but always from the outside looking in!

And gone with it, she told herself staunchly, was the arrogant Mr. Ramsay—banished forever from her mind. But the sea breeze was soft as a man's touch on her hot cheek, the sun beamed down no brighter than his smile, and above her golden head a kittiwake circled and swooped and screamed derision. Whenever she glanced back at the shoreline, slipping fast away, Bainter himself seemed to be standing there, grinning at her in his lemon silks.

Dorinda's blue-green eyes glinted and her fingers gripped the rail. The winds of fate blew strangely. Look where those winds had brought her: from London to Williamsburg and now to Philadelphia! It was not beyond imagining that the elegant Mr. Ramsay might someday cross her path again and if he did—Dorinda's white teeth clenched into her soft lower lip almost drew blood—*if he did, she was going to straighten him out!*

At night I hear the rustle of your touch upon my gown
And, thrilling, feel the rasp of silk as it goes sliding down,
And wake to find the moonlight shining in as bright as day,
And learn that I was dreaming—for you are far away!

PART TWO

The Beautiful Waif

Chapter 20

Philadelphia was something new in Dorinda's experience. The "little London" she had envisioned of nights in the dim starlight as she paced the *Swallow*'s swaying deck, she found did not exist. Philadelphia was neither London nor Williamsburg—it was a world of its own.

After London's narrow streets and twisting alleys, the regularity of Philadelphia's checkerboard of wide unpaved cartways, often deep in mire but edged with neat brick sidewalks, seemed strange. And to a girl who had stood wistfully on the outskirts of an easygoing planters' aristocracy in Virginia, this raw new "city of brotherly love" that disapproved of theatrical performances and claimed it had neither beggars nor old maids, seemed odd and decorous. The Quakers wore rich clothes; fine silks and taffetas rustled by her in the streets—but they were of subdued colors. Restrained dark greens and plums and dull blues seemed the mode and looking about her at this prosperous decorous world, Dorinda's wild young heart sometimes yearned for the bright colors and lightsome ways of the easygoing Virginia gentry. The colorful balls and masques that she had glimpsed through candlelit windows on Duke of Gloucester Street seemed very far away here, the backstairs gossip was not nearly so exciting. William Penn's city was an orderly one and to Dorinda, who yearned for gaiety and romance, not quite her cup of tea.

She cared for the servants the Blores gathered about them even less, for once arrived in Philadelphia John Blore promptly bought an expensive brick house on a shady street, hired five servants besides Dorinda, and set himself up as "gentry." To her disappointment, Dorinda learned that she was too young and inexpert to become Elissa Blore's personal maid—*those* duties went to a vivacious young French girl named Simone, who spoke indifferent English and snubbed Dorinda. Cook was a taciturn woman with a bad back who turned out delicate feasts but groaned as she worked. The butler, Crowley, was a man with a cold face and fishy eyes interested only in what he could steal—Dorinda learned to beware of him early. The footman she avoided as well because he was always pinching her black and blue. The chambermaid, Emmy Tubbs, was a young girl from a large Birmingham family who had emigrated to America and discovered they didn't like it—they hated country life, feared the Indians, considered Philadelphia miserably provincial, and lived for the day when they could return. All in all, the household was not Dorinda's cup of tea either.

In point of fact, she preferred her employers to their staff. They were vain, foolish and inept—but they were neither bad nor unkind. Elissa Blore continued to wear her stays too tight, and she continued to faint. John Blore continued to manifest impatience with everybody and to stir about a great deal, yet managed to accomplish almost nothing himself.

Dorinda, almost superfluous now in this well-staffed household, tried to be unobtrusive and nobody seemed to care. The Blores had a small but excellent library and she hid herself away with the books and read all she could, trying to teach herself French and Latin and mathematics from the books she found there.

Before he had been in Philadelphia a month John Blore bought a chandler's shop, which Dorinda seldom saw. At home she was mostly an errand girl to be ordered about—although she took every opportunity to observe the way Simone, the French maid, arranged Elissa's hair. She would watch Simone at work and then she would slip away to her room and practice doing the same waves and curls until she began to achieve really elegant effects—effects which were carefully hidden under a conservative white mobcap, for Elissa Blore did not approve of servants who looked like "hoydens with their hair flying about!"

Dorinda would always remember that first Christmas in Philadelphia. Christmas fell on a Tuesday that year and on the Sunday before it had snowed and continued snowing lightly right through Christmas Eve. Dorinda woke to a white shining world with sleigh bells tinkling outside and small boys running by dragging sleds and ice skates and laughing as they ran.

Christmas dinner for her was in the servants' hall (which Elissa persisted in calling the large pantry off the kitchen in which the servants gathered to eat, for while the "reception rooms," as Elissa called them, were capacious enough, the kitchen was by no means large and Cook was forever complaining about it). They drank wine and ate the same wild turkey that had just been brought on its silver charger from the master's dining table (it was huge; Cook muttered they'd be eating it for a week!).

The master and mistress dined alone and in state in the large wainscoted dining room which lay to the left of the front hall just behind the front study. They were elegantly dressed in ivory satins for the occasion and faced each other smiling across their gleaming board. Dorinda helped serve the flaming plum pudding, which was topped with a sprig of holly. She reported back excitedly to the kitchen that Mistress Blore had told her husband "that King Henry VIII had once had a plum pie baked nine feet long that weighed 165 pounds!"

"I pity the baker!" muttered Cook gloomily.

But that was the only gloomy note because then they were eating their own plum pudding and toasting each other in mock imitation of lords and ladies, Simone sang Christmas carols in French and even the dour butler, Crowley, kissed everyone he could catch under the mistletoe.

That evening Dorinda struck up a friendship with the French maid, Simone, for Simone had had too much wine and was friendly with everybody.

"La, la, we mus' all dance, *n'est-ce pas?*" Simone waved at Dorinda to help her push back the kitchen table and began executing difficult dance steps in the center of the room. Dorinda watched, fascinated, and applauded energetically as Simone finished.

Flattered, Simone essayed to teach her to dance and those lessons that began during the holidays were to continue all year until Dorinda was herself an accomplished dancer in the best French style.

It was an eventful Christmas season for another reason, for it was during the Twelve Days of Christmas that Emmy Tubbs took Dorinda home to meet her family—all fourteen of them. And eighteen-year-old Robbie Tubbs promptly fell in love with Dorinda. He was awkward and shy and he blushed when he kissed her under the mistletoe, but he took her ice skating— for the first time ever—and she nearly broke her neck on borrowed skates. After that he called regularly to take her to church, but Dorinda, although she liked the big blond lad, could not return his almost puppylike affection.

His devotion got her over a lot of bad moments though and she tried to focus her thoughts on Robbie whenever she would wake up shivering from a dream of Bainter Ramsay.

Not till spring did Dorinda learn what was the matter

with her employers, the false note, that nagging something that always seemed to her not quite right. For in the spring Elissa Blore caught her high heel in a chink of the brick sidewalk outside the house and fell, injuring her right hand. She could not write legibly for months and it was suddenly remembered that Dorinda had claimed she could read and write.

Called to assist, Dorinda dutifully penned what Elissa dictated—all letters innocuous enough to English relatives, but Elissa insisted that they all be copied over on expensive vellum and the red sealing wax imprinted with her gold signet ring. It was this copying over after the mistress had swished away that gave Dorinda access to Elissa's little slant-topped walnut writing desk in which she kept her correspondence. It was stuffed with letters and Dorinda shamelessly read them all, for life was basically dull in the Blores' establishment and she could not resist reading letters left lying about. Their contents opened her eyes.

John Blore had come to America with "all the money his father was ever going to give him for he'd already frittered away more than his brothers and sisters would ever receive." Why he could not have made a success as a linen draper with everybody lending assistance his father never would understand—there was more but Dorinda put the letter down in some alarm. For John Blore, experienced supposedly as a draper, had just bought instead a chandler's shop—a business about which he knew nothing!

Elissa's letters were always apologetic. They were doing "the best they could," she would announce vaguely.

Dorinda felt sorry for her kindly overdressed employers, for through reading those letters she had come to understand them. John Blore and his wife were English "discards," unsuccessful fringe people on the edge of the burgeoning new mercantile aristocracy that was growing up in England. Failures in their own land, they'd been sent to the Colonies—sent with money for a new start and the heartfelt hope that they would make it in America since they hadn't in England.

John Blore checked in briefly at the chandler's shop every day—Dorinda knew that for she heard him report it to his wife. Elissa would always ask dutifully if things were going well and he would answer vaguely that Elias Zachary (who ran the shop for him) said things were going as well as could be expected. After which they both plunged happily into their abundant social life, a constant round of calls and dinners and parties. Dorinda wondered uneasily if John Blore was ever going to learn candle making—or if he really wanted to!

By summer Elissa's writing hand was well enough for her to take up the pen again and Dorinda lost track of their English relatives. By summer too Robbie Tubbs, grown bolder now and seizing her and kissing her every chance he got, was pressing her to marry him. And when she refused, his sister was furious.

"You led Robbie on!" she accused.

"I didn't!" protested Dorinda.

"You did, and now you broke his heart!" screamed Emmy and stomped away from Dorinda on her big flat feet.

Emmy stopped speaking to Dorinda for a month, she was never really friendly again, and Dorinda was almost glad when that autumn the entire Tubbs family moved back to England. Dorinda learned they had all of them except the young children signed articles of indenture to pay for the voyage home.

Emmy was not replaced. Dorinda took over her duties.

The next Christmas was a difficult one for the Blores. The chandler's shop was not doing well, they had written home to England for money and the money was not forthcoming. That Christmas they dismissed all the servants except Cook and Dorinda took over as Elissa's personal maid as well.

Actually she enjoyed it. It was fun handling the lovely

fabrics of Elissa's beautiful clothes, sorting out her lace kerchiefs and perfume bottles and pomades and fans. Elissa's own hair was no problem—it was straight and sparse and fine and covered with a wig. Both her husband's wig and hers represented a major expense, however, for they required cleaning and curling at frequent intervals. As an economy measure, Dorinda learned to do both.

"You're such a clever girl, Dorinda," Elissa would sigh, turning from powdering her face at her dressing table to smile that sweet vague smile at Dorinda. "What would we do without you?"

Dorinda wasn't sure how they'd manage without her. She managed to do so many tasks that the Blores were able to keep up appearances even though they had had to sell their carriage and horses and now walked everywhere. But Dorinda had only two years left to go on her indenture and she didn't intend to be a bound girl forever. She hoped the Blores would be able to get their muddled affairs straightened out somehow.

They did not. Things got worse.

In the summer they were down to a more or less steady diet of pigeon pie for the butcher had cut off their credit and the meat of the chesty seventeen-inch-long birds that flew over in flights numbering in the millions, breaking down huge trees when they settled down to roost, was cheap. Wine was no longer served at table except when they had company—which wasn't often.

That was the summer Elias Zachary found other employment and Blore was left with a run-down chandler's shop with two overworked apprentices and no manager. Dorinda overheard his troubled conversation with his wife.

"We cannot hire a replacement for Zachary," he explained, "because there's no money to pay anyone. That's why Zachary left. Hartzel, the oldest apprentice, is willing to take over but he says they need another hand at least to keep going—and there's no money to get anyone."

"Doesn't the candle making business bring in *any-thing*?" asked Elissa plaintively.

"Not enough to meet expenses," said Blore gloomily.

At that point Dorinda came into the room. "I couldn't help overhearing," she said. "Would it help if I worked mornings in the chandler's shop? I could at least take care of the customers and run errands and help out."

The Blores considered that a marvelous idea and Dorinda was promptly dispatched to the chandler's shop each morning. The shop was small and squarish and low-ceilinged and there was a place out back for melting tallow and dipping the wicks. Dorinda had dipped candles before at the White Hart but here she was learning the trade. Here various types of candles were made, some were called spermaceti candles which were made of wax from the heads of the great sperm whales that were being slaughtered in ever increasing numbers and making New England sea captains rich. Spermaceti candles gave three times as much light as the tallow candles Dorinda was used to and didn't smoke as badly. They were in great demand.

But in even greater demand were the lovely fragrant bayberry candles—as Dorinda learned from her customers. And the Blores' shop contained none.

"We should make bayberry candles," she told John Blore eagerly. "I'm told there are plenty of bayberry bushes about for they thrive near the sea."

That autumn, while John Blore—a great comedown for him—tended the shop, Dorinda and the two apprentices, Hartzel and Kyle, took several days off and roamed the lovely countryside around Philadelphia, gathering great quantities of berries. They brought the baskets of berries back in a cart and threw them into boiling water, skimming off the wax. It congealed to a dirty green and Dorinda thought it of a consistency somewhere between wax and tallow. But melted and refined it took on a beautiful transparent green color. Dorinda and the boys became very expert at making these fragrant, almost smokeless candles and sold them as fast as they could make them to the wealthy merchants whose homes might use forty candles or more in an evening.

By winter—for the first time—the chandler's shop showed a profit.

Dorinda was exhausted but elated. The Blores promptly perked up and Christmas was a merry time with part-time help hired from among the new settlers who poured in, waves of them it seemed, with every ship to cast anchor in the port of Philadelphia.

That Christmas was remarkable for another reason too. John Blore's ne'er-do-well nephew, also named John Blore, paid them a visit. He was heavyset, dissolute, and raucous—none of the refinement of the Philadelphia Blores had rubbed off on him. Dorinda took an instant dislike to him—partially because she heard him pressing his uncle for a loan she knew he could not afford. And when "Jack," as the elder Blores called their nephew, followed her to the chandler's shop and reached up under her skirt while she was dipping candles to pinch her bare bottom, Dorinda whirled around and threw some hot wax at him. The wax missed him but Jack complained bitterly of her behavior, and there was a wild scene that night in the drawing room with both Jack and John shouting at each other. Elissa had the vapors and fainted. Jack left in a huff shouting that he'd not be back, and they did not see him again at the house, although Dorinda did see him once or twice later staggering about near the waterfront. But she knew from something she overheard John say to Elissa that Jack had not left empty-handed—he had taken with him a goodly amount of the family plate that they could not afford to replace.

That spring Hartzel, the oldest apprentice, asked Dorinda to marry him. She was now a sixteen-year-old beauty, but that beauty was well masked and hidden beneath the sturdy linsey-woolsey clothes and enveloping gray linen smock she wore in shop. Dorinda, completely absorbed in the Blore household and with no social life at all, said no. Hartzel was taken aback; plainly he had expected her to accept for he was a handsome lad. He pointed out that when they were both free, they could have made a fortune as chandlers! Dorinda, whose one all-consuming desire at the moment was to make this particular chandler's shop a success, gave him an impatient look and after that they never went back to their former camaraderie. She knew that Hartzel had not forgiven her.

That summer they took on a third apprentice and began to expand their sales. They paid the butcher's bill and their diet grew more varied. They gathered more bayberries that fall and there among the bayberries the newest apprentice, a tall awkward boy named Blassing, proposed to Dorinda.

She said no to him too.

That winter John Blore's health began to fail. He had always been a heavy smoker and in the past year he had developed a deep hacking cough which never left him.

Before Easter he was dead.

And that one single happening overturned Dorinda's world, for it brought his half-sister Ada into her life.

When John Blore died, letters flew thick and fast between England and Philadelphia. John and Elissa had never had any children and Elissa would have only her "widow's mite"—all the rest would go to his English relatives. This was a very damp period for Dorinda, for Elissa wept incessantly, and Dorinda, numbed by running the chandler's shop, keeping the books, taking care of the customers—and then coming home to a dizzy round of combing her employer's wig and doing the housework, began to feel edgy. She realized that Elissa was the kind of woman who leaned and her leaning post had been taken away. Dorinda had liked

John Blore well enough but she wished bitterly that he had not been so thoughtless—at least he could have made a will and left to his wife the property she had naturally expected would be hers!

By now Dorinda had pretty well taken over the house, for Elissa was in no condition to decide anything, not even what she wanted to have for dinner, which they now shared in the big dining room while the apprentices ate in the kitchen. Summer found Dorinda tired and thinner—and unprepared for the terrible outburst of tears and woe that greeted her on her return from the shop one day in early summer when Elissa waved a letter at her and cried, "Oh, this is terrible! They're sending out Ada!"

Gradually Dorinda pieced together from her hysterical employer what had happened. By trading about among themselves, the Blore family had signed over their parts of the inheritance to Ada. Ada would be coming soon, from Jamaica—to take over.

"And she will!" wailed Elissa. "Oh, she's a terrible woman—John hated her!"

"Is she married?" asked Dorinda, thinking that perhaps Elissa, who had a quality of sweet helplessness that was sometimes very appealing, could turn to Ada's husband for aid.

"Ada married? Oh, heavens, no. Ada always said she'd never hand over the reins to any man, she wanted to run things herself!"

Dorinda began to get a grim picture of Ada as the days went on. Ada had "made a great success of her sugar plantation in Jamaica; she got twice the work out of her bond servants as they did at the next plantation!" Hearing that, Dorinda grimaced. She could well imagine how that had been accomplished! Ada did not believe in fine clothes and had always criticized Elissa for wearing them. Dorinda noted, pityingly, that Elissa was beginning to hide her favorite gowns away in trunks pending Ada's arrival.

And then abruptly Ada was upon them.

She came in like a West Indian hurricane, a large commanding woman with small very bright brown eyes, a square jaw, and a hard expression.

"Well, I see you are as always, Elissa—in tears," was her scathing greeting to Elissa. It was her kindest remark of the week.

Everything was wrong about the house. It was badly run—and mortgaged to boot. She promptly cut Cook's wages and Cook quit. She hired someone off one of the ships that docked regularly, a tall German woman who didn't speak English and sometimes misunderstood her instructions but who cooked very well indeed—and bragged she had got her for half the price. She made the apprentices' lives miserable.

Of Dorinda she had no criticism. For Dorinda grimly kept her temper and, for Elissa's sake, continued her mad whirl of endeavor.

"John did a good day's work when he bought that girl's articles," Dorinda heard her tell Elissa. "I'm amazed he had the sense to do it."

"Well, we needed someone," said Elissa humbly. "All the servants had left us—and after we'd paid their passage over, expecting them to stay."

"That's what I mean," said Ada crisply. "John never thought ahead. Indentured servants are the only thing to have in the long run—they can be brought back if they run away."

Dorinda, remembering how Ada had doubled the production on her sugar plantation with bond servants, shivered. From the newest apprentice, Blassing, she had heard terrible stories of life in the West Indies, for he had lived there for a time. He told her of bond servants who, when their seven-year-period of indenture was about to end, were starved, beaten, and even threatened with death if they did not sign articles again. Most did, he told her gloomily, some more than once. Ada, Dorinda surmised, could be such a bondmistress.

And then Ada surprised everyone by bringing in Josiah Carp.

Chapter 21

Dorinda surmised that Josiah Carp, a big swarthy man with an unkempt beard whose articles of indenture Ada had purchased from a drayman, had been brought in not—as Ada maintained—to do the heavy work, but to strike fear into the hearts of the apprentices, who had been complaining about eighteen-hour days and an impossible workload. Dorinda did not like the bold way his hard speculative stare swept over her and his complete lack of expression was unnerving. The apprentices were nervous when he was around and tried not to meet his eyes. *Completely cowed*, she thought, and understood how Ada had done it. She could easily imagine hulking Josiah in the West Indies bringing down a whip on the sunburned sweating backs of Englishmen transported to the islands as bond servants for crime. She knew that if she stayed she was going to have to one day step between Josiah and the apprentices— but she had no intention of staying.

Her last day as a bound girl passed pleasantly enough. The apprentices were glum that she was leaving and she tried to cheer them up, singing as she helped them dip candles and almost caroling her greeting to customers whose entry jangled the little bell above the door of the shop.

She had rather expected to be invited to sup with Elissa on this last day, but when she walked by the dining room Elissa saw her and abruptly ducked her head. That meant no doubt that Ada wouldn't approve, for Dorinda's pleasant custom of dining with her mistress—which she had done ever since John Blore's death—had ceased abruptly with Ada's arrival. Oh, well, nothing could spoil this day for her! Tired as she was, she almost danced out to the kitchen.

She woke the next morning and stretched luxuriously. She was free, free! She could lie late abed, collect her things and the money due her from her days of bondage—surely Ada would not block that! And then she could be off on her own to wander about Philadelphia for the first time as a free woman! Perhaps she would seek employment in some chandler's shop in the city, she thought—just until she could make her plans.

Her winging thoughts were interrupted by a knock on her door. "Oh, Dorinda!" Elissa burst in, wringing her hands. "Hartzel has burned himself with the hot wax!"

"What?" Dorinda sprang from her bed for Hartzel was supposed to take over as manager of the shop today. "Is he badly hurt?"

"I don't know. Blassing just said he'd been burned."

"I'll be right there!" Dorinda forgot all about being a free woman. She told Elissa "not to worry" and dashed down to the shop. As she left she heard Elissa saying to Ada, "You see? I told you Dorinda would take care of it!" And wondered if Elissa really expected Ada to appreciate Dorinda's staying to help out in an emergency.

The emergency turned out to be minor. Hartzel's burn was inconsequential but it had excited Blassing, who had raced to the house seeking Dorinda. Dorinda felt a kind of nostalgia creep over her as she smoothed things over and got the shop on an even keel again.

Now that she was free it was tempting to linger, and she did.

She had meant to wear her best gray bodice and kirtle today, she thought blithely as she strolled home in the summer heat. But in her hurry to get to the shop and aid Hartzel, here she was on her first day as a free woman clad in her old smock and with a mobcap hastily stuck over her touseled hair, for she had dashed off without taking time to comb it. The sun was beating down and it was a relief to turn into the familiar shady street where she had lived these past three years.

But as she reached the big brick house a restlessness to get on with her life seized her. She took the front steps two at a time—and ran full tilt into a tall man just coming out of the front door.

As she catapulted into him, his arms reached out instinctively to prevent her from falling and caught her to him. Dorinda collided with a skirted broadcloth coat that smelled ever so slightly of one of the better blends of Virginia tobacco and through that coat she could feel the strong steady beat of his heart. In that moment the arms about her tightened and she was held for the flutter of an eyelash imprisoned by them.

Then he let her go and she looked up, startled, past a dashingly tied white Steinkirk cravat, into a face darkened by wind and weather but lit by a roguish grin. She guessed instantly that it was a face much given to smiling for there was a gleeful look about the gray eyes that stared down at her from beneath straight dark brows.

"Did I hurt you?" he asked in a pleasant rather deep voice.

Dorinda, who had nearly lost her mobcap in the encounter, felt foolish. "No, of course not," she mumbled in confusion.

The gentleman with the skirted coat kept his grip on her still. "You are sure?" he insisted.

"Certainly I'm sure!" Indignation was beginning to

set in for he still solidly blocked her way. She was also sure they must all be watching from inside and it had not escaped her notice that the arms that had held her were long and strong, or that they belonged to a tall jaunty fellow in his prime with hair of a rich dark brown, almost raven here in the shadow of the trees.

"I do not see how you can tell," he murmured with a grin. "For if you usually come through doors in this fashion, you must be black and blue underneath that flimsy smock from encounters like this!"

Dorinda gave him an affronted look and pushed past. To her relief, no one was watching, the hall was empty. She went directly to the living room. Through the doorway she could see Elissa sitting there in her most subdued costume, a mauve silk elegantly trimmed in point lace. She moved directly to her.

"Who was that man who just went out?" she asked Elissa as she entered.

"Oh, he was just someone asking to see John," said Elissa vaguely. "And when I told him John was dead he looked quite startled and said the matter was of no moment, he would not bother me. *Oh, not that table, Ada!*" Her voice grew piercing as if she were in pain and Dorinda turned to see Ada crouched down at the far end of the room inspecting the underside of a small gateleg table of which Elissa was enormously proud. "Ada is inspecting the furnishings to see what will bring a good price," explained Elissa miserably. "Oh, Dorinda, do explain to Ada that I use that table when I serve tea!"

Why not? She was no longer a bound girl here, no longer subservient. "'Tis true," she told Ada. "That table is always used for the tea—Elissa really does need it."

Ada ignored her. "Rosewood," she muttered in an assessing voice. Then she looked up. "We will have no impertinence here," she said heavily. "You will refer to

Elissa as 'Mistress Blore,' and you will address me as 'Mistress Blore' also."

"I will not be addressing either of you after today," said Dorinda crisply. "My indenture was up yesterday. I'll be leaving."

"No, we can't let you do that," said Ada, frowning again at the rosewood table.

"I'm afraid you don't have a choice," said Dorinda pleasantly. "I've come to tell you that under the terms of my articles, now expired, I'm due a new kirtle and bodice, a new petticoat, money in the amount of—"

"But we need you, you know that," Ada interrupted. She had picked up a silver candlestick and was weighing it in her hand.

"I realize you need me," said Dorinda carefully. "But I need me too and I must get on with my life."

"We will talk about it later—in the fall."

"Are you saying," asked Dorinda slowly, "that you won't live up to the terms of the articles?" She was wondering if she would have to take the matter to court and, if so, how, for she knew nothing of courts or lawyers.

Ada turned to face her then. She seemed to rise and rise until she towered over seventeen-year-old Dorinda. "We'll have no talk of leaving. Tomorrow at your usual hour you will be back in the shop—working." She paused, her small brown eyes glinting. "Josiah will escort you there."

Now Dorinda knew why Josiah had been brought in—not just to keep the apprentices in line, to keep *her* in line.

"But you cannot keep me here," said Dorinda in amazement. "Neither you nor Josiah! This is not some godforsaken sugar plantation—this is Philadelphia! I don't doubt you can have Josiah drag me to the shop but I will tell every customer who comes through the door that I am being held against my will! The law will be on my side!"

"Oh-h-h-h!" wailed Elissa. She was swaying in her chair.

"Don't you dare faint!" cried Dorinda. "Tell this woman she can't do this to me!"

"Oh, Dorinda, do as she says," cried Elissa. "For otherwise she is going to make you marry Josiah!"

"And Josiah," finished Ada triumphantly, "is bound to me for four more years. A wife must stay with her husband and travel where he goes."

Dorinda felt shaken but amused. "But you cannot drag me to the church and make me agree to marry Josiah!"

"You are right," said Ada surprisingly. "But I am impressed with your capacity to work, Dorinda. So of course there is an alternative. If you choose not to continue in the chandler's shop, Josiah will take you to my sugar plantation in Jamaica."

By force! The implication was plain. And since the plan was crude, the methods would be crude. Carried on shipboard unconscious, perhaps to wake in Josiah's arms, a shipboard marriage with the captain's connivance.... A cold wind seemed to have crept in around Dorinda and her imagination plumbed frightening depths. She swung around to Elissa. Elissa could help her, *should* help her! But Elissa's gaze dropped away from hers—that hunted look, those darting eyes that searched about for a means of escape were answer enough. It was almost as if Elissa had screamed out: *If I go against Ada's wishes, she will cast me out!*

Dorinda stared at her former employer for a long time. Contempt and pity mingled in that look. But fear had made her feel cold and alert—the alertness of a rabbit when the hawk is near. This was no time to rage and scream and rail at fate—that would only get her tossed into Josiah's bed! The moment for subtlety was at hand.

She let her shoulders slump and turned to Ada. "I would far rather continue in my present employment than have Josiah forced upon me," she said dryly. "I will go on with my work as usual."

Elissa's head came up. She had expected a wild scene and was agape at such a mild response from spirited Dorinda. But Ada, who was used to bending others to her will, only squared her heavy shoulders and laughed. "I knew you would see reason," she said. "Tomorrow Mr. Hopkins will bring over new articles of indenture and you will sign them."

Just like those unfortunate bond servants in the West Indies. Ada had learned her lessons well!

Dorinda nodded meekly. She turned again to Elissa. "I will go up and straighten up the bedrooms now," she said in what she hoped was a defeated voice.

"But your dinner!" cried Elissa tearfully. "You left without breakfast!"

Dorinda marveled. Having no regard for Dorinda's future, Elissa was still tearfully concerned about her dinner.

"I'm not hungry," she said shortly.

"You see?" she heard Ada crowing as she left the room. "What did I tell you? It was no trouble at all! Oh, *do* stop crying, Elissa!"

And from Elissa a fresh burst of tears.

Dorinda went up the familiar stairway with her heart pounding. In the front hall she could see Josiah, smirking, lounging against the front door—guarding it! Had she headed for the kitchen he would undoubtedly have followed her there to prevent her running out the back way. And he was a powerful man—he would enjoy wrestling her to the ground. Her scalp prickled slightly.

When she reached the second floor she went directly to Elissa's front bedroom and quietly latched the door behind her. For a moment she leaned against that door and closed her eyes and shook. Then some inner strength on which she could always count gave her courage. She would escape them, but she would not leave here attired in a smock! They did not choose to pay her what was due—very well, she would collect it herself! With interest!

She plunged toward the big clothes press that held Elissa's best garments. Much had been removed and hidden away but Elissa had left out one glorious gown for great occasions. The next few moments were a flurry of feverish activity. Dorinda stripped off all her clothing and dressed from the skin out in Elissa's clothes—too loose at the waist for all Elissa's lacing and too tight at the bust but, thank heaven, they were the same height! She slipped on the delicate lawn and lace chemise with its spill of fragile lace at the cuffs, slid—for the first time ever—silk stockings over her elegant legs, and ribboned garters. She fastened around her waist the marvelous blue-green petticoat so encrusted with glittering silver embroidery that it looked almost to be made of repoussé silver. Next came the fragile blue-green silk gown that Elissa had once remarked exactly matched Dorinda's eyes. Dorinda had always yearned just to try it on—now she would wear it! Low cut and elegant, it was Elissa's newest gown made to mimic a Paris fashion doll—and now that Ada had taken over, it would probably be her last. She felt a momentary pang at the thought of Elissa's wail at the loss of her gown—and then hardened her heart. Three years was a long time to work for no more than food and lodging and the cheap coarse clothes on one's back! Something was owing for that—and besides she had done the work of three people here! If Elissa had begged her to stay and help out, she might have done so, but threatened by Ada—never!

Swiftly she swept her hair up into the most stylish coiffure she could concoct on a moment's notice—and told herself it was a pity she couldn't wear Elissa's slippers, but they were two sizes too large and they threatened to slip off her feet. Oh, well, she would just have to wear her old worn slippers!

Buoyed up by excitement, she stuck her head out the

open window. It seemed a perilously long drop from the second floor to the hard brick sidewalk below, but she had to chance it.

Fortunately there was no traffic on the pleasant tree-shaded street at the moment. In the summer heat that had settled like a blanket over everything, everyone was indoors having dinner. Not till later would they come out to stroll. Dorinda fervently thanked the builders that there were no porches for people to sit on nearby, only steps running up to the front doors.

She had to take a chance that no one was in John Blore's study at this moment for it was the room directly under this one. The "drawing room," as Elissa persisted on calling it, was on the other side of the front hall. And Josiah would wait for her to come down, he would not leave his post at the solid front door.

Dorinda jerked the bedcovers and pillows from the bed and tossed them to the street below—and then the blankets which were stored in the top of the big press. After that she tugged the feather mattress from the bed and somehow squeezed it through the window.

She threw her silk-stockinged legs over the sill and for a moment quailed. That pile of bedclothes, even with the addition of the feather mattress and pillows, seemed inadequate.

She thought of Josiah . . . waiting. Waiting to drag her to his bed and clutch her shrinking flesh to his. It was enough.

Carefully Dorinda eased her body over and held onto the sill until she was suspended from it full length. Then she gave herself a push outward from the brick wall with her feet as she let go.

She landed rolling and for a moment thought she had broken all her bones. She seemed to be in the midst of a snowstorm. Then she realized that she was still intact, although the shock of her landing still echoed through her body. The snowstorm was the down from the feather mattress which had burst, loosing a cloud of white goose feathers into the air.

Choking, fighting her way clear of the feathers, Dorinda ran on her soft slippers down the street. She never stopped running all the way to the docks.

She knew she had very little time until they discovered her absence and began to look for her. God willing, there would be a ship about to sail.

She found one: the *Roving Gull*. To her surprise, she made it aboard without difficulty. Passengers were crowding aboard, tearful farewells were being said, husbands clasped wives and promised to be home soon, mothers clasped daughters and made them promise to write, people swirled about her. Dorinda melted in among them, mingling with the throng. Not wearing traveling clothes, not carrying so much as a small reticule, she was obviously seeing somebody off. Indeed in the tumult of those about to sail and trying to get their boxes stowed on board, little attention was paid to her. She moved about wondering where she could hide, and suddenly a solution to that problem was presented to her.

The captain came out of his cabin and through the open door behind him Dorinda could see a large sea chest. It stood carelessly open and the back of the lid was presented to her view. It was large enough to hold a person. A moment later the captain dashed past her, shouting at a child who, unattended, was attempting to climb the rigging. Dorinda took advantage of the excitement with everybody looking up at the child, to dart inside and close the door behind her.

It could not be more than an hour, she told herself, before they would sail. They would clear away the well-wishers, they would check out the passenger list—and they must not find her. Biting her soft underlip, Dorinda considered the sea chest. Somehow close up it did not look to be the haven it had seemed from outside. It was filled with a jumble of clothing. She was going to be very cramped in there. She guessed—and rightly—that the captain would probably not be coming back into his cabin until the ship was actually underway. That gave her time. She walked restlessly about, looking at all the nautical things that occupied this masculine domain. The captain, she told herself nervously, was old enough to be her grandfather but he had a stern face.

How would he feel about a stowaway? If he found her before he was well away from land, he might put her ashore—and that would bring a terrible retribution from Ada. Or he might bring her back in irons on his return voyage and turn her over to the authorities. That would be just as bad for Ada would manage to claim her.

Of a sudden the ship gave a great lurch. There was a creaking and groaning and a loud crack as the white sails billowed out to take the wind.

A sense of relief flooded Dorinda. She had surmounted the first hurdle! The ship was underway!

Now she must deal with the captain. Which brought her thoughtful gaze back to the open sea chest.

Now that she had had time to think about it, the sea chest did not seem such a good idea. It was undignified at best. She wished she had had time to search the ship for a really safe place to hide, but she did not know where the ship was going (she had been afraid to ask on deck) or how long the voyage would take. No matter where she hid, she would eventually be discovered for she had brought neither water nor provisions and thirst would drive her out in time.

While she was debating this with herself there was a step outside. That decided her. Without hesitation Dorinda plunged for the sea chest, quickly lifted up the top layer of shirts and smallclothes and jumped inside, pulling the garments down over her head. She only hoped the whole did not bulk up sufficiently high to attract attention.

A measured step came into the cabin. From her crouched position stuffed in among his undergarments, Dorinda could not see the captain but she identified him by his walk. It was not the walk of an old man even though his weathered face had identified him as having been on this earth for a long time. She had heard his name mentioned in the shop and knew him to be a widower of impeccable reputation. In a way that frightened her. A man of iron-clad rectitude would not be susceptible to a stowaway's breathless story. He would realize that her handsome clothes were stolen—and condemn her for it. Inexorably he would—take her back? Send her back? Turn her over to the law somewhere else? What happened to stowaways? Dorinda had never known their fate. Hearing him pace about the cabin, she quaked.

Suddenly the toe of a boot connected with the lid of the sea chest and it was slammed down over her. Dorinda, her nerves on edge, almost screamed. She waited a moment in the stuffy darkness, crammed in among the shirts and smallclothes, and then very gently tried to open the lid a crack. It did not budge. The clasp must have caught when the lid was slammed down.

Panic overcame Dorinda. She would suffocate in here! Suppose the captain went out and spent many hours on deck? He would find a dead woman when he opened his sea chest!

"Help!" she screamed, her voice incoherent as she fought the shirts away from her mouth. She began to beat lustily against the lid and to wail at the top of her voice.

It was a pity Dorinda could not have seen the captain's face just then. It was the very picture of amaze as he turned to find his sea chest speaking to him and—as Dorinda threw her body this way and that against the side, hoping to overturn the chest—bouncing a little on the clean-scoured floorboards.

Captain Winslow was a man of action. Action had been his life. He could not quite understand the muffled wails that were coming from the chest, but it sounded like caterwauling. In his lifetime he had made enemies. It occurred to him that someone might have slipped a wildcat into his sea chest and he silently padded over to a small locked wall cupboard, took out a key and unlocked it. From the cupboard he extracted a large pistol and cocked it.

The caterwauling continued. Whatever it was in there, it resented his having slammed down the lid. He lifted the pistol, having in mind to put a ball through the side of the sea chest and then paused. This was a good sea chest and he'd hate to ruin it. Besides, a shot would panic the passengers.

Very cautiously, holding the pistol at the ready, he threw open the lid.

What rose up from the chest widened his blue eyes even farther. Gradually emerging from an avalanche of shirts and neckpieces and smallclothes was a fashionably coiffed young lady dressed in elegant clothes. Her face was very white and for a moment he thought this aqua and silver apparition was going to faint and disappear once again into the trunk. The capricious thought occurred to him that if she did and he closed the lid over her, she might be gone like a puff of smoke when he opened it again. But basically the captain was a hard-headed man who did not believe in magic or goblins or genies—sea serpents, yes, and possibly mermaids. But not in sea chests! He reached out and seized Dorinda's hand in a firm grip and she stepped out of the chest, almost tripping herself up in the sleeve of his best coat, which had been crushed beneath her feet at the bottom of the sea chest.

"Where did you come from?" he demanded bluntly of this vision.

"Philadelphia," said Dorinda in a shaky voice.

"And you're going right back there! I'll have no

runaway baggage stow away aboard my ship—I'll have ye rowed back!"

"Wait—oh, please wait." Dorinda's hand on his sleeve detained him. "Hear my story first," she pleaded.

A ruse perhaps to allow the ship to sail too far away for her to be returned, he thought. But the wench looked so frightened and he judged her to be still in her teens. Wealthy, to judge by her clothes. What could have driven her to such a pass? Was she running away from a betrothed? A strict guardian?

"Be quick about it," he said brusquely and sat down, letting Dorinda stand.

If ever she was to be persuasive in her life, now was the time. Dorinda told him the whole story, words tripping over each other. She left nothing out. She told him about John Blore and Elissa and Ada. And about Josiah—oh, especially about Josiah. And what would happen to her if she were to be returned to Philadelphia.

Captain Winslow listened thoughtfully, his weathered face almost without expression. He had listened so to sea tales, to patent lies, and sometimes—as now—to the unvarnished truth. Dorinda began to fear that he had but half heard her, that he was paying no attention to what she said. Silent now, she waited for his answer.

It was a while in coming—and even when it came it was not conclusive. "We'll have a bite of supper," he said, "while I think over what you have told me."

"Where is the ship bound?" she asked timidly.

He shot her a wry look. "You mean you did not inquire?"

"I was afraid to," admitted Dorinda. "And besides, I was in a tearing hurry."

To her surprise, he laughed. "Youth," he murmured. "There's nothing like it! The *Running Gull* is bound for Williamsburg, little wench."

Williamsburg! She could not believe it. The only other town she knew on this whole continent—and the ship was going there!

"And what would ye plan to do in Williamsburg, little wench, if ye should get there?" the captain shot at her as they shared supper in his cabin. "Don't you realize that a woman as determined as you describe this Ada to be will advertise for you? She will charge that you stole those clothes—and the advertisement will describe the very gown you are wearing?"

"Yes, she probably will. I have been thinking of that," said Dorinda soberly. "And I have decided that the only way to avoid having the gown recognized in that case is to be above suspicion."

He cocked an eye at her. "Above suspicion?"

She had decided more than that. The world was never going to view *her* as a homeless serving girl again! She would assume the title once held by her tragic but glamorous grandmother, Rinda of the flame-red hair. She looked up and met Captain Winslow's gaze calmly. "I intend to announce myself to be the Countess of Ravensay."

Astonishment warred with amusement in the weathered face that studied her. "And did you pick that title out of a hat?" he wondered.

"Oh, I came by it honestly enough." And she outlined for him her tenuous claim to the title.

When she had done, he shook his head and sighed. "I have known some wild things to happen as I've sailed the seas," he admitted. "But nothing so harebrained as this scheme of yours to pose as a countess has ever come my way. I wish ye luck, little wench. Faith, ye'll need it!"

"Then you'll—you'll let me stay aboard?"

He gave a short barking laugh. "Oh, I've no intention of putting ye ashore—nor of making ye swim back. But the ship's full to capacity." He ruminated a minute. "You can sleep here in my cabin." At her startled look, he raised a dignified hand. "On a pile of blankets there in that corner. Your bones are younger than mine—I need the bunk! And you can sleep sound for I'm no despoiler of untried wenches, and that I take you to be." Dorinda's eyes dropped in embarrassment before his keen look and he sighed. "The life you'll go into with your adventuring ways will deflower you soon enough, I've no doubt, but I'll not be the one to do it. For your own protection, I recommend that you stay inside the cabin during the voyage. Don't mingle with the passengers—then there won't be those in Williamsburg to remember that you have just come from Philadelphia, in case this Ada does advertise for you—for she may offer a reward and there are always those who are eager for easy money. You can take your meals here and walk about on deck by night after most of the passengers have gone to bed. Your name will not appear on the list of passengers, indeed the owners of this vessel need not know ye were ever aboard and, if aught is said, why then I but carried a wench along in my cabin to pleasure me during the voyage." A sardonic grin lit his weathered features. "Faith, 'twill enliven my reputation at every port of call, for I'm thought to be well past it!"

Shakily, Dorinda realized how very lucky she was. For this was a small tight coastwise vessel and a captain was in complete charge of his ship. It could have been a very different story.

He was looking at her meditatively. "Is there anything you need?"

"Yes," said Dorinda instantly. "You can give me a needle and thread for I wish to adjust this bodice so that I can breathe!"

Captain Winslow gave his stowaway an admiring look. He had half expected her to ask him for money—and the truth was he had none. He had been set upon and robbed in an alley shortly before coming aboard. He got her the needle and thread and went out on deck. When he came back Dorinda's bodice fitted her supple figure superbly. She twirled before him and then, with his comb, seated before a tiny mirror, she did miraculous things with her hair. He watched her, amazed.

"You can set yourself up as a hairdresser in Williamsburg," he remarked at last.

"Yes." Dorinda smiled. "Perhaps I will do that—although I do think I know more about candlemaking!"

Dinner brought an astonished cabin boy whose mouth fell agape at the sight of the captain dining in his cabin with an elegant young lady—but breakfast, with that same young lady looking refreshed and dewy-eyed, made him more round-eyed still.

"Now he'll trot down to the galley to carry tales to Cook of the captain's young mistress," Captain Winslow chuckled after the boy had departed. "I wonder if Cook will believe him. . . ."

Although the voyage was short, Dorinda caught up on her rest, sleeping by day. The food was good. And by night she took strolls along the deck, steering away with head ducked down from any night-strolling passenger and passing the ship's watch like a shadow. She was aware that the crew members watched her curiously—sometimes she saw disbelief mirrored in their eyes.

"I thought the captain was nearing his dotage and now he's got himself this young sprig of muslin!" she heard one burly sailor mutter to another as she passed. Dorinda hid a smile. Let the crew think what they would! Not for worlds would she have robbed Captain Winslow of his triumph!

Dorinda had not realized how tired out she was from her exertions in Philadelphia, but this restful voyage gave her time to scheme and dream. Staring at her glittering reflection in the captain's tiny mirror, she told herself that no one would recognize in this splendid bird of paradise she had become the shy little wren of a serving girl who had blacked boots at the White Hart! Those magic words, "Countess of Ravensay," would open doors that had been closed to her. She thought of all those windows she had passed in Williamsburg, gazing wistfully in at satin-clad dancers bathed in candlelight—now *she* could go to those balls and dance the night away! How she would live, how she would support herself, all seemed beautifully unreal during the voyage. Ah, it would be a romantic venture and it would have a happy ending! She was young, she was strong, perhaps she would set herself up as a candle-maker! Overhead the wind sang in the rigging and Dorinda's heart leaped ahead on that wind. She had left Philadelphia and her shabby life there far behind her—she could hardly wait to arrive in Williamsburg!

Reality did not crowd in upon her until it was time to leave the ship. It had all seemed a joyous venture till then. They had reached their journey's end in flawless weather. A fleecing of white clouds raced across the azure summer sky and somewhere in the green that lay just ahead upriver was Williamsburg.

In his cabin Captain Winslow bade Dorinda a formal farewell, resisting the urge to blow his nose, for in the course of this brief voyage he had grown fond of the little wench and he would miss her. "Here," he said abruptly, reaching into his pocket and dropping a pair of gold coins into her hand. They were his good-luck pieces that he had kept in his sea chest for thirty years but she need not know that. "This will help keep you while you decide what to do."

Dorinda swallowed as she looked down at the coins. She had already heard the story of how he had been robbed just before boarding and knew that these coins must mean something to him. "It is very kind of you, sir," she said huskily. "Some day I will repay you."

"No need for that," he said in a gruff voice.

And suddenly she threw her arms around him and pressed a swift breathless kiss on his weathered cheek. Then her blue-green skirts were swishing away from him and he followed her through the door.

In silence he watched her go, walking jauntily along the deck with the wind blowing her bright hair. In a moment she would be over the rail and down the ship's ladder into the waiting longboat. Suddenly it came to him why she appealed to him so much. In his youth he had known such a girl. She hadn't looked like this girl, but they had shared the same reckless view of the world. Her name had been Trinity Blake and she had been far above him, a captain's daughter when he was but a lowly cabin boy. He had loved her with all the passion of youth. The moments they had shared when Trinity had been able to steal down to the ship from her big house on the hill had been some of the best in his life. He remembered—and it wrenched him still— how Trinity had wept hot tears when she told him her father had betrothed her to another sea captain's son. He had urged her to run away with him then, but she had not. She had been taken with a sudden fever and while she was confined to her bed his ship had sailed and he with it. While he was gone on his long voyage she had married the other man, borne him a son and died of it. Dear lost Trinity, the mosses long had grown on the handsome stone that had been raised above her. But always, always he had carried her in his heart.

Belatedly he realized how strikingly like his lost Trinity this girl was—gallant, unafraid.

Of a sudden he was galvanized into action. He hurried forward, pushed aside the sailor who was eagerly offering to help Dorinda over the side and lifted her up himself.

"Countess," he said with a grave smile as her hands clasped the rope, preparatory to descent.

Dorinda looked up and gave him a flashing smile. Somehow that single word, that acceptance that she could indeed be a countess, had given her courage.

"Captain Winslow," she murmured. "I will never forget you."

A sailor reported it later in the crew's mess, shaking his head in wonder. "'I'll ne'er forget ye' was what she said to him as he set her over the side. And he called her 'Countess!' "

There was a rumble of amaze and all agreed over their pints of ale that old dogs were sly dogs and ye never knew what a man might do when he'd a mind to! And all agreed that their captain walked with more elasticity in his rolling stride these days. It amused Captain Winslow and his step was the firmer for the respectful awe he saw in their eyes.

That buoyancy carried him all the way to Charles Town—his next port of call, for he had stopped by Virginia only to disgorge passengers; Carolina was his real destination, and he would return from there direct to Philadelphia.

He supposed he would never see her again and the thought made him sigh, for the girl's wild heart had reached him and it would have been nice to have learned what happened to her.

Some are born to lie at ease beneath the summer sun,
Some are born to find each day their work is never done,
Some are born to virtue, some are born to sin,
And some are born to overturn the very world they're in!

BOOK V

The Dangerous Deception

Would ye seek a lover, lass? Fall starry-eyed
   upon the grass?
Old and rich? Or young and strong? What then
   would ye choose?
Daughter of adversity, burdened still with
   chastity,
Wild of heart, you're born to love—and surely
   born to lose!

PART ONE

The Man from Philadelphia

Chapter 22

Dorinda had not been in Williamsburg five minutes
before she realized that what had seemed a plan of last
resort aboard ship was in reality no plan at all. If
nothing else turned up, she had planned to become a
roving chandler, drifting from plantation to plantation
carrying on a packhorse a lot of jangling metal molds
that would efficiently make up her customers' accumu-
lated wax and tallow into candles. Even if she received
her pay not in coin but in wax, she had reasoned she
could make the wax up into candles and sell them door
to door in town. Now the patent folly of that reasoning
became apparent. She had not the money to buy a
riding horse, much less a packhorse—even the expense
of metal candle molds to start up was beyond her! The
two gold coins Captain Winslow had given her would
buy her temporary accommodations at an inn but after
that she would be on her own. And penniless.

Suddenly the joy went out of strolling, bravely gowned,
down familiar streets lined with square gambrel-roofed
or steeply roofed rectangular frame houses with their
brick chimneys and outside shutters, alternating with
small but handsome brick houses whose decorous in-

310

side shutters showed through small neat panes. No longer did she feel so free and excited as she had when she had stepped on shore. Still it was pleasant to realize that passing gentlemen were bestowing upon her admiring glances and that one had even stopped to stare and nudge his companion. And after all, who among them would ever recognize in the glittering aristocrat she had become the tired thin coltish little slavey who had blacked boots and filled endless tankards at the White Hart?

Which brought up another problem that she had not envisioned aboard the *Running Gull.* She had not even a change of clothing—and how was she to apply for a job looking like this? Any chandler would indeed rush forward to serve her, but he would look askance at a woman so fabulously gowned importuning him for employment in his shop. She would be turned down— uneasily, for no one wanted to hire a runaway and that was what they would guess her to be. And then if Ada advertised for her and offered a reward, she would be remembered. . . .

Faced with this new and unforeseen problem, Dorinda's walk slowed. Best, she decided, to stop in at a coffee-house and sit a few minutes and think.

The place she chose was crowded at this time of day. As she came through the door she was nearly crushed between two fat ladies who flew at each other, one crying out joyfully, "But I thought you were not aboard the *London Queen,* Emma! How did I miss you?" Many people there were discussing the voyage of the *London Queen,* which had arrived from London but yesterday after a rough passage with many gales. "Nearly capsized twice!" a large red-faced man in stained velvet kept shouting. "Thought we were sped for certain! Women praying, children crying, torn sheets flapping above us—!" His voice was lost in the din.

Dorinda paused a moment to get her bearings and assess the throng, and a smirking serving maid carrying a tray of tankards nearly plummeted into her droning, "Let me pass, good sirs, let me pass."

Over in a corner of the low-ceilinged room a group of young men were paying off wagers and wrangling over the results of a horse race held a short time before. Above the babble a shrill voice could be heard lauding a play that had recently been held yet villifying one of the actors, whose trousers were so tight they had actually burst on the stage "woefully embarrassing poor Molly." Dorinda thought it might have embarrassed the actor even more and hid a smile. Williamsburg might not be so lax as London, she thought, but it was certainly a lot less buttoned down than Philadelphia where theatres were forbidden and young men spent their time in debating societies instead of wagering on the endless horse races that seemed to be held impromptu wherever Virginians met.

She had some difficulty working her way through the throng but eventually she found a seat between two animated groups, talking loudly to make themselves heard over the noise. It took her a long time to get served in this crush and that gave her leisure to listen idly to the conversations flying back and forth about her.

To her right two lanky fellows in buckskins, who grinned widely when she came in and kept watching her out of the corners of their eyes, were having an animated discussion about a daring local highwayman they called "The Blade."

"Robs only the best people," one drawled with an engaging look at Dorinda. "Stole the governor's horse and gold. Next he ambushed the magistrate just outside of town and robbed him." He laughed. "Faith, he's a bold rogue!"

"Aye," agreed his comrade, draining his pewter tankard and wiping his lips on the back of a buckskin sleeve. "And took Burgess Peter Bellamy's horse and picked his pockets clean only last week, I hear—and that was near town too! The cheek of the fellow!"

"Who're ye talking about? The Blade?" An old gentleman in a grizzle wig sitting nearby inclined his ear toward the pair as if he were hard of hearing and put aside his clay pipe. "Better ye should be shaking your heads over such a rogue instead of admiring him as ye do, for he'll be dangling from a rope soon enough!"

Dorinda turned away from this gloomy prediction as her coffee arrived and—to avoid the buckskinned pair's too obvious interest—turned her attention to the satin-clad couple on her left.

"Poor Mr. Merryvale—I shall miss him," the woman, of middle age and wearing a profusion of jet jewelry, was saying pensively. "And to die leaving behind neither chick nor child!" She shook her head so that her graying curls bounced.

"Joshua Merryvale was happy enough in his bachelorhood," pointed out her companion, a dignified man of indeterminate years. As he spoke he moved ever so slightly so that he could view Dorinda out of the corner of his eye. "He told me that Merryvale Plantation was all that mattered to him and he had no wish to marry. He never spoke of any relatives in England so I assumed he had none."

Dorinda, listening absently, was watching the graying woman's hairdo come perilously near to falling down every time she shook her head.

"But to leave such a fine house and all that land and have no one to leave it to—it's regrettable, I tell you!"

Dorinda was drinking it all in along with her coffee. But her blue-green eyes kept roving the room for familiar faces—and she was relieved when she found none. Plainly there had been an enormous influx of new people into Williamsburg during the three years she had been gone for there seemed to be not a face she knew in all this crowd.

She got up thoughtfully, with nothing decided. It was

too hard to think in all that stifling din, she told herself, and left, wondering what her next move should be.

She strolled out into the hot sunlight and found her feet almost of their own will drawn irresistibly down Duke of Gloucester Street, walking east toward the White Hart, where Lady Soft Paws might be luxuriously sunning herself in the innyard at this time of day— although perhaps in this heat she had sought more shade and might be curled up somewhere. *On the back stairs,* she could hear Jeddie say resignedly, *where everyone would have a good chance to trip over her*! Dear Lady Soft Paws. So much time had passed, would the cat even remember her? Jeddie had always maintained that cats had no proper memory—that they were like men, they took your favors and forgot you, but Dorinda knew in her heart that this was not the case. Lady Soft Paws would not forget her, just as *she* would never forget her small furry friend.

It could do no harm to take a look at the inn, she told herself as she approached the familiar building, even though warning bells were clanging in her head. Of course she would not risk going inside, for someone there might recognize her, but she might at least catch a glimpse of Lady Soft Paws, or perhaps see Jeddie's familiar form walking by one of the windows.

There seemed to be no one about except for some little boys playing noisily in the street. It seemed so safe. What could be the harm? A glimpse and then turn back the way she had come....Irresistibly drawn, she moved closer until the familiar green door lay dead ahead.

The door opened abruptly and two gentlemen came out. Both were tall. The one on the left had a head of thick dark hair and a rather formidable look to him. He walked with a swing, an easy grace that came of great strength. He wore a maroon coat with gold buttons and a dashingly tied white Steinkirk cravat.

Dorinda froze. It was the man she had crashed into returning home on her last day in Philadelphia—the one who had come to the house inquiring about John Blore only to learn he was dead. She could only hope that he would not recognize her.

And beside him, swaggering along in fashionable rose damask with a half-contemptuous smile on his dissolute face, was Bainter Ramsay!

Dorinda stood rooted to the ground of the innyard. Like a hare when the hunter is near, she did not move a muscle. They were talking and laughing—perhaps if she stood very still they would pass on by, taking no more notice of her than if she had been a tree or a parked cart.

But even that faint hope was abruptly dashed. From the pack of clamoring children swirling about in the street, two little boys detached themselves and ran toward her rolling a cart wheel. Just as the pair of strolling gentlemen came abreast of Dorinda the cart wheel wavered on the uneven ground and veered toward her. She took a hasty step to avoid it—and once again collided with the man from Philadelphia.

And just as in Philadelphia, his strong arm reached out to catch her. But it was a moment too late because as she jumped aside her ankle turned under her. She gave a little exclamation as pain shot through it and grasped wildly at his broadcloth coat as she fell.

His reflexes were excellent for he had scooped her up almost before she struck the ground. Dorinda, looking up, saw those same level gray eyes she had seen before in Philadelphia—only this time they were grave and had lost their merriment.

"Are you all right, mistress?" he demanded.

"I—I think so," she gasped, unwilling until the pain had subsided to give up her grip on the broadcloth of his coat.

At least Bainter did not recognize her! She could not tell if the man from Philadelphia did or not. His gray eyes were unreadable and he was staring squarely at her while Bainter's gaze was merely pleasantly admiring.

"You are very pale," observed the stranger in his rich voice.

"My—my ankle," she admitted faintly. "I seem to have turned it."

"Perhaps you should come into the inn with us and have a glass of malmsey to restore you?"

Bainter reached out to take her other arm. "An excellent thought."

"But gentlemen," protested Dorinda, mindful suddenly of the proprieties that went with her newly aristocratic appearance. "I do not know you. I—"

"That is easy remedied," said the man from Philadelphia. "Allow me to present myself. I am Tarn Jenner and this gentleman with me is Bainter Ramsay."

All thought of passing herself off as a countess fled before his cool gaze. "I am Dorinda Mer—" she began before she thought. She had almost said "Meredith" but she changed it quickly to the first name that began with "Mer" that came into her head, the name of the planter she had just heard had died. "Dorinda Merryvale," she said nervously.

"Mistress Merryvale, your servant." He bowed crisply, but the grip he had on her arm would be hard to shake off. "And now to your restoration, for we cannot let you stand out here and possibly collapse in the street." His hand beneath her elbow lifted her up as well as urged her to proceed. "Lift up, Bainter," he added jovially. "We'll speed Mistress Merryvale into the inn without her feet touching the ground!"

Thus lifted up and irresistibly propelled forward between the two men she felt least prepared to meet at this moment, Dorinda's wits were working wildly. She was swished into the inn past Buxton's wife who, she saw, had grown no more charming with the passing years, but who scarcely looked at her as she went swiftly by.

Wine was promptly ordered and Dorinda stole a look at Bainter. He looked just the same, his handsome dissolute face still tugged at her heartstrings, she still yearned to kiss that slightly cruel mouth.

But the man from Philadelphia was more of a problem. "Have I not seen you somewhere before?" he wondered. "Faith, you have a familiar look to you, you do!"

"Perhaps in London?" suggested Dorinda, trying to sound casual. At least she could speak intelligently of London, having spent her early years there. "I spent some time there before I embarked."

"You are fresh from England then?" he asked quickly. Dorinda nodded.

"Strange," he murmured. "I am sure we have met somewhere before."

Dorinda's dainty chin went up. "We have never met," she said firmly and turned to Bainter Ramsay. Desperation at that moment furnished her with a desperate plan. "I am in the most terrible trouble," she said appealingly. "I really do not know where to turn."

"You must tell us about it," said Tarn Jenner.

She flashed an uneasy look at him and saw that he was bending forward intently. She took a deep breath. Now was the time to throw out the dice!

"I am Joshua Merryvale's niece," she said, drawing on the gossip she had heard at the coffeehouse today. "I arrived but yesterday on the *London Queen*. I was eager to get on to my uncle's plantation so I hired a cart and driver to take me there along with my luggage. It was rather late when we got started and the cart broke down and the moon came up. And we had gone but a few miles when suddenly a man on horseback came out of nowhere and held us up at gunpoint. He ordered me down off the cart and made the driver throw down my luggage. And then he told the driver to go with all speed back to Williamsburg or he would shoot him dead on the spot. The driver near overturned the cart wheeling the horses around and taking off. I tried to leap into the cart but the highwayman detained me. He forced me to open my luggage there on the road and to go through it and hand to him all my best petticoats—and they were *very* valuable."

There was a strangled sound from one of the gentlemen. At the moment she didn't know which. Both were looking at her in fascination.

"It would seem you have encountered 'The Blade,'" murmured Bainter.

And the man from Philadelphia added imperturbably, "Tell us, what did he look like, for no one hereabouts can seem to give a decent description of the fellow?"

"Oh, he was—he was very large and very fierce," said Dorinda. "I was *terrified* of him. He threatened to search me unless I gave him all my money and I promptly did and he rode away with my money and my petticoats—" her voice rose to a small wail—"leaving me alone by night in that godforsaken spot!"

"The devil take the fellow!" cried Bainter. "No gentleman would have done a thing like that!" His voice rang with bluster.

"Well, after all The Blade is a highwayman—not a gentleman," pointed out Tarn Jenner. There was a slight note of amusement in his voice but his face was suitably grave. "Do not tell me you were forced to walk all the way back to Williamsburg?"

"I was," sighed Dorinda. "And I was so tired, being so recently off a ship that had nearly battered us all to death with its rough passage, and so terrified of the dark in that strange place, that I hid beneath some overhanging branches until the sun was well up and then walked back to town. And the first thing I heard when I reached here, penniless and stripped of all my valuables, was that my uncle was dead." She was so excited now by her own fabrication that she looked about to burst into tears.

"There, there," said Bainter masterfully and patted

her hand. "But your boxes left upon the road—we must send for them!"

" 'Twould be no use," said Tarn. "The Blade will have spirited them away by now. Ah, here is our wine. This should restore you." Coolly he poured her a glass.

Dorinda felt she should pile agony on agony. "And as if all that were not enough, I have ruined my shoes on that bad road," she cried, aggrieved. At least that would explain the disreputable state of her footwear!

"Do you have relatives in England, Mistress Merryvale, who could be acquainted of your plight?" asked Bainter, quickly solicitous.

Ah, it was a very different thing to be a lady without funds than a slavey without funds! thought Dorinda with sudden spite. She wondered abruptly if Bainter would offer her a new petticoat this time. . . . If only he did not look so golden, sitting there! She took a quick sip of wine. She had left Williamsburg with an over-powering desire to straighten this man out and now that she was back and he was looking at her with admiration and respect in his tawny eyes, she felt an overwhelming sense of power.

"No, Uncle Joshua was my only living relative," she said. "And now I do not know what to do. I am without a roof for my head, without funds, without friends, I find myself in a strange land—and my only living relative is dead."

"The first leg of your problem is easily solved," smiled Tarn Jenner. "I'll take a room for you here at the inn."

"No good," objected Bainter. "I heard Innkeeper Buxton telling someone an hour ago that he was filled up."

"Ah, then you can have my room," smiled Tarn. "And I'll sleep down here in the common room along with all those other gentlemen who can't find rooms."

Bainter brushed that aside. "I've a better solution," he said, eyeing Tarn. "Mistress Merryvale will want to see her uncle's estate—after all, she was on her way there when this Blade fellow interrupted her travels. And since my plantation of Haverleigh is only slightly downriver from Merryvale Manor, and since I am journeying back there this afternoon, she will be my guest at Haverleigh!"

"You are too kind," protested Dorinda, almost carried away by this longed for invitation. "But really I cannot impose on you—"

"Indeed he is *entirely* too kind," agreed the man from Philadelphia on a note of irony. "And of course you cannot accept his kind invitation because your reputation would suffer if you were to journey alone to a bachelor establishment and take up residence there. You'd do better to take up my offer." He gave Bainter a bland smile.

"Perhaps you did not know, Jenner," laughed Bainter. "But the Riddles, brother and sister—after that disastrous fire at their plantation that near took their lives— are staying at Haverleigh while their house is repaired. They came into town with me and Mistress Riddle will provide excellent chaperonage not only at Haverleigh but on the way there."

"No, it would seem you forgot to apprise me of that," said Tarn Jenner carelessly. The ghost of a frown played for a moment between his straight dark brows. "But we are both forgetting Mistress Merryvale's injury. She will doubtless wish to repair herself to a doctor who will of course advise against a jolting trip upriver."

"We'll go by boat," countered Bainter. "Only way to travel these days. By the river. Faster, smoother. You can prop up your ankle on a pillow as we travel."

She was going to Haverleigh as Bainter's guest! Going chaperoned like a lady! The very thought almost overcame Dorinda.

"I—I do believe my ankle is a bit better," she said cautiously. "I believe I could stand on it now."

Tarn Jenner was looking at her with a gleam of

amusement in his gray eyes. "But you will be without luggage," he murmured. "Surely you would prefer to stay in Williamsburg overnight and buy some necessaries at the shops tomorrow? And for that, my offer of a room here at the inn is still open."

"Oh, but I have no money to buy anything," protested Dorinda.

"That will not be a problem. I could advance you money for what you may need."

Dorinda hesitated. There were many things she would need if she were to carry out this charade—including a new pair of shoes to replace her worn ones!

"Nonsense," objected Bainter heartily. "As her neighbor now that she will no doubt become the new owner of Merryvale Manor, I insist on doing her this small service. Mistress Merryvale can return at her leisure to purchase anything she needs."

"But all purposes can be served at once," pointed out the imperturbable gentleman from Philadelphia. "Mistress Riddle and Mistress Merryvale are welcome to share my room between them this night. You and Riddle and I can lounge down here in the common room. And tomorrow, if her ankle is up to it, Mistress Merryvale can have at the shops to replace her missing wardrobe."

"Oh, that would be wonderful!" cried Dorinda, excited at the prospect of having the best of both worlds. "But of course—" she hesitated and cast a look of sweet confusion at Bainter—"if you do not think so—?"

"Nonsense, of course he does," said Tarn Jenner blithely. "Do you not, Ramsay?" Without waiting for an answer, he went on. "Well, 'tis decided then. I will escort you up to my room when you're ready, Mistress Merryvale, and get my things out of your way, and Ramsay can wait here for the Riddles to explain they'll be spending the night. Would you care for another glass of wine, Mistress Merryvale? No? Then perhaps we should hie us upstairs for you will want a bath sent for and to rest no doubt before dinner. No, don't get up, Ramsay. I will support Mistress Merryvale up the stairs if she's feeling faint."

Leaving Bainter Ramsay fuming behind him, the overwhelming gentleman from Philadelphia guided a dazed Dorinda, walking slowly on an ankle that still twinged a bit, through the common room and up the wooden stairs.

"You left Mr. Ramsay to pay for the wine," she said suddenly, shooting an oblique look at him as they reached the head of the stairs.

"I did, didn't I?" he said with a grin. "I thought stopping to pay for it might slow him down if he decided to chase up here after us. And I wanted a word with you alone."

So that was it! Dorinda felt her heart give a sickening lurch. He had recognized her after all! At least he had not unmasked her publicly in the common room. He was being considerate, waiting until they were alone in his room to do it. There he would no doubt suggest that she withdraw quietly, possibly by the back stairs, and forget all about the mad things she had told them.

Feeling miserably dejected, because for a moment there she had felt herself soaring to the heights, a lady at last, Dorinda turned down the hall she had trodden so many times carrying pitchers and trays and mops.

"No, in here," he said, indicating a door to his right.

"Why, you've one of the large front rooms!" she gasped, astonished that a single gentleman should have been given one of the large front rooms that usually housed families.

He looked startled, pausing momentarily before the closed door with his hand on the latch. "How could you know that?" he wondered, and Dorinda cursed herself inwardly for evincing too much knowledge about a place supposedly new to her.

"Because—because you said it would accommodate both this lady from upriver and myself," she said faintly.

"Ah, yes, I said that, didn't I?" he responded gravely, but the gray eyes that looked down at her were still puzzled.

With what aplomb she could muster, Dorinda lifted her small determined chin and preceded Tarn Jenner's tall form through the door he held open for her. The square room with its big bed and its blue and white coverlet was indeed one of the inn's nicest—and largest—rooms and must be costing the imperturbable gentleman from Philadelphia a fortune, she thought, for Innkeeper Buxton always packed in as many as he could.

" 'Tis not always mine alone," Tarn Jenner told her. "The innkeeper here, like others of his calling, reserves the right to saddle me with an assortment of traveling gentlemen who are in need of bed and board for the night."

Dorinda knew that was the custom. Perhaps he was not as rich as Croesus after all!

"What did you want to talk to me about?" she asked nervously.

"About Ramsay," he said. "He's a devil with the ladies. I thought you should be warned."

So surprising was this remark—after expecting him to denounce her—that Dorinda wanted to give a shout of laughter. She managed to keep her gravity with difficulty. "It was very kind of Mr. Ramsay to offer to take me in," she pointed out.

"Yes, but there might be a price to his kindness. Are you prepared to pay it?"

He asked the question easily but Dorinda's eyes widened. "I cannot imagine what you mean," she said frostily for Bainter was after all her idol and—and he would have *changed* in the three years since she had been gone. He would have sown his wild oats by now. "I am sure Mr. Ramsay has only the kindest of motives," she reproved.

"Perhaps." He was watching her brightly. He seemed

in no hurry to go. "You know," he said suddenly, "you remind me of my stepgrandmother. Beautiful, vivacious—she's had a wonderful life. Married my grandfather—he was called 'Wild Nick' in those days—and led him a chase." He gave Dorinda a genial smile. "Always willing to lend herself to mad schemes, is my stepgrandmother. Tell me, Mistress Merryvale, do you lend yourself to wild schemes?"

Dorinda gave him a nervous look. "Of course not!"

"Hm-m-m," he said, as if gnawing that over.

She tried to look aristocratic—and distant. "Was there anything else you wanted to speak to me about?"

"No." He was moving about the room, deftly removing his personal possessions and stuffing them into a small chest, which he closed with a snap and locked, put the key in his pocket. "Now," he said, rising from that task, "you and Mistress Riddle can disport yourselves here as comfortably as if Innkeeper Buxton had had a room to spare!" He was moving toward the door. "I'll have a bath sent up."

"Thank you," smiled Dorinda. "And please tell Mr. Ramsay that I thank him too."

"Oh, I'll be sure to convey your felicitations." He paused. "About that Blade fellow, you didn't give us a very good description and I'm sure the town would appreciate knowing what he looked like?"

"He was—tall," said Dorinda reluctantly. It seemed a safe guess.

"Tall," he repeated expressionlessly. "Dark or fair?"

"Oh—dark, I think. I'm not sure. It was dark."

"I thought you said the moon had come out."

"Well, it had, but he—he was wearing a hat and besides he had a kerchief tied around his face."

He studied her for a minute. "That matches the governor's description," he said, apropos of nothing, and went his way, closing the door behind him.

Left alone, Dorinda gave a twirl of pure joy on her good ankle—and winced as she put her weight on both feet. She threw herself upon the bed and lay there looking with dancing eyes at the ceiling.

He had not recognized her—neither of them had! Not even Innkeeper Buxton's wife, who had boxed her ears so many times, had seen in this elegant lady the thin little bound girl she had been. And now she would have new clothes, so even if Ada advertised for her and described her clothing as "stolen," she would be wearing other things and no one would remember!

Whatever happened now, she was bound for Haverleigh Plantation where she would be in close proximity every day with Bainter Ramsay—she would have her chance with him on an equal footing at last!

The White Hart
WILLIAMSBURG, VIRGINIA
Summer 1717

Chapter 23

Now that Tarn Jenner had gone clattering down the stairs, Dorinda was free to look for Lady Soft Paws, the gentle pussycat with whom she had shared her attic room and who had gotten her through so many bad moments in her days as a bound girl here at the inn. Familiar with the cat's habits, Dorinda headed for the back stairs. For the cat was often to be found mousing there where bits of bread and cheese were carelessly dropped by serving girls bringing up trays to the inn's patrons.

Making sure she was alone, Dorinda called softly, "Lady Soft Paws! Kitty, kitty!"

To her delight the cat dashed up the stairs, lured upward by that familiar voice, and rubbed her furry body against Dorinda's gleaming skirts.

"Oh, Lady Soft Paws!" Dorinda bent and picked up the cat and held her purring gray and white body against her cheek. "I was afraid you'd have run away or been run over by a cart!" She carried the cat back to her room and sat down on the bed. Lady Soft Paws was quite content to curl up in Dorinda's lap and purr.

She was still there, purring, when Dorinda's bath was brought up. Dorinda had forgotten about the bath and it was a shock when she saw that it was being brought in by Jeddie, who was staggering under the burden of the metal tub, a huge pitcher of hot water, sponge and towels and soap.

Dorinda almost started forward with a cry of "Let me help you!" but she realized in time that such a move wouldn't be in character with the part she was now playing of Joshua Merryvale's undoubtedly pampered niece. Best that Jeddie not recognize her. She cast her eyes down and pretended to be entirely occupied with the cat.

"That cat don't take to people usually," remarked Jeddie, setting down the metal tub with a bang and beginning to pour the hot water into it. "And she's been wilder since Buxton's wife drowned her kittens last month."

"She did that?" cried Dorinda. Her head came up and her indignant gaze flew to Jeddie's face. She saw Jeddie's jaw drop as her suddenly relaxed fingers nearly let go of the pitcher.

"Dorinda!" Jeddie whispered, tightening her grip on the pitcher just in time.

There was no point denying it. Jeddie's blue eyes were starting from her head. And it would be good to have someone she didn't have to pretend with, someone to talk to.

"Yes, it's me, Jeddie," she said. "But if you give me away, I'll never forgive you. I'm flying under false colors now—everybody thinks I'm Dorinda Merryvale, Joshua Merryvale's niece."

"I can't believe it!" Jeddie looked confused. "You left here a bound girl—"

"I'm no longer bound. But I got into other trouble—in Philadelphia."

"You're pregnant?" guessed Jeddie.

"No, no. Oh, Jeddie, it's too long a story to tell now.

You'll hear it all later. But in the meantime, try to remember that I'm Dorinda Merryvale and you never saw me before."

"I don't think I'd have recognized you except for the way you got upset about the cat," admitted Jeddie frankly. "You sure have filled out and you look—different. More grown up. Prettier."

Dorinda flashed a smile at her. "Oh, Jeddie, how have you been? I've missed you!"

Jeddie shrugged. Then she sighed. "I guess I've changed. At first it was all right, slipping out of nights and enjoying myself for all that it would make me sleepy fit to die the next day. And then in early summer I got me a gentleman friend and I really thought that maybe him and me—" she broke off, looking wistful. "I'd slip out to meet him, but then a fortnight ago Buxton cornered me in the pantry and he was trying to force his hand down my bodice when his wife came up behind him and pulled him back by his collar. And then she called me a slut and fetched me an awful whack on the side of the head." Jeddie's hand went instinctively to her head as she recalled the blow. "My head rang like a bell! And the next day I broke a crock and she beat me with a barrel stave!" Jeddie looked aggrieved.

"Is Buxton—hard to hold off?" Dorinda asked hesitantly, remembering her own despair when she'd expected Buxton to rape her and his wife to kill her for it.

"Sometimes," admitted Jeddie. She pushed back her thick auburn hair with a frown. "At first he'd just give me a pat or a pinch, but now...."

Getting bolder.... Dorinda felt cold fear for Jeddie who she viewed as being in what had once been her own shoes.

"How much longer on your indenture, Jeddie?"

"Not quite a year." Jeddie looked discouraged. "It's a long time to go!"

It was indeed! Dorinda's heart went out to Jeddie, trapped in the same terrible situation that she once had been.

"And your gentleman friend?"

"I really thought he cared for me," sighed Jeddie. "I was supposed to slip out to meet him the night Buxton caught me in the pantry, and I couldn't because Buxton's wife locked me in and she's locked me in of nights ever since! I guess it must have made him angry because he stopped coming by the White Hart altogether. Maybe he decided he was above me and thought things had gone far enough...."

"Oh, Jeddie, I'm sorry."

"Well, that's as may be," said Jeddie, whose unquenchable spirits were never downed for long. "What do you think of Williamsburg now you're back? New people have been pouring in ever since you left. Some of them drift upriver to the falls and beyond, but others stay around here."

Dorinda remembered how crowded the coffeehouse had been. "There are more houses now too—I saw a big new house that's been built next door to the Red Lion."

"Walter Claridge built that for his bride," said Jeddie, who was always a great source of gossip. "But there's them as says there's others besides himself that beds her there when Walter's not looking!"

Dorinda flashed a smile at Jeddie. She had seen Lucy Claridge riding by in her carriage back when she had been Lucy Winters, and had burned with jealousy because that carriage always stopped when Bainter Ramsay strolled by.

"You can bring me up to date, Jeddie," she told her homespun-clad friend. She chose her words carefully, trying to sound casual. "I'm surprised Bainter Ramsay hasn't married. It can't be for lack of interest in him!"

"Oh, no," agreed Jeddie. "He's seen with this one

and that one—but he never follows through. There's some as expected him to marry Lucy Winters but he didn't—and some said it was because she had no money of her own and her father had six girls to marry off and raise dowries for. But Lucy was the pretty one and he didn't need to raise no dowry for *her.* Walter Claridge took her without one."

"And has Bainter—prospered?"

"There's some as says his is the worst run plantation on the James," said Jeddie frankly. "I heard the governor himself say right here in this inn that it was 'manned by lazy louts.' But I don't credit it, no matter what they say, for Bainter's always showing up here in new clothes and he always has lots of ready money to drink and gamble. He wagers large sums, they do say."

"And loses?"

Jeddie shrugged. "How would I know? He don't do it here. Loses and wins, I guess."

"What about Tarn Jenner? What do you know about him, Jeddie?"

"Not much." Jeddie laughed. "He's good looking!"

"But what does he do?"

"He comes and goes. I don't know what he does."

"I ran into him in Philadelphia and I was afraid he'd remember me."

"But he hasn't?"

"No."

Jeddie was looking at her satirically. "And you can't decide whether it's worse not to be remembered or to have your game spoiled, is that it?"

Not till Jeddie stated it so baldly had Dorinda realized that was exactly the way she felt. "I think I'm afraid of him," she admitted.

"But not *too* afraid of him?" jibed Jeddie slyly. "I mean, this *is* his room you've moved into!"

A slow flush spread over Dorinda's cheeks under Jeddie's amused scrutiny. "I *haven't* moved in with him," she said with as much dignity as she could muster. "He very gallantly offered me his room for the night which I'll be sharing with Mistress Riddle and then I'll be journeying up to Haverleigh Plantation and staying there."

"With your old flame Bainter Ramsay?" Jeddie chuckled. "Well, you are the sly one, aren't you?"

The flush on Dorinda's cheeks deepened. "I'm not moving in with him either," she said clearly. "He's just making me welcome at Haverleigh because my 'Uncle' isn't here to receive me."

"Your 'Uncle,'" derided Jeddie. "How easy that rolled off your tongue! Are you really going to keep on pretending you're Joshua Merryvale's niece?"

"I have to, Jeddie!"

"Well, you certainly *look* rich," sighed Jeddie, surveying Dorinda's stylish coiffure and rustling silks. She looked about her. "Didn't you bring no trunks or boxes?"

"Oh, I told them I arrived yesterday on the *London Queen* with lots of luggage and that I hired a cart driver to take me to Merryvale Manor, but that highwayman The Blade set upon us and robbed me."

Jeddie's jaw dropped open. "Whyever did you say that?"

"I had to explain why I didn't have any money, not even a change of clothes, didn't I?"

"I suppose so. So you claimed The Blade stole your petticoats?" Jeddie dissolved in laughter. "That's rich! Wait till *that* story gets around!" She wiped her eyes. "The Blade will probably pounce on you for making a fool of him!"

Dorinda frowned. "I wasn't thinking about that. I'd overheard him being discussed and it was the first thing I could think of to explain just appearing like this without any luggage. What do you know about The Blade?" she asked seriously. "Have you ever seen him?"

"Nobody has—save them he's robbed. Comes and goes like a ghost, it seems."

"Tarn Jenner asked me what The Blade looked like. I was hoping you'd know."

"Not me," said Jeddie cheerfully. "He's robbed the governor and some other folks, so they say. Why don't you ask one of them?"

"Because I'm supposed to have seen him, Jeddie," retorted Dorinda, vexed. "I can't very well ask!"

"Well, them as tells lies gets caught up in them," offered Jeddie cheerfully. She refused to take Dorinda's situation seriously. "You going to keep the cat up here with you?"

"Yes. Just tell that Buxton woman if she asks that one of the guests has taken a fancy to the cat and would like to take the cat with her when she leaves."

"The Buxtons won't mind." Jeddie shrugged. "They're tired of puss here having kittens all over the place. Last week a ship's cat strolled in, a big yellow tom, and they were talking about getting rid of puss."

Dorinda shivered. It would seem she'd come back just in time to save her pet!

"I'll get you some more hot water," said Jeddie. "And you'd better get in the tub. It's getting cold."

"And bring up some milk and chicken for Lady Soft Paws, won't you? If Buxton's wife wonders about it, I'll pay for it—I have enough for that."

Jeddie cocked an eyebrow at her as she went out, but she came back with a bowl of milk and a small plate of chicken for the cat, who attacked her meal greedily.

"She acts starved," said Dorinda, who had undressed by now and was easing into her bath.

"You know," said Jeddie, who had obviously been thinking as she ran up and down the back stairs, "I'm awful tired of this place. If you do stay, and if you do end up rich, will you buy up my articles of indenture from Buxton, Dorinda? I wouldn't mind being bound to you."

Jeddie's voice was so wistful that it tore at Dorinda's heart. No one knew better than she what it was like to look ahead at endless years of servitude! "Of course I will, Jeddie," she said warmly. "It's the first thing I'll do!"

Jeddie smiled down at the girl in the tub. "I still can't believe you're back," she marveled.

"You don't think Buxton or his wife or any of the servants will recognize me, do you?" worried Dorinda. "I mean, *you* did!"

"No, they'll not recognize you." Jeddie shook her head wisely. "For in your fine clothes and all filled out and with your hair done up that way, you look so different!"

In her heart Dorinda felt so too. She couldn't help thinking that her only real danger now was the possibility that Tarn Jenner would remember where he had seen her.

He was a very irritating man—but gallant too. He had pressed this room on her and ordered up her bath. But was that just to taunt his friend, Bainter? Because there had been something in his eyes when he looked at Bainter that wasn't at all friendly.

Meditatively, Dorinda soaped herself with the same perfumed French soap that she had once brought up those back stairs to Bainter Ramsay—and for which the guests paid extra. She picked up the big sponge and squeezed it and let warm water run down over her back and realized that this might be the very tub she had brought him for his bath that day three years ago. His lean rump might well have reposed where her softer one did at this moment, on the metal tub's flat bottom. The thought sent a quiver through her.

And when she got up and dried herself off with the big towel and dressed again, she sat there stroking Lady Soft Paws, who was now taking her own bath, daintily washing a white paw and rubbing her furry ears with it.

Jeddie was right, she thought. It *was* all unbelievable. As if some fairy queen had waved a magic wand over her at midnight and suddenly changed her life.

Tonight she would dine with Bainter Ramsay and Tarn Jenner and the Riddles. They would accept her as a lady of fashion and fortune. She would eat fine food and drink fine wine and tomorrow she would go shopping for the clothes that would befit her new station!

She was living out a fantastic dream, beyond imagination. And she had even regained Lady Soft Paws!

She was smiling until it came to her that of all the things she had just enumerated only the gray and white cat was substantial and real—and hers. She was wearing a name not her own, clothes not her own, and if the truth were known about her, all her newfound friends would draw away from her. She might even face prosecution!

She bit her lip and frowned down at the happily bathing cat. She was playing a dangerous game and the stakes were high, but perhaps she could brazen it out. If only the man from Philadelphia did not trip her up!

She looked up as the door opened and an elderly lady bustled into the room. Beneath her flaxen wig, the lady was a pink and white confection of thin taffetas and lawns and starched white lace. She moved with a bounce and her infectious laugh pealed as she saw Dorinda petting Lady Soft Paws.

"Ah, I see you've managed to catch the inn cat! Isn't she a pretty thing? And a wonderful mouser, I'm told. I'm Gladys Riddle and you're Dorinda Merryvale, they told me about you downstairs. Terrible about your uncle dying like that before you could arrive and get yourself established, but we'll all do all we can to help. Bainter tells me you were attacked by that dreadful highwayman—what's his name?"

"The Blade," supplied Dorinda, able at last in this rapid-fire monologue to get a word in edgewise. "He—"

"Yes, that's it, The Blade. The roads simply aren't safe these days, not safe at all." Mistress Riddle shuddered. "Fortunately we'll be returning upriver by water. So much better." She peered at Dorinda. "How very pretty you are! It will be a pleasure to help you shop for all the things you'll need. We do have excellent shops here, what with ships arriving all the time."

"I'm sure you do," agreed Dorinda. "They—"

"So nice of that—what's his name? That Mr. Jenner, to give us his room for the night. I don't know anything about him, do you?"

"No, I only just met him," admitted Dorinda. "He—"

"But he's certainly very handsome, don't you think? In a sinister sort of way, of course. I'm told he talks very little about himself."

"No," Dorinda managed to get in with a wicked grin. "I think he prefers to talk about his stepgrandmother."

"His stepgrandmother?" Mistress Riddle fixed Dorinda with a pair of astonished pale blue eyes. "How very odd indeed! What does he say about her?"

"Mainly that she led a wild life married to his grandfather who must have been a great rake."

"Odder and odder," said Mistress Riddle, who was now struggling with her bodice hooks. "Will you help me with these, my dear?" she gasped. "I must bathe before dinner and these pesky hooks always defeat me!"

Dorinda leaped forward to help the older woman, thinking ruefully how many stout ladies she had "helped with their hooks" in this very room! "Mr. Ramsay has offered me shelter at Haverleigh Plantation until I get established," she volunteered.

"Yes, I heard all about it." Mistress Riddle bobbed her wigged head. "Oh, thank you, my dear, *now* it will come off." She struggled out of her bodice. "Oh, these stays are absolutely stuck to me! Haverleigh is huge, my dear. Plenty of room for all of us. Bainter has offered us shelter too until our house is put back in order—the fire, you know."

"Yes, I heard you were burned out," said Dorinda sympathetically. "It's terrible."

"Oh, not really *burned out*," corrected Mistress Riddle. "But the fire gutted the east wing. It—" she shook her flaxen head as if to dispel visions—"it frightens me to look at it somehow, all blackened like that. I refused to stay there until it is rebuilt and put back in order, although nothing of course will restore to me my letters and keepsakes that were destroyed by the fire. My brother Isham wanted me to stay, said we could sleep in the reception rooms, but I would not hear of it. Bainter was there the very next morning, he had heard about our trouble and he insisted I stay with him during the rebuilding since it upset me to be there. Well, naturally my brother was not going to let me go alone to a bachelor establishment, so he went along. I do not know why people do not *like* Bainter Ramsay more." She shook her head in bewilderment. "He is certainly most kind."

"Oh, don't they like him?" Dorinda had been too dazzled with Bainter three years ago to have gained any impression of what others thought about him.

"Well, the gentlemen don't seem to," conceded Mistress Riddle. She ceased talking as her bath was brought and a great to-do was made over the water not being hot enough. Finally it was deemed ready and Jeddie left with a sniff.

Dorinda waited patiently until the older woman got her plump sides into the tub. "Why don't they like him?" she asked.

"Who, dear?"

"Bainter Ramsay. You said the gentlemen didn't like him."

"Oh, there was something about a card game at the Wallaces'. One of the guests felt he was cheated at cards. There was almost a duel over it but I'm told that

Evan Wallace made good his guest's losses to avoid having bloodshed spoil his twenty-fifth anniversary supper! But of course, it *did* cause talk." Dorinda could imagine it would!

Mistress Riddle soaped herself meditatively. "And then there was something about a horse race. Bainter won but his opponent, Carter Sedgefield, did not like the way he won it. I can't remember but there were those who agreed with Carter." She sighed. "Bainter is *so* charming and so elegant and I'm sure that he's totally misunderstood. After all, he's obviously quite well off. Why would he need to cheat at cards?"

Why indeed? Or was it a game to him, to see what he could take from the world? Dorinda felt a sizzle of excitement quiver down her spine. She was dining with two dangerous men tonight, the "sinister" gentleman from Philadelphia and the elegant Bainter Ramsay of the tarnished reputation.

"I am surprised he has not married," she volunteered.

"Oh, there are many young ladies who'd have him—and widows too!" laughed Mistress Riddle. "My dear, would you mind pouring the rest of that pitcher of water over my back and shoulders? Ah, that's perfect! But Bainter remains a confirmed bachelor."

"Why is that, do you think?"

Mistress Riddle paused in struggling from the tub. "Well, I really think," she confided, "that those he'd marry are restrained by their families, and those he wouldn't keep hoping in vain!"

Dorinda felt a sudden rush of sympathy for Bainter, misunderstood, harassed by enemies male who were determined to keep their sisters and daughters from his bed. She remembered now how determinedly three years ago Roger Charington had swept his two sisters away from Bainter in the courtyard of this very inn. Well, if that was the treatment accorded him, no wonder he had not married!

"Then you believe all this talk about Bainter Ramsay

has no foundation?" she shot at Mistress Riddle, who was energetically toweling herself.

"Oh, none whatsoever. Indeed, I'd be much more ready to believe bad things about Tarn Jenner—despite the fact that he's gallantly let us have his room for the night. There's such a *sinister* look to him, don't you think?"

Dorinda was not quite sure what she thought about Tarn Jenner. But the prospect of having dinner with two such disreputable characters was certainly intriguing!

Chapter 24

Dorinda dressed her hair that night with enormous care. She piled it in heaps of gleaming gold, mounded as handsomely as any lady's of the French court, with one long fat curl falling carelessly down to caress the white column of her neck.

"I must say, you do that awfully well!" remarked Mistress Riddle, eyeing this young heiress's hairdressing skill with amazement. "One would think you had been born and bred to it!"

Dorinda hid a smile. Born to it she might not have been, but her tireless hours of mimicking Simone's clever technique in Philadelphia was certainly standing her in good stead here. She gave a last pat to an already perfect coiffure, rose and smoothed out the blue-green folds of her silken skirt, moving sinuously over the glittering silver embroidery of her petticoat. She was aware of the picture she made, freshly combed and bathed and powdered lightly with Mistress Riddle's finely ground alabaster powder, gliding down to dinner in the common room of the inn where she once had walked unnoticed as a servant. It was enormously satisfying to see men who had ignored her, or brushed by her carelessly, turning to stare.

And it was doubly satisfying to see Bainter Ramsay come to his feet along with Tarn Jenner, both their faces mirroring instant admiration.

"You look as cool as lime ice on this hot night," grinned Tarn, offering her a seat.

"Beautiful as the moon," whispered Bainter huskily, as Dorinda sank down between the two men while Mistress Riddle occupied Bainter's other side next to her brother.

Dorinda gave them both a cool look and touched her hair in a way that let the dainty lace ruffles of her chemise cascade like a waterfall over her slender forearm from beneath her blue-green sleeves.

Tarn Jenner's grin deepened.

"Minx," he murmured in a voice that only she could hear as he proffered her a glass of wine.

Dorinda took the wine and gave him a level look. There was something veiled in his glance—perhaps he *did* remember her! Her heart skipped a quick beat and then stilled again. Either he was going to expose her or he wasn't, and nothing short of a sudden declaration of her real identity was going to spoil this glorious evening! She turned to Bainter with a winsome smile. "I am *so* dying to see Haverleigh Plantation," she told him meltingly.

"Oh, I'll wager you are," murmured Tarn's amused voice in her ear. "And Merryvale Manor too!"

Dorinda ignored him. She was certain no one else could hear these low-voiced maddening asides, but she kept her blue-green shoulder turned to him nonetheless.

"I am told you enjoy racing," she added, taking a sip of wine.

"Oh?" Bainter regarded her lazily. "And where did you hear that?"

"Oh, I told her," interposed Mistress Riddle happily. "And that you gamble as well. After all, Dorinda is a young impressionable girl and she must not view you as a saint just because you are offering her your hospitality!"

"I see I am found out." Bainter was regarding Dorinda's soft curving mouth. His tawny gaze passed still lower, gliding down the smooth skin of her throat to concentrate on the soft rise and fall of her white bosom.

Dorinda squirmed slightly under that direct scrutiny.

"I do not ride," she admitted. "But I do adore watching men race their horses."

All eyes turned on her instantly. "You do not ride?" demanded Mistress Riddle, scandalized. "Why, I was brought up on a horse!" And Dorinda was abruptly reminded that all the gentry rode.

"It was—my mother's fault," she said lamely. "After my father broke his back in a fall from his favorite hunter, she was terrified of horses and refused to allow me to learn."

There was a general acceptance of this rather novel explanation and Tarn Jenner leaned forward.

"And where is your mother now?" he inquired.

"Both my parents are dead," said Dorinda in a quivering voice. "Back in England. When my mother died, she told me to go to my Uncle Joshua—and now I find him dead as well!" She blinked her eyes as if she were about to burst into tears.

"Don't bring up unhappy memories, Tarn," said Bainter irritably. "You can see how it affects her!"

"I offer my sympathies," said Tarn Jenner solemnly. "And my kerchief as well." He thrust a square of white cambric toward her and Dorinda pushed it pettishly aside. He was mocking her, she could tell it from something in his gray eyes, some inner mirth.

"Thank you, but I am well enough," she insisted.

"But you will be better by the time you have spent tomorrow shopping and emptied Bainter's pockets of their coin," laughed Tarn and Bainter gave him a frowning look. "Come now, Bainter," he rallied. "We've a shining lass here, a gem who needs naught but a setting to dazzle our eyes as she's dazzling them now. I trust ye've brought enough gold to Williamsburg to turn the trick? Or d'ye feel in need of a small loan perhaps from me?"

"I feel equal to raising any amount Mistress Merryvale may care to spend," said Bainter haughtily. "And my credit is good everywhere."

"Is it now?" cried Tarn Jenner. "Everywhere? Ah, then ye've traveled a deal! Come now, regale us with tales of your journeys. D'ye know this coast well, for instance?"

"My travels were mainly in Europe," growled Bainter.

"So far away?" said Tarn pensively. "Are we to infer that you stay rooted to Haverleigh now?"

"Damme, Tarn, ye're to infer anything ye like!" Bainter's voice had grown testy. "Ye're boring Mistress Merryvale here with your infernal questions!"

"Am I? I hadn't noticed." Those steely gray eyes turned to Dorinda. They had, she thought, an extremely tranquil expression. One would not have thought their owner to be baiting a man with Bainter's reputation for temper.

"No," she said hurriedly, her fingers toying nervously with the cutlery that lay beside her empty pewter trencher. "You are neither of you boring me. But I vow that I am hungry enough to eat these lace ruffles. Perhaps one of you could tell me what's for dinner?"

"The girl is coming with it now," said Tarn, nodding toward Jeddie who was edging her way through the crowd carrying a large tray piled high with the seafood that was so plentiful here.

Dorinda was glad it was Jeddie who was serving them. The less contact she had with the inn servants the better. Jeddie knew the truth about her and would not tell—she might not be so lucky with the others who would consider the notion of a bound girl returning as an aristocratic lady a secret too good to keep. But she felt her body go tense and almost spilled her wine on the tablecloth when Jeddie, as she carefully placed the big pewter bowls and chargers piled with steaming seafood before them, leant down and muttered conspiratorially, "Shall I feed the cat or will you?"

"Oh, you do, if you please, Jeddie," said Dorinda, glad that Mistress Riddle's loud delighted exclamations over the variety of the seafood before them had temporarily claimed Bainter's attention. But she was blushingly aware that Tarn Jenner had overheard and was looking at her as if due an explanation. Under cover of Mistress Riddle's prattle, she gave him one. "I have appropriated the inn cat," she murmured.

"What, the big yellow tom?"

"No, Lady——" She had already begun, she might as well finish. "Lady Soft Paws," she said defiantly.

"Oh, you mean that nice little gray and white pussy that always purrs against my boots."

Dorinda, helping herself to scallops and shrimp from the bowls being passed, gave him an astonished look. Generally the cat did not let men get that close! "Lady Soft Paws prefers purring against skirts to purring against boots!"

"Indeed? I hadn't noticed." Tarn Jenner paused a moment as if fascinated. "You have not yet a permanent roof over your head yet already you have acquired a cat." He took a large helping of oysters and gave Dorinda a bland look. "Tell me, do you intend to acquire a brace of hounds as well?"

"I do not!" Dorinda stabbed at her boiled shrimp and missed.

He smiled as he observed her chasing the shrimp around her trencher. "You will be taking the cat with you then when you go?"

"Of course!"

He grinned at her. "That should be interesting. One

squirming terrified cat clinging to the side of the boat and meowing!"

"I shall take her in a box, of course," said Dorinda frostily.

Tarn Jenner hid a grin. Beside them the conversation had inevitably drifted to that focal point of Williamsburg interest now—The Blade. What had he done lately?

"I was hoping Mistress Dorinda could give me a better description of the fellow," said Tarn Jenner wistfully.

"That's right, you were the first to be robbed by The Blade," said Bainter, his interest suddenly aroused.

Tarn Jenner nodded moodily.

So he had been testing her! Dorinda felt a little shiver of fright but she rose to the occasion. "If you were robbed by him yourself, why on earth would you require a description of him from me?" she demanded tartly.

The man from Philadelphia gave her a restless look. "My situation was a bit different," he said. "I was riding along in the outskirts of town when my horse threw a shoe. I dismounted near a clump of trees and bent down to inspect the hoof when suddenly I felt a sharp point pressed against my back and a voice told me to toss back my purse. I did so and I heard him laugh as he picked it up with what out of the corner of my eye looked to be the point of a rapier."

"Why didn't you turn on him then?" demanded Bainter.

"From my kneeling position examining the horse's hoof, that would have been difficult," was the dry rejoinder. "'Thank you, sir,'" he said. "'And this is compliments of The Blade!' And with that he struck me from behind—I think, with the hilt of his rapier, for it felled me like an ox! When I came to myself I was lying in the road with my horse grazing nearby, minus my purse and with the worst headache of my life!"

"You were fortunate," shrugged Bainter. "He took the governor's horse as well!"

"Perhaps my horse was too conspicuous for him. He has very distinctive markings, easily traced." Tarn turned soberly to Dorinda. "So you see why I yearned for a description of the fellow. I had no chance to get a look at him."

"But the governor must have seen him," protested Dorinda.

"It was pouring down rain—sheets of it. The governor was huddled beneath a tree trying to shelter himself from this cloudburst when he was suddenly seized from behind, mauled, trussed up, his purse, his ring, his watch, and his horse all stolen!"

"The magistrate fared no better," put in Isham Riddle, who had been listening intently. "He was seized on the way to the Amberley ball upriver and forced to dismount and hand over his valuables."

"To dismount?" wondered Bainter. "But I am told this fellow operates with a sword rather than a pistol."

"A gentleman thief," murmured Dorinda, dimpling.

"Except in your case." Tarn Jenner threw her an amused glance. "However Bainter does bring up an interesting point. Why did not the magistrate promptly put spurs to his horse and depart the area?"

Isham Riddle shook his head. "I would have thought that too, but the way he tells it, he was passing under a low branch at the time when a hand reached down and grabbed him by the scruff. Then a blade snaked down from the leaves overhead and pressed against his windpipe. 'Twould have been death not to do as he was told!"

"He's an impudent rogue," laughed Bainter. "What happened then?"

"Then suddenly the magistrate was spun around by that hand that had him, twisting his cravat, he was struck on the head even as you have described, Tarn, and probably by the hilt of that same rapier, and sent sprawling on his face in the road while the scoundrel rode off on the magistrate's horse!"

"One would think the horses would turn up," Bainter mused.

"Do not think there is no watch out for them," said Isham Riddle. "The governor tells me he has sent men up both the York and the James."

"Of course," pointed out Bainter, "they could have been ridden hard to some coastwise sloop, loaded on, and be off to—who knows? Charles Town? Philadelphia?"

Tarn Jenner sighed. "And now there are reports that The Blade has robbed two planters far upriver."

Isham Riddle turned to him alertly. He was a small pink-cheeked man, stout like his sister, and—like her—wearing a flaxen wig. "I had not heard that. Faith, I must warn my neighbors!"

"There is little need, I would say. These fellows do not stay long in one place. By next week he will probably be harrying the Post Road out of Boston and have forgotten all about Virginia!"

"I wish I could be as optimistic as you are," said Isham Riddle with a frown.

"Come now, gentlemen," admonished Gladys Riddle, who had kept silent during this discussion. "You are frightening this lovely child and me to death. We have been upriver, cut off from the world. Is there no gossip worth repeating?"

Tarn Jenner laughed. "Well, the talk of the town just now is the beautiful Mistress Merryvale, for word of her beauty and her misfortune is even now spreading throughout Williamsburg. I heard her name mentioned when I went over to the Raleigh Tavern just now."

"Did you indeed?" cried Mistress Riddle in delight. "There now, Dorinda, you see what a success you are going to be? You are the talk of the town even before the town has met you!"

At the moment Dorinda would have preferred anonymity. She cast her eyes down and tried to make herself a little smaller at the table.

"Modesty becomes a woman," spoke up Isham Riddle. There was an approving note in his gruff voice. He turned to his sister. "Gladys, you talk too much, you are embarrassing Mistress Dorinda."

"I never knew a girl to be upset by being admired," declared Mistress Riddle merrily. "Come, Mr. Jenner, tell us all the gossip!"

The conversation lapsed into small talk, then Mistress Riddle began to badger all three bachelors about how remiss they were in not getting married. As her brother remonstrated with her, Tarn Jenner turned to Dorinda.

"I have made inquiries and your cart driver seems to have vanished along with your trunks," he said.

"Oh, do you think something has happened to him?" Dorinda's blue-green eyes were wide and guileless.

"No," he said cryptically. "I do not. I think he will be found in the same place as your boxes and trunks."

Which was nowhere, thought Dorinda in panic.

"Have you made plans, Mistress Dorinda, for what you will do with Merryvale Manor?" wondered Isham Riddle.

"Why—why, no." Dorinda's poise was shaken. "I haven't even laid eyes on it. What do *you* suggest I do with it?"

"Well, most young ladies would sell it but I am hoping that after having experienced life along the James, you might even be persuaded to become one of us."

"Oh, yes, do!" cried Mistress Riddle heartily. "Stay and become our neighbor! For Merryvale Manor is just upriver from Riddlewood. We could see each other often!"

"You do make it sound most tempting." Dorinda smiled at her. "And I vow I *am* looking forward to all the balls and dances that Uncle Joshua described so vividly."

"And never attended," murmured Tarn Jenner.

Dorinda was brought up short. "Oh, but he *heard* all about them from other people," she insisted with her sweetest smile.

"And wrote you just what sort of ruffles the ladies were wearing, I've no doubt?" Ironically.

"Why, no!" Dorinda's smile now had a touch of vinegar. "He wrote me who the pretty ones were and I was left to imagine what they were wearing."

Bainter heard that and laughed. "Touché, Jenner! Just what a man *would* be likely to write!"

"A man pushing ninety?" came Tarn's gossamer whisper in her ear.

Pushing ninety! Dorinda froze. She would indeed have to watch her step. In panic she dived into her boiled shrimp and began to comment wildly on the food.

"You were treading on thin ice there," he muttered in her ear.

By now Dorinda's hands were shaking. The rest of the meal passed by in a kind of nightmare as she waited for him to denounce her, to turn to the others and say casually, "This lady is not what she seems. When last I saw her she was wearing a mobcap and a smock smeared with tallow—and that was in Philadelphia."

But he did not. Indeed he seemed to be enjoying his food and he relaxed afterward with a long clay pipe just as did Bainter. She had a strong desire to box his ears.

As she bade both gentlemen good night at the base of the stairs, under cover of Mistress Riddle's effusive good nights to Bainter, Dorinda muttered, "If you have something to say, say it!"

The face Tarn Jenner presented to her was bland. "Why, then," he murmured. "I'll say that I knew your relative slightly better than you seem to—at least I had met him!"

Dorinda gave him an affronted look and marched off to bed with Gladys Riddle puffing along in the rear.

So he intended to keep on torturing her!

He was still at it the next day when, to Dorinda's surprise, all five of them went shopping in Williamsburg.

Plump, bright-eyed Gladys Riddle led the way, excited by the prospect of "completely outfitting" a young lady of beauty and substance.

"Of course, 'tis not like the London shopping you are accustomed to, Dorinda," she said deprecatingly. "But you must needs make do with it until you can send overseas for what you want."

Dorinda thought of the lean days of her childhood in London when she had stood outside of shops gazing with yearning upon other more fortunate children who strolled in and out accompanied by doting mammas or governesses or footmen. She thought of the elegant young ladies, plumes swaying on their hats, alighting from coaches and chairs and walking past her on satin-shod feet emitting in their wake a drifting scent of perfume. Well, now *she* would be one of those ladies! London or Williamsburg, what did it matter?

"Oh, I am sure I shall make do with it excellently!" she declared in a happy voice.

At just that moment Tarn Jenner cocked an eye at her and she was brought sharply back to earth. She was no goose girl suddenly elevated to princess like some character of a fairy tale. She was a penniless vagabond, wanted in Philadelphia for the theft of the very clothes she was wearing, playing out a dangerous game as make-believe heiress to a property she had never even seen!

"I *will* make do with it," she said in a voice of challenge and he grinned delightedly.

"I have every confidence in you," he assured her. As if she had asked him!

She was half of a mind to respond to his mockery in kind when Mistress Riddle interrupted with a sigh. "There is one thing I do miss when I stay in Williamsburg. At home I always rise before dawn and collect the dew that has fallen on the grass by night and dampen my face with it."

"Why?" wondered Dorinda, who much preferred to sleep until hunger dragged her out.

"Oh, did you not know? Dew does wonders for the complexion. Indeed it is to the constant use of dew that I attribute the clarity and smoothness of my skin! You must try it when we get to Haverleigh!"

Dorinda gave the older woman a doubtful look. Mistress Riddle's round face was indeed smooth and clear but Dorinda was inclined to attribute that more to heredity than dew since Mistress Riddle's brother had exactly the same pink and white complexion and she doubted he rose at dawn to drench his face in dew!

"Mistress Dorinda needs no assistance for her complexion," pronounced Tarn Jenner, looking down at her critically.

"Indeed she does not," agreed Bainter, who had been lost in thought and now joined in the conversation. "Her complexion rivals the rose and her eyes put the stars to shame."

Dorinda felt slightly dizzy at such an extravagant compliment from the man she most admired. It irritated her that Tarn Jenner gave him a sardonic look.

Up and down Duke of Gloucester Street they went. It was a day of drifting clouds and bright sunshine and once, crossing the street, they had to step nimbly to avoid a huge cart of "venture furniture" which had been crafted in New England and sent south to Virginia in payment for fine Virginia tobacco. While Dorinda was being measured for boots and trying on slippers, Mistress Riddle dragged her brother off to a silversmith's to see if he could make her some table silver of the same design that had been lost somehow—"probably melted down and lost among the rubble" during the fire in the east wing of Riddlewood. "And they were of a most pleasing design," Gladys Riddle had mourned. "The knives were very heavy at the haft and the spoons were very long and rather pointy with a large 'R' engraved on the handle of each." She trotted away still chattering volubly and Dorinda was left to try on an assortment of brocade and satin slippers.

Bainter Ramsay was at the front of the shop conversing with the leathern-aproned bootmaker about ordering a new pair of boots. Dorinda was browsing in the back of the shop where the wall was hung with different size wooden lasts over which the shoes would be formed. Tarn Jenner had followed her back there.

"Ye need have no fear of shoddy workmanship here," he assured her. "For the law of this Colony prescribes that well tanned and curried leather be used and good thread well twisted."

"I know," said Dorinda absently. "And the penalties are fierce. . . ."

"You know?" His dark brows shot up quizzically. "Faith, but you have a massive knowledge for one who arrived on our shores day before yesterday!"

Once again Dorinda cursed herself for displaying too much knowledge of a place she was supposed never to have been. "Uncle Joshua wrote to my mother about it," she improvised rapidly. "He was very particular about his boots."

"Not when last I saw him," murmured Tarn. "Cared nothing for dress, and his boot leather was cracked."

Caught up again! Dorinda could feel her ears burning as she bent hastily over a pile of shoes all too large. "That was in his earlier years," she amended.

"Oh, I see," he said gravely. "Those you're looking at won't fit. Now here's a pretty dancing slipper that might fit you." He held out a tempting creation in emerald green satin, garnished with a delicate rosette.

"What I really need most is a good pair of walking shoes." She eyed the delicate satin slipper doubtfully.

"Yes, one needs good leather underfoot if she is to flee from an overzealous suitor with any reasonable hope of escape," said Tarn pleasantly.

Dorinda shot him an oblique look as she bent over and slipped the satin slipper onto her foot. It fitted her superbly. "And what makes you think I will need to escape from an overzealous suitor?" she demanded tartly.

He grinned at having nettled her. "Oh, I think you might," he drawled, looking significantly at the front of the store where Bainter was arguing over the height of a boot heel.

Dorinda's brows elevated haughtily. "And what makes you think I would care to escape Mr. Ramsay?"

"Perhaps I was not thinking of Mr. Ramsay," he countered whimsically. "Perhaps I was thinking of myself. Or perhaps I was thinking of all the elegible bachelors of Williamsburg, who will be hot on your trail once they have discovered you!"

"If there is to be such a crush pursuing me, indeed I believe I will make my escape by coach!" she sniffed.

"A coastwise vessel might be more practical," he suggested and she gave him a sharp look.

"These fit very well," she said. "I will take them."

"Oh, do try these as well." Tarn had been rummaging about and now he handed her a pair of green calfskin shoes with red heels.

They were very smart and Dorinda took them from him with delight and slipped them on.

"They fit excellently well!" she cried and the bootmaker came hurrying back, leaving Bainter frowning down at a sample of leather.

"I am sorry but those are not for sale," he told Dorinda. "I made them up for one of John Carstair's daughters and she will be calling for them at the end of the week."

"Ah, but you will have time to make another pair for Carstair's daughter," suggested Tarn. "While you have a chance to sell this pair now today rather than let the lady go across the street to your competitor to seek a pair."

The bootmaker saw the sense of that. "Indeed, if they suit you so well?" he said tentatively.

"Oh, they do!" cried Dorinda, standing up shod in both and taking several fast steps.

"Then you shall have them," said Tarn masterfully. He winked at the still doubtful bootmaker. "And since you have been so nice to her, Mistress Merryvale will no doubt be back to find a matching pair of slippers for every gown she chooses, for we are outfitting her today head to toe!"

"The boots and satin slippers and these with red heels are more than enough," Dorinda protested to Tarn as the happy bootmaker went away to wrap up her purchases. "You are too generous!"

"Oh, there is no end to my generosity," he said in a bantering tone. "Especially since Ramsay over there is paying the bill!"

Dorinda flushed and gave him a resentful look. "I will not so impose on Mr. Ramsay."

"Oh, do impose upon him by all means. Let us see of what sort of stuff Mr. Ramsay is made. I am told he has been known to welsh on his debts. Let us see how he pays in cash."

"He is your friend and he will hear you," she said in a resentful tone.

"Oh, he is a very newfound friend," was the cool response. "And men are what they are, as you will no doubt learn. As to his hearing me—" Tarn chuckled— "Bainter is lost in contemplation of a new pair of boots and every seam is of consummate interest to him. It cannot have escaped your notice that you favor a bird of plumage?"

Dorinda's chin lifted. "I think it is a good thing for a man to have a care for what he wears," she said, giving a missing button on Tarn's maroon coat a pointed look.

"Ah, I see you have noticed that," he said, following her gaze. "I was hoping that you would offer to sew it on for me."

"I will be delighted to," said Dorinda stiffly, reminding herself that she was beholden for her sleeping quarters to this man. "But I cannot understand why you have waited until we were so busy shopping to ask me. Since it was also missing yesterday at dinner, why did you not ask me to sew it on then?"

"You seemed to me too absorbed in every word dropped by our foppish friend here." His sardonic nod encompassed Bainter, now arguing with the bootmaker over the sheen of the leather. "I hated to spoil your concentration on the elegant Mr. Ramsay."

Irritation gave crispness to Dorinda's voice as she pronounced herself ready to go. She might have come to blows with the tall annoying gentleman who hovered nearby but that Mistress Riddle and her brother arrived just then.

"The silversmith said he could not match a pattern he had not seen," she announced in a disappointed voice. "But I have ordered new cutlery anyway—though I doubt I will like it so well as the first. Ah, I see you have decided on some shoes, Dorinda. You will doubtless need other pairs once you have chosen your gowns." Tarn's merry gaze met Dorinda's and she flushed. "Well, come along, do. There will be need for alterations, I don't doubt, so we must speed ourselves to the dressmaker's." As she spoke she was hustling them out into the street.

Tarn was carrying Dorinda's packages, Bainter had said carelessly, "Send the bill to me at Haverleigh," and Dorinda was finding pleasure in seeing again the familiar brick and frame houses with their kitchen gardens and their flower gardens and their neat brick or marl paths that led more often than not beneath fruit trees that she remembered as being a dazzling burst of blooms in spring. These properties were miniature plantations really, she thought, with their service areas and their outbuildings, little self-contained units. She paused to admire a shrub trimmed to imitate a tall vase and admired as always the evergreen hedges, the box and holly.

" 'Tis a green town, is it not?" said Tarn. "It is hard standing here to believe that out to the west, past the river-edged plantations, past the blue mountains, stretches some vast unexplored wilderness."

"Yes," agreed Dorinda. "It is hard."

Before the morning was gone they had purchased for Dorinda a dainty yellow and green sprigged muslin gown with wide flaring skirts, an elegant ball gown of emerald silk trimmed in brilliants, a fitted riding habit of thin forest green taffeta (although Dorinda had protested again that she did not ride, "You will learn of course, my dear," Mistress Riddle had insisted), a sweeping hat with emerald plumes, a lemon silk shawl heavily fringed and embroidered, two sheer lace-trimmed chemises which Mistress Riddle had made the men turn their backs as they inspected, a light emerald silk cloak, and a brace of petticoats, one of almost tissue-thin palest green velvet, the other of embroidered yellow silk to wear with the sprigged muslin, a painted ivory fan, tall pattens for rainy days, a light dressing gown of lemon silk, and some pins and combs for her hair. All of which Bainter paid for.

"But surely you will not let Mistress Dorinda go upriver to Haverleigh without the comfort of a wig?" cried Tarn Jenner in mock dismay. "She will need at least one—possibly more!"

Bainter Ramsay turned to him with the ghost of a frown on his face. It was one thing to advance clothing money to a temporarily embarrassed heiress, but wigs were prohibitively expensive.

"Oh, yes," cried Mistress Riddle. "We had forgotten that! You will need a fine wig indeed if it is to rival your own hair!"

"Thank you," said Dorinda dryly. "But I prefer to wear my own hair."

"But my dear, fashion demands—"

"Fashionable or not," said Dorinda in a voice of finality.

"A wig and a mask can change a milkmaid into a marquessa or a duchess into an orange girl," laughed Tarn and Dorinda bit her lip. If she wished to flee, it was true a wig would be a great help—particularly if the hair were of some color other than her own. Ah, well, it was too late now to change her stand on the matter!

"Mistress Dorinda should not wear a mask and hide her lovely features from the world," declared Bainter gallantly. He looked rather relieved at not being forced to buy a wig.

"I couldn't agree more," said Tarn carelessly. "Perhaps a kerchief?" he suggested, holding up several lace-trimmed ones.

Dorinda was about to reply tartly that she would not mask her face with a kerchief either when Mistress Riddle intervened. She pounced on the kerchiefs with a cry of, "Of course, I was about to forget them!"

"And she'll need this as well." Tarn picked up a green brocade purse trimmed in silver embroidery.

"To carry the money I do not have?" Dorinda's brows lifted.

"To carry these kerchiefs!" said Mistress Riddle energetically. She thrust both at Bainter. "Most necessary! And we must have ribands as well—yellow for the sprigged muslin, green or black for the emerald silk. Where are my wits that I would forget them?"

Tarn Jenner hid a grin, but when they were ready to climb into the open carriage which would take them to the barge that would convey them upriver, he said, "Wait a minute. I have just remembered something Mistress Dorinda will find most useful." He left them, striding away on his long legs with Bainter Ramsay glowering after him, and returned in short order carrying a wide-brimmed straw hat of a light taffy color. "This was made in the islands," he told Dorinda. "You will find it cooler than that plumed affair you were so taken with."

At Dorinda's cry of delight, for she had been thinking much the same thing and was already regretting the heavy elegance of the hat that now crowned her head, Bainter frowned and promptly excused himself.

"I wonder where he is going," muttered Isham Riddle. "He kept telling us we must hurry else dark would catch us on the river!"

Suddenly Dorinda remembered Lady Soft Paws, fed to near foundering by Jeddie and waiting for her at the inn.

"I just remembered—I left something at the inn," she cried. Unceremoniously she thrust her straw hat into Mistress Riddle's plump hand, gathered up her skirts and dashed off, crying, "I'll be right back," over her shoulder.

At the inn she found Jeddie.

"I got you a box like you said," Jeddie told her brightly. "It's a wig box but I punched holes into it so she can breathe. Buxton's wife was glad to be rid of her, but does Bainter Ramsay know you're bringing the cat?"

"No, he doesn't," said Dorinda anxiously. She gave the wig box a couple of bashes to make the holes look less studied and more as if they'd been made by unfortunate accidents, and looked down hesitantly at the sleeping Lady Soft Paws. Suppose Bainter didn't like her? He had never observably stroked a cat in her presence; indeed she had a vague memory that she had once seen him brush aside an alley cat with his boot when crossing the street.

Still...she thought of Buxton's wife and the drowned kittens. That should not happen to Lady Soft Paws again! Nor would she be bullied by that big tom whose rapacious appetite snapped up all the best food before Lady Soft Paws could get her dainty teeth into her morsel—Jeddie had told her about that. Whatever happened, Dorinda told herself, their fates were linked. She lifted the sleeping cat and deposited her in the box. Lady Soft Paws opened her big aqua eyes and identified Dorinda. She gave a sleepy lick to the hand that stroked her, yawned, stretched, and went back to sleep.

"You should've seen what she ate for breakfast," said Jeddie in an awed voice. "You'd sleep too!"

"And yet she's rather thin," pointed out Dorinda, frowning.

"It's been a bad season for mice," sighed Jeddie. "They've all gone out in the fields where the pickings are better. And that big new tom that Buxton's wife likes so well—"

"Eats up her food before she can get it. I know." Dorinda carefully tied the box with a wide pink riband which hid some of the holes that could be unveiled later, hugged Jeddie and took off. She found her little group still waiting for her by the carriage and heaved a sigh of relief, for Bainter Ramsay was nowhere in sight.

"Whyever did you run away like that?" scolded Mistress Riddle. "We could have sent the driver back for any box you'd left."

Dorinda cast a look at the driver, sitting slumped in resignation with the sun beating down, but ready to go on command. "Oh, 'twas the thin petticoat I usually wear beneath this one," she whispered, afraid to tell the truth lest Mistress Riddle cry out and alert the driver who in turn might tell Bainter; she could not risk the chance that Lady Soft Paws would be exiled again to the inn. "I was afraid the chambermaid would think I had thrown the petticoat away for 'tis a trifle worn," she fabricated quickly, "and I did want to take it with me. And she gave me this battered box, which was the best she had, to carry it in, and tied it with pink riband to boot!"

"Oh, a petticoat? Oh, I see, yes, I do see!" Mistress Riddle subsided, frowning. She could not for the life of her recall seeing Dorinda peel off an extra petticoat when she had undressed for bed last night—no, nor

recall seeing an extra petticoat at all this morning.
Perhaps she was getting old, she scolded herself, not
noticing things. Or perhaps, as her brother often insisted
when she sewed a button on wrong, her sight was
failing. She supposed she'd end up wearing spectacles
and losing them off the end of her nose as her father
had! She sighed. "Oh, this sun is unbearable! I must
get me to some shade."

"You could sit in the carriage, Gladys," suggested her
brother.

"An open carriage won't give me shade!" she cried.
"Come here, all of you. Let's go stand under that big
tree over there." She beckoned and they followed her,
Isham Riddle audibly wondering why Bainter was taking so long.

"The carriage driver and the horses could use some
shade too," said Dorinda. "I think I'll go tell him to
drive on down the street."

"Oh, no, don't do that." Mistress Riddle touched
Dorinda's arm warningly. "For all he's so charming,
Bainter's very hot-tempered and strict with his help."

"Ha!" said her brother fiercely. "He lets them run the
plantation any which way they please!"

"But if a horse is not brought at the moment he says,
or a carriage not left exactly where he expects it to be,
he might well flog the driver," insisted Mistress Riddle.
"He insists on absolute obedience in these matters."

A cloud drifted overhead, giving them some relief.
Above them a bald eagle seemed to hang suspended
motionless, wings outspread. Dorinda was uncomfortably
aware of Tarn Jenner's amused gaze focused on the
box. She shifted it in her arms, irritably aware that he
had guessed its contents.

Isham Riddle turned irritably to Tarn. "I was surprised to find that Ramsay's a friend of yours, Tarn,"
he said bluntly. "Wouldn't think you'd care for the cut
of his jib."

"I don't," said Tarn easily. "But I cultivated his acquaintance because I was curious to know how a gentleman planter could spend most of his time carousing in Williamsburg, have reportedly constant failures in his tobacco crop—"

"That's true," agreed Isham gloomily. "Never saw a plantation so badly run."

"—yet still seem to thrive as Ramsay does! He loses large sums, he wagers on anything, he has just ordered another suit from his tailor. How does he do it, Isham?"

Isham Riddle shook his head and looked down at his toes, but his sister suggested, "Perhaps he has income from another source?"

Isham Riddle looked up and caught Tarn Jenner's eye. A worried look passed between them.

"If you mean, does he have an income out of England, none profess to know of it nor does he claim any," said Tarn slowly.

"Aye, that is what I thought," sighed Isham.

"I think it is terrible to speak so of your host!" remonstrated Mistress Riddle.

"He's not my host by choice," complained her brother, turning on her. "When you refused to spend another night at Riddlewood until the wing was rebuilt, I wanted you to go to the Barclays."

"But the Barclays did not offer and Bainter Ramsay did!"

"The Barclays would have offered, had you given them the chance. Instead, just because Ramsay happened by that morning and felt impelled to offer us shelter, you have put me in the position of sleeping under the roof of a man I do not like—indeed I *must* sleep there or leave you alone in the house with him!"

"Ridiculous! I'm perfectly safe—a woman my age? I assure you, young Mr. Ramsay has no designs on me!"

"There's the matter of propriety, Gladys! How would it look? And it requires me to keep men hauling me up and down the river so I can hold the property together! Why couldn't you go to the Barclays? Why can't you go there now and take Mistress Dorinda with you and let me get back to Riddlewood where I belong?"

"Nonsense," said his sister sharply. "The Barclays are overcrowded as it is."

"They would make room for you!"

"Indeed they would and it would put them out! What with a new baby on the way and those English cousins suddenly piling in on them. No, we are very comfortable at Haverleigh and there we shall stay. For the present."

As Isham muttered, Gladys turned regally to Tarn. "Have you had any luck in finding the plantation you wish to purchase?"

Dorinda's eyes widened in surprise. "How large a place are you looking for?" she asked.

"I'd prefer ten thousand acres with a suitable house." He smiled down at her. "Or less acreage if there's enough good tobacco land."

"You can have mine soon," growled Isham. "If I'm not there to mind it!"

His sister gave him a quelling look. "I would think that Merryvale Manor would fit your needs exactly," she hazarded.

"Well, I thought so too—but then an heir turned up, so there's a question now as to whether it will be sold." Tarn looked directly into Dorinda's eyes. "*Are* you going to sell it?"

Dorinda's gaze slid away. "I—I'm not sure," she said vaguely.

"Well, after all she hasn't seen it yet," protested Mistress Riddle, her arch glance suggesting that if they got married they could *share* the plantation.

Dorinda felt the pressure of Tarn's keen gaze. It seemed to probe beneath her bodice, caress the silkiness of her breasts, and ferret out all her secrets. What would it be like to marry him? she asked herself breathlessly. A dangerous man, an exciting man!

Suddenly into that breathless pause Isham Riddle

cried, "Well, there he is at last!" and they saw Bainter Ramsay striding down the street toward them.

"And look what he's brought you, Dorinda!" cried Gladys Riddle excitedly.

Not to be outdone by Tarn's gift of a hat, Bainter had come back swinging a delicate ruffled parasol of shimmering lime green silk that he must have gone to some trouble to get. With a brief formal bow he presented the parasol to Dorinda. "I believe this will better shield you from the sun than a hat made of flimsy straw," he observed. "Consider it a gift from me."

Mistress Riddle tittered, her brother cleared his throat disapprovingly, and Dorinda, faced with the patent incongruity of the situation, was hard put not to laugh. She felt herself to be a veritable belle of Williamsburg as, twirling her new silk parasol and clutching the disreputable box that contained the cat, she was handed into the carriage.

Bainter's talk was urbane, he was quick to point out places of interest as they passed, but Dorinda could not resist a last look back at the man from Philadelphia she was leaving behind her.

He stood watching them depart, a tall and resolute figure with his dark hair blowing as a sudden light breeze caught it. Seeing her turn, he waved at her. Then the same breeze that was blowing his hair caught hers and swept it in a shower of gold over her eyes. When she had pushed it back again, the tall figure was gone.

"Something else you've forgotten?" asked Bainter solicitously.

"No, nothing," she said, but she felt a sudden unaccountable sense of loss as if a worthy adversary on whom she counted to sharpen her wits had suddenly departed her life.

"If you were looking at Jenner, he will be off to the taverns to find himself a willing barmaid for the night," said Bainter in a slightly spiteful tone.

Willing indeed, Dorinda thought with an absurd sense of sorrow. *The barmaids of Williamsburg would no doubt count themselves lucky to be held in such arms!*

Determinedly she turned her face away, upriver toward Haverleigh and her destiny. Whatever he knew or suspected, Tarn Jenner had not betrayed her. He looked to be the roving kind, she thought regretfully. After all, he had no roots, he was staying at an inn. If he did not find the plantation he wanted, he would doubtless be moving on. She would probably never see him again. She remembered as Williamsburg receded in the distance that she had forgotten to sew on his button and felt a sudden sharp stab of regret.

He'll speak you fair
Till he gets you to bed
And then he'll forget
That he asked you to wed!

PART TWO

Of Danger—and Dreams!

Chapter 25

The trip upriver had been uneventful. The green banks had slid by as they were rowed up the James in stately fashion in a long barge. Six men strained at the oars and Bainter and Isham Riddle stood in the prow while Dorinda and Mistress Riddle sat on seats beneath an awning in the stern.

Beside Mistress Riddle reposed a box of sugared muffins and now she waved one. "Look there, Dorinda!" She was calling Dorinda's attention one by one to the handsome homes that lined the river, homes with grassy lawns and big spreading trees and boxwood and smaller dependent buildings that marked them as the great independent plantations they were.

Dorinda was watching Bainter's handsome figure in the prow. He stood there, a majestic figure in rose damask, glittering in the sunshine. If his pose was a bit studied, Dorinda did not mind. He was the man of her girlish dreams and it was magical that she should at last be actually gliding upriver to Haverleigh in his barge.

Beside her Mistress Riddle kept up a running flow of conversation. At the moment she was bemoaning the fact that the fire at Riddlewood, which had absorbed all their attention, had kept her from visiting a cousin newly arrived in Boston. "And the post is so slow," she was wailing. "It takes four weeks for a letter to reach us from Boston in the summertime—and twice as long in winter!"

Dorinda nodded but she was not really listening. She was half dreaming in the shade of the awning. Before her the river stretched onward, draining down from the high peaks of the Alleghenies, but she gave it no thought. Her soft gaze floated over the verdant green shoreline with its pines and hardwoods—here a cluster of oaks mixed in with red cedars, over there a poplar grove, there a tall beech or a hickory. They passed walnut trees towering over redbuds, with gray squirrels flashing through their branches, and endless dogwood. Sometimes cattle or horses were grazing in the marsh grass and looked up curiously as the barge went by, and once an otter played in the water near them. Dorinda looked up as a golden eagle flew over, soaring high, and then swooped down—and she saw his prey, a red fox which took off running. Above Mistress Riddle's pattering voice she could hear the song of the mockingbirds and the angry squawk of a jay whose territory had been invaded. It was lovely country, she thought, leaning back. She leaned over the side, intending to trail her hand in the water—and drew back as a water moccasin swam by.

She looked up at Bainter suddenly. The thought had occurred to her that while this was beautiful country, it was not without its dangers.

She wondered abruptly, could Bainter Ramsay be one of them?

But the upriver journey ended with the sun still shedding its golden rays and Dorinda stood at last on the green lawn of Haverleigh Plantation, sloping gracefully down to the James. Behind her lay the silver river, before her the broad expanse of Haverleigh—that house about which she had dreamed through so many exhausted nights with Lady Soft Paws clutched in her arms to comfort her.

Haverleigh was as beautiful as she had imagined—and considerably more imposing. Massively built of brick on the H-shaped plan so beloved by Elizabethans, it stretched before her. The main floor was reached by a wide outside stairway which seemed to go up and up, rising directly at the crossbar of the H. Four chimneys were grouped at either end and rose like miniature towers from the multiple hipped roof. Breathless with delight, she saw that those massed chimneys carried arches and a balustrade—and there was a promenade that connected them! What a lovely cool place to stroll on summer nights! Flanking the huge central house were service buildings. From the chimney of one of them smoke was rising and she guessed that was the kitchen, from which servants would dash across the lawn carrying hot food. The long brick stables lay to her left—Bainter's pride, no doubt!

But it was the magic of the gardens that most caught her eye. Beneath great elms and yews and tall syca-mores that shaded a blaze of roses were green lawns and double lines of box forming stately walks. Magnolias and crepe myrtle were everywhere, lilacs twisted in exotic shapes and smoke trees gave the whole a roman-tic blur. Among dogwood and mock orange drooped wisteria vines, and guelder roses gave up their fragrance.

"In spring there are fringes of daffodils and purple iris and over there—no, you can't see it from here—a little tea garden," Bainter told her proudly as he led her up a wide green corridor formed by the overarching tree branches toward the house.

"It's wonderful," she said dreamily. "I can't see why you would ever leave it."

He gave her an amused look. Beside her, Mistress Riddle clucked along, pointing out her favorite yellow jessamine and pattering on about her own herb garden at Riddlewood, and how she would be only too glad to share her precious herbs with Bainter, whose herb garden was sadly overgrown. "For this was another bachelor abode before Bainter inherited it," she whispered significantly.

Bainter, Dorinda noted, did not seem much interested in herbs. Plainly he was more interested in the delights of town, and the taverns of Williamsburg were more to his liking than the simpler delights of the country. For some reason she found that disappointing.

He sneezed suddenly, and Mistress Riddle was all sympathy. "You are catching a cold," she told him severely. "And summer colds are as dangerous as any other. You should hop right into bed and let me bring you a poultice!"

"I don't need a poultice," protested Bainter, sneezing again. "There must be a cat around someplace. I always sneeze when there are cats around—God knows why!"

Dorinda was guiltily aware of Lady Soft Paws, stuffed with tasty tidbits from the inn and sleeping still in the wig box she carried. She adjusted the box to her other arm and made certain that the holes she had punched in the top for air were out of Bainter's line of vision.

Up that broad outside stairway they went, past the small windows of the half cellar and passed beneath the simple brick pediment of the main entrance and into a hall thirty feet square. Ionic pediments separated the pine panels of the walls with their recessed bookcases and Dorinda looked up at the coved ceiling, entranced.

"There are five main rooms on this floor," Bainter told her matter-of-factly.

"And passages lead off into a pair of rooms in each wing," added Mistress Riddle. "My brother and I are occupying that wing." She nodded.

"I occupy the east wing," Bainter told her. "If you will let Mistress Riddle show you about, I will have a room prepared for you."

"Oh, I would love to show Dorinda about!" Mistress Riddle said delightedly. She promptly took Dorinda on a tour of the house ("That stairway at the end of the east passage is the only inside stairway leading down.") Dorinda felt that Bainter liked occupying that spot; it gave him command of his castle. But what enchanted her most lay above their heads, a vast attic extending over the whole of the main floor, and a winding way that led to the rooftop promenade.

It was there that she left the box, now open at the top, containing the still sleeping Lady Soft Paws. "I was afraid to tell you in town because the driver might have heard, but it was not a petticoat I went back for but my cat," she told Mistress Riddle conspiratorially. "And since I now learn that Bainter insists they make him sneeze, I think it best that I leave her up here until I can smuggle her down into my room!"

"Indeed, I would have warned you against bringing her had I known," said Mistress Riddle in some alarm. "For Bainter hates cats and you will observe that there are none on the place. For myself, I adore cats and have fifteen of them at Riddlewood. All of them good mousers—and their kittens are in great demand, I can tell you."

Dorinda felt a little chill at learning that Bainter detested cats. But, she told herself sturdily, Lady Soft Paws had winning ways and could melt the coldest heart. And once Bainter got used to her, he would no doubt stop sneezing (for medicine was in its infancy and allergies not understood). Thus bolstered she went back downstairs and discovered that she had been given a bedchamber lovelier and far larger than any she had dreamt of.

"All the furniture was already here," Mistress Riddle told her conversationally, indicating the handsome dark carved Jacobean furnishings with a wave of her plump hand. "The Ramsays were a very wealthy family and all of these things were brought over from England. Bainter is the last of his line."

"I must get some food for poor Lady Soft Paws," said Dorinda. "She will be ravenous when she wakes up."

"We do not dine until eight-thirty," Mistress Riddle told her. "Haverleigh is very fashionable! But I will take you out to the kitchen and you can find her some tidbits."

Dorinda was impressed by the kitchen. Its huge fireplace dwarfed even that of the White Hart and could easily have been used to roast an ox. Two female servants looked up as they entered. Neither of them looked happy, but they brightened as Mistress Riddle paused to exchange pleasantries with them and to collect a bowl, a small pitcher of milk, a pewter plate and some roast venison. Lady Soft Paws would dine in style this day!

"Bainter does not understand the handling of servants," Mistress Riddle confided. "He is far too harsh with the kitchen help. The whole place needs a woman's touch. I have scolded him that he should take a bride." She gave Dorinda a bright expectant look. "Perhaps now he will...."

Dorinda blushed. "If I should decide to stay on at Merryvale Manor," she said carefully, "I will count on you to teach me all those things I do not know. About herbs and how to run a house as large as this."

Mistress Riddle picked that up at once. "Oh?" she said in surprise. "You did not have a large house in England?"

"Only when I was very small," said Dorinda quickly. "After that we lived in a London town house. It is very different living in town, from living in the country."

Mistress Riddle, who had never lived in town, could not dispute it.

That night at dinner in the large dining room, Isham Riddle looked up from his sturgeon and boomed out, "When you ladies were in Williamsburg, you did forget one thing."

His sister gave him a startled look. It was eight-thirty

and in the late summer dusk four candles glittered on the long board. "Why, I thought we had overlooked nothing," she exclaimed. "Pomades, petticoats, gloves, fans—what did we forget?"

"You forgot to see about probating the estate."

"Oh—yes," said Dorinda vaguely, suddenly losing her taste for the sturgeon.

"Oh, pooh! She will want to see the estate first, Isham! And that's easily managed—we can take you there tomorrow, Dorinda. Once he learns who you are, the estate manager will let us in."

Isham Riddle subsided, grumbling that they should have consulted old Merryvale's attorney while they were in Williamsburg. Dorinda felt swept along by the tide. Having announced that she was Joshua Merryvale's niece, she could hardly refuse to view her "inheritance."

"Nonsense, she can see him day after tomorrow at the Claridge ball—I am sure Bainter will want to take you, Dorinda," twinkled Mistress Riddle.

Bainter frowned. "I had not yet decided to go."

"Oh, do let's go!" cried Dorinda, to whom the prospect of attending a ball with Bainter just as she had so often done in her childish dreams was irresistible.

He smiled at her across his wine. His amber eyes seemed to pick up lights from it and grow tawnier, more golden. "If you like, we'll go," he agreed easily.

His gaze upon her was so intense that she felt flustered by it and turned abruptly to Mistress Riddle. "Will we stop by Riddlewood on the way to Merryvale Manor?" she asked the older woman. "I remember you said it was the neighboring plantation, and I'm looking forward to seeing your herb garden and your cats."

"Oh—" Mistress Riddle looked confused for a moment. Then, "Of course we will see it!" she exclaimed energetically. "Isham needs to see how the work is proceeding on the east wing and I must make sure that my cats are being well taken care of." She smiled brightly at Dorinda but just for a moment Dorinda felt she had glimpsed something dark.

A wild thought leaped unbidden to her mind. Could it be that Mistress Riddle was afraid of her own house?

Bainter did not accompany the Riddles and herself on their trip to Merryvale and Dorinda was glad that he had not. She had very mixed feelings about accepting this inheritance she had in Williamsburg so blithely claimed. There she had had an excuse—the fear of immediate exposure. Now that she had had time to think, she felt guiltily that she might be fleecing some unknown heir who would be found if only somebody instituted a diligent search—which they would not do, of course, if they believed her to be the sole heiress.

That she could even carry it off, she had some doubt. After all, lawyers were supposed to inquire into such things and would not her ignorance of Joshua Merryvale be glaringly apparent to Joshua's lawyer? How easily he could trip her up, trap her. The future seemed full of spiked glass over which she must tread with care.

The Riddles' barge, while not so large and impressive as that of Haverleigh, being manned by only four oarsmen instead of six, had nevertheless an awning of a coarsely woven material and comfortable seats. Mistress Riddle was dressed today in a sensible blue linen dress with a neat white collar and a blue hat with a brim. Dorinda wore her new yellow and green sprigged muslin. As she left the house she put on the wide-brimmed straw hat Tarn Jenner had given her and she saw Bainter eyeing it with a frown. But surely he wouldn't expect her to carry that parasol everywhere! It occurred to her suddenly that he was jealous and the thought so buoyed her spirits that she turned and blew him a kiss as she gathered up her light skirts and ran down the bank to catch up with the departing Riddles.

"I am surprised you had your barge at the ready," Dorinda said as she clambered in.

"Oh, it comes down every day to fetch Isham up to Riddlewood," explained Mistress Riddle. "And brings him back in the evening."

"That must be a problem on rainy days," laughed Dorinda, for having decided that Bainter was jealous of her had put her into irrepressibly good spirits. "This awning is grand for shade from the sun but doesn't the porous material leak when it rains?"

"It's made of Virginia cloth," sighed Mistress Riddle, "which is coarse stuff at best. Everything worth having has to be imported!"

But not this air, and not this sun, and not this beautiful Virginia countryside! thought Dorinda.

"My sister would not know whether the awning leaks when it rains or not," growled Isham Riddle. "She is seldom under it!"

"Isham is annoyed that I go with him so infrequently," explained the older woman.

"Infrequently?" He gave a short laugh. "One would think you had become Ramsay's housekeeper!"

"Well, I do feel beholden to him for taking us in like this," said his sister defensively.

"Taking us in? As I keep telling you, we have no need to be taken in by anybody. There are excellent rooms in our own home just waiting for us to occupy them!"

"Oh, Isham, you're upsetting me," cried Mistress Riddle. "Oh, see the otter!" she cried in an attempt to divert him. She pointed to a furry streak that went by them in the water, giving them a quick glance from its bright eyes. "I love to watch them."

Her cry brought Dorinda to lean over the side of the boat. Dorinda loved wildlife and was delighted to see a deer pausing to drink as they were rowed upriver. Muskrats played and darted into the water and once she saw a large mud turtle sunning himself. She could not but think how very bountiful life was here, the tobacco fields burgeoning, meadows waving green, the rustling woods full of deer and wild turkey, the great

migrations of waterfowl and passenger pigeons that
sometimes darkened the sky, the enormous variety of
fish and shellfish that could be taken from the river.
And lining the river at discreet distances from each
other—for some numbered ten thousand acres or more—
elegant plantations where fashionable gentry laughed
and played: a paradise.

"I doubt me we'll have a good year for our tobacco,"
said Isham Riddle gloomily as they passed an area
cleared for tobacco plants. He cast a glance at his sister.
"With me away so much and using four men needed
for the tobacco to row me endlessly up and down, up
and down."

"You could stay the night at Riddlewood if you choose,"
his sister responded tartly. "Dorinda and I can chaperon each other."

"Bah!" was her brother's fiercely delivered rejoinder.
"Ramsay has the devil's own reputation—I'd not leave
either of you alone with him overnight."

Mistress Riddle sighed and gave Dorinda a shrug
that said while it was nice to be so well taken care of, it
could be very annoying at times. But Dorinda had been
reminded that tobacco was king here, tobacco was the
cash crop that bought the silks and laces for the planters' ladies. "Is Merryvale Manor very large?" she asked
suddenly.

The woman beside her gave her a startled look.
"Why, didn't your uncle tell you?" she exclaimed. "It's
all of four thousand acres and much of it good tobacco
land!"

Dorinda sat back feeling frightened. If Merryvale
had been naught but a cottage and garden plot she
would have felt herself to be a thief—as it was, she was
a grand thief!

They let Isham Riddle off at Riddlewood, which
Dorinda could only glimpse through the elm and
broadnut trees in the distance.

"Come along, you can see Riddlewood on the way

back," Mistress Riddle told her briskly, pulling her back onto her seat in the barge. "And Isham will appreciate some time without us too, for he frets over all that may go wrong in his absence."

True to the older woman's promise, a short row took them to Merryvale and Dorinda disembarked with trepidation and nervously advanced through a grove of locusts across a spacious lawn. Directly before the house was a clipped circle of box, dark green against the emerald grass. The house itself was low and rambling, of white painted hand-hewn clapboards overgrown with English ivy. The roof shingles were slate-colored and scroll shutter dogs held the apple green shutters in place.

Dorinda paused unhappily beneath a stately elm that stood like a tall lonely sentinel amid the grove of graceful locusts. She felt like an interloper.

"Just wait, I'll get the keys from the agent for I know that when poor Mr. Merryvale died they locked up the house," she called to Dorinda.

Dorinda's gaze swept from the broad lawns to the pines and cedars that edged this part of the James. It was lovely country, this, and she could indeed make her home here. *But suppose a real heir turned up? What then?*

And suppose one did not? *Could she go through life being ever watchful? Could she go through life living a lie?*

She saw that Mistress Merryvale was coming back, bringing with her the estate's manager, a Scotsman who was all smiles. Dorinda could hardly face him.

But face him she did and then Mistress Riddle took her on a lengthy tour of the house, from the basement kitchen with its bake oven and brick fireplace to the big attics at the top.

In the pleasant dining room, Dorinda looked up at a rectangular wooden frame which surrounded a picture of a dour erect man with straight black hair neatly parted in the middle and a brush of gray-black whiskers around his firm chin—Joshua at middle age no doubt. It was a face of great rectitude and Dorinda felt condemned by that level painted gaze.

."It is—Uncle Joshua, isn't it?" she asked. And then quickly, "You see, we had no picture of him."

"Yes, that's your uncle." Mistress Riddle bobbed her head. "Looking as he always looked, right straight at you. Sometimes people would twit him that he should go back to England and spend his declining years, but he'd always say, no, this was a new land and he had thrown in his lot with it, whatever happened."

Dorinda, facing his painted likeness, felt ashamed. She wished she could beg his pardon.

"You will want to look over the linens and silver, I suppose?"

Dorinda shook her head. She felt suffocated.

"Oh, well, 'tis no great matter. Being a man and alone for so many years, he was not much interested in linens and silver. He often said pewter plate was good enough for a man, that only women cared to slave and polish to keep silver shining!"

"I think I have—seen enough," choked Dorinda the interloper. As they left she was haunted by the sight of the big square bed with its steps to climb up, where Joshua Merryvale had died, by the rather empty but sunny rooms and the almost barrackslike neatness of Joshua's bachelor abode.

"Come, you'll want to see this before you go," said Mistress Riddle briskly. She led Dorinda down a southeastern slope through the garden, already becoming overgrown with neglect now its owner had gone, and Dorinda stiffened as she saw she was approaching the family graveyard.

"Of course, so far it contains but a single grave," Mistress Riddle told Dorinda as the two women came into the shady little enclosure already overrun with blue-flowered myrtle and dark green English ivy. "Your uncle's." Her tone implied that someday Dorinda herself and all the children she would one day have would be buried here. "Perhaps you might like to pick some flowers from the garden to put on his grave?" she suggested kindly.

Feeling every inch a fraud, Dorinda picked some fragrant musk roses from the overgrown garden and walked to the raw new stone that said "Joshua Merryvale, gentleman. Born London, England 1640, died Virginia Colony 1717." Tarn Jenner had exaggerated. "Uncle Joshua" had been seventy-seven when he left his beloved manor. He had been born in the time of the Stuart king, Charles I, and had lived to see him executed. He had survived the revolution and the England of the Puritans under Cromwell, the joyous restoration of another and more licentious Stuart, Charles II, to the English throne. He had lived through the Great Plague and the Great Fire and the Monmouth Rebellion and had come to America and built here a home to be proud of.

Dorinda knelt and with gentle fingers laid the big fragrant white roses, whose perfume had scented the English countryside for so many centuries, upon the grave of an Englishman turned American.

She would not have been surprised if they had shriveled at her touch.

It was a relief to return to Riddlewood, to climb from the barge and shake off some of the guilt that had enveloped her like a cloak at Merryvale Manor.

Isham Riddle was not there to meet them; he was closeted in the plantation office with his estate agent going over the books. But they were greeted nonetheless, for a motley collection of cats came running as Mistress Riddle called, "Kitty, kitty!" in her high squeaky voice. Cats of all descriptions swarmed about their feet as they walked across the enormous lawn shaded by stately elms and lacy willow oaks and handsome broadnut trees. Tabby cats, calicos, tiger-striped, two-tones, all raised their voices almost in shrieks in an effort to gain their mistress's attention as the two women approached the T-shaped house with its four chimneys and steeply curbed roof. Mistress Riddle clucked at them as she walked, calling each by name. "They wander in," she admitted. "I suppose they're attracted by the crowd."

"Yes, it must be like town living to them," laughed Dorinda, who had been eyeing the nearly flush dormers and thinking how light and bright Riddlewood must be inside. "A town of cats!"

"Do you think they're hungry?" worried Mistress Riddle as they approached one "L" of the "T" and entered the house through a porch tucked in the angle. "I left strict orders to feed them."

The cats followed them in and Dorinda found herself in a wide hall with a handsome cornice and staircase.

"I wonder if Puss has had her kittens yet," said Mistress Riddle, stumbling over a big black and white tom as she opened the door into a paneled room. "Yes, she has!" she exclaimèd delightedly, going over to a large padded basket where a cream and brown tabby cat looked up and yawned. Her four fluffy kittens were busy nursing and she flexed her paws and purred. "And fine kittens they are, Puss," approved Mistress Riddle, stroking the cat's soft ears. She turned proudly to Dorinda. "And every one of them spoken for by my neighbors! They're aware of our reputation as mousers, aren't they, Puss?"

Dorinda held back her mirth for Mistress Riddle, with her short nose and plump body and fluffy wig looked a bit like a "mouser" herself. She felt real affection for the older woman pour over her. Here at last was someone who didn't have a single bad thought in her head! It occurred to her that the Riddles had been driven out of their home by fire and she had so far seen no evidence of it.

"Where is the part of the house that burned?" she asked.

"Here," said Mistress Riddle promptly. She opened a door as lovely as the walls' rich paneling and Dorinda found herself suddenly looking out on a tall blackened chimney rising from a mass of tangled charred beams and rubble against a backdrop of gardens and trees. "The east wing," said Mistress Riddle solemnly. "*This* was our dining room. Ah, I had such a lovely cherrywood table and such fine salts! And there were lovely round arches on each side of the fireplace and such nice deep window recesses!" She gave a little whimper and Dorinda's heart went out to her. "My bedroom was just upstairs over the dining room. I had eaten a heavy meal," she added almost apologetically, "and I was fast asleep."

You were stuffed and you were sleeping like the dead—and you nearly ended up dead, thought Dorinda.

"Luckily Isham, whose room was down the hall, woke up and he was hungry and he decided to go down and try potluck in the kitchen. It was then that he smelled smoke and when he opened the door into the hallway it was filled with suffocating black smoke. He had the presence of mind to wet a towel from the basin and put it over his face and he fought his way through the smoke to me. Everything in my room was in flames. Even my bed had caught fire and Isham dragged me from it. Indeed when I came to myself I thought I was in hell and the devil had me in the pit!" Mistress Riddle's voice rose to a wail. "I was so confused I fought with Isham and he struck me and dragged me out."

"And saved your life," whispered Dorinda, her own scalp prickling as she imagined how it had been. "But how did you put the fire out? From this much destruction—I mean, this whole wing is gutted—I'd have thought the whole house would have gone up!"

"It almost did," shuddered Mistress Riddle. "Indeed it would have, save that we had a sudden torrential rainstorm. It was the thunder and lightning that had waked Isham up, you see. Water poured down like a waterfall and cascaded over the roof and Isham had the presence of mind to marshal the servants and have them bring buckets and wet down the door here and the wall. You can see watermarks if you look, and most of the furniture was ruined. All the cloth has to be replaced—you can see that I took the draperies down because they were so smoked and water-stained, and anything overstuffed has to be recovered and still smells musty—but I couldn't bear the sight of any of it and I had it all stuffed into the west wing! But the very worst thing was losing the dining room because it was my pride and joy! All my dishes were broken when the beams collapsed and fell upon the cupboard and I suppose my silver is in there somewhere, melted down and unrecognizable, but Isham has had the servants poke about and so far no one has found it." She looked about to cry. "Oh, Percival, don't do that!" she wailed, trying to shake off a half-grown tiger striped cat who was climbing ambitiously up her skirts.

Inspiration seized Dorinda, a way to pull Mistress Riddle out of her despair. "Let's find something to feed the cats," she suggested, gently extracting the young tiger cat's claws from Mistress Riddle's taffeta skirts. Those skirts bore the marks of other claws, she noted critically as she set the cat down upon its paws.

"That's a good idea," said the older woman in a more normal voice. "*Then* perhaps they'll stop bothering us."

With the cook's help—and Dorinda could not but notice the compassion and affection with which both Cook and scullery help treated the plump little spinster—they found a large bowl of scraps ("I was about to feed them, ma'am.") It was a wild scene. A large crock of milk was poured into round wooden bowls and the eager cats shouldered each other aside and fought for position as they drank. They snarled playfully over tidbits and slapped each other's furry faces—sometimes with real force. And when it was over, they purred and licked milky whiskers and strolled out onto the lawns and found favorite spots to lie in the shade and groom their elegant coats.

But even the distraction of the hungry cats could not keep Mistress Riddle from veering back to the subject that was on her mind.

"People said it was the lightning," she told Dorinda when Cook had gone and they were left alone. "They said that lightning struck the house and set it afire and that the noise woke Isham up. . . ." Her voice trailed off.

"But you don't think so?" Dorinda gave her friend a penetrating look.

"I was only half-conscious and choking and Isham was pulling me down the stairs and I caught a glimpse through the window outside and—and I saw someone standing there in the fire's light. All I could see was his red coat—glowing in the light of the flames. And something glittering in front of him."

"Perhaps the buttons on his coat?" suggested Dorinda.

"And no one on the plantation has a red coat."

Dorinda felt her scalp prickle. "But didn't you find him? Afterward?"

"No," wailed Mistress Riddle. "Isham says I was scared to death—which was true—and so shocked I was imagining things. He said there wasn't any man, that lightning did strike the house. But he admits he didn't look out the window as he dragged me down the stairs. And how could the house have gone up in flames so quickly? And why wasn't the roof burning at first? Why did the fire start from below, in the dining room? Why haven't they found the silver?" Her plump body began to shake with sobs, and Dorinda's arm went around her comfortingly. "That's why I'm afraid to come back," she choked. "I think someone deliberately set the house afire. I'm afraid that someone will try again."

"But—but *why*?" gasped Dorinda, feeling totally inadequate to meet this new problem. "Do you have any enemies? Do you think the Indians—?"

"There's no Indian trouble." The plump little woman stopped crying and begn to wipe her eyes. "And Isham is well liked and I think I am too. We haven't an enemy in the world that we know of. And—and we've been here twenty years! If someone hated us, why wouldn't they have tried to kill us before? And to think, we put in all that paneling after we bought the house and now so much of it is burned!" She began to cry afresh.

"The former owners," said Dorinda, clutching at straws. "Could they have had enemies? Could someone have returned and thought they still lived there and set the house ablaze not knowing you'd bought it?"

Mistress Riddle stopped sobbing as she considered this novel possibility. "No," she sighed finally. "We bought it from a widow who was returning to England after her husband died. They were well liked too." She gave Dorinda a despondent look. "Don't mention what I told you to Isham. He thinks I'm foolish. *But I know what I saw—a man in a red coat holding something shiny.* So now you know," she sighed. "You know why I don't hurry the rebuilding, why I stay on at Haverleigh—oh, I *leaped* at the chance when Bainter Ramsay came upriver the morning after the fire and offered us his hospitality! Once the wing is fully rebuilt, I'll have no excuse for staying on!" She began to wring her hands. "Oh, I'm so afraid, so afraid. I have nightmares about it and I wake up hot and shaking and feeling the flames all about me. It's as if I'd died and gone to hell!"

The Claridge Ball
WILLIAMSBURG, VIRGINIA
Summer 1717

Chapter 26

No party she attended later would ever quite match for Dorinda the excitement she felt as the barge pulled away from the landing at Haverleigh Plantation for the Claridge ball in Williamsburg.

The morning had been spent in plebian tasks. Mistress Riddle, who tried, Dorinda knew, to oversee some things on this ill-run plantation to repay Bainter's hospitality, had insisted this day on supervising the servants in the making of soap and Dorinda assisted her.

"I always have good luck with my soap," Mistress Riddle told Dorinda importantly. "So many people fail with it. Not I! And my secret—and you must remember this, Dorinda—is always to stir the soap in one direction as it boils—never change directions, it will ruin it utterly!"

Dorinda resisted telling Mistress Riddle how much soap she had made in her life. Some of it had indeed "failed" but she had attributed that to the poor quality grease she had had to use. This combination of bear grease and fish oil and deer fat should give no trouble. But the terrible odor, when all that grease was boiled with lye, as always, drove her back from the big iron pot that had been set up outdoors.

" 'Tis awful!" she gasped.

The older woman gave her a patient look. "Try to stay upwind of it," she said.

"But why are we making soap at all when we all use perfumed imported soap?"

"For the servants," said Mistress Riddle dismissingly.

Dorinda saw the serving girls who were busily stirring the contents of the iron pot with long wooden paddles give each other resigned looks. The harsh soft soap reddened and coarsened their hands.

"It will harden if only we dash some salt into it," she told Mistress Riddle hopefully. "And make nice light bars!"

"A shocking waste of salt," reproved the older woman. "Do you know what salt costs?"

"Oh, do let me show you!" Dorinda, who had made "special soap" at the inn for those guests who could not afford the imported variety, ran and brought some salt. Skillfully she added just the right amount of salt and stood back while the girls stirred. One of them turned to give her a grateful look. This bar soap, they were sure, would be much easier on their hands!

And then they were dressing for the ball—Dorinda in her elegant new emerald green silk gown. Brilliants sparkled from her tight bodice, highlighting the shapeliness of her firm young breasts and her sixteen-inch waist. Over her shoulders for the barge trip downriver was draped the embroidered lemon silk shawl with its rich gleaming silk fringe. And on her feet were the green satin dancing slippers that Tarn had recommended. She wondered if he would be there. And thinking of him, she unconsciously patted the tall upswept coiffure that had taken her three hours to perfect.

"You look ravishing," Bainter told her appreciatively. "No lady of the French court could look more elegant!"

Dorinda gave a breathless little laugh. Bainter had been paying her extravagant compliments ever since she had arrived at Haverleigh, but so far he had made no move to touch her. Plainly the tawny Bainter had a different approach for heiresses and chambermaids!

"Yes, that dress becomes her well," chimed in Mistress Riddle, who was herself a miracle of lavender silk flounces and had made her flaxen wig a forest of pink and purple rosettes. "I did think Dorinda should wear a rosette or two in her hair though," she added regretfully. "But she thought that just a simple black satin riband was enough."

The black satin riband wound gracefully through Dorinda's huge gleaming curls and was caught at two strategic points by a winking brilliant. Its black sheen brought out the gold of her hair in a dramatic way that would cause heads to turn. Just now the length that spilled down alongside the fat graceful golden tress that nestled alongside her neck and curled a short way down over her white bosom seemed to fascinate Bainter. He kept staring at it so fixedly that Dorinda thought nervously that he was going to start toying with it but he did not.

"Have you given any more thought to what should be done for Mistress Dorinda in the matter of Merryvale Manor?" he asked Isham Riddle without looking up.

"Aye," was the ready response. "George Peabody, Joshua Merryvale's attorney, is sure to be at the Claridge ball. I expect to buttonhole him there and ask him to see to what's necessary."

Dorinda felt some of the joy go out of the evening. She looked out upon the silvery water gliding by in the gathering dusk and wished from her divided heart that she could both disclaim the Merryvale fortune yet keep the social acceptance that being an heiress had brought her. She sighed.

From a seat nearby, Bainter's topaz satin form turned toward her. "You are pensive tonight," he observed.

And she thought he had not noticed! "Yes," she said carefully.

"You are homesick for England?" he guessed.

It was on the tip of Dorinda's tongue to blurt out that indeed she was not homesick for England, that she had been little better than a street urchin in London, and that Virginia was to her a paradise found. But of course she did not. Too much was at stake. "I miss— many things," she said diffidently. *Things she had never had, not things she'd known!*

"I will try to make you forget England," he said, and for the first time took her hand.

Mistress Riddle beamed on them both. She was sure she had made a match and meant to boast of it this night. That would settle all those girls who were setting their caps for Bainter Ramsay!

The new house Walter Claridge had built for his bride next door to the Red Lion was the pride of Williamsburg and Dorinda, like the others, was dazzled by its eighteen-pane windows and handsome brickwork, a basket-weave effect of Flemish bond. Above their heads rose a denticulated cornice, garnishing the hipped roof. Through those many-paned windows now blazed a forest of candles, sending out slanted golden light into the street, and torches had been stuck into the iron railing outside. Picking up her emerald silk skirts, Dorinda accompanied her party up one side of the double brick stairway and through the open front door into a blaze of light.

In the wide wainscoted hallway their hostess, a pretty woman in her early twenties gowned in cream-colored taffeta shimmering with silver stitching and with a powdered wig, stepped forward and embraced Mistress Riddle warmly, asking her how the rebuilding was coming along at Riddlewood.

"Slowly," Isham Riddle answered for her. He might

have said more but that his sister gave him a reproving look and promptly presented Dorinda to her hostess and to Walter Claridge, a rather preoccupied gentleman, meticulously got up in sky blue satin, who stood beside his wife, gravely receiving his guests.

"Yes, I heard that you had arrived—and in such tragic circumstances too!" Attractive Lucy Claridge seized both of Dorinda's hands. "If you tire of this dreadful rake—" she gave Bainter an arch look—"you must come to town and stay with us!" Dorinda muttered confused thanks as her hostess greeted other new arrivals and then turned back to her.

"And now you must come and meet all our guests, Mistress Merryvale, for I do declare you are the only person here who does not already know everyone!" she cried merrily.

Leaving her husband Walter to greet any new arrivals, Lucy Claridge swept Dorinda the Newcomer into the candlelit drawing room which was already crowded with people. Dorinda had a swift impression of paneled walls painted that soft tone which would one day come to be known as "Williamsburg green," of candles in shining brass wall sconces, mirrored to reflect the light. Over the carved wooden mantel was gracefully draped a twisted garland of roses and ivy, the red flowers glowing from out of the dark waxy green leaves. Through the open door of the next room came the slightly discordant sounds of the musicians warming up. Wafting about her was the scent of expensive perfumes mingled with Virginia tobacco, the popular sweet wines and the tangier scent of stronger spirits. Dorinda was whirled about the room, her new green satin dancing slippers tripping lightly over the soft blue "Turkey carpet" as her energetic hostess made introductions right and left. Gentlemen in pastel satins with shining gold buttons and tight-fitting waistcoats and knee breeches bowed and made a leg to her. Ladies waving ivory or feather fans, some of them set with jewels or tiny mirrors,

ladies with their elegant gowns adorned with brooches
and earrings of coral or amber or seed pearls or
jet—striking against their light satins and brocades—
expressed their delight at meeting her, although many
pairs of bright eyes were hard put not to display their
envy and many a smiling mouth tightened at sight of
this striking newcomer in their midst. All of them went
by Dorinda in a bright excited blur.

Except for one. Midway through the crowd she was
suddenly aware of a smiling sardonic face above her,
and that face atop a gentleman of stature.

The man from Philadelphia.

He looked very fit tonight. He had abandoned what
must have been a favorite maroon coat for another of
scarlet silk handsomely adorned with gold buttons—
none of them missing. His muscular legs were encased
in dove gray silk breeches and his silk-stockinged
calves were as handsome as any in the room. When
she had seen him last he had been wearing boots but
tonight he wore black leather shoes with silver buck-
les. A ruby ring set in gold flashed from his finger as
he tossed down a glass of wine. Around that sardonic
face his thick dark hair was tied back military fashion
in a neat queue—a style that vastly became him. He
was arrogant, debonair, a man women would always
pursue.

As they were pursuing him now, she saw, and a tiny
frown appeared between her high winglike brows. He
had not seen her yet. He was occupied with—indeed
surrounded by—a little knot of admiring ladies who
parted reluctantly to allow their hostess to pass through,
sweeping Dorinda along with her. The rather acid
looks that were directed at Dorinda over ivory fans or
from the corners of long-lashed eyes spoke their annoyance at this interruption.

"Mistress Merryvale," cried Lucy Claridge, using the
same arch look and coy tone she had used a few
minutes ago with Bainter. "I must present to you an-

other newcomer to our shores, Tarn Jenner. Mr. Jenner has not been with us very long but we all do hope he will stay, don't we?" She included the group encircling Tarn with her light nod and there was a rippling of assent.

Tarn Jenner looked down on Dorinda from his great height, his cold gray eyes taking in appreciatively the golden sheen of her hair, the radiant beauty of her countenance, the delicate luster of her bosom which needed no alabaster powder to give it a pearly sheen as it rose and fell above the emerald silk of her bodice, alight with brilliants.

"Mistress Merryvale and I have already met," he told his hostess lightly. "Indeed having met her once, one could never forget so lustrous a lady!" Gallantly, he made a leg to her and bent to brush his lips over the back of Dorinda's outstretched hand.

He had kissed her hand! Dorinda felt a tingle go through her at his touch and admitted, her color somewhat heightened, that she was indeed acquainted with Mr. Jenner.

"Well, we must not let Tarn monopolize you," declared her hostess, and promptly led her away to another group, dominated by three elderly gentlemen who were wrangling over this year's probable price of tobacco, what was to be done about the Indians "north of the falls," and whether the perpetual battles between clashing Indian tribes who used the Shenandoah Valley as a hunting ground would ever cease.

Lucy Claridge entered into an animated discussion with one of them about the danger to the settlers beyond the falls and Dorinda, slightly annoyed that Tarn Jenner had not followed her, found herself catching snatches of conversations nearby.

"—and of course that girl Jonas was so infatuated with in Yorktown was only a bound girl with nothing behind her, no family, no standing in the community, he couldn't be *expected* to marry her," a lady in bronze taffeta and jet was saying.

"But he ended up marrying such a colorless little thing, so pitifully dull, I wonder Jonas can stand her company for an evening, let alone a lifetime!"

"Ah, but that was for her money—at least the money she was reputed to have."

"Yes," sighing. "It did lend her a certain glamour, I will admit—"

The chatting ladies wandered out of earshot but Dorinda could feel her own ears burning. She felt as if she had been stripped naked to public view. *She* had certainly been a bound girl and that same Bainter Ramsay who was paying court to her now had considered her unworthy of respect because of it! And whoever the colorless little thing was that Jonas had ended up with, it was the money she was *reputed to have* that had lent her the glamour needed to make the match.

Williamsburg was full of eligible young ladies, many of them heiresses, and Bainter Ramsay had somehow managed to evade them all. What had they lacked?

She was pondering this as Bainter's tall form loomed beside her and of a sudden a wild scheme occurred to Dorinda. She would separate the men from the boys! She would cut Bainter out of the pack and make him her own, just as she had once dreamed she would do—and now she knew exactly how she would do it!

Bainter was sipping a glass of wine as he sauntered up to them and now his topaz satin figure bent toward his hostess.

"On such a glorious night when the air is soft and warm and there are musicians in the next room, did you not intend dancing?" he asked Lucy.

Lucy's lashes fluttered. "I had not intended it," she admitted in her high light voice. "But of course if it

would please you, we will by all means take up the rug
and have dancing."

Bainter was laughing down into Lucy's eyes. "You
know as well as I do that you always intended to have
dancing, Lucy," he said in a voice as intimate as the
rustle of sheets. "You just wanted everybody first to
walk over your new rug and exclaim over it and *then*
you were going to call final attention to it by having it
taken up, were you not?"

Lucy Claridge's eyes sparkled and her cheeks reddened
a trifle beneath the rouge. She struck Bainter a playful blow with her fan. "You are a dreadful man,
Bainter!" she declared. "Such a thing never occurred
to me! But since you ask it, I will certainly have the
rug taken up and we will dance the night away." She
spun away from him laughing in a swirl of ivory skirts
and called gaily to her servants to take up the "Turkey
carpet."

Bainter stood beside Dorinda—indeed he hovered
over her as the servants quickly took up the blue rug
and cleared the floor for dancing. "Would you not like
a drink?" he asked. "Or will you share mine? To have
your lips touch the glass is to give the wine a sweeter
taste."

"Not yet, thank you," said Dorinda, who was not used
to drinking and hoped she could get through the
evening on a single glass. She remembered Jeddie's
gossip and wondered suddenly if Bainter had slept with
Lucy Claridge. There had been something intimate,
clandestine between them just now. "Are you always so
successful with ladies?" she asked, giving him a slanted
look.

"Oh, you mean Lucy Claridge?" He laughed. "But we
are old friends. I do not count the Lucy Claridges," he
murmured, moving closer. "I only count—"

"The innocent girls that you seduce?" She backed
away a step, smiling.

He paused and looked hurt. "Now what have I done

to warrant that?" he demanded in mock dismay. "Damme, Dorinda, but you're as prickly as a thistle!"

The music struck up just then, the governor led Lucy Claridge out upon the floor and Bainter set down his glass on a tiny rosewood table and turned to Dorinda. "May I have the honor?"

Dorinda, flushed and lovely and with the most elaborately coiffed hair in the room, made him a deep curtsy that swept out her emerald skirts. With Bainter in topaz satin, they swirled and sparkled among the dancers like twin jewels in the candlelit room, the golden woman and the tawny gentleman.

"You dance like a Frenchwoman," he said abruptly.

"I had a French dancing teacher," was her breathless reply.

That answer seemed to satisfy him and he was silent for a while, whirling her about. Dorinda saw that across the room Tarn Jenner was dancing with a tiny girl in a red dress. As they spun by she saw the girl's inky curls fly out and heard her laughter tinkle. For some reason she could not quite explain to herself the sight annoyed Dorinda. Tarn Jenner, she told herself firmly, was nothing to her—it was Bainter Ramsay who interested her! And was she not living out a dream, dancing with him tonight?

Dorinda was not unaware of the swift envious glances on the faces of several women there and when Bainter, over her shoulder, cast a smile of truly lascivious sweetness upon one young thing in pink satin with powdered hair and a beauty patch beside her dimple, Dorinda decided so to divert him that he would have eyes only for her and make the women of Williamsburg green with envy.

She would invent a past for herself.

"My life has been full of heartbreak," she sighed, noting that Tarn Jenner's dark head was bent rather close over that of the little dark girl.

"Tell me about it," said Bainter absently. He was still

looking over her emerald shoulder at the flirtatious pink satin confection.

And she would invent that past in such a way as to explain everything yet still maintain her social position!

"I was betrothed as a mere child of twelve to the richest man in Kent," said Dorinda clearly.

That got his attention.

"And he was killed when his horse balked at a stone fence. I—I was there," she added with a realistic quaver for Tarn Jenner had just danced the little dark-haired girl out the door into the garden.

"How tragic," said Bainter gravely. "The richest man in Kent, you say?"

"And then when I was fourteen," Dorinda rushed on, "I was betrothed again—this time to the Earl of Arden, who assured me he had homes in six counties."

"Indeed?" murmured Bainter, but he was looking at her now with more respect. "But I take it you did not marry this Earl since your name remains Merryvale?"

"Oh, I cannot talk about it," sighed Dorinda. *What could they be doing out there?* "I cannot. What happened to him is too awful!"

She had at last aroused the burning curiosity of the man in topaz satin. "Of course you can tell me!" he urged.

"No, no." Dorinda turned her head away from him. She was trying to focus on the garden door, to see if Tarn and the little dark girl had returned, but the effect was to show to advantage the lovely lines of her neck. Bainter viewed that white expanse that stretched down her flawless bosom to her straining bodice with a glint in his amber eyes.

"I will tell you some other time for I—I must not burst into tears," she said in a shaky voice for they had just returned and the little dark girl was covered with blushes, while Tarn Jenner looked his usual jaunty self.

"You will tell me now," said Bainter, leaning over and looking this time intently into her flushed upset face.

Dorinda had been thinking so hard about Tarn Jenner that for a moment Bainter's tawny face blurred before her.

"Very well," she said in a distracted voice. "I—" she looked away, saw that Tarn had surrendered the little dark girl to a peach-garbed fellow and was leading a tall statuesque redhead out upon the floor. They seemed to be laughing a great deal. Dorinda took a deep indignant breath. She had to trust someone. *She was going to trust Bainter.* "I married him," she said grimly.

Bainter lost a step.

"Where is he now?" he inquired politely.

"In the family crypt at Elsington, his main seat. Our wedding day was so stormy that there was some thought of calling off the wedding, but people had come so far that we felt we must not postpone. We beat our way to the church in a driving rain. There was terrible thunder and lightning all through the ceremony. I almost had to scream 'I do' to be heard against the din. And no sooner had we been pronounced man and wife than lightning struck the church. The wedding guests scattered. I was running too, almost tripping over my bridal gown."

Bainter was hanging on her words now, she could imagine how furious her competition must be. Unfortunately Tarn Jenner, completely absorbed by the statuesque redhead, did not seem to notice.

"And then—?" demanded Bainter tensely.

"Part of a cornice fell and struck my bridegroom." Dorinda shuddered, wishing doom upon Tarn's dancing partner who had just thrown back her head and was laughing vivaciously at something Tarn had said. "He was killed instantly."

"So the marriage was never consummated!"

Dorinda dragged her attention away from the dancing couple nearby and focused on Bainter. She gave him a tragic look from her big blue-green eyes.

"But it was a marriage nonetheless," she told him disconsolately.

"Then you are a countess!" he exclaimed.

"Yes," said Dorinda, and her voice rang with sincerity. "I am in truth a countess." For was she not well and truly Countess Rinda's granddaughter, and should not that count for something?

"Well, then we should call you 'Countess,'" he said in amazement. "I wonder that you did not tell me this before?"

"There is more," sighed Dorinda. She saw Tarn glancing in her direction and she lifted her head haughtily. *Now was the time to take the plunge! But with Bainter—not Tarn!* "Oh, Bainter," she cried, the emotion she had felt at watching Tarn dancing with other girls coloring her voice, "could we not go somewhere more private so that we can talk without fear of being overheard?"

"Of course." With alacrity he led her from the floor and interested eyes followed them. She hoped spitefully that Tarn had noticed her leaving with Bainter!

Bainter took her strolling in the long narrow garden with its fragrant climbing roses and clipped box. "Now then," he said when he had reached the end of the garden. "What is it that you wish to tell me so privately?"

Dorinda took a deep breath. She was taking a long chance but then she had ever been a gambler by nature. She felt that she had left the old life behind her and had become a new woman. If a romantic past was desirable, then she would have a romantic past. But here before her, bathed in moonlight, was the man she had wanted for so long—wealthy, desirable, *single*. She put away from her any pulsating thoughts about the irritating Mr. Jenner. She wanted *Bainter*—not Tarn! —to ask for her hand in marriage, she wanted to be Bainter's bride just as she had dreamed she would be so long ago at the White Hart, *but she wanted it all to be right*. She could tell him these glib romantic lies for they could all be disclaimed later and laughed over. But if Bainter was to ask for her hand—and she sensed that he would—she could not let him go on believing the one big lie, that she was the Merryvale heiress.

Her chin lifted. "I am not the Merryvale heiress," she said. "Not in truth."

His face had gone very still. "And how is that?"

"My name is not Merryvale. The young earl I married was named Merryvale. Joshua Merryvale was not my uncle—he was my husband's uncle."

"You mean old Joshua died an earl and didn't know it? But there must be family estates in England!"

She nodded her head dolefully. "Joshua Merryvale did indeed die an earl and you are right that he did not know it. But as to family estates in England—! My father discovered those estates were so heavily in debt as to be beyond redemption. I was not wealthy, you understand, and launching me into society had beggared my father. He had a weak heart and the disappointment killed him."

"I thought you said he broke his back in a fall from his horse?"

"I did say that," said Dorinda hastily. "But it was a heart attack that made him fall—a heart attack brought on by bitter disappointment."

Bainter was staring at her.

"All I know of Joshua Merryvale is what I have read in letters directed to my late husband—and they did not come from him, they were *about* him. Among other things. With both my parents dead, I was practically destitute—a young widow, damaged goods! I wracked my brain for what to do, and finally decided that I would come to America—I had money enough for that—and throw myself on Joshua Merryvale's mercy."

"And arrived to find him dead," he murmured.

"Yes. And when all of you leaped to the conclusion that I was indeed his blood relation and sole heir, I—I saw that as a convenient answer to my problems." She hung her head and whispered with real sincerity, "I am so ashamed."

She waited in silence for him to condemn her, to take her in his arms and tell her it did not matter, they did not need the inheritance. He did neither.

Suddenly he was convulsed with laughter. "You are an adventuress," he choked, bringing his fist down delightedly into his open palm. "I have been taken in by an adventuress!"

Dorinda took a step backward, offended. "I do not consider it funny!" she said sharply.

"No, of course it is not," he gasped, wiping his eyes.

"I was but asking your help as to what to do about the terrible trouble that I am in!"

"Trouble?" His expression changed and he was looking down at her now with some astonishment. "You are in no trouble that I can see."

"But I am claiming something that is not rightfully mine!"

Bainter shrugged his topaz shoulders. "So your claim is somewhat left-handed. Who is to know that? Tell me, have you been so foolish as to tell anyone else this story?"

"No, but the passenger list of the *London Queen*—" She had been about to say "will have no record of my name" but Bainter did not let her finish.

"Do not worry about it," he said briskly. "I will arrange to have that passenger list destroyed. Meantime, you will stick to your story, you will inherit Merryvale Manor and all of Joshua Merryvale's goods and chattels, you will sell it to me for something less than it is worth and you can go back to England with money jingling in your pocket!"

Dorinda felt her breath taken away. She had expected anything but this calm assumption that she would go through with it and carry her masquerade to its final conclusion! She felt trapped.

"Come, we have been gone long enough. This is no time to compromise your reputation!"

"But—" cried Dorinda.

"Trust me," he said, and marched her back to the ball.

Chapter 27

Dorinda went back inside feeling stunned. Nothing had turned out as she had expected. She had blurted out her confession—albeit sugar-coated with lies—*and Bainter had laughed.*

Some of the glitter went out of the ball for Dorinda; the candles seemed to burn less brightly, the colors dimmed.

It was with feelings rubbed already raw that she was claimed for a dance by Governor Newbold—and dancing with the governor was something that ordinarily would have made her catch her breath. The governor was a handsome widower with silver gray wings in his dark hair, impressive tonight in black silk trimmed in silver braid. He danced Dorinda about the floor with stately grace. Two of his daughters in England had married earls, but Governor Newbold, it was said, could abide neither of his sons-in-law. To escape their scrapes and their harassment, it was whispered, this vastly wealthy senior statesman had sought this appointment across the sea in Virginia and was now buying plantations on the York River and lands upriver near the falls of the James.

"I haven't seen beauty like yours since I was sent to the West Country during the Monmouth Rebellion," he told her appreciatively as they danced.

Dorinda, who had scarcely been following what he was saying, her mind was in such a turmoil, looked up at the words "West Country."

There was a melancholy look on the governor's face. "There I glimpsed a red-haired beauty in a red dress riding like the wind and leading a horse with a man who looked more dead than alive in the saddle. They were escaping the Battle of Sedgemoor. I was a young officer then. I should have shot them of course, or at least taken them prisoner, but I was blinded by the lady's beauty—she looked very like you. My pistol was raised and she rode directly for me—I have never seen a woman look so wild or so lovely. And when I lowered the barrel and she saw I was going to let them pass she flashed me a smile and gave me a lighthearted salute. And—" *No, he was not going to tell this young English girl staring up at him how the wind had come up at just that moment and blown those light red silk skirts billowing over long white legs, or how a young officer's heart had gone out to that valiant woman, or how he had envied that man half dead in the saddle that she was so obviously trying to save.* His voice grew husky. "I have never forgotten her—and you look so like her as she was then, save that your hair is more gold. Tell me, do you have relatives in the West Country?"

"I am from London," said Dorinda truthfully. "But—I think you may have seen my grandmother, the Countess of Ravensay. She was seventeen when she snatched her lover from the battle, but she is believed to have died on her way to France."

"Too bad," he sighed. "I would have liked her story to have a happy ending."

So would I, thought Dorinda pensively as the gallant governor swung her about the floor. *Oh, so would I.*

"You look quite wild tonight," murmured an appreciative voice in her ear and Dorinda, who had finished her dance with the governor and had now been separated from him by the crush of people eager to talk to him, turned with a start to see Tarn Jenner at her elbow. Her blue-green eyes were glittering as she looked up at him and they flung him a challenge, for had she not danced with the governor? And did not that same governor actually remember her grandmother? Let him try matching his dark minxes and statuesque redheads against that!

He was looking down at her and she could not read his sardonic expression. She could not know how he had fought to stay away from her—this girl who so obviously preferred the wealthy planter, Bainter Ramsay, to himself—or how irresistibly he had been drawn to her side.

Dorinda realized that he expected an answer to his comment. "I *feel* quite wild," she muttered. In point of fact she felt bewildered. Her gamble with Bainter was not precisely lost but it had certainly gone astray.

"Do you also feel like dancing another measure?"

Without waiting for an answer he took her hand and led her out upon the floor. If Dorinda and Bainter had sparkled like emeralds and topaz, Tarn and Dorinda flashed like emeralds and rubies—she with her scintillating wide skirts whirling, he with the candlelight gleaming off his broad scarlet shoulders. Dorinda could almost feel the eyes upon her back—although fans waved and heads were wont to turn casually away when she whirled about to face them. *And why not?* she thought miserably. *Was she not doing her best to alienate every unattached female in the room?* First she had taken Bainter's ever-roving attention on the dance floor, then disappeared with him into the garden, and now she had captured what many must consider—next to the governor—the other most eligible bachelor in Williamsburg, the sinister but apparently wealthy Tarn Jenner.

She had been stung by that chance overheard remark

about a bound girl and she had been behaving very badly. She had no doubt that she would pay for it.

"What makes you so silent and sad?" wondered Tarn, studying her keenly.

"I have led a tragic life," said Dorinda ironically. "I have been betrothed to many men and they have all come to bad ends."

"Oh?" he said skeptically. "What happened to them?"

"They met violent deaths," she told him, not caring what she said.

"They displeased you and you shot them?" he hazarded.

Dorinda looked up at him wrathfully, met his twinkling gray eyes, and all of a sudden she saw the funny side of what had happened. She had been caught in her own net. She burst out laughing and he threw back his head and laughed too and suddenly she felt much better. What had been said could be unsaid—when the time was right. Meanwhile Bainter would keep her secret—indeed she was but following his instructions. All would be well.

"A lightsome lass like you should not be touched by tragedy," Tarn said caressingly. "She should spend her days in joyous laughter, mocking this foolish world we live in!"

"I do agree," said Dorinda, attempting—after her outburst—to be again demure.

"I take it that perhaps Bainter said something to offend you when you lured him into the garden?"

She gave him an affronted look. "How do you know that *he* did not lure *me*?"

"Oh, I know you too well for that," he chuckled. "You have set your sights on the vastly eligible Mr. Ramsay and you intend to let nothing on God's earth stand in your way!"

Dorinda's good humor departed as rapidly as it had come. She gave the irritating Mr. Jenner a cold look. "Are you staying in Williamsburg long?" she asked pointedly. "I had half expected to have found you gone before the Claridge ball."

"Trying to get rid of me, ay?" His gray eyes glinted. "Well, I am not ready to go just yet. Indeed I have found Williamsburg more interesting than I would have thought possible."

"Perhaps it is your unmatched popularity with the ladies of the town," she suggested flippantly, for it still rankled that he had chosen so many others to dance with before asking her.

"Ah, so you have noticed that?" he said with an enigmatic smile that made her grit her teeth. "But then the master of Haverleigh is popular too—at least with our hostess. Had you noticed?"

Dorinda had indeed noticed but she did not care to discuss it. "Bainter is a man of the world," she said stiffly.

"Yes," he agreed with lifted brows. "He is most certainly that. But of just what world—"

The music ended and she would have torn free from his grip but that he held onto her.

"I am tired of dancing," she said.

"You will dance with me one more time," he said grimly, "for I have something to say to you."

"I always feel as if you are—are threatening me!" she panted.

His expression did not really change but something in his eyes did. "Now how could that be?" he asked silkily.

"I do not know," she said. "But I do not like it." She would have wrested free but that the music started again and she allowed herself to be whirled out onto the floor again rather than make a scene. The sweeping skirts of other ladies brushed against hers, the skirted coats of the gentlemen whirled stiffly out as they turned about in the dancing and Tarn Jenner held her in a grip that would brook no departure.

"It is not my intention to harm you," he said in an

altered voice. "But surely I am as free as any other man to pursue a pretty girl."

"And you have certainly been pursuing them tonight," she flashed. "All around the room—brunettes, redheads!"

He looked pleased that she had noticed.

"Blondes too," he murmured, looking down at her gleaming fair hair.

"Bah, you pursue everyone!"

"But I pursue you with more—passion," he said whimsically.

She felt that she was being mocked. It infuriated her. She sought for a chink in his armor. "When I first saw you at the inn," she challenged, "I thought that you were Bainter's friend, but now I do not feel that you are his friend!"

"You do not? And why is that? Because I felt I should warn you that not all the young ladies who go upriver to Haverleigh return as chaste as when they left Williamsburg?"

"You are mocking me!" she cried.

"I am warning you," he said lightly. "But you do not seem to care to heed my warning. You are a woman of gold, Dorinda." His voice had grown caressing and he held her a little more tightly. "Not only the spun gold of your hair, but the hard clinking gold that the sale of Merryvale Manor will bring you. Without that gold—"

"Are you suggesting that Bainter is a fortune hunter?" she said furiously.

"Just so," he said.

"That's ridiculous!" she snapped. "Half the girls in Williamsburg would be delighted to wed him!"

"Undoubtedly true, but you will notice that wiser heads in the form of fathers and brothers and guardians hold them back. At least those few Bainter would consider, the wealthy ones."

"But he is so rich himself," she gasped. "What you suggest is madness!"

The gray eyes looking down into her wide angry

blue-green ones glinted. "I am saying, Dorinda, that should there be any hitch in your inheritance you will find yourself left at the church door."

"Oh-h-h!" She could hear her teeth grinding.

His scarlet shoulders shrugged. "Of course nothing may go wrong, but I warn you to have a care. Those who play with Bainter Ramsay are playing with fire."

It was fortunate the dance had ended for she had had a strong desire to kick him on the shin.

A young gentleman with a name that sounded vaguely like "Havelock" that she remembered meeting earlier came up promptly to desire the next dance and Tarn Jenner, with a sardonic look, surrendered his angry beauty to him.

Dorinda was whirled about the floor by first one young buck and then another. She sipped glasses of wine and set them down and forgot them—or let her current companion finish them for her. She laughed and flirted and twirled her fan. But she found herself deserted not only by Tarn Jenner, who now stood among a group of men surrounding the governor and watched her keenly over his glass, but also by Bainter who had disappeared somewhere. She looked about for her hostess. Lucy Claridge had also disappeared somewhere. Dorinda began to fan herself rather too energetically. Could it be that upstairs in one of those bedrooms she had never seen, behind a locked door, Bainter and his hostess—?

"Brightest eyes I ever saw," someone commented, looking at her.

Dorinda's blue-green eyes were indeed very bright. At the moment she was not sure who irritated her the most—Tarn Jenner gazing at her fixedly across the room thinking who knew what about her, or Bainter Ramsay off somewhere seducing his hostess and probably not for the first time!

Intent on her personal concerns, and making short distracted answers to her current companion's sallies,

Dorinda had all but forgotten estates and lawyers until Isham Riddle's voice behind her said, "Oh, here you are, Mistress Dorinda. May I borrow the lady for a moment, Will?" He took her away from the discomfited young planter who had been extolling the virtues of his particular plantation. "There's someone I want you to meet," he said.

A moment later she found herself swished across the room where as she arrived she heard a white-haired old gentleman in worn purple silks and a gravy-stained waistcoat, his ear inclined as he shouted into his younger companion's face, say, "I hear she's not only heiress to the Merryvale fortune, George, but has family estates in England as well."

Dorinda was astonished. How in the world had her simple remarks about England been blown up into this?

Too prudent to protest and sharply aware of the annoyed look that passed over Isham Riddle's generally placid countenance, she saw the old gentleman stab an admonishing thumb into the ivory waistcoat of his younger companion and bawl, "You should have gone after her, George! Instead I'm told that Ramsay fellow's got her."

"George's" ruddy face darkened with embarrassment as Dorinda was propelled forward by Isham Riddle, who gave the older gentleman a lowering look.

"Mistress Merryvale," Isham said crisply. "Allow me to present George Peabody—Junior and Senior."

George Peabody, Junior, a nervous-looking man of about forty, promptly made a leg, but his rotund father inclined his large white head and shouted, "Who? Who did you say? Penny-ale? What's this about 'penny-ale?'"

"I fear I must apologize for my father—he's quite deaf," murmured the red-faced George Junior as Isham dutifully squalled, "Merryvale! I said, this is Mistress Merryvale, George!"

"That's quite all right," smiled Dorinda, dropping him an enchanting curtsy.

George Peabody looked charmed. Beside him his father regarded Dorinda with a daunting stare. "Pretty little baggage, ain't she, Isham?" he commented in what he obviously considered an aside but which was delivered with deafening power.

George Junior winced but Dorinda could not keep a smile from curving her soft mouth.

"Mistress Dorinda," said Isham Riddle hurriedly, wiping his brow. "George Peabody here—the younger, not this old chap who can't seem to get you off his mind—was your Uncle Joshua's attorney. He'll be handling the Merryvale estate and I think you'll want him to take over your affairs and straighten things out for you."

Nobody could straighten things out for her, Dorinda thought hopelessly, thinking of the tangled web she had spun for herself. But she gave George the Younger what she hoped was a look of confidence.

"Unless of course you'd prefer your London solicitors to handle matters for you," interposed the meticulous Williamsburg attorney.

"No, I wouldn't dream of bothering them," said Dorinda, hoping she would not be called upon to recite her London solicitors' names! "You are on the home ground, as it were—I'd much prefer to have you handle things."

George Peabody looked even more charmed. "Then I—" His voice quavered as his father clapped him on the back with a force that almost sent him plummeting into Dorinda, and shouted, "You're a fool, George. Always were!" and was dragged away by Isham Riddle who was shouting into the old man's ear, "They need to discuss business, George!"

"You were saying—?" said Dorinda helpfully.

"That I'd be glad to assist you in any way I can." George the Younger cleared his throat. Although he'd celebrated his fortieth birthday last week, George Peabody

Junior was still afraid of his father. Always would be. Dominated by him. All his life George Senior had destroyed his son's self-confidence, nicknamed him "Rabbit Face." George Junior had had no luck with girls, too bumbling. So he had buried his "rabbit face" in musty law books and was by now the most knowledgeable lawyer in Williamsburg and with an expanding practice. But he still feared to strike out on his own.

Earlier this summer he'd fallen in love with a bound girl at the White Hart, but his ego had been so blasted by his father's lifelong badgering that when she'd failed to show up to meet him one night, he'd promptly decided she didn't care for him—after all, who could love a bumbling "rabbit face?" And he had skulked away and once again buried himself in his law books. So seldom had he gone out since that his pleasant face was pale from it.

This party at the Claridges' was a novelty for him and he'd come only out of a sense of duty to his former client, Joshua Merryvale, for the Merryvale heiress was sure to attend—and indeed here she was. But this whole miserable evening had been haunted for him by ripe generous Jeddie with her robust laugh and her merry blue eyes and her wonderful zest for living. He'd been too shy to more than steal a kiss although her full lips had been wondrously inviting. Many the night he had tossed and turned on his narrow bed—that same bed he had occupied since boyhood, grown lumpy now with age—and wished Jeddie could have loved him in return. He knew of course that they couldn't have married any time soon, not till his father died—lord, his father would disown him at the mere thought! And a scandal such as his father—with that roaring voice that could be heard, George Junior was sure, a good quarter mile—would make of his son's "marrying down" would destroy him with the local gentry. He wouldn't be able to make a living! Unless of course he moved away somewhere.

The thought of that disaster had panicked George, for he was the last man to step out and try something new. But he knew in his heart that once his father was gone to the family plot he'd have taken the step and gladly, no matter what Williamsburg's plantation society thought of him. He'd have married Jeddie, all right, and brought her home to his white frame house on Queen Street and tried to make her happy. If only she had loved him. . . .George came back to the present and turned his full attention to the gorgeous creature who stood before him in the person of Dorinda Merryvale. "I understand you're staying at Haverleigh Plantation?" he said.

"That's right."

"If you would prefer, I could arrange for you to stay at Merryvale Manor while the estate is settled."

"Oh, no, I'd feel a stranger there," said Dorinda quickly. "And I don't know people yet. I'd really prefer to remain at Haverleigh. With Mistress Riddle to keep me from being lonely."

The attorney nodded his head as if that made sense. "I understand you came over on the *London Queen*?"

"Yes," lied Dorinda, adding, "It was a rough voyage." She was aware that Isham Riddle had joined them again.

"So I heard." George Peabody looked pensive. He would have liked to have talked with the *London Queen*'s captain, cleared up a few things, such as what luggage there was that had been later lost to that highwayman fellow, things that would no doubt upset Mistress Merryvale if he brought them up now. "The *London Queen* has already set sail for Barbados," he said. "She was loaded quickly."

That at least was good news, for the captain of the *London Queen* could have tripped her up. George Peabody might have asked to see the passenger list and the name "Dorinda Merryvale" would not have been on it!

"That's too bad," she said insincerely. "It would have been nice to see the captain again."

"Yes," he said. He sighed. "Well, you must tell me if there's anything I can do."

"There is," cried Dorinda, on sudden inspiration. "There's a girl—Jeddie Turner. She works at the White Hart. I would like to buy her articles of indenture from Innkeeper Buxton."

Both men looked startled, but George Peabody was thunderstruck. Jeddie? His Jeddie? For he still in his heart thought of her as his for all that she had, to his way of thinking, "abandoned" him. This sparkling young lady before him wished to buy up Jeddie's articles?

Isham Riddle's flaxen wigged head swung round. "Are you sure you want to take on an indentured servant before you decide whether you're staying on?" he demanded.

"Yes, I'm quite sure I want her," said Dorinda firmly. She herself might come to grief but at least Jeddie would have her freedom! "Her name is Jeddie Turner. She is of medium height." (*A perfect height,* George Peabody was thinking with an inward sigh. *Standing on tiptoe Jeddie could look directly into his eyes.*) "She is rather stocky." (*Oh, that was not the word he would have used for that ample voluptuous feminine figure!*) "And she has thick auburn hair." (*George trembled as he remembered how he had once or twice daringly run his hand through its thick shining strands.*) "And blue eyes." (*The bluest!*) "And a nice smile." ("*Nice*" *wasn't a good enough word to describe Jeddie's smile— she had a* wonderful *smile!*) "Do you know who I mean? You must have seen her if you've supped at the White Hart?"

"Yes, I believe I know who you mean," said George Peabody vaguely. Hearing his beloved thus coolly described had shaken him to his foundations. His world was whirling. Suddenly he brightened—this would give him a perfect excuse to see Jeddie again! But then ... if this Merryvale heiress bought Jeddie's papers, Jeddie would be moving upriver—when would he get to see her? And would Jeddie like being employed so far from town? "It does seem—rather a big step," he ventured cautiously.

"Explain the problems to her, George." Isham Riddle sounded disgusted.

George gave Dorinda an uneasy look. "You do realize you'll have to house and feed the girl and you aren't yet set up to—"

"I like Jeddie very much," interrupted Dorinda crisply, now as eager to rescue Jeddie as she had been to rescue Lady Soft Paws. "And I'm quite sure Jeddie likes me. Her situation there at the White Hart is intolerable. Buxton's wife recently beat her with a barrel stave—"

"What?" cried George Peabody.

"And she locks Jeddie in at night." Dorinda paused, alarmed by the change in him. She would not have judged George Peabody at first sight to be a man of so sensitive a nature but she could see he was actually trembling with indignation and his fists were clenched.

"The woman should be up on charges!" he cried wildly, and Isham Riddle's sandy brows elevated in amazement at such heat.

"I agree with you." Dorinda's voice was dry. "But I'd rather rescue Jeddie than do battle with the Buxtons. Jeddie confided her problems to me and I think it's high time that she was gotten out of there and settled in with people who care about her."

George Peabody got hold of himself with an effort. "I would of course be willing to advance you the money," he told Dorinda hoarsely. "Joshua Merryvale died leaving plenty of cash lying around." He paused. "Do you have any idea what Buxton would be asking for her articles?"

Dorinda looked blank. She had no idea what an indentured servant such as Jeddie was worth. "I haven't a notion," she admitted with charming candor. "Would you—would you arrange it for me, Mr. Peabody?" she asked appealingly. She gave him a winsome smile. "I am no good at bargaining, I am afraid. I am sure you will strike a much better bargain than I ever could."

Would he arrange it? It took all George's willpower to keep from dashing to the White Hart right now and demanding that Buxton sell Jeddie's articles to him! And if he refused, to beat the fellow with a barrel stave until he did!

"I'll do my best," he heard himself say in a voice whose calm tone in no way reflected the tumult roiling within him. "Indeed I'll stop by the White Hart first thing tomorrow morning and ask Buxton what he will take for the girl's articles."

"Point out to him that Jeddie has but a short time to go on her indenture—less than a year, I think. So it won't be all that much—I mean, he'll be saving himself having to give her a new kirtle and bodice and a pair of new shoes—all those things he'd normally have to give her when she finishes her indenture."

"I'm surprised you know so much about Jeddie," blurted George, astonished.

Once again she had displayed too much knowledge! "Oh, she's very open-hearted," said Dorinda vaguely. "She brought up my bath there at the inn and we got very friendly and she sat down and told me all about herself. I was very taken with her."

Well, the Merryvale heiress did sound as if she liked Jeddie and would give her a good home, and that was the important thing. George Peabody reminded himself that he had seen nothing of Jeddie since the night she had not showed up to meet him—locked in, he'd never thought of that! Anyway he'd been seeing nothing of her here—he could hardly see less of her if she lived upriver!

"I'll bring her upriver to you at Haverleigh if I'm able to buy her articles from Buxton," he promised.

"Good," smiled Dorinda, thinking that at least one

good thing would come out of all this deceit—Jeddie's freedom.

"No need for you to go to all that trouble, George," interposed Isham Riddle, who had been listening in silence and whose experience with lawyers had always been that they charged and charged high for the "extra" things they did. "I've some business in Williamsburg day after tomorrow. I'll be coming down in my barge. My sister will be coming with me and Mistress Dorinda can come along and take the girl back with her then, George, if you're able to make the deal."

George Peabody was hard put to hide his chagrin. His prominent front teeth, which had caused his father to nickname him "Rabbit Face," almost bit through his lower lip. Devil take Isham Riddle anyway, robbing him of a lovely trip upriver with Jeddie!

Oh, God, his father was bearing down on him again! George Junior's face was again red with embarrassment as George Senior's big voice boomed out, "Well, did you ask the heiress to sup with you, George? Ay? Ay? This was your chance, George, don't tell me you muffed it again!"

But Dorinda, to George's choked relief, was already out of earshot and it was only several of his good clients and their wives who had to turn their bewigged heads to hide their mirth.

When it was time to go and Dorinda went to get her shawl, she ran into Tarn Jenner. His scarlet form was lounging in the hall and she had the distinct impression he might have been waiting for just this moment.

"So you're buying Jeddie," he said.

"News travels fast." Dorinda came to a halt. "And who told you anyway?" she demanded with asperity.

"George Peabody told me just now. He was asking me what I thought Buxton would take for her. I told him."

"Well, thank you very much," said Dorinda and would have passed on by but that he caught her by the arm.

"First a cat, and now a bond servant," he murmured.

"And all before you move under a roof of your own. Tell me, Dorinda, if I were a homeless stray, would you take me in too?"

"I would not!" she said, shaking off his arm.

She could hear him chuckle as she walked on by, her young back very straight.

Dorinda was silent on the moonlit trip back upriver. The Riddles thought it was because she was tired but that was not the reason. Every time she looked at that white moon sailing so serenely overhead she found herself thinking treacherously of Tarn Jenner and his suddenly penetrating gaze as he said, *Tell me, Dorinda, if I were a homeless stray, would you take me in too?* A man like Tarn Jenner would never be homeless, she thought. He would simply elbow his way in somewhere! Not that he would ever have to, for he seemed well off, living in the best room of the inn, wearing fine clothes—even if sometimes buttons were missing. She smiled. Careless of him. . . .

She caught herself up short. He was a dangerous rake, she could see it shining out of his eyes. And he looked at her boldly, as if he felt he could possess her. It was very aggravating.

She glanced over at Bainter Ramsay, slumped down in his seat in an amber heap with his mouth open, snoring. He had drunk too much and now was noisily sleeping it off. She gave him a look of sudden slight distaste and then caught herself. Many gentlemen drank. Many who drank, drank too much. From time to time, of course, not habitually. Bainter was no worse than the rest.

She asked herself suddenly if she had changed. Gliding upriver beneath a pale white moon on a summer night, the only one except the oarsmen who was really awake, for the Riddles were dozing beside her, she watched the dark shore where occasionally the green or golden eyes of some little wild creature caught the light. . . . And all the while her treacherous heart was leaning toward the man from Philadelphia, a man who mocked her, who frightened her, and yet who seemed to call out to her in some deep primeval way....

She shook her head to clear it and one of her hairpins fell out. She picked it up carefully for hairpins were expensive. Tomorrow she would arrange her hair in a different style.

Day after tomorrow she would have Jeddie with her. A Jeddie saved from the wrath of Innkeeper Buxton's bullying wife. It would be good to have someone to confide in, someone who knew the real truth about Dorinda Meredith! That it might also be dangerous to have someone about who knew the real truth about her Dorinda did not at that moment consider. Instead she faced the one truly dark thought that had been with her all evening, ever since she had talked to the lawyer George Peabody.

Up to now it had been a masquerade and no harm done. Tonight the whole picture had changed. Tonight she had in effect let George Peabody advance her money. Money for a good purpose, of course, money to buy Jeddie's articles and rescue her from a bad situation, but money nonetheless that she was not entitled to.

Her position tonight had subtly changed. It was no longer a merry sort of joke from which she could withdraw if she chose. Nor was it like the clothes she had absconded with in Philadelphia, which were in justice only a payment for services rendered.

This she had done with her eyes wide open. This a court would not excuse. She had—or would by day after tomorrow—have accepted money from the Merryvale estate. To pay for Jeddie. She was in it now—in it too deep to extricate herself.

She would have to be Dorinda Merryvale of Merryvale Manor all of her life—or until the law brought her down.

Chapter 28

Bainter was perfectly charming the next day. He apologized for having been drunk the night before and set out to entertain her. Nothing was said about her false inheritance, but then she was never alone with him—Mistress Riddle always tagged along, chatting merrily. Dorinda did not tell Bainter that she was purchasing Jeddie's articles and she noted with some surprise that neither Isham Riddle nor his talkative sister told him either. Perhaps they felt as she did, that in theory Bainter might not approve of Dorinda buying a bound girl who would be brought upriver and housed with him, but that when it was a fact accomplished he would accept it with good grace.

The following day Dorinda accompanied the Riddles downriver in their barge to pick up Jeddie. The barge had called for them early, before Bainter was up. They were walking down the lawn toward it when Bainter called to them from his open window, "What, off to Riddlewood already?" And when Dorinda called back, "No, we're off to Williamsburg. The Riddles are going on business and I have some shopping. Why don't you come with us? We'll wait!" Bainter looked for a moment as if he might go with them. But even at this distance they could see that he looked hung over and worn. He made a dismissive gesture and turned away.

"He looks tired," observed Dorinda as she got into the barge. "And he shouldn't be, we all went to bed early."

Isham Riddle snorted. "*We* went to bed early. Ramsay sat up half the night drinking, I don't doubt—*that's* why he's tired!"

"Drinking alone?" Dorinda was slightly scandalized. It was one thing to match your friends merrily glass for glass, and quite another to sit alone at night tossing down goblet after goblet—as Maud Whatton had done during those terrible last days in London. Gin and discouragement and age had gotten to Maud— but Bainter? He was young, strong, rich—he had everything!

"Didn't you know?" sighed Mistress Riddle, tucking her skirts around her against the breeze as the barge began its journey downriver. "Bainter always drinks. Pass by him any time of day—you'll smell liquor on his breath."

That was true! Dorinda remembered suddenly that three years ago, when Bainter had seized her and kissed her so forcibly at the White Hart, there had been liquor on his breath. The memory of his kisses had since gone dim, but the smell of the liquor lingered.

"You must not be too hard on Bainter for that, Dorinda," admonished Mistress Riddle. "We live in a drinking age and it is considered only sociable for a man to be frequently in his cups!"

Her brother snorted.

"Bainter must be very unhappy to drink so much," murmured Dorinda.

"Can't see what would make him unhappy," grunted Isham. "He always seems to have money and women running after him."

Something in his past, thought Dorinda. *Something that didn't bear mentioning. Something a good woman could make him forget.* . . . Subconsciously, her heart softened toward Bainter.

She was gazing pensively toward the shore as the barge sped downriver and from a marshy stretch a big marsh hawk suddenly fluttered up and drifted overhead. There was something elegant about the bird, she thought, looming so majestically above them, something wonderful about this new land that now she felt had always waited for her. Suddenly she *wanted* Merryvale Manor, wanted it with a deep and desperate yearning. She wanted to put down roots here in this green Virginia countryside and marry and bear children and make a home here for her family. She wanted to cast in her lot with these lighthearted yet valiant Virginians who seemed to have brought with them the luster of London yet left behind its inbred quarrels. She had heard of cruel punishments in the north, but they were much milder here in Virginia—a tolerant people. She felt she would fit among them well—yes, and she would make even Joshua Merryvale proud of her if he were watching, as proud as if she had been his own blood niece!

If only something did not go wrong. . . . Of a sudden, worry seized her, and plagued her all the way to Williamsburg.

She hardly glanced up when Mistress Riddle, eyeing a large plantation gliding by on their right, said, "Well, I see the Allenbys have finished their rose arbor at last. In time to have their daughter walk beneath the rose arch to be married!" She laughed. "I remember last year her mother vowing that she would not let Letitia be married until that rose arch was in place, for she herself had had naught but a hasty wedding on shipboard after they set out for America and she intended to pretend that it was herself and not Letitia walking beneath that arch!"

"It's hard to realize that this was strong-held Indian country or that bloody wars were fought here," muttered Isham Riddle, viewing the peaceful vista before him, the lawns stretching up to a handsome brick house.

"Listen to those songbirds," said Mistress Riddle. "What a racket they make! Indeed you'll find that the mockingbirds set up such a chatter at Merryvale Manor that they'll keep you awake." She peered at Dorinda. "Well, why do you look so sad?"

"I'm very concerned about Jeddie," admitted Dorinda. "Perhaps Innkeeper Buxton won't be willing to part with her."

"Innkeeper Buxton would be glad to sell anything he owns for enough money—including his wife," pronounced Isham Riddle—and closed his mouth suddenly.

"Really, Isham!" His sister gave him a reproving look for uttering such sentiments in Dorinda's presence.

Dorinda sighed and tried to sit back in the barge and watch the green banks slide by, but she was still impatient and nervous when they reached Williamsburg—and terribly relieved when they went into the gambrel-roofed white frame building where the Peabodys, Junior and Senior, lived, and a beaming George Junior told them that he had indeed been able to buy Jeddie's articles, and at a good price too. He did not mention that a surly Buxton had declared the girl "unruly" and "unmanageable" and that he'd be glad to be rid of her, nor did he mention that it had taken all his control to keep from clenching his white academic knuckles and making a real attempt to knock Buxton's teeth down his throat. "Jeddie," he added in a real understatement, for Jeddie had taken the news as a gift from heaven, "was overjoyed."

"Then she's mine?" Dorinda was so relieved she wanted to hug George Peabody and her brilliant smile reflected it.

George Junior gave her a dazzled look. "She is indeed. I have her articles of indenture right here, signed over to you." They were all standing clustered around a large wooden table in his office as he spoke and he said diffidently, "If you'll just sign a receipt for the articles, and for the hundred gold guineas I'm advancing you from the estate? I need these things for the court, you understand, at probate." He pulled out a chair, handed Dorinda a turkey quill pen and indicated the small slant-top writing desk that he had placed atop his table.

A hundred gold guineas! And every one of them worth twenty-one shillings! To a girl who had never owned more than two gold pieces in her life it seemed an incredible sum.

Dazed, Dorinda sat down at George Peabody's ink-stained writing desk, dipped the point of the quill into a small brass pot containing ink made from vinegar and ox gall, and scribbled her name on the parchment receipt George had prepared.

She wrote "Dorinda" with a steady hand, hesitated a moment, then firmly wrote "Merryvale."

The die was cast! Dorinda felt she had signed her life away!

"Are ye making good progress in settling up the estate, George?" she heard Isham Riddle ask as she watched George carefully pour sand over her signature to blot it.

"Aye, good progress." George nodded as he expertly poured the sand back from the paper into its container. He handed a folded paper to Dorinda. "The articles. And the guineas." He counted them out and poured them into a small green silk purse which he handed to Dorinda.

Isham Riddle lifted his eyebrows as he saw the elegant little embroidered purse. Had George been giving *him* a hundred guineas, he'd simply be expected to pocket them. Isham never guessed the purse to be what it was—a small token of thanks for befriending

Jeddie. Instead he leaped to the obvious conclusion—
George Peabody must be very taken with the Merryvale
heiress!

"Is there anything else I can do for you just now,
Mistress Merryvale?" George asked Dorinda a trifle
wistfully. He was wishing for the impossible—that Dorinda
would say it was inconvenient for her to take Jeddie
back with her because the barge would be too full of
her parcels and the Riddles' goods, and would he mind
delivering Jeddie to Haverleigh himself?

But Isham Riddle interpreted that wistful note to
mean something else and hid a grin. He thought it
would be excellent if Dorinda chose to marry George
Peabody. He was an attorney, he'd be able to handle
all her legal matters for her! And with her American
holdings and the lands and manors he'd heard at the
Claridge ball that she held in England, she'd be needing
a good lawyer! (For gossip had magnified Dorinda
into an heiress of enormous fortune both here and
abroad.)

It was on the tip of Dorinda's tongue to tell him that
she was feeling a bit faint and to ask him to bring
Jeddie to her here. But suddenly she had a better idea.
From where she sat she could see through the small-
paned window out into the street and a lady had just
strolled by wearing a mask. Masks were fashionable for
ladies for street wear, both here and in England. Why
should she go to the White Hart bare-faced and court
recognition?

"Oh, no, there is nothing else—at the moment," she
said in her sweetest voice and gave George Peabody a
bright smile.

Isham Riddle coughed to hide his chuckle at George's
disappointed expression as they left. Quite bowled him
over, the lass had! He hurried off to take care of his
business and left the two women to collect Jeddie.

But Dorinda was of no mind to go directly to the
White Hart. "On our way," she said, turning to Gladys

Riddle, "do you know where I could purchase a face mask? This sun is beating down so! Even with my hat shading my face I can feel its glare reflected upward from the bricks. I must be mindful of my complexion."

"Oh, if you would only do as I told you and use dew on your face, you will need nothing else!" cried Mistress Riddle eagerly, for she did not care for masks.

"No, it must be a mask," said Dorinda decisively. "I do not care to rise at dawn to soak my face in dew."

"But you will not have to! Now you have a bond servant who, I presume, is to be your personal maid. *She* can rise at dawn and collect dew in small jars— enough for both of us!" She beamed.

"Well, we will see. But in the meantime, before I go all the way to the White Hart in this glaring sunlight, I will need a mask," said Dorinda stubbornly. It occurred to her that if Jeddie resumed her old nocturnal habits that had sent her stealing out of the inn to return heavy-eyed at dawn, she might be delighted to collect dew on the grass and then fall into bed!

So there was nothing for it but that Dorinda should purchase a broadcloth face mask. She chose several in colors to match her dresses and it was wearing a green mask that she strode into the White Hart and con- fronted—this time with more confidence—Innkeeper Buxton, who had, she noticed, a bruised face and a swollen eye and a very surly expression.

As they entered Buxton turned to a tall quiet serving girl whom Dorinda had never seen before. "Meg, go get Jeddie."

Meg returned shortly with Jeddie behind her, car- rying her few belongings tied up in a linen square. Jeddie also sported a black eye and she flounced by the innkeeper, giving him a resentful look as she passed.

"Good riddance," he muttered. And then to Dorinda,

"Ye'll find she's no bargain, this one. 'Tis my advice to you to beat her soundly if she does not obey you!"

Jeddie turned to snarl something and Dorinda laid cool fingers on her arm. The touch quieted Jeddie, who walked meekly out with them.

"What happened to you, Jeddie?" she asked, when they reached the street.

"Old Buxton was in his cups night before last and he tried to rape me in one of the pantries," said Jeddie. She gave Mistress Riddle a doubtful look. "Beggin' your pardon, ma'am, but I was in no mood for his clumsy pawin'! So I hit him in the face with one of the apples I'd been sent to get." *His eye,* thought Dorinda. *That explained it!*

"Is that when he hit you?" she asked.

Jeddie nodded energetically. "And *that's* when I kneed him in the groin!" Jeddie's blue eyes flashed and Gladys Riddle leant forward and gazed at her in horror. "And he'd have striped my back for me the next day but that was when George Peabody arrived and said Dor— Mistress Merryvale wanted to buy my articles. They closed the deal on the spot and I was signed over, but when George Peabody said you—" she looked at Dorinda—"weren't going to collect me till today, Buxton smirked and said that was good, he ought to 'discipline' me before he let me go anyway. And that's when George Peabody raised his voice. He said if there was a scratch on me, now that he'd bought my articles, he'd have Buxton up before a magistrate for assault. After that Buxton had me locked in my room and I haven't been out since!"

"Have you had anything to eat?" asked Dorinda.

Jeddie sighed. "Bread and water. Nothing to hold body and soul together."

"My goodness!" cried Mistress Riddle, scandalized. "The man should be whipped himself!"

"This time we'll let bygones be bygones," said Dorinda quickly, for she had no desire to stir up a hornet's nest that could bring them all into court where someone might indeed recognize her, for she felt a magistrate might well desire her to remove her mask. "Meantime Jeddie can run to the bakery and get us all some cakes. Bring them to Mistress Stevens, the dressmaker's, Jeddie. We're going to buy you some better clothes. And tonight you shall dine in the common room of the White Hart with us—" at Mistress Riddle's frown, for servants did not dine with their masters, she amended that to, "Of course you'll have a small table by yourself, but you'll have the same dinner we have and you can forget all about dining on bread and water!"

Jeddie's face broke into a wide grin. "It'll kill old Buxton!" she cried. "He'll be hard put to find me the worst cut of gristle!"

"He'll do no such thing," said Dorinda sharply. "For I intend to select everything on your plate myself and to pass it over to you!"

Mistress Riddle looked dazed at this reversal of master-and-servant role, but Jeddie's deep blue eyes filled with tears. "Oh, I do thank you, Dor—Mistress Merryvale," she cried, looking with wonder at the golden guinea Dorinda dropped into her hand, and fairly danced off to fetch the cakes.

Mistress Riddle accompanied them to the dressmaker's and then for a while went off on her own pursuits. When she came back she drew Dorinda aside.

"Isham says we must spend the night in Williamsburg. He wants to inspect some goods brought over on the *Mary Louise* to replace things we lost in the fire and her captain says it will be morning before the hold will be unloaded enough that we can view them properly. He's taken rooms for us at the White Hart. Knowing how they'd treated poor Jeddie, I should have insisted we stay someplace else." She sighed.

Which meant she'd again come under close inspection by the Buxtons—without her mask for it would be conspicuous to wear the mask to dinner. Dorinda felt her scalp prickle a bit.

She ran the gauntlet of that inspection when Mistress Riddle stepped on the hem of her own skirt and tore it. "Oh, dear me, I'll have to go back and fix it," she said, and Dorinda and Jeddie accompanied her back to the White Hart.

In the common room, Mistress Riddle ran into old friends and Dorinda, who wanted to speak to Jeddie privately, made her excuses and took Jeddie up the front stairway—that same wooden stairway that had been the scene of her disgrace as she pitched down it. She passed Innkeeper Buxton on the way and he gave Jeddie a sullen look but never looked at Dorinda in her fashionable mask. Dorinda took heart. She was going to be safe after all!

Quickly she drew Jeddie into the bedchamber that had been assigned to them. "Jeddie," she said. "We haven't much time, but I wanted you to know that I'm going to free you. I'll sign over your papers to you."

Jeddie's jaw dropped. "But you give good money to buy my articles," she gasped. "And you're entitled to my work for well on another year."

"I know, Jeddie," said Dorinda gently. "But I want to free you now before something goes wrong and the Merryvale estate is snatched away and everything is sold under the hammer! Don't you understand, Jeddie, your articles could be sold along with it? You'd be considered a chattel!"

Jeddie's square chin had assumed a stubborn set.

"What I understand," she said, "is that you took the first money they give you—for George Peabody told me that I ought to appreciate it, your very first act had been to buy my articles—you took that very first money you got and you saved me from the Buxtons."

"But Jeddie," protested Dorinda, "don't you realize you could go right back there? If your articles were sold under the hammer, the Buxtons—or somebody even worse—could buy them!"

"What I realize," said Jeddie stubbornly, "is that you're in deep trouble for all that everything seems to be going so fine and I'm sticking with you to get you through it!"

"Oh, Jeddie!" Dorinda threw her arms around the other girl. *Did anyone ever have such a friend?* she thought.

"Besides," confided Jeddie with a cheerful grin. "Money's never stuck to my fingers. With me it's easy come, easy go. If you did give me my freedom and let me go—"

"But I'd employ you then! For wages."

"You'd be the talk of Williamsburg," Jeddie reminded her. "Nobody ever did nothing so odd! And I'd spend it as fast as I got it and if anything happened to you, I'd probably be in debt and I'd have to indenture myself to someone else to keep out of debtors' prison. No—" she moved restlessly—"I'd as soon be bound to you until I marry. Then—" her blue eyes twinkled—"you can free me right enough!"

"I'll free you any time you want to marry, Jeddie," Dorinda told her huskily. "That I promise! Now go find a needle and thread because Mistress Riddle and her torn hem will be here any minute."

Dorinda not only outfitted Jeddie indulgently that day, but she bought gifts: a handsome cravat for Isham Riddle, a beribboned walking stick for Bainter who, she knew, fancied such things, a purple petticoat for Gladys Riddle who gasped over it in delight and, as an afterthought, a set of gold buttons suitable for a man's coat for Tarn Jenner, which she left with the dressmaker.

"Mr. Jenner has lost a button from his maroon coat," she told the astonished dressmaker. "Will you please send a messenger to the White Hart and ask Mr.

Jenner to stop by your shop and have his full set of coat buttons replaced by these?"

"That was very thoughtful of you," smiled Mistress Riddle, who had a soft spot in her heart for the dashing Mr. Jenner.

"Oh, well," laughed Dorinda. "I did promise to sew his button on for him and then I forgot all about it!"

Mistress Riddle gave her a penetrating look. How anyone could ever forget anything about the masterful Mr. Jenner was a mystery to her. "'Tis a fine gift," she said dryly. "I'm sure Mr. Jenner will be suitably impressed!"

"I wish to thank him for giving up his room to us," said Dorinda in a hurried voice.

Gladys Riddle cocked her flaxen head at her. "Or perhaps you just wish to see him again?"

Dorinda flushed and looked about her, glad that Jeddie had been too far away to catch that remark. She wouldn't care to have Jeddie teasing her about the rakish Mr. Jenner.

They saw him again as they came down the stairs at the White Hart for supper. Dorinda was wearing a gown she had purchased only today, a light creamy silk over a tangerine petticoat that brought out the red highlights in her golden hair. Beside her Jeddie was almost as showy. She was wearing a dress of her own choosing, of thin indigo blue linen ("It's very serviceable, won't have to be washed much—won't show the dirt at all!" Jeddie had said imploringly when she saw the dress. Dorinda had been glad to buy it for her even though she guessed it was not the dress's serviceability that appealed to Jeddie, but the way it matched her dark blue eyes.) The dress also showed off to advantage her slightly stocky but voluptuous form. Beneath Jeddie's excited face, aglow with anticipation at being for once a guest instead of a servant, was spread the wide expanse of a frosty white collar edged with stiff point lace, and beneath the wide skirt, caught up in panniers at either side, was a brilliant scarlet petticoat embroidered around the hem in white and indigo blue. Jeddie had urged the petticoat upon Dorinda with a wistful, "See, it's very useful—it has a pocket." She didn't add that George Peabody loved her in red!

Mistress Riddle had frowned at Jeddie's selection. "The girl will think she's above herself," she had muttered in an aside to Dorinda.

"Oh, that's all right," Dorinda had laughed. "Poor Jeddie's had a terrible time—she deserves something nice."

"Well, I'll allow the girl does look very neat in it, and with a large white linen apron over that bright petticoat, she'll look fine serving tea when you're settled in your new home." For Mistress Riddle was now taking it for granted that Dorinda would settle at Merryvale.

Dorinda gave the older woman a restless look. "I'm worried about Lady Soft Paws," she said, to change the subject. "I left her plenty of food but I hadn't intended to leave her overnight."

"You should have taken my advice and brought her up to Riddlewood where she'd have lots of cat company."

Yes, but suppose she didn't like the cat company? Suppose the cats already there didn't take to having a newcomer dropped in their midst? "I was afraid she'd run away and try to find me and get lost," she told Mistress Riddle frankly.

"Well, of course she's your cat." Mistress Riddle sighed.

Now, coming down the stairs at the White Hart, Dorinda was able to nod to people about the room, people she had met at the Claridge ball. It was a wonderful heady feeling—*to belong.* She smiled winsomely.

And met Tarn Jenner at the foot of the stairway.

He was wearing the same scarlet silk coat and gray trousers that he had worn to the Claridge ball and he stood out, she thought dizzily, from every other man in the room—head and shoulders above. His hard face was smiling as he bowed to the Riddles and nodded to

Jeddie, but it was to Dorinda that he turned the daunting weight of his full attention.

"I am beholden for a gift of gold buttons, Mistress Dorinda," he began. "But 'tis too handsome a gift to be accepted."

Mistress Riddle gave him an approving look but Dorinda, who had never had any money of her own before and was spreading it about with a free hand, said lightly, "Of course it is not. I am very beholden to you, sir, for I would not have known what to do had not you and Bainter rescued me! I trust the dressmaker sewed them on for you?"

"She did not," said Tarn.

"Oh, I'll be glad to do it," offered Jeddie eagerly.

"Unless your sewing has vastly improved, Jeddie, he'd be losing another!" laughed Dorinda and realized instantly from Tarn's startled expression that she had again displayed knowledge she shouldn't have. "Jeddie has told me of her unsuccessful bouts with a needle," she said quickly. "Anyway, I insist you accept them," she added with an imperious toss of her head. "For I did promise to sew on your lost button and I left without doing it!"

"And do you always keep your promises?" he asked in a timbred voice.

Of a sudden the world seemed very still, the din of the surrounding common room sank to a murmur. There was only herself and this tall smiling man looking down keenly into her eyes as if he saw through to her very soul.

"Always," said Dorinda huskily. *And it was true, wasn't it?* she asked herself. *She'd told scandalous lies, but fate had forced her into that. She could not remember ever having broken a promise.*

"Come, Isham." Mistress Riddle briskly patted her brother's coffee-brown satin arm with a plump hand. "Let us find a table. I think these young people have something to discuss."

Tarn Jenner turned upon her a look of gratitude. "Indeed Mistress Dorinda and I have much to talk about," he agreed. "I wonder, could I borrow the young lady for the evening? I had already engaged supper at the Raleigh and would be delighted if Mistress Dorinda would accompany me."

"Oh, yes, do go," urged Mistress Riddle. "The food is really much better and we'd go there too but I see the Barclays over there. I wonder what they are doing in Williamsburg? Good heavens, Miranda Barclay is *showing* so! Does she plan to have the baby here?"

"I think she has come into town to sign some legal papers," said Tarn. "I was just talking to them."

"I would love to go with you to the Raleigh," said Dorinda. "But I had promised Jeddie that—"

"Never mind, *I'll* look after Jeddie," said Mistress Riddle. "I'll see that she sits among the gentry and doesn't get shuffled off to the kitchen!"

"Dressed like that, Jeddie," grinned Tarn, "it would be a pity not to show yourself off to the town!"

Jeddie beamed at this unexpected compliment and Dorinda let Tarn sweep her away to the Raleigh Tavern on the north side of Duke of Gloucester Street. It was exciting for Dorinda to be ushered by Tarn into the many-dormered frame building whose kitchens only she had glimpsed when Buxton's wife, who never baked enough buns, would send her off to fetch more from the dome-shaped red brick ovens at the Raleigh. And it was a triumph to sweep into the Apollo Room at his side to the accompaniment of kindling looks from the elegant gentlemen gathered there.

"It's lovely!" she cried breathlessly as they were seated at a sturdy table scarred by dice boxes, for Virginia gentlemen were a gambling lot, sometimes recklessly wagering an entire crop or even a plantation on a throw of the dice.

"You become the setting well," Tarn told her in a caressing voice. His smile reflected the beauty of the woman before him with her shining blue-green eyes and her deeply cut creamy silk gown that displayed a breathtaking vista of pearly bosom. "I wanted you to see the best of Williamsburg, as exemplified by—" he nodded at the gilded motto over the mantel that read *"Hilaritas Sapientiae et Bonne Vitae Proles."*

"'Merriment, child of prudence and good living,'" she said in free translation.

He looked at her quickly. "You are educated," he murmured.

"A smattering only." She thought of those stolen hours in the early days in Philadelphia when she had perused books of Latin and French and tried desperately to educate herself. Philadelphia with all its tribulations seemed very far away. Reality was the Raleigh's Apollo Room, eating scalloped oysters and fried chicken and Virginia ham and Sally Lunn bread—and being toasted in fine Madeira by the elegant gentleman who sat opposite her.

"I will be hard put to it to set so good a table as this at Merryvale Manor," she said lightly as the food was served.

"You have decided then to occupy Merryvale rather than to sell it?" he asked alertly.

Her blue-green eyes challenged him: *If you know any reason why I shouldn't, speak now!* "Yes, I plan to make my home here in Virginia. At Merryvale Manor."

He smiled. "I am delighted to hear it."

Puzzled, she studied that dark saturnine countenance that lit up so startlingly when his white teeth flashed. She must have been wrong about him, he did not remember her from Philadelphia; he just enjoyed teasing people and her story had indeed been a strange one.

In the warmth of that smile she relaxed and enjoyed the evening as never before.

"Are you staying long in Williamsburg this time?" he

asked her caressingly as he brought her back to the White Hart and bade her good night at her door.

"Only till tomorrow," she said regretfully. "And then I take Jeddie back with me upriver."

"Oh, yes," he murmured. "Jeddie." He reached out and delicately toyed with one of Dorinda's shining curls. She felt breathless, having him so close in the empty hallway. "What interests me most," he admitted whimsically, "is not so much when you take Jeddie upriver as when you will return downriver again yourself."

"Oh?" murmured Dorinda, studying him through slanted lashes. "And is when I return so important?"

He chuckled. "Witch!"

And of a sudden she was in his arms, his lips were pressed warmly against hers, his arm around her slender waist had curved her lithe young body against him—and the world was a magic place. His kiss had a lingering tenderness that called to her heart. A rake he might be—and a dangerous one at that—but in that moment Dorinda did not care.

She went into his arms as if she belonged there and for a few moments out of time forgot that she was living a lie, that she was in deep trouble and could lose everything. She was for the brief span of that kiss a woman who had but one thought—and that thought to make this man her own.

A booted footstep sounded down the hall, a faint jangle of spurs. Tarn was more alert than she was. He let her go quickly.

Dorinda reeled out of his arms, suddenly aware of the approach of those booted feet.

"When will I see you again?" Tarn murmured.

"Come calling at Haverleigh," she challenged him.

"I think not," said Tarn. "The elegant Mr. Ramsay and I might come to blows over you."

Down the hall a door opened. The booted feet disappeared into it. They were again alone in the hall.

Tarn was leaning closer. He looked of a mind to kiss her again.

"Then come to Merryvale Manor day after tomorrow," Dorinda whispered and opened her door.

"I'll be there," Tarn told her with kindling eyes. He watched her go inside.

Dorinda breathed a last good night through the crack of the door and dreamily closed the door. The sound of snoring greeted her from Mistress Riddle's side of the big square bed. In the light of the single candle Dorinda could see Jeddie, still dressed, sitting cross-legged on the narrow cot that had been put into the room for her to sleep on.

"I waited till you got back, but can I go out now?" Jeddie hissed, with a glance at the sleeping woman. "I saw my gentleman friend again this morning—and I think it's still on with us." She dimpled and considered letting Dorinda in on her secret, then remembered George's anguished *"Tell nobody!"* when he had for a moment got her aside. "And I want to say good-bye to him proper like—I haven't seen much of him lately!"

"Of course, Jeddie." Dorinda ran her hands through her hair and stretched luxuriously in a way that made her silk dress ripple. "I'm glad you're back together. Stay out as long as you like."

"I'll scratch at the door when I want to come back in," said Jeddie as she left.

"Scratch loud enough for me to hear or you'll end up sleeping downstairs on a bench!" laughed Dorinda, who was at peace with all the world tonight.

She felt like a ship, long lost on strange uncharted seas, buffeted by terrifying storms, when suddenly the sun broke through and the longed for shore of some verdant tropical isle was sighted. Glittering, desirable, beautiful as all Virginia, her future stretched out before her.

Not with Bainter Ramsay, drunken master of Haverleigh Plantation. With Tarn Jenner, the rake who as-

pired to be a planter and had his gray eyes set on
Merryvale. She could tell him the truth if things went
far enough, he could buy Merryvale for her, they could
live there forever and ever.

Her little ship, buffeted for so long, was coming in
for a landing on a golden tropical isle.

Dorinda had forgotten that in dazzling tropical waters
lurked saw-toothed coral reefs capable of sinking any
craft!

Her world this rascal now can turn about
And defeat her with a single laughing shout!
She should hate him—why does it disturb her so
That this dashing fellow might get up and go?

PART THREE

The Laughing Rogue

Chapter 29

When they arrived back at Haverleigh, their host met them at the pier. He was dressed in orange satins that became him devilish well but his tawny eyes were blood-shot and he walked with a slight stagger.

"So you stayed the night," he grumbled, looking at Dorinda. "To bring back this?" He shot a contemptu-ous look at Jeddie, who flushed resentfully. She had been out all night and was looking a little bleary-eyed herself!

"'Twas my business kept us overnight," stated Isham Riddle briskly and his sister added nervously, "We should have let you know, Bainter."

But Bainter's gaze had returned to Dorinda. She looked steadily back at him. "I have brought back not only Jeddie but the inn cat which I have adopted." She held up the hatbox containing her new hat as if it contained Lady Soft Paws. No need for Bainter to know that the cat was probably roaming the big attics at this moment!

"A cat?" he exploded. "Can't have a cat here. They make me sneeze, devilish beasts!" He glowered at her.

"I do realize it's an imposition." Dorinda eyed her handsome host warily. "But I hoped we could stay here yet a day or two—until I can arrange to remove to Merryvale Manor."

He stopped short and blinked at her. "Remove to—?" he began.

"Yes, I am planning to stay in Virginia." She gave him a defiant look. "And reside at Merryvale."

He shook his tawny head as if to clear it. Then, "But you've no need to remove any time soon," he said heartily. "You're all welcome to stay as long as you like."

A gracious host! Mistress Riddle melted, but Dorinda said carefully. "That's very kind of you, Bainter, and I do promise to keep my cat out of your way, but now that I have Jeddie with me, I'll be moving up there as soon as the estate is settled. After all—" her smile flashed—"I can't impose on your hospitality forever!"

Bainter's bemused expression was a picture to see, but Mistress Riddle cut in with an exuberant, "We're all so glad Dorinda has decided to stay! Merryvale Manor will come into its own at last—it was such a silent place when Joshua Merryvale lived there alone!"

Being of no mind to be pulled aside and asked questions, Dorinda walked on up the lawn with Jeddie following in her wake. She was glad that Bainter had not noticed the new gold locket suspended on a delicate gold chain around her neck. Tarn had given it to her just before she climbed into the carriage in Williamsburg for the drive to the Riddles' barge.

"Wear this for luck," he had said as he slipped it around her neck. And when Dorinda would have protested, he had murmured, "A gift for a gift. Bear in mind I'll be wearing your gold buttons!" and they had both laughed.

Behind them the Riddles were already in the carriage and talking animatedly about the goods Isham Riddle had bought and was having shipped up to Riddlewood.

Her own voice was entirely overridden by Gladys Riddle's glad cries of, "Ironstone? Oh, Isham, you've bought me some dishes to replace those I lost in the fire! Blue and white, you say?" Dorinda said shyly, "It's a lovely locket." She opened it and found it empty. "But there's no picture inside!"

Under cover of Isham's rumbling response to his sister, "Now maybe you'll come back home to Riddlewood where you belong!" Tarn smiled at her. " 'Tis ready for a picture of your lover—when you decide who he is."

Dorinda flashed him a bright enigmatic look. "Yes, it is, isn't it?" She gave him a gamin smile. "Tomorrow at Merryvale then?" She let herself be boosted into the carriage and it was with a delightful feeling of power that she looked back at him as he watched them go. The two most eligible bachelors in Williamsburg—and she had them both!

Tarn's sardonic smile suggested he might have guessed what she was thinking. He responded to her light-hearted wave, then turned on his heel and strode back to the White Hart. He had some heavy thinking to do.

Mistress Riddle's sharp eyes had not failed to notice the locket. " 'Tis a lover's gift!" she had exclaimed. "The next step is a betrothal ring, is it not, Isham?"

Her brother grunted. "A better choice than Ramsay," was his dry comment.

Jeddie, seated beside Dorinda with her worldly possessions tied in a linen square and reposing on her lap, drank it all in. Although she had voyaged across the sea, she had never been up the James by barge and the trip thrilled her. A country girl, her sharp eyes spied out the countryside, and she would break into the conversation to carol, "See the 'possum in that tree over there?" Or, "There's a mother raccoon teaching her babies to cross water," indicating a rivulet that ran into the James. And once she claimed to have glimpsed a black bear, "Right there in those cedars—oh, you can't see him now!"

Isham Riddle remarked that she must have been mistaken, bears were getting scarce and so were wildcats, and then the barge was passing a white pillared manor house and Jeddie was all "ohs" and "ahs" as she speculated aloud on the marvelous lives of those within. Her running conversation had kept them amused all the way up the river and now, hurrying over the sloping front lawn of Haverleigh, she caught up with Dorinda.

"I never seen anything so grand!" she cried, looking up at the sweeping brick manor house. "I didn't know Bainter Ramsay lived like this!" Her face was solemn.

"Well, he does," laughed Dorinda.

"Is Merryvale this fine?" asked Jeddie, impressed.

"Maybe not, but I love it," said Dorinda.

"Then so will I," sighed Jeddie. She danced a couple of steps beside Dorinda. "Oh, I think I've died and gone to heaven—first last night and now this!"

"What happened last night?" asked Dorinda, remembering that it had been dawn before Jeddie had scratched discreetly on the door. When Dorinda had roused sleepily to let her in, she had come in giggling and smelling of wine.

"Oh, I spent my evening with my gentleman friend," Jeddie giggled conspiratorially. "A very good friend!" She tossed her auburn head thoughtfully. "Maybe I'll decide to marry him!" And then as Dorinda turned to give her a curious look, Jeddie said swiftly, as if to ward off questions, "Why'd you tell Bainter Ramsay there was a cat in that hatbox when the cat's been up here all along?"

"That was in case he runs across Lady Soft Paws," Dorinda said ruefully. "It would seem the master of Haverleigh has no love for cats!"

"I warned you about that," insisted Jeddie. "But you *would* bring her along!"

"Yes," said Dorinda, giving Jeddie a level look. "And

if Lady Soft Paws isn't welcome here, I shall repair me to Merryvale Manor with or without the court's permission and let George Peabody sort it all out!"

They had by now gone up the wide steps and through the big front door and Jeddie muttered, "Look at this!" as she found herself in the thirty-foot square paneled room. She gazed around her in awe.

"Wait till you see the rooftop promenade!" said Dorinda. "We haven't used it yet but imagine a party there!" With Jeddie trailing her and gawking about, she led the way to her spacious bedroom and Jeddie gave a happy cry and tossed her things down rapturously. "Oh, 'tis grand!" she breathed. "Twice as big as the biggest bedroom at the White Hart!"

"Well, space there is at a premium," laughed Dorinda. "And here no one thinks of charging for the room!"

"That's true," said Jeddie absently. She stalked toward the big square bed, eyeing it warily, and then turned to Dorinda with a look of appeal. "I know they'll be bringing in a cot for me," she muttered, "but could I just—?"

Dorinda guessed what Jeddie was going to do and laughed. "Go ahead, Jeddie."

Jeddie took a flying leap and landed sprawled face down in the middle of the big bed. The feathers sank with the impact of her body and closed around her, almost making her disappear. "Real goose feathers!" came her ecstatic muffled cry.

"Yes, it's really goose down," laughed Dorinda. "Now get up before Mistress Riddle comes in and decides we're a couple of children!"

With a sigh, Jeddie fought her way up out of the enveloping feather mattress and straightened out the green and white coverlet, patting it smooth.

"You were telling me about your gentleman friend?" said Dorinda, as she stood on tiptoe to put the hatbox containing her new hat with the tangerine plumes on a high shelf in the big cherry clothes press.

Jeddie straightened up from patting the coverlet smooth. "Here, let me do that," she cried. "I'm supposed to be a ladies' maid now, and helping you!"

Dorinda laughed. "I'm afraid it will take time before I can adjust to that, Jeddie. I'm too used to doing things for myself." She went back to the subject of the gentleman friend. "Have you known him long?"

"Not too long." Jeddie's ruddy complexion deepened a shade as she thought about him and her deep blue eyes glowed. "He told me he thought I wasn't interested in him when I didn't come to meet him and kept to my room like that, and when I told him I'd been locked in of nights he looked kind of relieved." She gave Dorinda an arch look. "I guess he was jealous, thinking I was stepping out with some other fellow!"

"This sounds serious," smiled Dorinda.

Jeddie looked down and picked at her skirt. "Well— we'll see," she said. "I used to think that men were just after one thing, but this one, well, he's different. I know there's a lot of difference between his station and mine, but—" she gave Dorinda a challenging look—"I could learn to be a lady, couldn't I? After all, you did!"

Dorinda winced. For a little while she'd forgotten that while she was born of aristocratic lineage, the world had never been willing to accept it—not of a bound girl. They were a pair of bound girls, both of them, and Jeddie—like herself, when she had worked at the White Hart—was hoping for better days.

"Who is this paragon?" she asked Jeddie dryly.

Jeddie hesitated. "He said I mustn't say nothing about my seeing him—not just yet. Not to anyone. That's on account of his father wouldn't never approve of us getting married. But his father's old and when his father dies, he wants to marry me right and proper!" Her face glowed as she looked at Dorinda, and Dorinda with all her heart hoped that Jeddie's "gentleman friend" was not just leading her on.

"Jeddie," she said. "When Isham Riddle goes upriver tomorrow, I'm going to ask him to take me to Merryvale Manor. Would you like to go along?"

"Oh, yes," breathed Jeddie.

"Good," said Dorinda, who was convinced that Isham Riddle would not allow her to go to Merryvale unchaperoned. Better Jeddie, who would conveniently disappear and leave her alone with Tarn when he arrived, than Mistress Riddle who would stay with them every minute! "I'm going upstairs now," she said, "to rescue Lady Soft Paws."

She found the cat purring on the torn bit of blanket she had provided to make a soft bed for her.

"Did you catch a mouse while we were gone?" Dorinda hugged the forgiving gray and white bundle of fur and cuddled her in her arms, for poor Lady Soft Paws had been a prisoner of the big attics and the rooftop promenade since they had left, even though she had had plenty of food and water. With the cat in her arms she came downstairs to meet a shining-eyed Jeddie.

"They've given me a room of my own," Jeddie informed her excitedly. "A real room—not like that cubbyhole I had at the White Hart!"

"That was nice of Bainter," said Dorinda, glad he was making Jeddie welcome.

"Oh, it wasn't Bainter Ramsay—it was Clem the butler who assigned me the room." She giggled. "I think he likes me."

"Be careful of him," warned Dorinda, who didn't care for the way big Clem looked at her when Bainter wasn't watching. She handed the cat to Jeddie with instructions to take her down to the big kitchen and feed her.

"Shall I take her outside afterward?" Jeddie liked the cat and took her from Dorinda's arms with affection.

"For a little while," said Dorinda. "But before dark you must bring her back in and take her back to the attic. I wouldn't want her roaming the countryside at night. She might be killed by some wild animal."

"Wolves," muttered Jeddie, her blue eyes big and dark. "Or bears!"

Dorinda gave her a whimsical look. She very much doubted that Jeddie had seen a bear today. "And I certainly wouldn't want Lady Soft Paws to bother Bainter," she added. "It seems cats make him sneeze!"

But Bainter was not on her mind that night as she drifted through dinner eating the indifferent food and hardly noticing what was said to her. She was thinking of tomorrow and of seeing Tarn Jenner again.

In the morning, after their usual breakfast of runny omelet and cold coffee, Dorinda found Isham Riddle more than willing to take her along with him so that she might visit Merryvale. Jeddie jumped into the barge with glee. But to Dorinda's vexation, plump Mistress Riddle also joined the party, saying happily that she would accompany them to Merryvale and be their chaperon.

"Tarn Jenner is meeting me at Merryvale," muttered Dorinda to Jeddie. "Try to help me get rid of her for a while, won't you?"

Jeddie nodded, bright-eyed. She was all for intrigue!

They reached Merryvale early and Tarn Jenner was not there. Mistress Riddle went to see the agent while Dorinda and Jeddie stayed under the locusts on the front lawn, ostensibly to gather flowers. They were still there when Tarn arrived, and went down to the landing to greet him.

Tarn had eyes for no one but Dorinda, but Jeddie stuck her auburn head forward to ask wistfully, "Can I speak to you before you go?" She was thinking of sending George Peabody a message and turned away contentedly when Tarn gave an absent nod.

Dorinda hardly noticed. "Jeddie, go try to keep Mistress Riddle busy," she said breathlessly. "Tarn, would you like to see the house? It's unlocked."

"I would," he said, and followed her inside.

In his company, the house looked entirely different

to Dorinda. It had been light and bright before, but now it seemed positively to glow. She walked about, happily pointing out things she liked, things she would change.

"So you're not moved in yet but already you're planning to redecorate?" he laughed. "How like a woman!"

"Ah, but can you deny that the dining room would look lovely painted a soft green and the walls of the living room a soft blue, I think—with white painted wainscoating?"

"Or perhaps a scenic French wallpaper," he suggested, cocking an eyebrow at her. "You could be one of the first to use it and have all the ladies of Williamsburg green with envy!"

"Yes, that would be fun," admitted Dorinda. She was looking straight at Joshua Merryvale's portrait as she said that and she met his accusing painted gaze defiantly.

I am going to make Merryvale a showplace, she silently told that dour painted face. *Whether you like it or not!*

Tarn had stopped before the portrait. "A good likeness," he observed. "I saw him but once or twice—and he was older of course than when that picture was painted."

"Oh—yes." Dorinda's gaze slid away from the portrait. "Come, I must show you the bedrooms! The linens of course are quite inadequate, but I thought I would ask Lucy Claridge to advise me—after all, she was kind enough to invite me to her ball."

"I see you will have no difficulty making your way here socially," he grinned. "Lucy Claridge, for all her faults, carries a lot of weight here."

Dorinda gave him a contented look, and pointed out the beauty of the balusters "when polished as they should be!"

She had been running up the stairs ahead of him and now she flung open a paneled door to reveal a spacious bedroom with a lovely view of the river.

"This is the nicest bedroom. I mean to take it when I come to live here. The view is wonderful, don't you think?"

"The view will be even more wonderful when you are lying in the center of that big bed with the bedclothes thrown off because of the heat," he said wickedly.

"If I am too warm, I will simply fan myself with one of those big palm leaf fans from the islands," was her airy response.

He leaned closer. "Ah, but even so the air will be close and hot—"

"There will be a breeze from the river," she mocked.

"Little tendrils of your hair will be stuck to your damp neck and shoulders and you will brush them off and toss and turn and your chemise will ride up—"

Dorinda caught her breath. This had gone quite far enough. She edged away from the impudent Mr. Jenner. "No chemise of mine would dare to ride up," she told him haughtily, and he gave a great laugh and reached for her.

Dorinda struggled in his arms. There was a small scuffle and then his lips found hers and it was the magic of that kiss at the inn all over again. She sagged toward him and a wild refrain seemed to play in her head. The big bed seemed the only piece of furniture in the room. In another moment she knew he would urge her toward it.

A voice broke into their reverie.

"Are you two upstairs?" caroled Mistress Riddle's voice, and they heard her footsteps pattering up the stairs.

Tarn let her go and they stared at each other. Both had been shaken by that kiss and at the moment neither felt like laughing.

"Oh, there you are!" Mistress Riddle came bustling in. "Isn't this a lovely room, Mr. Jenner? I do think, Dorinda, that you will want to change that coverlet. It's quite worn, and I don't think puce is a very good color for a bedspread, do you?"

"No, I don't," agreed Dorinda, her rapt gaze still on Tarn Jenner's face that for a moment had lost its sardonic expression and looked quite boyish. "In fact, I don't care for anything in puce!"

"In that," laughed Tarn, "you agree with my step-grandmother. She dotes on all shades of red—except puce! She met my grandfather in Paris where he had fled when his estates were confiscated. He was a young widower then, and had left his small son in the care of his sister. And when he met this English girl in the forest of Versailles where he was strolling—he said she was bathing in a stream at the time and he watched her for quite a while without her knowing—she quite took his breath away."

Mistress Riddle looked scandalized but Dorinda laughed. "I can see she might!" she declared merrily.

"She came out of the stream and he made himself known to her. It must have been love at first sight for they were married very soon after that. They had but a handful of florins between them but my grandfather was not called Wild Nick for nothing. He was a handsome devil and bold as brass. They took their florins to a gambling hell and came away with enough to live for a month. After that their path was clear. They took assumed names not to shame their relatives back in England. He called himself "Nick Forsythe" and he christened her "Elsinore." He always bragged that she had a man's cool daring and a woman's velvet charm. And I think she really gained her dislike of the color puce in Brussels—they toured the great capitals of Europe gambling for a living until my grandfather's estates were restored to him and he could return to England—but it was in Brussels that a mad Frenchman in puce velvet took exception to the play and would have run my grandfather through with his dagger save that Elsinore saw the blow coming and knocked up the blade with her arm. She bears the scar yet...." He sighed. "He was a good man, was Wild Nick, and they loved each other to the day he died."

"Do you have a large family?" wondered Mistress Riddle.

He shook his head. "Elsinore and I are all that's left."

Dorinda had liked the story of his stepgrandmother. "Your grandfather called her Elsinore," she said curiously. "What do *you* call her?"

"Oh, I call her Elsinore too," he replied cheerfully. "For she will have it no other way. She seems to have the secret of eternal youth—her step is light, her laughter is catching, she still has a steady hand on a pistol or a deck of cards."

"I wish I could know your stepgrandmother," sighed Dorinda.

"Perhaps you will," he smiled. "Someday."

Mistress Riddle was torn between shock and admiration. She herself was old enough to be a grandmother but she would certainly not allow her grandchildren—not even a stepgrandson like Tarn—to call her by her first name! She brought the conversation back to the bedchamber in which they stood. "This room is a trifle plain. Joshua Merryvale had no use at all for frills."

"Mistress Dorinda is bent on redecorating," Tarn assured her. "It seems she plans to enlist your aid and that of Lucy Claridge in the project."

"Oh, that's splendid. Lucy Claridge has marvelous taste. Did you note what she was wearing at her ball? The latest thing from Paris!" Mistress Riddle sighed. "I do wish Isham cared more for fashion."

She accompanied them on their tour of the house, pointing out all the changes that *she* would make were Merryvale hers, and the two of them were silent mainly, watching each other in a guarded way. Not until they were back downstairs and Mistress Riddle announced that she was tired and must sit down and rest her feet

did they have a chance to escape to the garden where
they could be alone.

"It's lovely here, don't you think?" Dorinda asked
him dreamily as he strolled beside her through a clipped
circle of box, the small green leaves dark against the
emerald of the grass. "I love this countryside along the
James." She sighed. "Oh, I do think I shall be very
happy here."

He caught at her hand and she let him keep it. It felt
small inside of his. The garden was warm—and private.
Nearby a mockingbird was singing its heart out.

"Dorinda," he said. "I am not yet in a position to
speak of marriage, I do not yet have a holding here in
Virginia."

"Would that matter?" she asked softly. "You could
marry and share one." *This one, for instance.* The offer
hung plain between them.

"I would offer you my name," he said soberly. "Are
you saying that you would share Merryvale with me?"

"Oh, gladly," said Dorinda, her words coming in a
little rush. "Oh, Tarn, I *want* you here with me. I—"

She could not finish for she was already crushed in
his arms and he was kissing her, uncaring whether
Mistress Riddle was observing them from the windows
or not. Dorinda felt the blood rush to her head with the
force of her response to him. Her lips moved beneath
his, her whole body was aglow, tingling with desire. If
he had asked her at that moment to come into the
woods with him, to find some quiet private glade, she
would have gone.

After a while he let her go and she sensed a change
in him. He was gazing down at her very resolutely now.

"Dorinda," he said, and she sensed he was choosing
his words carefully. "Suppose I did not want to reside at
Merryvale? Suppose I asked you to come away? Would
you be willing to give it up?"

"You mean—sell it?" She gave the rambling house

with its painted clapboards and its luxuriant ivy a wistful look.

"Or even—abandon it." He was watching her keenly.

"Abandon it?" She stepped back and gave him an indignant look, for she had wound her dreams around Merryvale now and in her heart it was already hers—whether that portrait gazed at her accusingly or not!

"Too much to ask?" he murmured, and she could not read his smile.

"I—I don't understand why you'd ask it?" she said, confused. For she had by now convinced herself that Tarn had long forgotten that chance encounter in Philadelphia.

He leant down and lightly kissed her forehead. "Maybe I won't have to." But she sensed that he had drawn away from her somehow and he frowned down at the grass.

She might have told him then, she might have blurted out everything she had done and been, she might have asked him what she should do—but Mistress Riddle chose that moment to patter out of the house and join them and the moment was lost. Dorinda hoped that they could break free of her but they were unable to. She chattered along beside them as they paced the garden paths or paused beside the handsome boxwoods. And her coy admonition to Tarn, "You had best be about your courting, Mr. Jenner, or Bainter Ramsay will get there ahead of you! Indeed, I think our Dorinda already fancies him!" had a chilling effect.

"Does she indeed?" murmured Tarn, with a curious glance at Dorinda.

Dorinda could cheerfully have shaken Mistress Riddle, but she could think of nothing appropriate to say. Indeed she felt a guilty flush creeping over her cheeks that she had been more honest with Bainter than with Tarn—telling him she had no real claim to Merryvale. Vexed at his narrow gaze, she changed the subject. "I think I will plant clumps of daffodils in the front lawn so they will bloom next spring in a shower of gold, as I am told they do at Haverleigh," she said crisply. "What would you say to that?"

"I would say that showers of gold have always appealed to me," Tarn said dryly and Dorinda gave Mistress Riddle an irritable look.

That lady promptly responded by announcing that she needed Dorinda's help in pinning her petticoat that she had just ripped on some rose thorns. And once they were inside the house, she told Dorinda in a stage whisper, "You must not mind what I say, my dear. I am only encouraging a backward suitor."

"Tarn Jenner could hardly be considered backward in anything," Dorinda sighed, for she felt that somehow a wedge had come between them.

"Well, he has not yet pressed you to marry him, has he?" Tartly.

Dorinda hesitated. He had mentioned marriage. Certainly he had not *pressed* her to rush into it! "Not in so many words," she said cautiously.

"Well, then?" was Mistress Riddle's triumphant response. "'Tis obvious he needs prodding! Isham thinks you should marry Mr. Jenner," she added, as if that were the last word on the subject.

"Mistress Riddle, I do wish you would leave off prodding him," sighed Dorinda. "And now if you will give me a pin, I will see what I can do about your petticoat," she added.

"That is the trouble," bewailed Mistress Riddle. "I simply do not have a pin—to spare, that is. I cannot use the pin which is even now holding my chemise top together!"

"No, we cannot use that," agreed Dorinda hastily, her mind alive with visions of Mistress Riddle's chemise retreating in billows to her stout ankles and having to be retrieved by all of them. "Come, let us see what we can find upstairs. Mr. Mer—Uncle Joshua must surely have had such things lying about!"

As they searched for a suitable pin in what had been Joshua Merryvale's spartan bedchamber, Dorinda glanced through one of the front windows. She saw that Jeddie had found Tarn and they were standing by the river, talking closely together. Their forms were dark against the silver sparkle. She felt a flash of irritation at Jeddie who had wandered off somewhere, instead of managing to keep Mistress Riddle occupied.

"Oh, I've found a pin I think will do," cried Mistress Riddle, holding it up for Dorinda to see, and Dorinda turned away from the window to help her.

When she and Mistress Riddle, the latter's petticoat now neatly pinned, again emerged onto the lawn, Jeddie quickly broke away from Tarn and hurried back toward the big kitchen where she had apparently made friends with the help. And Dorinda and Tarn fell in step beside the short-legged older woman and walked about until it was time to go back downriver and pick up Isham Riddle at Riddlewood.

At Riddlewood, Mistress Riddle insisted Tarn accompany them back to Haverleigh for dinner. "Why, Bainter would feel quite slighted if you went right past him downstream at suppertime!" she cried, shocked. "Any river planter would!"

Tarn smiled. Hospitality was indeed a fetish here in easy-going Virginia. "He may not be so overjoyed as you think," he said wryly.

"Oh, what if he's not?" grumbled Isham Riddle. " 'Twill be a relief to have your company, Tarn."

"He means," Mistress Riddle told Dorinda in an aside that was loud enough to be heard by all, "that Bainter and Tarn are both competing for your favor—and he favors Tarn's suit." She gave Dorinda a significant look.

Dorinda moved her shoulders uncomfortably in her light sprigged muslin and her color deepened. Tarn grinned and then Isham buttonholed him and kept him deep in a conversation about tobacco all the way downriver to Haverleigh.

Bainter Ramsay did indeed look startled to see Tarn Jenner alight with the others. But he hid his feelings well and came down jauntily to the landing to welcome his caller.

"We could not let Mr. Jenner go downriver without supping," cried Mistress Riddle, beaming on them both.

"Indeed, I agree," said Bainter instantly. His orange satin suit was impeccable but he hiccupped once and Dorinda realized he had been drinking. "Dinner should be ready soon. Come have a drink with me before dinner, gentlemen, while the ladies freshen up."

"Thank you but I've had a rough day, and feel the need of a short nap before dinner," said Isham Riddle curtly. And as he accompanied the women away Dorinda heard him mutter to his sister, "We'll see what cook has mangled for us tonight. I wish you'd leave off being a guest and go back to managing your own household, Gladys!"

"Hush, Bainter will *hear*," chided his sister. She leant toward Jeddie. "When you've finished helping Dorinda I do hope you'll help me with my hooks?"

"I don't know why the Riddles stay here, as nice a house as they've got," Jeddie said wistfully once she and Dorinda were in Dorinda's big bedroom.

"Oh—they have their reasons, I don't doubt." Dorinda was not about to share Mistress Riddle's frightened confidences with garrulous Jeddie. She stood quietly while Jeddie helped her with her hooks so that she could change to her light cream silk. "I wish you could eat with us, Jeddie," she said apologetically.

"Oh, don't worry your head none about that," laughed Jeddie. "There's better food in the kitchen than ever reaches the dining room!"

Dorinda blinked. She would have gone into that at more length but she was in a hurry to join the gentlemen for she felt that Tarn and Bainter might well be coming to blows in the drawing room.

She need not have worried. When she arrived, slightly

breathless and with her hair not done quite so perfectly as it would have been had she taken more time, they came to their feet smiling, with glasses in their hands. Indeed, they seemed the best of friends.

Slightly taken aback, for she had expected them to be quarreling by now, Dorinda gave them her best curtsy and accepted a glass of Madeira.

"The Riddles will join us presently," she said. "Jeddie is helping Mistress Riddle get dressed."

"A gigantic job," observed Bainter dryly, for he detested stoutness in women.

"She likes you," said Dorinda in a level voice and he shrugged as if to say, *That's her privilege; the liking doesn't necessarily have to be returned!*

Dorinda turned with a frown to Tarn, who was watching her very pleasantly over the lip of his wine glass. "I will hear nothing against Mistress Riddle," she announced frostily to the room in general. "She has been a good friend to me since I have come here!"

"Oh, you'll hear nothing against her from me," shrugged Tarn. "I have a certain fondness for the lady."

Their voices were stilled at the sound of approaching footsteps for that would be the Riddles. The Riddles arrived, Bainter offered Dorinda his arm and they went in to dinner. And there, suddenly, over execrable food, Dorinda was on her bad behavior.

She was not quite sure what had annoyed her. Was it because she had expected the two men to fight over her—and they had not? Or was it because Tarn had so neatly brought her feelings for him out in the open without making any firm commitment on his part? Well, she would stir them up! She leaned maliciously toward Bainter.

"Merryvale was lovely today," she taunted. "You should have come with us, Bainter."

Mistress Riddle gave Tarn a stricken look—it was plain to see where *her* feelings lay. Her brother continued to stare wistfully down at his food, as if remembering other better meals.

Tarn seemed quite untouched by it. "Yes, Ramsay," he challenged. "Why weren't you there?"

Bainter's tawny gaze flicked toward him. "I have no hold over Mistress Dorinda," he said lightly.

"Have you not?" wondered Tarn softly.

"She may go where she pleases!" snapped Bainter.

"Yes, it *was* a lovely day," cried Mistress Riddle, distressed. "Indeed you *should* have gone with us, Bainter."

"Why?" Bainter's voice was blunt as he turned to Dorinda. "Did something transpire that I should know about?"

"Of course not." Dorinda's answering gaze was serene, guileless. She shrugged. "It was the kind of a day for doing daring things."

"Daring things . . ." he repeated, with a dark look cast at his unwelcome guest.

"Yes," smiled Dorinda. "A wonderful day. For you, Bainter, it would have been a day—to race your favorite horse, I would think. Have you ever raced against Tarn, Bainter?"

"Once," supplied Tarn humorously. "Ramsay lost."

Bainter's lips drew back from his teeth. "My nag went lame," he grated at Tarn. "I'll race ye again the next time I'm in Williamsburg and have a nag beneath me that is worth his salt!"

"Any time," was the urbane response.

Dorinda could feel the underlying current of animosity here. She had indeed stirred things up. For some reason it delighted her.

"I always hope the best man will win in any contest," she said clearly into the silence. "I believe absolutely in 'winner take all.'"

"The winner usually does," observed Tarn dryly.

"When I occupy Merryvale, I intend to hold jousts on the front lawn. The ladies will watch from a summerhouse which I shall have built as the gentlemen vie for their favors."

"You have a romantic nature," murmured Tarn, amused.

Bainter laughed. "You'll not find enough energy left among these planters to wield either sword or lance after they've spent the day worrying over how to get more out of their tobacco fields!"

It was a wrong note. Dorinda gave him a cold look and Mistress Riddle, sensing that they were headed for trouble, entered the conversation and hardly stopped for breath until Tarn announced regretfully that he must depart.

"Ye're welcome to stay the night," Bainter was quick to say, though unsmilingly.

"Thank you for dinner, but no, I am expected back in Williamsburg and I see through the window that the boat that took me upriver has now tied up at your landing, Ramsay. The men will be eager to push off—they have families in Williamsburg who expect them home tonight."

So it was in the company of others that Dorinda saw Tarn off. She felt a deep sense of disappointment—and perhaps of shame at her recent behavior for she really *had* been trying to set them at each other's throats! She had felt so close to Tarn this morning, she thought regretfully, and now he was going—and she had somehow expected him to declare himself more *definitely* before he left, but he had made no attempt to get her aside.

She walked a few steps ahead, feeling disconsolate to be seeing him off, and at the last minute he turned to her. "Dorinda—"

"Yes?" she whispered, for she thought she saw a yearning light in his eyes. Moonlight, of course, is deceptive....

She thought he was going to speak then, to say something memorable out of the hearing of the others who lagged behind, something that she could hug to her through the night and cling to all the next day. But he did not.

"Take care," he said lightly, and was into the boat. The men were casting off. Dorinda waved. Then she turned to rejoin the others—and saw that a little ways behind the group, Jeddie was waving too.

Chapter 30

Not till the next afternoon did the blow fall. It happened quite by chance. Jeddie had come into Dorinda's room. She was making a great show of hanging up Dorinda's clothes (for she loved to play at being a lady's maid) when her apron, badly tied, came off and as it fell to the floor something shiny rolled to Dorinda's feet where she sat at her dressing table.

"Oh, dear," cried Jeddie, without turning around. "What have I lost now?" For she was always losing things, it was a standing joke between them that Jeddie would lose her head if God had not seen fit to attach it firmly to her shoulders!

Dorinda was at that moment holding a necklace of blue glass beads that she had bought in Williamsburg and which she had decided was after all not the right color for her. She was toying with the idea of giving the beads to Jeddie to match her blue eyes when the shiny object rolled toward her slipper and she bent down to retrieve it.

She picked it up and saw that she was looking down at a gold button. A very distinctive gold button that she remembered all too well. It was exactly like the one she had promised to sew on Tarn Jenner's maroon broad-cloth coat.

And with the sight, it came to her in a rush all that finding that button in Jeddie's possession entailed. Tarn Jenner then was Jeddie's "gentleman friend," the one who was so above her in station, whose very name must be kept secret! And Jeddie had been gone all night after Tarn had left Dorinda at her door at the White Hart in Williamsburg—Jeddie must have spent the night with him! She remembered how yesterday from the window at Merryvale she had seen Jeddie privately conversing with Tarn, their heads confidentially close. And Jeddie had rushed out of the house last night to wave good-bye to Tarn when he left.

The evidence was overwhelming. She had been had! *He wants us both!* she thought, appalled. And Jeddie, obviously, was willing to share.

In a convulsive gesture, Dorinda's grip on the blue beads broke the strand and the glass beads showered to the floor like frozen tears, rolling everywhere.

"I'll get them," cried Jeddie, who thought the neck-lace quite beautiful. "Here, some of them rolled over in the corner—I'll find them!"

Dorinda let the gold button drop from her nerveless fingers to the floor and roll away from her. Let Jeddie find it among the beads, whatever it meant to her—talisman? Keepsake? She looked up and saw reflected in the mirror a stranger's face. Older somehow, pale. And very, very bleak. Over in the corner Jeddie was scuffling for the beads. Fortunately the girl's back was turned away from the grim-faced woman staring at her reflection in the mirror.

Dorinda's first instinct was to scream at Jeddie, to hurl a hairbrush at her. But, she asked herself in fairness, how could she blame Jeddie for being led astray by a man that she herself had found attractive? And Jeddie had found him first for had she not said that she had met him "earlier in the summer?" And

Tarn Jenner was a relative newcomer—Jeddie could have met him shortly after his arrival! Jeddie—the thought shriveled her—was sharing her lover with *her*! That Tarn was toying with the girl and had no intention of marrying her, she had no doubt. Still what did she really know about him except that he chose to charm into his bed those ladies who crossed his path?

Her gaze fell suddenly to the little gold locket that rested upon her bosom. It seemed to leer at her, an evil glimmer. With sudden fury, she jerked it from her neck, breaking the delicate gold chain. The chain flew to the floor and lay there as Dorinda tossed the locket contemptuously to the dressing table.

So did he always give his light loves golden trinkets? How many such had he scattered around? Perhaps Lucy Claridge of the roving eye had a pair of gold earbobs from him! Perhaps—! She jumped up, shaken by the images that flitted through her mind.

Jeddie had by now picked up all the glass beads she could find in the corner. "When will we be going back to Williamsburg?" she asked breathlessly as she got up off her knees.

"We won't." Dorinda hardly recognized her own voice, so harsh did it sound in her ears. "We're stayng right here until we move into Merryvale."

Jeddie looked up and caught sight of Dorinda's face. "What's the matter?" she gasped.

"Nothing's the matter." Dorinda shook out her skirts. "What could possibly be the matter?" she demanded in a brittle voice.

Leaving an open-mouthed Jeddie behind her, Dorinda stalked from the room, swishing her skirts up into the big attics to find Lady Soft Paws and carry her up to the rooftop promenade. There she sank down disconsolately in a corner and leant against one of the big chimney pillars and stroked the cat's soft fur.

"Oh, Lady Soft Paws," she whispered. "I thought he

cared for me...." And the cat looked up questioningly as hot tears fell upon her fur.

When Dorinda came downstairs carrying the cat she found Jeddie waiting for her in her room.

"I found all the blue beads," Jeddie said eagerly.

"We can restring them later," said Dorinda, who wanted Jeddie's happy face banished from her sight just now. "You'd best take Lady Soft Paws outside for an airing," she added in a curt voice.

Jeddie gave her mistress a hurt look and departed, bearing the cat, and Dorinda was left to her private misery.

Jeddie took Lady Soft Paws outside to the garden. She was holding the cat close in her arms as she went lest she get away and run through the big rooms and have a possibly disastrous confrontation with Bainter Ramsay. And Jeddie was frowning.

This paradise into which she had been thrust seemed suddenly to have developed cracks in its structure. They were a strange lot in the kitchen and Jeddie did not like what she was hearing. True, they had welcomed her as "one of them," but Jeddie had found that she did not feel like one of them—indeed she did not think she could ever become one of them.

She had already discovered thieving in the kitchen. Part of the reason for the poor quality food that was served was that the best of it was spirited away by big Clem the butler to Williamsburg and there sold to various inns. But everyone was afraid of Clem—too afraid to speak out. And besides, the food the help ate was somewhat better than those burnt offerings and half-cooked morsels served at the master's table, which tended to keep them quiet. Jeddie had debated with herself whether to take this knowledge of Clem's blatant thievery to Dorinda, who would undoubtedly tell Bainter and thus arouse the household, when Clem began to show an overt liking for her. He hinted broadly that "the master would overlook anything"

where he was concerned, and he winked when he
added with vague menace that he "knew things."

What things? Jeddie had not liked his tone, nor the
broad wink he had given her. She wished her "gentleman
friend" were here to consult—he knew all about the
law!

She set the cat down on one of the overgrown garden
walks and Lady Soft Paws promptly set off on a mock
chase of a butterfly, sending her gray and white body
twisting lightly up into the air as the golden winged
thing fluttered always out of reach.

Yesterday when Clem had cornered her in one of the
pantries and suggested they get better acquainted, Jeddie
had nervously used the excuse that "Mr. Bainter" would
hardly approve of that. Clem had laughed and said,
"Won't he now? With what I know—!"

"What do you know?" she had asked bluntly.

Clem had winked and patted her shoulder with a
hamlike hand. "I could tell you things." His hot gaze
had run scaldingly over Jeddie's lush figure. "Like
about Felix Blair, for instance."

Felix Blair, Jeddie knew, was a fellow who had two
years ago come out of nowhere to inherit the Blair
property when the Widow Blair had died suddenly of a
stroke. Two months later he had been found drowned
in the James and Bainter Ramsay had showed up with a
deed to the property, dated a week before the drowning.
There had been some nasty talk at the time and it was
one of the reasons so many of the planters did not like
Bainter Ramsay, but the talk had all died down. Jeddie
herself had never put much stock in it. Talk was cheap
in Williamsburg.

Now something shuttered and evil in Clem's voice
sent chills down her spine. "What—about Felix Blair?"
she asked.

Clem had winked again. "I know what I know," he
said loftily. "And that's why Bainter Ramsay won't never
fire me no matter what I sell downriver—even if it's the

meat off his table!" He had laughed uproariously and slapped his heavy thighs and Jeddie had said quickly, "I think I hear my mistress calling," and made her escape.

On her way back through the pantries that day she had bumped into Tressa, a pale beaten-down serving maid that Jeddie privately considered the best of the lot.

"I thought you might need an interruption to help get you away from Clem," Tressa said, indicating the pail of milk she was carrying. "If I saw you was in trouble, I planned to pretend to trip and throw this milk all over him."

Jeddie gave her a grateful look. "Clem scares me," she admitted.

"He scares everybody." Tressa rolled her brown eyes. "I'm lucky he doesn't like me—says I'm too thin."

"Well, he couldn't say I'm too thin!" Jeddie looked down at her voluptuous body uneasily. "He talks like he could get away with anything here!"

"He does," nodded Tressa. "And if the master knows, he looks the other way. I think Clem has got something on him."

"He mentioned Felix Blair. I know there was talk some time ago."

"Yes." Tressa shivered. "I don't know nothing about it and I don't *want* to know. I wish I'd never come here but—jobs is hard to come by." She indicated the foot that had been twisted in infancy and that would never be right, she would always walk crooked.

"I think Bainter Ramsay wants to marry my mistress," said Jeddie seriously.

"Heaven help her then." Tressa shook her head. "For he's a bad man. He wasn't content with sacking Wilbur Hull the day Wilbur tripped and accidentally drenched him with cider when he was about to leave for Williamsburg—he broke Wilbur's jaw and knocked out a lot of his teeth!"

"What about—women?"

"Oh, he doesn't bring them here—leastways not any more. He has a flock of them in Williamsburg, according to the help here. Married or single, ladies or scullery maids—he takes 'em all on!"

Now, thinking about Tressa's words, Jeddie stood pensively in the scented summer garden and watched the cat at play. She'd meant to tell Dorinda today what Tressa had told her—and what she suspected, which was even worse—but Dorinda had acted so strange and distant she'd decided against it. And maybe, she thought uneasily, Dorinda was still in love with Bainter Ramsay. If she was, she certainly wouldn't appreciate hearing servants' gossip about him.

Jeddie sighed. If only she could talk to George Peabody! She thought of the gold button Tarn Jenner had given her when she had passed him, going out, that night at the White Hart. He had stopped and looked down at her.

"You're going upriver to Haverleigh as Mistress Merryvale's personal maid, aren't you, Jeddie?"

Jeddie, clad in her new clothes and impatient to go out and meet George, who'd be skulking in some nearby alley, had allowed that was so.

Tarn had taken several pieces of eight from his pocket and given them to her. She had gaped at him. "What's this for?"

"That's for keeping quiet about what I'm about to ask you, Jeddie. Tell me, can you write?"

She had shaken her head regretfully.

"No matter." He had fished in his pocket and found there a gold button, had pressed it into her hand. His face had been very grave. "If you should decide your mistress is in any sort of trouble, Jeddie, send that button downriver to me right away."

Jeddie had guessed—wrongly—that Dorinda must have told him about her deception and how she wasn't really who she said she was—and he was planning to save her if things turned out wrong. Jeddie warmed to him. This was the kind of man to have! Dorinda must love him....

Now, remembering Dorinda's harsh pronouncement that they wouldn't be going back to Williamsburg and how thick she seemed to be getting with Bainter Ramsay, she wasn't so sure.

And now she wasn't even sure she had done the right thing by running across the lawn at Merryvale the moment Dorinda and Mistress Riddle had left Tarn alone and asking him to deliver a message to George Peabody.

"A message to George Peabody, Senior?" Tarn had asked, for he passed the old fellow occasionally in the common room of the White Hart where he sometimes came to drink with friends or play cards.

"*Oh, no,* sir!" Jeddie had colored to the roots of her auburn hair. "I'd not be interested in a man so old!" She choked at the words her indignation had caused her to blurt out and promptly put a horrified hand over her mouth.

A smile had curved Tarn Jenner's sardonic mouth as he realized he was being asked to carry a message in an affair of the heart. "I see," he said gravely. "And what would you like me to say?"

"Just say—oh, please, sir, do remember I'm watching Dorinda for you so you should keep my secret for me!"

"I'll be discreet," he promised.

"Just tell him there'd be no harm in his finding some business to transact upriver. He could say he wanted to check out something at Merryvale—we go up there most every day. And I could meet him there. And do be careful where you tell him, for his father mustn't ever know."

"I'll tell him most privately," promised Tarn, wondering how many colors George Peabody would turn when he received this message!

Now in the gardens of Haverleigh, watching Lady Soft Paws stalk a blowing leaf, Jeddie was having second thoughts about having sent that message even by a man she trusted as much as she trusted Tarn Jenner. It had seemed such a golden opportunity at the time, but now she wondered: Would George be furious? After all, he had said *"Tell nobody,"* and now Tarn Jenner knew....

Life was getting very complicated.

More to give her hands something to do than anything else, Dorinda spent the afternoon elaborately dressing her hair. Clad in her becoming new cream silk panniered gracefully over her tangerine silk petticoat, she went down to dinner as regally as any queen.

Bainter came to his feet at sight of her. "Ye look like a duchess!" he cried admiringly.

Flattery was balm to Dorinda's sagging spirits just now. She smiled at Bainter. "I had forgot the gift I brought you from Williamsburg," she said, bringing the beribboned walking stick out from behind her and presenting it to him.

"O-ho, very elegant!" Bainter postured with the orange ribboned walking stick and turned to her with a boyish laugh. He was completely different tonight, she thought, from the man who had glowered at them over breakfast this morning. She wondered if he had braced himself with enough hot coffee to rid himself of his hangover of the night before or if just the passing hours had done it. In any event, he did not seem to be drinking now. "I missed you when you were gone," he said.

It was a very simple statement but it struck straight to Dorinda's battered heart.

"I had not meant to be gone overnight," she admitted. "I but went along with the Riddles to see George Peabody."

"About the estate—I see. And did Peabody persuade you that you needed a bond servant?"

"No," sighed Dorinda. "I thought of that all by myself." And now in many ways she was regretting it. For Jeddie would be a constant reminder of Tarn

Jenner's treachery. She blushed to think how he had led her on at dinner at the Raleigh when all the time he was planning to spend the night with Jeddie!

Bainter gave her a puzzled look. "You don't look happy about it," he said frankly. "Is the wench giving you trouble? If so, I'll straighten her out."

"No—no trouble," said Dorinda. "I suppose I just realized all the responsibilities I'm taking on."

"Too many." He grinned. "You should sell the place. You will anyway," he added confidently, "after you've tried living there. You'll find it's isolated out in the country when your heart's in town. I've found it so here at Haverleigh."

"Oh?" she rallied him. "And is your heart in town?"

"My heart is where there are dice to be thrown and horses to be raced and pretty ladies to be danced with," he told her. Real sincerity rang in his voice. And Dorinda thought, *At least he doesn't lie to chambermaids and make them think he's going to marry them! He's a rake—but he's honest about it!*

At that moment the Riddles joined them and they went in to supper.

"I hope you've made your cat comfortable," Bainter said courteously and Dorinda warmed toward him still more.

"Yes, I have," she said, smiling. "Jeddie has been feeding her—and I'm sure she'll more than earn her keep mousing in your attic."

"Oh, indeed she will," agreed Mistress Riddle comfortably. "Dorinda, I don't see how you can do your hair so handsomely yourself. Look at it, Isham; have you ever seen the like?

Isham Riddle grunted but Bainter smiled caressingly at Dorinda. "She is indeed remarkable, Mistress Riddle—on many counts. I never thought to find such a woman."

Dorinda flushed and addressed herself to her roast capon. It was underdone and she was reminded that Mistress Riddle had said that if she didn't herself see to things at Haverleigh, the slovenly servants would lie about, letting everything go!

"Perhaps you can advise me." She directed her remark to Bainter. "When I settle in at Merryvale, I will need servants. Where did you get yours? Or were they already here when you took over?"

"No, no, the servants who used to be here had all found good positions elsewhere before Bainter came," Mistress Riddle spoke up irrepressibly. "Bainter himself employed this group."

"Really?" said Dorinda, still addressing Bainter. "Where did you get them?" *So I can avoid hiring them from the same place!* she was thinking as she struggled with a dull knife to sever a bite from her underdone chicken.

He shrugged. "I picked them up here and there, from local taverns mainly. 'Tis a skeleton staff, true, but then I run a bachelor establishment and am seldom here anyway." *And did not care what happened when he was away, his careless tone implied.*

"You should have a wife," said Mistress Riddle severely.

"So I have been thinking of late." Bainter's gaze rested softly on Dorinda. "A lady to share my—interests."

"And what interests are those?" wondered Dorinda, for indeed she had yet to find that Bainter had any real interests save an interest in gaming and wenching and drink. "I do not ride," she added hastily, remembering that he enjoyed racing.

"Oh, there are other ways to travel besides on horseback," he said easily. "By coach, for instance, or by ship. I have in mind to see the great capitals of the world, to drink their wine and dance their dances, and perchance when I find a spot that interests me, to lease a villa for a time—or even to buy one if I find the perfect place."

"How delightful!" cried Mistress Riddle, who thought travel quite marvelous. She had been born and bred in Williamsburg.

"You'd spend half your life retching over a ship's rail

in inclement weather and the other half being jolted black and blue over rutted roads, if you could, Gladys," declared her brother gloomily.

But Dorinda's gaze—just as Bainter had expected it would—had gone dreamy. *The great capitals of the world....* She saw herself elegantly gowned and in a gilded coach gliding over the cobblestoned streets of Paris, Rome, Brussels, or floating in a flower-decked boat down a canal in Amsterdam, or being rowed by gondola through the canals of Venice.

"Would you really do that?" she asked wistfully.

"Of course," said her genial host. "I've done a lot of traveling in my life. Indeed Williamsburg is the first place I've lingered since—" he hesitated.

"Since?" pursued Dorinda.

"Since a certain lady deserted me," he muttered and Dorinda thought, *Ah, that is why he drinks!*

"Your—wife?" she asked hesitantly.

"She was once." His voice roughened. "Now she's dead." Abruptly he changed the subject, and Isham Riddle gave his underdone chicken a last vicious jab and launched into a tirade against the high prices of imported goods.

Dorinda listened but she did not really hear. She was watching Bainter wistfully, seeing in him the things she had seen in him three years ago. There was something gypsylike and transient in his smile. Like a butterfly glistening in the light, it seemed to rest upon his lips and then depart, never quite reaching to his roving amber eyes. There was an instability in him, she supposed she had always sensed it. And now at last she had discovered its base: He had loved a woman once and he had lost her, and he was trapped in remembering.

Dorinda, toying with her undercooked capon and burnt bread and indifferently prepared and seasoned vegetables, felt her heart go out to Bainter in a melancholy way. *Both of them, unlucky in love....*

"I will promise you a treat for tomorrow night,

Dorinda," he said, his tawny head swinging toward her with sudden determination.

"What is it?" she asked.

"It's a surprise," he smiled. "One you will like."

And neither Mistress Riddle's eager questions nor Dorinda's smiling ones would cajole it out of him. "It is something both of you ladies will like," he said with an expansive wave of his hand.

"I do think we must be promised something exciting," whispered Mistress Riddle as they trundled off to bed that night. "What do you think it can be?"

"I have no idea," said Dorinda. *Make it some kind of magic,* her heart pleaded. *Make me love him once again as I did when I was young and foolish. Make me forget Tarn—with Bainter.*

The next day was spent pleasantly enough supervising the making of candles—at which Dorinda excelled. Bainter slept late, keeping to his rooms till afternoon, but when he did come out he was all smiles and teased them about his surprise which would be presented "after supper."

They found out after a meal of charred turkey and soggy bread and watery custard, followed by some very good wine.

"Now," said Bainter, impressively. "We will repair us to the rooftop promenade." He led the winding way through the large attics, sneezing once or twice, and Dorinda looked nervously about for Lady Soft Paws but did not see her—Jeddie must have her somewhere.

Tall ladderback chairs had been set up in one of the "summerhouselike" enclosures of the long promenade. Dorinda felt as if they were seated in an open square tower of sorts, looking out upon the Virginia countryside, mysterious by moonlight. The trees were awesome shapes in the darkness, the river glittered silver. Bats swooped through the night, dark shapes against the moon and somewhere a sleepy bird twittered to its mate. The air was soft and somnolent. Dorinda felt her senses lulled by it. Caught by the magic of the night, Dorinda felt she was drifting, far from shore upon some nameless sea. And in the distance across the wild waves she seemed to hear the mermaids singing, calling, telling her of another life somewhere that she might have, if only she would seize the moment.

Bainter seated them all and then clapped his hands once. Instantly the plaintive music of the *viola da gamba* filled the air and Dorinda was reminded of something Jeddie had said on her first day at Haverleigh: "Jake Finnegan does the cooking—he used to work at the White Hart before you came. He plays the viola." Here Jeddie had laughed. "Plays it better than he cooks," she had admitted ruefully.

But for now the magic of the moment had seized Dorinda. Bainter stood up and bowed formally before her. "May I have the honor?" He swept Dorinda into a dance, in the soft night air with the moonlight bathing their bright hair, their faces silvered in its radiance, the whole long length of the promenade from "square tower" to "square tower," from musician to guests.

Dorinda knew that she had fallen under the spell of Haverleigh, caught by an enchantment its builder had perhaps envisioned of summer nights here atop the building, lost in a world above and beyond everyday life.

Up and down, up and down the promenade they danced. Until finally Bainter, just now out of sight of the Riddles, buried his face in her thick upswept hair and whispered hoarsely, "I want you, Dorinda. Oh, God, I want you!"

Dorinda's senses, which had seemed to be drifting through all this unreality, sizzled to wakefulness. "I think you should dance with Mistress Riddle," she murmured warily. "She's been tapping her feet and looking wistful ever since we started dancing—Isham doesn't dance, you know."

"Your wish is my command!" Bainter led Dorinda

back to her chair and whisked a delighted Mistress Riddle into a skipping dance all the way down the promenade and back.

"I declare I'm quite winded," cried Mistress Riddle, when they came back. "But 'tis a wonderful place, is it not, to entertain one's guests?"

It was indeed. The spell of the night had an unreality about it, a feeling that anything could happen. Isham Riddle, who had eaten too much of the indifferent food, dozed in his chair and Mistress Riddle, winded, wafted her fan vigorously. Bainter watched Dorinda intently.

He knows the effect all this has on me, thought Dorinda in sudden misery. *He thinks me to be an adventuress—as indeed I am. He thinks to seduce me by magic, he who once thought to take me by force. The end result is the same—his way of going about it is just more subtle!*

"It was indeed a wonderful surprise, Bainter," she said, rising. For the beauty of the night was almost unbearable. Under its spell she might be led down paths she was not yet sure she cared to tread.

"Oh, you're not leaving?" cried Mistress Riddle.

"Yes, I find that I am very tired—I think it was all that candle-making." *That excuse would do as well as any other!* "I will say good night."

She was gone like a wraith. She fled down the winding way through the attics and when she had reached her room she latched the door and leant against it, feeling the smooth wooden panels cool her hot cheeks. *He is just one more who would take my virginity and laugh and fling me aside,* she told herself. *But she could not be sure. There was a single-mindedness about Bainter, a headlong concentration that made her feel like a quarry who would be pursued until caught.*

She started as the latch gave a faint rattle.

"Dorinda." Bainter's voice. And then more insistently, "Dorinda, let me in."

Dorinda drew away from the door. "No," she whispered. "I feel—confused. It was a lovely evening but—good night." She turned and fled across the room, stood looking out the big windows toward the moon-washed trees.

There were whispering sounds at the door. She thought they had a wheedling, pleading note. And then abruptly they were gone. The master of Haverleigh had taken himself elsewhere. To walk restlessly about? To drink? To fall asleep and forget her?

These thoughts tormented Dorinda. *And who was Tarn Jenner pursuing tonight?* she asked herself disconsolately.

Chapter 31

Dorinda awoke from a deeply satisfying dream. She came to lazily there in the big square bed of her big square bedchamber at Haverleigh. Sound asleep, Dorinda had conjured up a wedding held right here at Haverleigh. She had drifted into the paneled great hall on the arm of the governor himself, and it was the governor who gave the bride away. She was wearing a lovely gown of layered sheer white silk overlain with silver tissue. The bodice was tightly fitted and came dramatically to a tiny waist, then flared out into an enormous skirt held out by wide panniers. The bodice was embroidered with a rose leaf design in tiny seed pearls, a design that was repeated on the stiff white satin petticoat and all along the hem of the gown. Elbow-length sleeves exploded into a froth of sheer white lace at the elbows, while around her beautifully dressed hair she wore an intricate circlet of lace rosettes garnished with seed pearls and white roses.

In the long drawing room where the guests were assembled, her bridegroom waited. He was elegantly dressed in heavy dove-gray satin and although she could see perfectly well the lace ruffles that spilled from his wide cuffs, and the frostiness of his cravat, some floating mist that must have drifted in from the river seemed to obscure his face. In her dream that did not seem odd at all and she floated toward him with love shining from her blue-green eyes.

Abruptly her dream changed and flashed to her wedding night, spent (not too surprisingly, since many couples chose to spend at least their first night of wedded bliss at home after all the dancing and merriment) in this very room. She was pulling off her white bridal slippers and for some reason she began to feel very nervous.

"I want you to know—" she began, and before she could go further a pair of strong arms went round her and a pair of lips pressed softly down into her hair. His voice was muffled, it seemed to reach her on a whisper through the perfume of her hair.

"There'll be no need for explanations between us," he said. "I'll always understand."

And that dream Dorinda felt welling through her a tide of perfect happiness.

"Oh, my dearest—" She choked and squirmed around and flung herself against him, her wet cheek pressed against his as he bent tenderly over her. "I never thought I could be so happy."

His hands were warm as, still holding her against him, he swiftly undid the hooks that held her bodice. Dorinda would have helped him save that she was too occupied holding his face close to hers with both hands and kissing him.

"Oh, Tarn," she whispered. "Oh, Tarn...."

Dorinda came up from her dream to a thundering noise. She was still whispering rapturously, "Oh, Tarn...." as she realized that Mistress Riddle was knocking on the door and telling her that she'd be late for breakfast.

But that *"Oh, Tarn..."* echoed in her mind as she called, "I'll be there in a minute."

She sat up and stared about her. *She had been dreaming*

she was marrying Tarn Jenner—and in her dream she had been deliriously happy about the whole thing! She had quivered to his touch, felt his flesh tingle against her flesh, felt her body flaming with desire! She put her hands to her face and rocked with the humiliation of it.

She must forget Tarn Jenner! If she had a future with anyone here, it was with Bainter Ramsay!

Still under the influence of her disturbing dream, Dorinda leaped out of bed and began excitedly pacing up and down. Her fingers clenched and unclenched as, unbidden, she remembered what it had been like in her imagination to be caressed by Tarn, loved by him.

She would not, *she would not* spend any more time thinking about that worthless rake! she told herself, and pulled on her clothes so fast she almost ripped them. Attired in her light sprigged muslin, she ran down the hall and through the big front doors, down the wide outside stairway and stood on the front lawn, breathing hard.

It was there Bainter found her.

He had quite obviously not been drinking. He looked hard and fit and determined and he gave her a smile as bright as the sunlight glaring down upon the James which reflected it back with mirrored brightness.

"I thought about you all night," he said simply.

Dorinda gave him a hunted look. She had hoped she would not run across him quite so soon. She needed time alone to think. "Did you?" she asked inadequately.

"Yes." He caught her by the shoulders. "I want you to marry me, Dorinda," he said urgently. "Together we would be wonderful. We could travel wherever we like, do all the things you always wanted to do and—" he smiled—"don't tell me you haven't wanted to do practically everything because I'll know you for a liar!"

His lips were almost on hers when Mistress Riddle called out piercingly, "Oh, *there* you are!" and Dorinda flinched away from him. She turned to see the older woman waving from the doorway. "Breakfast is ready!" she caroled. "Hurry in, or your food will be cold!"

Bainter cursed under his breath, but Dorinda was glad of the respite.

"I'm coming," she called, and ran up the steps to go into breakfast with Mistress Riddle.

Bainter was right behind her. "If you're going to Merryvale today," he said, "I intend to go with you."

Dorinda was not so sure she wanted to tour Merryvale in Bainter's company. "Mistress Riddle plans to supervise the laundry today, and I—"

"Devil take the laundry!" said Bainter with a dismissive gesture.

"Very well," said Dorinda brightly. "Mistress Riddle, 'tis plain the master of Haverleigh does not wish to have the laundry done today."

"I care not a whit whether the laundry is done today or not," he exploded. "I would have you show me through Merryvale!"

Mistress Riddle, who had been looking puzzled, saw the light. "I think it may rain," she said. "And it would do the linens no good to get two soakings. I would be glad to accompany you to Merryvale, Dorinda, so that you may tell Bainter all the things you plan to do to the place." Bainter gave her a sulky look, but she ignored him. "So you shall have company on your way upriver, Isham."

Her brother nodded and addressed himself gloomily to his pancakes which were burnt on the edges but doughy in the middle. Dorinda gave him a sympathetic look. Poor Isham, would he ever get to live in his own house again?

On the way upriver while Bainter and Isham were in the prow of the barge talking, she asked about it. "Have you set a date yet for going back?"

Mistress Riddle shuddered. "I do not know if I can," she admitted. "I had another nightmare about it last night. I could see the fire ... and that figure in the red coat disappearing!" She shuddered again.

Dorinda thought about her own dream and her cheeks flamed. When Bainter came back to join the ladies, she made herself deliberately pleasant to him. That was the way to get her mind off Tarn—concentrate on somebody else.

Jeddie had been left behind, for Dorinda could not bear to look at her since coming to believe that the girl was having an affair with Tarn, but Mistress Riddle took her role as chaperon seriously. She left Dorinda's side only fleetingly all day.

Dorinda was rather relieved at that, for Bainter kept his hot gaze focused on her and it was not difficult to read his thoughts. He kept deriding Merryvale, and his objections confused Dorinda.

"It is too far from town," he said, the moment their chaperon left them alone for a moment. "Haverleigh is too far for that matter and this is farther yet. You would feel isolated, cut off."

"No, I wouldn't," protested Dorinda. "It's too beautiful here."

"Do you think you could live alone?" he demanded. "How would you supervise the plantation?"

"How do *you* do it?" countered Dorinda. "I would have an estate manager the same as you do."

He laughed and seized her hand. "Look about you. Would you live here if you could live at Haverleigh? Be honest now!"

"I would love either place," said Dorinda with perfect candor.

He laughed again. "At least you're honest. But suppose you could live in a chateau in France? A castle in Germany? A town house in London? What then would you choose?"

His suggestions took her breath away. "I had not considered those places," admitted Dorinda.

"Then *do* consider them," he urged. "For the world is wide for you and me."

Dorinda gave him a dazzled look. This was a new Bainter, the Bainter those other women had known.... She too found him fascinating.

"You drink too much," she said bluntly.

"For you I would change," he said on the instant.

"No, you wouldn't," she sighed. "People don't change. They just deepen in their ways."

"And what made you so wise?" he demanded, laughing.

His laughter was infectious and they were still laughing when Mistress Riddle joined them.

After that she felt easier in his company. Some ice had been broken between them. Half-drunk and irritable, he had suffered by comparison with the imperturbable Tarn Ramsay. Now, working at being charming, he was beginning to seem again the man she had fallen so desperately in love with three years ago.

Time seemed to fall away, and she could remember how she had felt whenever he crossed her field of vision, how she had suffered whenever he had even looked at another woman, how hurt she had been, when he had not noticed her, and then how shocked she had been when he had noticed her at last but in a cruelly contemptuous way.

And he was still Bainter Ramsay, the man who once had held her heart in keeping.

She was silent and melancholy as they drifted downriver to Haverleigh, the oars dipping almost silently into water the long rays of the evening sun had turned into molten gold. She had loved him once—and he had rejected her. And now that he wanted her, she wasn't sure....

Tarn Jenner's sardonic face floated up before her and she ran her fingers restlessly through her hair, wishing she could forget him. Completely. Forever.

"It's a warm evening, isn't it?" Bainter was lounging back in the barge, a handsome figure in lemon satin garnished with green rosettes. He looked lazy and bored.

"Yes," she agreed. "It's warm."

She wondered treacherously if Tarn Jenner was finding the afternoon warm in Williamsburg, and whether Jeddie had managed to send a message to him, luring him upriver while she was gone. The thought was gall to her. She turned to Bainter.

"Are we to have musicians on the rooftop promenade tonight?" she asked.

"I hadn't planned to," he said lazily. "Tonight I thought we'd walk in the garden and I could tell you how lovely you are."

She gave him a shadowed look. She would walk with him, talk with him, but if he kissed her it would be someone else she kissed. . . .

Bainter carried through his promise. After supper, when Mistress Riddle, who looked somewhat worn after her long day of chasing the young people about, declared herself for bed and her brother stalked off as well, Bainter caught at Dorinda's hand as she would have followed along.

"Stay a bit," he urged. "Stroll with me outside."

"It may rain," protested Dorinda weakly. "Mistress Riddle insists she can feel rain in her bones and she's been predicting it all day."

"It may indeed rain," he smiled. "But not before we've walked a while in the moonlight. Not before I've told you I love you."

Love . . . She looked at him uncertainly. It was the first time he had spoken of love. Was it possible he loved her?

They went outside. Clouds flitted from time to time across the moon but in between the gardens were a silvered miracle of flowers and box. The trees whispered softly as a light breeze blew them and the scent of roses was overpoweringly sweet. A night for lovers.

"It is at moments like these that I feel I would like to

stay at Haverleigh," he told her frankly and for a moment his hard face was young and torn. In that moment Dorinda felt she knew him very well.

"I know," she said softly. "When I first left England I thought I could never love any other place, but now. . . ."

"Now?"

"Now I do," she said. And suddenly she knew it was true. It was not money or the four thousand acres that made her want to inherit Merryvale. *It was because she loved the place, the river life, Virginia itself.* She wanted to belong to it, to know that she belonged.

"If I married you, would you stay here?" she asked suddenly.

"If you married me, I would do anything you asked!" he cried. "But oh, Dorinda, there is so much more in the world." His lips found her hair although she nervously turned her face away, for the night was tempting and she did not want to be beguiled by it. Undaunted he caught her by the shoulders and his tawny gaze held hers, raptly. "Marry me," he said intensely. "Marry me and let me show you all the great capitals of the world, Dorinda! Marry me and let me take you everywhere and then if you want to come back here, we can do that."

The pressure of his gaze held her riveted. She felt a dreaminess stealing over her. Yes, that was the thing to do. To go away. Now. With Bainter. To forget Tarn. To seek foreign diversions and when she had come back Tarn would probably be gone, he would be only a memory that she might take out from time to time and dust and put back in its place along with a box full of other memories.

But tonight his memory was very much with her and it must be exorcised if she was ever to be happy!

"Oh, Dorinda," Bainter said huskily. *"Marry me!"*

She nodded, as if hypnotized. "I will marry you, Bainter," she heard herself say.

For a moment he looked surprised. Then that tawny

gaze kindled and a note of triumph crept into his voice. "Then why need we wait?" he murmured. "I'll carry you over the threshold now!"

She caught her breath at what he was suggesting. It was too fast, too unplanned, too—no, it was not. It was exactly what she needed to banish forever Tarn Jenner's mocking sardonic face!

"I'll—I'll leave my door ajar," she said shakily.

At that moment came Clem's voice through the shrubbery from a few yards away. So concentrated had been their attention upon each other that they had not heard him approach.

"Mr. Ramsay, there's a man here to see you," he said. "Said he has to see you personal."

"I'll get rid of him," Bainter told Dorinda, letting his hands drop reluctantly from her shoulders. "Go on up. I'll join you presently."

What have I done? she thought as she fled from the garden and into the house. *I have promised to marry Bainter. I know what he is but I have promised to marry him anyway—no, maybe it is partly because of what he is that I have promised. Because I feel that I can mean something in his life—something I would never have meant to an arrogant fellow like Tarn Jenner.*

A sob escaped her lips. Tarn Jenner again! Would she never be free of him?

She hurried into her room, automatically reaching for the latch to latch it behind her.

And then her hand fell away from the latch. She had promised to marry Bainter and he had taken that promise as license, and she had not protested. She had said, "I will leave my door ajar"—with all that that entailed. She opened it a crack.

With shaky hands she lit a candle—and then she blew it out. This was something that must be met in the dark, where her faltering courage would not show upon her face. She heard a step in the hall and for a panicky moment she almost ran back to the door and latched it against him—as she had last night.

And then she turned again to the window and her back siffened. She would see it through! It was the only way to exorcise that devil Tarn Jenner from her heart and her mind. She would open her arms to Bainter, she would let him make love to her, she would marry him—her mind traveled no farther than that. Where they would live, where they would go, that was for tomorrow. Her mind whirled and seethed. Hers was a turbulent heart—and it had been hurt. All of her being wanted to strike back at Tarn and was this not the perfect way to do so? *Tomorrow,* she told herself staunchly, *she would have forgotten Tarn Jenner!*

A widening shaft of light from the candlelit hall told her that the door was being opened. The light narrowed, then disappeared, telling her that he was now in the room. There was a tiny sound as the latch fell into place. Dorinda kept her back turned, facing the window with her heart pounding. She was still fully dressed.

She looked very appealing there silhouetted in the moonlight in that dark bedchamber—and to the man who watched her intently, devastating. On silent feet he crossed the room toward her.

Dorinda felt his presence behind her and a tiny quiver passed through her delicate body. This was the moment!

Chapter 32

His arms went round her, and even as they did a random cloud hurried by, obscuring the moon. In sudden warm darkness she felt herself turned gently around and the big head that she could more sense than see in that dark bedchamber lowered toward her.

She might have drawn away at that moment, she might have drawn back from her promise so hastily given, from all that she was about to do. "Bainter—" she whispered—but she never finished her sentence for a warm pair of lips closed down over hers, a pair of lips expert in love that moved adroitly across her own, leaving a trail of stardust. And now as he settled her body more easily to fit his own, she felt with shock a warm tongue probing between her softly parted lips, exploring touching, ardently seeking.

Dizzily she realized that since she had been back in Williamsburg, Bainter had never kissed her, not even once—he had tried but always she had eluded him. This sweet assault was very different from the time when he had tried to overpower her at the inn. These tender loving lips were nothing at all like the hard almost contemptuous remembered pressure of his lips three years ago at the White Hart. He was entirely different tonight. *He did love her, he did—his lips were telling her so!*

Her arms went round him and her body responded eagerly to his as she stood on tiptoe and curved her slender form the better to fit herself to his. The searing ardor of his kisses, the very felt need of him, was making her gasp with delight. Oh, she had not thought it would be like this! It was Tarn Jenner's kiss all over again only better! Or was it only better because her emotions were so sharp-honed tonight, her every nerve end tingling?

Gently he was pulling her toward the big bed, only the faintest of shapes in the darkness. Now, if ever, was the time to break away. To tell him that she needed more time, to tell him he must wait until after the banns had been cried, the wedding bells rung.

But something wild and uncharted in Dorinda did not want to break away. Some earthbound madness born of the summer night had seized her. From the moment his warm lips had brushed her own, she had known, *she had known there would be no turning back.* The magic was here for them tonight—such magic as they might never know again.

He had pressed her legs against the side of the bed now, had eased her body up over it and she had sunk down, lost in its enveloping feather softness. His own tall body was between her and the window, an only slightly lighter rectangle against which his image blurred. Dorinda closed her eyes. She knew from the small sounds in the room that he was taking off his coat and probably his waistcoat. There was a slight clang of metal as the sword he always carried was laid down and two clunks as his boots hit the floor. If she was going to speak, to protest, she must do it now before . . . But she did not. She made no sound, but lay there waiting, entranced.

And then he had joined her in the bed. Her eyes

fluttered open but her lashes were pressed against his cheek. His breath smelled fresh—and she was grateful for that; he had not been drinking. There was a clean masculine scent to him, strength and vigor in the springy muscles of his arm that her fingers found so hesitantly.

The bodice of the light silk she had worn to supper opened down the front, and now his clever fingers were working the hooks—and still he had not spoken. She felt his fingers rove across her breasts as he pulled open her bodice, and her senses, already atingle, awakened even more fully to glorious life as those fingers cupped her breasts. She knew a gasping delight as his head was lowered to plant soft tongue-touching kisses on each tingling nipple. Overcome with desire, she moved restlessly in his arms and now she felt one of his hands reaching down and easing up her skirts.

Tension built up in her. She was a maiden standing on the brink of womanhood and for a swift shattering moment she was terrified of all that lay ahead. Her eyes, which had been closed in delight, snapped open, staring up at him. But his thick hair had fallen like a screen between her and the moonlight that had come back for a moment and all she could see was—she thought—an ear, that moved slightly to be replaced by a mouth that pressed a soothing kiss between her arching brows.

Quieted, reassured by that kiss, her lids fluttered shut again. He had not spoken, nor made her speak—and she was grateful for that. Her voice would have trembled and she, who had so much fierce pride, would have been ashamed of that.

Her skirts had ridden up now making her feel strangely bare and vulnerable, and now she could feel his strong muscular legs pressing against her thighs. Gently his hands eased down her chemise to her waist so that her breasts rode free and he rested his head for a moment upon them. Her pliant waist he gripped and lifted, and one long leg moved easily between her thighs that parted to receive him.

At the first pressure of his masculine hardness, she made a slight involuntary moan and she heard, low in his throat, an appreciative chuckle. There was a joy in him tonight that she had never imagined he possessed, an eagerness that seemed almost boyish, a tenderness that she had not dreamed he had.

And then with a quick thrust that sent a shock wave of pain reeling through her and made her momentarily weak, he took her from girlhood to womanhood. He paused then, as if to question, his lean body asking silently, *Have I hurt you too much? Do you want me to go on? Or shall we wait a bit?* But her proud nature would not admit the pain and besides her blood was singing in her ears. Strange yearnings filled her tonight and they cried out to be fulfilled.

In a silent answer to a silent question, she twined her arms about his neck and tenderly nuzzled his throat with her face. Those sinewy arms about her tightened and she found herself embarked upon an unfamiliar journey as—experienced lover that he was—he took her with him down new and breathless paths, paths with splendid twists and turnings that opened up new vistas, new delights. Sinuously, sensuously, he was exploring all her secret places and she melted against him, almost sobbing in her excitement, content that it should be so.

On, on he went and her soul soared with him. Every touch, every thrust seemed to lift her to the stars. This was madness, this was splendor—thunderous, devastating, intimate! She thrilled against him, responding with every fiber of her being to his lovemaking, feeling as if she would break apart from the very intensity of her ecstasy.

And then in a soft magical explosion they reached the brink—and plunged over into a world shatteringly sweet, a place of wondrous splendor that Dorinda, lost in enchantment, had never dreamed existed.

From that golden summit of crested passions, she felt herself floating magically down and down through endless starlit space until at last she lay spent and trembling, her body still glowing with remembered beauty. Her eyes were still closed. So soul shattering had been this experience that she hardly dared look at him.

I was right to do it, her heart sang. *Oh, I was so right!* And had not his masculine body, more clearly than any spoken words, told her that he loved her?

She lay beside him, every sense within her still shuddering gently with remembered thrills, and felt his lean bare hip against her own. Her arm had somehow come entirely out of the sleeve of her bodice and her chemise was somewhere down around her hips—she knew that by the cool breeze from the open window that played over her bare breasts and torso.

Lazily she reached out to him, meaning to pull him to her again, meaning to shower him with kisses, meaning to set the date for a wedding that could not be held too soon to please her, meaning to tell him breathlessly that wherever they lived, here or London or the moon, it was all right with her.

"Bainter . . ." she whispered.

"Dorinda," said a caressing voice. "Witch of my heart . . ." And that warm pair of lips that had so excited her pressed down upon one breeze-cooled nipple.

But that was the wrong voice speaking!

Dorinda's blue-green eyes snapped open. The moonlight was bright now, for the storm had gone round them and taken itself away to rumble out at sea. And in that white moonlight she saw a smiling face just lifting itself from her naked breast and a pair of too-well-remembered gray eyes beneath straight dark brows looking quizzically into hers. It was a dark head of hair and not a tawny one that was making gooseflesh of her torso as it drifted over her silky skin.

Not Bainter Ramsay—Tarn Jenner was smiling down on her!

"You!" she gasped and gave him a push away. Her senses reeled. Those lips, she should have remembered those lips—she *had* remembered those lips, but she had thought they were Bainter Ramsay's! She had been amazed at their likeness to Tarn's, but she had never thought, here in Bainter's house—oh, dear God, she had gone to bed with Tarn Ramsay! And where was Bainter?

All of this and more swirled through her confused head at that moment. And her lovely face, at first incredulous, turned scarlet as she realized what she had done.

"Oh!" she cried. "How could you?" And grasped at her chemise to cover her breasts from his view.

He quirked an eyebrow at her. "I will admit that I came upriver in part to assure myself of your safety, but when you fell upon me as you did—"

"*Fell* upon you?" she gasped. "Oh, you seducer! You fraud!"

"As I say," he continued with a shrug, "when you fell upon me with such heat, I felt no real compunction to defend my honor. I let you have your way with me."

Dorinda glared at him, speechless. His strong muscular chest was bare to her gaze, his rippling shoulder muscles. He was, she thought bitterly, a magnificent animal—hateful as he was. Finally she found her voice and the breath to speak. "Since you have—" she emphasized the word solemnly—"*stolen* my virginity—"

"Stolen?" interjected the reprehensible gentleman who was leaning on one naked arm and looking at her lazily with such a twinkle in his gray eyes. "Say rather that I accepted what was freely thrust upon me! Come now, aren't you glad you've lost it? The whole world opens up for you!"

Dorinda, who had snatched up the light covering of her chemise to shield her naked form from his view, let it drop as she struck out at him. He ducked easily and his bright gaze rested in appreciation on the sight of her round pink-tipped breasts thus enchantingly revealed. She snatched back the chemise. "You had best leave!" she said stiffly.

He made no move to go. "No, I think we had best talk first, don't you? Ramsay won't be back until at least morning."

"How would you know?" she cried.

"Why, I had slipped through the shrubbery intending to see if I could find your room and perhaps speak with you—and lo and behold! There you were in the garden together, concentrating so fiercely on each other that you did not hear me come up. I was close enough to hear what you were saying. Then his butler interrupted and you rushed inside, obviously to jump into bed. Ramsay stalked off and I saw him handed a note. He read it, crumpled it, and took off downriver. It seemed a shame to let you wait for him, wondering why he did not come to you as he had promised. I decided it would be only fair to offer myself as a substitute—and I must say I found you delightfully eager." He grinned, and before Dorinda could form a suitably crushing reply, he leant forward. "Since Ramsay has gone off on some errand or other, why don't we simply nap here? We could greet him together on his return, tell him how we have formed this consuming passion for one another, and perhaps share his breakfast?"

Dorinda choked.

"Why did you really come here?" she demanded in a waspish voice. "Surely you did not come all the way upriver just to slip into my bedroom and—and—"

"What does it matter?" he asked crisply. "It seems you have become very thick with Ramsay—"

He was implying she was a loose woman! "Mistress Riddle is a perfect chaperon!" she cried, maddened.

"But not tonight," he murmured ironically.

Dorinda's teeth ground. "She is with me almost every waking minute!"

"How very annoying that must be," he jibed and for a moment he thought she would hurl herself at him in a passion and beat on him with her fists. But she did not.

"You are despicable!" she cried, trembling. "No gentleman would have—"

"Now whoever told you I was a gentleman?" he wondered silkily.

"Why," she gasped, "I assumed it from what people said of you, from your clothes, your bearing, your—your room at the inn!"

"Such trappings are deceiving," he agreed. "They bespeak money, however, not gentle birth. It may surprise you, Dorinda, but money is come by in other ways than through inheritance."

There was a sinister note in his voice as he said that but Dorinda was too angry to notice.

"You slip into Bainter's home like a thief, you steal into his betrothed's bedchamber—"

"And into her bed, don't forget that!"

"I could hardly forget it!" she stormed at him.

"No, I had hoped you would not." He nodded as if pleased. "I would like to feel I had made at least some impression on you. Since such impression as I made on you at Merryvale was far from lasting it would seem...."

How dare he throw that at her, when all the time he and Jeddie—! His cool look infuriated Dorinda. "If you do not go at once—" She was raising her voice with each word.

"Hush," he said, and would have raised a finger to her lips. Dorinda, remembering how the chemise had dropped when she struck at him and how that had pleased him, promptly bit at that admonishing finger. He grinned as his hand dodged her swift white teeth.

"Remember your reputation," he told her tranquilly. "None but the two of us know what transpired here tonight. But Mistress Riddle would be so dumbfounded if she were to arrive as the result of a commotion that I doubt me she would ever stop talking about it."

Prudently Dorinda lowered her voice. "You are a blackguard," she hissed at him. "Get out!"

"Oh, not just yet." He lounged back upon the bed despite her blushes as his masculinity came into view, and she considered striking him full in the face with her fist. She doubted it would do much good—even if the blow landed, which was unlikely. Worse, it might end up in another wild sweet assault upon her senses, another tussle among the bedcovers, with his warm mouth blocking her screams and his elegant masculine body proving once again to them both the sheer physical power he exercised over her quivering femininity. There was a terrible danger that even angry as she was, she would respond to him. Wildly. No, she must not risk that. She was shamed enough as it was. Best not to arouse him to fever heat again. She sat stiffly with the chemise held to her breast and looked daggers at him.

"Why? Haven't you had what you came for?" she asked sarcastically.

"Oh, not quite," he said in that tranquil voice, reaching out to caress her knee. Dorinda kicked at him half-heartedly and he subsided. "Although I must say it has been a most enjoyable evening—most unexpectedly so. But having learned so many intimate details about you, I am eager to learn more."

She gave him a bitter look from her blue-green eyes.

His smile was genial, his manner expansive. "Tell me about yourself, Dorinda," he sighed.

"You need know no more than that I am a woman about to do murder!" she told him in a shaking voice. "Get you gone!"

"Not yet," he said as if rebuking a schoolgirl. "I am positive I have seen you somewhere before. Could it be that you have seen me as well?"

"Certainly not!" cried Dorinda, but her heart was

beating violently. "I never saw you before that day at the White Hart!"

Suddenly it was a different face she looked into, a dangerous face.

"Tell me no more lies," he said angrily, seizing her by her white shoulders. "You worked in a chandler's shop in Philadelphia. Don't try to deny it, you had wax all over your smock when I ran into you at Blore's house. You arrived here not on the *London Queen* but on the same ship I did—the *Roving Gull* where I glimpsed you myself as you stood by the rail, though you were so wrapped up in your own affairs you looked neither to right nor left, but walked about head down, lost in thought. Word had it," he added whimsically, "that you were the captain's doxy."

"I was not!" she cried wrenching free. "How dare you suggest it?"

"Oh, *I* did not suggest it," he drawled. "Others did. It was rumored among the crew that the captain would keelhaul anyone who so much as spoke to you."

"I am surprised you let that deter you." Bitterly.

"Under other circumstances it would not have," was his cool rejoinder. "But it hardly seemed fair. An old man, who—"

"He was a kindly old man who helped me when I stowed away aboard his vessel. He saved me from being carried away to Jamaica and forced into bondage and worse!"

His gray eyes narrowed at this revelation. She could see he did not believe her. "A kindly old man you hoodwinked," he corrected her. "A man who called you 'Countess' as you left the ship. Come now, do you deny you passed yourself off to him as a countess?"

"I *am* a countess," she flashed. "By blood, not law!"

"Tell me about that," he said, fascinated.

"I won't! But I am a countess's granddaughter none the less!"

"I went to bed with an adventuress," he murmured.

"And now I find that I have seduced a virgin! And a countess to boot!" His gaze lowered at her.

"Seduced?" she cried wildly. "You took me by force!"

He gave a short laugh. "We both know the truth of that! You made an appointment with Ramsay. I was concealed in the shrubbery nearby and I heard you. He was called away and I kept that appointment. Do not pretend now to be shocked—I but seized the opportunity that presented itself."

"Do you always seize such opportunities?" she demanded with a resentful look.

"Always," he said sardonically, and there was something hot and wild in his gray gaze that told her this at least was so.

"You should be ashamed of yourself!" Indignation stained her cheeks.

"I am less ashamed than puzzled," he admitted, rising and pulling on his trousers. He had the grace to turn his back and Dorinda averted her gaze from the sight of his lean naked buttocks. Straightening up, he turned about and finished adjusting his trousers as he spoke. "Countess or not, you are plainly no niece of old Merryvale, who was as Puritanical an old codger as ever I've met. Just the wild look in your eyes would have sent him to his knees praying for his immortal soul!"

"Whose niece I am is no business of yours," she said fiercely. "The man has died leaving neither kith nor kin!"

"But you," he said meditatively, struggling into his boots, "intend to fill that gap."

"Who are you to meddle?" she cried. "Have you not harmed me enough?"

She looked so flushed and lovely sitting there in the middle of the big bed with her chemise off one bare shoulder and the pearly tops of her breasts staring at him that his hard face softened.

"I am sorry that you should feel that I have harmed you," he said reflectively, pulling on his white cambric shirt. "But look at it my way." He paused in the act of fastening his cuffs. "I take it that you sought to reach Ramsay's bed, a virgin bride?"

Her flush deepened. "Of course!"

"And yet," he said bitterly, standing hands on hips to look at her. "I seem to recall your saying to me at Merryvale, *I want you with me!* You were very definite about it. What of that, Dorinda?"

"That was before—" She stopped. She would not tell him she knew about Jeddie. Let him guess!

"Before what?" he demanded.

She tossed her head and her golden hair rippled, but her lips remained stubbornly closed.

"Tell me," he said slowly. "How did you come by this passion for Ramsay? Was it conceived suddenly at the inn or did you know him in his native Yorkshire?"

"I have never been to Yorkshire," she snapped.

"No, I thought not. Still, perhaps you will be good enough to enlighten me." He was shrugging into his coat, that same maroon coat she knew so well—and with the button still missing! That button that was even now in Jeddie's possession! It was a further insult!

"I should scream for the servants," she choked, "and tell them there is a man in my room trying to rape me!"

"A bit late for that, isn't it?" he inquired coolly. "Whether seduction or rape, the deed is done, and I'll wager you wouldn't care for the servants to hear about your recent past either, whether Ramsay knows of it or not!"

Dorinda gasped at such cool effrontery. "Bainter would run you through if he heard what you have done to me!"

A steely light glimmered in the gray eyes that were studying her so intently. "I would like to see him try it," Tarn murmured and she was suddenly aware of the extremely serviceable look of the sword he was even now buckling on. "Then you are trying to tell me that

Ramsay does *not* know of your deception? That you have fooled him too?"

"He believes me to be a—a left-handed sort of heir," she said indignantly, fury with him making her want to show Bainter as better than he was. "Bainter Ramsay would not have asked me to marry him if he thought I were a cheat!"

For a long moment the tall man before her studied her in astonishment. Then he threw back his dark head and his laughter pealed. She watched him uneasily, wondering if he had gone mad, and pulled her chemise up still higher as if to protect her quivering body.

She was glaring at him when at last he stopped laughing and seated himself upon the bed again, this time studying her with real amusement in his eyes. "Come," he said in a wheedling voice. "Tell me all about it. You might as well, you know. Anyone finding us together like this will believe the worst—and who knows, I might even help you!"

She gazed back at him in astonishment, amazed at this sudden about-face. *And why not?* she asked herself suddenly. *What did she have to lose?*

"My name is Dorinda Meredith," she said sulkily. And to give herself stature before that penetrating gaze that seemed to see into the heart of her, "I am grand-daughter to the Countess of Ravensay—of Grantland Manor, Dorset."

"Ah," he said politely. "A real countess, no less."

"Not quite," said Dorinda. "If life were fair—"

"It never is."

"No," she sighed.

"And what," he asked, "were you doing in Philadelphia attired in a wax-smeared smock?"

Dorinda gave him an angry look. "My mother died in childbirth—"

"And your father?" he interrupted.

"He was hanged," she flashed. "For killing a man who deserved killing! I was born in Newgate Prison."

"Ah," he breathed. "The truth at last. And how did you get mixed up with Ramsay?"

"A woman named Maud Whatton brought me up. She was a laundress when she wasn't drinking too much to work. She got into trouble with the law in London and bound herself for three years to pay for our passage to America. She died of a fever on the way over and on arrival in Williamsburg I was bound to Innkeeper Buxton for four years to pay for our passage. It was Buxton who sold my articles to those people in Philadelphia. My indenture was over, they were holding me there against my will and—I escaped by stowing away aboard the *Running Gull*."

He had been listening intently. "And are you saying that it was at the White Hart that you met Ramsay?"

"Yes," she said. "Although he does not remember— and I have never told him." Something sympathetic in the gray eyes that studied her made her continue. "I was very thin then and my clothes were awful and did not fit me. Well, actually he *did* notice me once but that was a great disaster." She stopped, unwilling to talk about that hurtful incident. "I—I had fallen in love with him and I—" her voice shook a little—"I had decided that if ever he crossed my path again *I would straighten him out!*"

The jaw of the man before her dropped in amazement. "*You would straighten him out?*" he repeated in amazement. "And just how did you propose to do that?"

She squared her dainty shoulders. "I intended to cross his path dressed as handsomely as a princess, proclaim myself a countess, and make him grovel at my feet!" she said tartly.

His gaze inclined suddenly upward and his lips twitched.

"Don't you dare laugh!" she cried. "You knew all the time who I was and you have taken shameful advantage of it!"

"I believe we have more in common than you know, Dorinda," he said genially. "Or should I call you 'Countess?'"

"Don't mock me!"

"Oh, I would never mock you," he said, and his fingers, reaching out, trailed gently along her bare shoulder, would have wandered down the smooth surface of her bosom to her white breasts, save that she struck his hand away. "Pray to remember that I let you make love to me thinking you were somebody else!" she said crushingly.

"Ah, so we now admit it wasn't rape but merely mistaken identity," he said politely, but he withdrew his hand.

Her blue-green eyes sent off sparks.

"I'll thank you to get out of here!" she said.

"Before I go," he said, making no move to leave, "there are one or two more things I yearn to have answers to. Whatever set you on this course to proclaim yourself old Merryvale's niece?"

"I was at my wit's end when I saw you and Bainter coming out of the inn," she admitted. "I was sure you would both recognize me! And when it seemed you did not, and began asking me questions, I but resorted to babbling about things I had heard a short time before when I stopped at a coffeehouse and heard various discussions going. One group spoke of a highwayman, The Blade. And another group was going on and on about a planter named Merryvale who had died leaving no heirs. Someone else came in and was welcomed by a friend who had arrived yesterday from England on the *London Queen*. I jumbled them all together and answered your questions with all the new things I had learned."

"Jumbled them quite handily, I'll admit," he told her with a sunny smile.

"I don't know what else I can tell you," she said

sulkily. "You surely must know more about me now than you care to!"

"Oh, I wouldn't say that," he murmured. "In fact the way your mind works still fascinates me."

She gave him a frowning look. "Then you will forget tonight ever happened?" And when he did not respond, "For I have been frank with you—I have told you all you asked."

His restless gaze passed over her. She would have given a deal to know what he was thinking.

"Ah, then I am not to be run through by a vengeful suitor?" he asked softly.

"Of course not!" she cried in exasperation. "If Bainter were to find out about this, he would probably not care to marry me!"

In silence he digested that. "I think you underrate yourself," he said at last. "He would find you a delectable morsel—as I did."

"And how am I to explain that I am no longer a virgin?" she flung at him.

"You'll think of something," he assured her. "With an imagination as vivid as yours, you're bound to! Anyway, we can discuss it further when you come down to Williamsburg tomorrow and visit me at the White Hart."

She gasped. "I'll do such thing! Indeed I have no call to go to Williamsburg at all, much less visit *you*!"

"Ah, but you do, Dorinda," he said, and for a moment his steely gaze upon her was wistful. "For 'tis really *I* who must give your hand in marriage, isn't it? I mean, suppose I decide not to let you marry Bainter? Do you think your recent betrothal would survive the knowledge that you were a penniless bound girl born in Newgate? Indeed, I think that news might strike him deeper than learning you'd been deflowered!"

"Oh, you wouldn't!" she gasped, her eyes widening in horror.

"Would I not?" His mocking smile flashed.

Dorinda's hands were tightly clenched in the chemise

she was holding up to hide her nakedness. Suddenly the delicate fabric seemed no protection at all from his bold gaze. "You are a blackmailer, sir!" she whispered.

"Call it what you will," he shrugged. "Tomorrow then at the White Hart?" He was opening the door or she might have thrown caution to the winds and screamed at him. As it was she struck her fist into the bedcovers so hard that the soft feather mattress enclosed her whole arm.

She would keep her appointment at the White Hart tomorrow, they both knew. For her, there was no way out....

Chapter 33

Bainter was still not back when Dorinda woke. She dressed and went down to breakfast toying with the notion of asking Isham Riddle to take her into Williamsburg in his barge. But she felt it was unfair to ask him when his own plantation needed him, and anyway under the circumstances Mistress Riddle's chattering company would have driven her mad.

Bainter's own barge, she saw, was still tied up to the pier—he must have gone downriver on horseback or in whatever conveyance the man who had arrived last night with a message had brought. Dorinda thought about that.

After breakfast, while Mistress Riddle energetically began her supervision of the laundry, Dorinda sought out Clem.

"I would have the barge take me downriver to Williamsburg," she told him.

Clem's swarthy face was surprised and uneasy. "I've got no authority to order out the barge in the master's absence," he protested.

"Nonsense!" snapped Dorinda. "I'll soon be married to the master! And I've shopping to do in Williamsburg!"

Clem frowned. It annoyed him not to know why Bainter had departed the plantation so suddenly. Made him feel he was standing on shaky ground. And now this gorgeous piece that Bainter was pursuing wanted the barge to take her to Williamsburg. Clem sighed. It went against his better judgment but he supposed he'd best do it.

And so it was that Dorinda, leaving behind both Mistress Riddle who was supervising the filling of the laundry tubs out back, and Jeddie, who waved at her wildly and ran along the bank entreating to be taken along, embarked in the Haverleigh barge for the trip downriver to Williamsburg.

She had dressed carefully for this new encounter with the unpredictable Tarn Jenner. She had considered wearing her sprigged muslin and trying to look demure and dewy-eyed and innocent—but he already knew her for a hot wench. Her face flamed as she remembered in vivid detail how she had responded to him last night! No, she must needs be a woman of authority if she were to best the blackmailing Mr. Jenner. She must wear a gown in which she looked not a girl but a woman to reckon with!

Accordingly she put on a dress she had purchased when last she was in Williamsburg, a vivid tangerine silk trimmed in rows and rows of black braid. The dress was very tailored and fit her figure as sleekly as the new riding habits which were all the rage. A splash of white lace cascaded at the neck and cuffs. The gold locket was conspicuously absent. She had considered bringing it along to throw in Tarn's saturnine face but decided the gesture would be lost on him.

She had plenty of time to think about what she would say to him as she was rowed downriver. Her fingers drummed on her tangerine silk lap as a number of suitably uncomplimentary remarks flitted through her mind. She discarded them all, however, divining that invective was unlikely to work with the imperturbable gentleman who held her future in the palm of his hand. Pleading might, but she had no intention of pleading with him.

She would bargain with him! But what did she have to bargain with? Another barge went by containing a planter's family she had met at Lucy Claridge's ball. They bowed politely but looked curious at seeing her gliding downriver unchaperoned. *Let them think what they liked!* thought Dorinda as she graciously returned their bows. *They* did not have to deal with the irritating Mr. Jenner!

The sun was beating down. She was glad of the awning overhead and wished she had brought her parasol, but the orange-plumed hat that sat so pertly on her golden head would have to do to keep the sun off! She told the oarsmen to wait for her in the Red Fox Tavern and soon she was making her way down Duke of Gloucester Street to the White Hart.

The common room had its usual complement of people, she saw, talking, eating, drinking, amusing themselves with cards or dice. Realizing that she had forgotten her mask did not improve Dorinda's temper and she nodded briskly to those she knew, glad to see that Bainter was not of their number, and ascended once again those familiar wooden stairs.

She had still not decided exactly what to say to Tarn and her heart was thumping as she knocked at his door, heard his deep voice call, "Come in," and entered.

He had been sitting at a wooden table by the window, writing on a little slant-topped writing desk that sat upon the table top, and he laid down his quill pen and rose as she entered.

"You are early," he murmured.

"Yes, I saw no reason to delay our conversation," she told him coldly, and shook her head as he offered her a chair. "I prefer to remain standing."

"Well, at least take off your gloves and hat," he said. "'Tis warm in here."

"I won't be staying that long."

"Oh, but I think you will." He gray gaze had gone steely again. He looked very handsome clad in the maroon broadcloth coat with its button still missing—that button Jeddie had in her possession! A pang went through Dorinda at sight of it. "You look very dashing," he added. "I like that dress."

"I did not wear it to please you."

"No?" He sighed. "Disillusionment is everywhere. I had hoped you had."

"What is it you want from me?" she cried. "That you would demand I come all the way to Williamsburg to seek you out?"

Amusement colored his tone. "Can't you guess?"

She gave him an affronted look and the plumes on her hat danced as she stiffened. "Even someone so reprehensible as you—" she began when he stopped her with a lifted hand.

"Let us not argue over who is the most reprehensible—you or Ramsay or me. The point is I want you to stay here. Overnight."

For a moment she was speechless, staring at him with incredulous blue-green eyes. Then indignation flared in what she said next. "You should be ashamed," she told him flatly.

He was looking at her wistfully. "Perhaps I am," he admitted.

She rushed on, her tangerine bodice heaving. "First to steal my virginity under false pretenses and now to demand—this! When all the world saw me walk through the common room just now! You would make it clear to all that I am your doxy, is that it?"

He winced. "I would take a room for you, of course."

"*And* expect to occupy it with me, I don't doubt!"

"I suppose I deserved that too...."

"Why did you not send upriver for your other doxy?" she cried in a passion. And when he looked puzzled, "Jeddie!" she flung at him. "Oh, do not think I do not know about you and Jeddie! She has told me about her fine 'gentleman friend' in Williamsburg who will marry her when he can! You should be ashamed of that too!"

"I take no shame for that," he murmured, but he was looking at her keenly now. "So this is the reason for your sudden change of heart toward me? Jeddie?"

She tossed her head and both her orange plumes and her bright curls danced delightfully. "I could not love a man who is so false!"

"And if I told you—" He stopped suddenly, frowning. "Ramsay, of course, is true, I suppose?"

Dorinda flushed. "If you are speaking about Lucy Claridge—!" she snapped.

"Lucy is only amusing herself," he cut in. "Her husband is occupied with other matters and has no time for her. No, I merely wondered if you are not jealous—of the others?"

Of the others! She had not known about the others. She had suspected, of course, but Tarn was stating it as a fact. Well, she would not accept it! "There are no others," she cried angrily.

He gave her a quizzical look. "And what makes you so certain?" he demanded bluntly. "Do you love Ramsay?"

"I—" Her head whirled at the impudence of his question. "Who I love is not your affair!" she cried. "You have forfeited the right to ask!"

He was still studying her, his gaze very intent. "Tell me, Dorinda, did you learn about Jeddie and me after or before the day we spent at Merryvale?"

"After!" she almost spat at him. "Do you think I would have allowed you to meet me there had I known?"

He seemed quite satisfied and while this bewildered her, it angered her the more. He gave her a crooked smile. "And how did you find out? Did Jeddie tell you?"

"I found the gold button!" sputtered Dorinda. "The trinket you gave your paramour! Oh, do not deny it, it is very distinctive and I can see it is missing—right there!" She stabbed a finger in the direction of the missing button on his maroon coat.

"A gold button..." he murmured, and sighed. "On such small rocks do the stoutest ships founder....."

Dorinda thrust her beautiful flushed face toward him. "Don't talk in riddles. I will *not* stay here and be your plaything! Send for Jeddie. *She* seems willing to share you—*I* am not!"

Her hot words seemed not to affect him. He was as debonair as ever. "At least have a drink with me before you go," he suggested. "A glass of wine to cool your hot head?"

She watched him warily. "I will have no drugged wine!"

"Ah, then you may pour it yourself. There are glasses over here by the writing desk and a bottle beside them. And if you like, I will drink first—a toast to your eyelashes!"

She supposed it could do no harm to share a glass with him. It was important to mollify this man because he could speak out against her and she would have no defense. She would lose Bainter, her chance at Merryvale, everything. Watching him out of the corner of her eye, she moved toward the table that held the bottle and glasses and several articles, the small slant-topped box-like writing desk on which he had been writing as she entered, some loose change, a silver porringer, and a spoon.

He moved aside and she poured the wine, trying to think what to do if he refused to let her go. Her frowning gaze passed over the parchment, reading what was on it.

"*Dear Elsinore,*" the letter began. "*I have found the perfect place for you. It is named Merryvale Manor, it comprises four thousand acres and it is handsomely situated upon the James.*"

Dorinda stared down at the letter indignantly. More treachery! Now he was trying to wrest Merryvale Manor away from her! That it was hardly hers to hold did not at the moment occur to her. She was trying to frame something suitably crushing to say to him when her meditative gaze passed to the silver spoon.

"The letter," he told her conversationally (for he guessed that she was reading it), "is to my stepgrandmother, she of the remarkable life." He went on, mentioning again Elsinore's beauty and poise, the many wild things she had done, but Dorinda was not listening. Her attention was focused on the spoon.

In mounting horror she realized that the spoon she was looking at was very long and rather pointy with a large "R" engraved on the handle—exactly such a spoon as Mistress Riddle had described as having been lost in the fire at Riddlewood along with the rest of the plate. Her hand holding the wine bottle seemed frozen in air.

"Where did you get this spoon?" she demanded.

"I found it."

She turned slowly to face him. "Found it where?"

"Lost somewhere in the grass," he shrugged.

Lost somewhere in the grass . . . at Riddlewood no doubt! Mistress Riddle had seen through the window a man in a red coat holding something that glittered—*this spoon!*

"The red coat!" she cried. "You own two red coats! Do not deny it, I have seen them."

He was looking at her steadily.

"I do not deny it."

"And this—this spoon! Something silver that glittered! *You* were standing at the edge of the trees at Riddlewood on the night of the fire!"

"I was." He gave the slightest bow of acknowledgment. "Your hands are shaking," he added. "You are going to spill the wine."

Oh, the cool rogue! Dorinda was so astonished that her legs nearly gave way beneath her. *"You admit it?"* she demanded incredulously.

"Of course." He was imperturbable. She believed he would not change a hair if she told him a Dutch fleet had just taken the town or that there was a warrant out for his arrest.

"You were there but you did not make yourself known," she accused. "You did not even offer to help when you saw the house was burning down!"

"I was about to when the heavens opened up and such a cascade of water poured down from the sky as almost to beat me to my knees. It was readily apparent that no blaze could exist in the face of such a cloudburst and besides the place was suddenly alive with servants with buckets, all of them running about in the downpour throwing water in all directions. I thought it best to make myself scarce."

"And why was that?" she challenged.

"Can't you guess?" he asked softly.

"Of course I cannot guess!" she said haughtily.

"Indeed? I think you have already guessed," he said, amused. "I was on my way to rob the governor. I was attracted when, riding by, I saw the blaze, but I felt compelled to get on. A wet purse of gold is better than no purse at all. The spoon was lying on the grass alone and unchaperoned. Naturally I picked it up and took it along."

The spoon suddenly dimmed into insignificance.

"*You* are the highwayman everyone is talking about?" she demanded incredulously. "*You* are the one they call The Blade?"

He bowed sardonically. "The very same."

So lightning had struck the Riddles' house after all. For it did not make sense that a highwayman out after a big haul would stop by and set a house alight! And Mistress Riddle had seen him from the window and naturally thought, when no man in a red coat turned up, that he was the arsonist! Oh, how simple the explanation was—and how dreadful! She had been consorting with a highwayman! She had even—dear heaven!—let him make love to her!

He cocked an eye at her. "I was understandably upset when you spread the story to the world that I had stolen your petticoats. I've never taken anything from a woman in my life except—" he grinned—"her virtue, freely given. Like yours."

Dorinda drew herself up. "You took me by false pretenses. I thought you were Bainter."

"So you gave me to understand," he said coolly. His narrow smile played over her. "Did anyone ever tell you that you had disastrous taste in men?"

"*You* do not represent my taste!" she flung at him.

"Just so," he said meditatively, glancing down at his boots. He looked up. "Surely the fact that I'm a highwayman will not come between us?" His face was bland. "I'd not have told you had I thought it would."

He was the most infuriating man she'd ever met! She felt dizzy with relief that he hadn't tried to burn the Riddles in their beds, horror that he should turn out to be a famous highwayman, and mingled with all that something else that could just possibly be fear for him, fear of what they'd do to him if he were caught. She put the thought directly from her mind.

"I see you do not wear a pistol." She glanced at his serviceable basket-hilted sword.

"No."

"Why not? I would think it would be standard fare for a highwayman!"

"I do not favor them." He shrugged. "Pistols make a blasted lot of noise. Blades are remarkably silent."

She shivered. "And to think," she said bitterly, "that I took you for a gentleman! A man of wealth and breeding!" Her tone was cutting.

"Well," he said reasonably. "A highwayman can be a man of wealth if he's lucky. I enjoy an excellent income. And by living well at fashionable inns I have a chance to overhear talk, to learn where people are going and sometimes where they will be next week, to find out who is rich and who is poor and who has something worth stealing. Of course," he admitted, "it's a bit chancy and I do have to move on from time to time."

She snatched at that. "Then you'll be leaving here soon?"

He shrugged. "Who knows? Perhaps tomorrow."

Now why should that upset her? "It cannot be too soon," she told him. "You have already overstayed your welcome here. The town talks unceasingly about The Blade, as you are called!"

"I am happy to have achieved such notoriety," he told her in an ironic tone. And then, more roguishly, "Tell me, Dorinda, where would you recommend I go next? And if I let you choose the spot, will you go with me?"

It had been on the tip of Dorinda's tongue to tell him he might go to the devil but at that latter comment two bright spots of color appeared in her cheeks. Her blue-green eyes snapped. He was the most insufferable—!

"How dare you suggest it?" she said between her teeth. "How can you believe I would do anything so disreputable?"

He gave her a look of mild amazement. "Well, you are sailing under colors as false as mine," he remarked gently.

"*I* was desperate!" she cried. "I had no clothes save those on my back, no money, no place to go—there was an excuse for me to do what I did!"

"Oh, I've made lots of excuses for myself too," he assured her genially. "None that would stand up in court, you understand, but I've frequently been desperate."

He was mocking her! Of a sudden a new thought occurred to Dorinda. It stood before her with crystal clarity. This new knowledge she had of him had changed everything. Now that she knew his true calling, Tarn Jenner no longer had any power over her! He would not dare to tell the authorities of her deception lest she inform them of his nocturnal activities! A highwayman pretending to be a gentleman and a former bound girl pretending to be an heiress—it was a standoff! She was free of him!

She lifted her chin with more assurance. "I will be leaving now, Mr. Jenner," she said regally.

"Oh, I think that after last night you might presume to call me by my first name," he said, amused. "After all, I shall continue to call you 'Dorinda.'"

"You will be calling 'Dorinda' to the empty air. For I will not be here." She made a lofty gesture, seeing that he now stood between her and the door. "Be good enough to let me pass."

He made no move to step aside. "You would let this Blade business come between us?" Mockingly.

She gave him an affronted look and would have brushed past him but that he swept her suddenly into his arms.

"Dorinda," he said. "Do you think I would have told you what I am had I not known that you cannot afford to denounce me? Your own ground is too shaky for that!"

"Let me go or I'll scream," she warned, wishing desperately that the very nearness of him did not so assault her senses.

"Scream away," he laughed. "And you'll rouse the inn and I'll suddenly remember where I met you—and what you were doing there. Poor George Peabody, who trustingly advanced you the money to buy your friend Jeddie's articles, will turn pale—but he will investigate. And he will find that you arrived on the wrong ship—"

"He won't!" She was struggling. "There is no record of me on board the *Running Gull* and Bainter is having the *London Queen*'s passenger list destroyed!"

"He is, is he?" Tarn looked grim. "Well, he can destroy the passenger list but not the captain's memory. Do you think a woman like you could be overlooked?"

She became still and stared at him.

"And thorough George will also discover that you arrived in Williamsburg in fine clothes—by the way, where did you get them?"

Dorinda caught her breath. Those clothes Ada would no doubt advertise she'd been wearing when she fled!

"Stolen?" he guessed.

"Not *stolen*," she choked.

"Unauthorized taking?" he amended politely.

She gave him an unhappy look. "They refused to pay me what was due at the end of my indenture, so I—"

"Oh, you needn't elaborate," he said, bending closer. "I'm on your side of the matter." He nuzzled her ear. "The trouble is, the law won't be. Could be we'd hang side by side."

She blanched and tried to wriggle away from him. "You wouldn't—tell them?" she said hesitantly.

"Of course not—any more than you'd whisper to Ramsay that The Blade is occupying the White Hart's best room! We have secrets, you and I, and we'll share them. In bed."

She was suddenly airborne as he tossed her to the big bed. She landed there spitting like a cat and he was right on top of her, preventing her departure.

"I won't!" she cried. "You can't make me!"

"Hush, keep your voice down," he reproved, holding her legs pinioned with the weight of his body and seizing her hands and irresistibly drawing them together so that he could capture both her wrists with one large hand. He began to run the fingers of his other hand lightly down her throat and bosom and inserted them gently under the tangerine silk of her low-cut neckline. Her bodice quivered as she felt those fingers play a little tune along her heaving breasts.

"Stop!" she cried angrily.

"You'll bring the inn down on us," he warned with a grin. "Innkeeper Buxton will break in, he'll see us making love, your reputation will be ruined, you'll lose that fine gentleman upriver whose plantation you so dote on—"

"I *don't* dote on his plantation!" She almost tore her bodice in her struggles to be free.

"Ah, Haverleigh does not please you?"

'Of course it pleases me, it's beautiful!"

"Well, then?" He bent down, roguishly nibbling her ear.

She jerked her head away. "I wouldn't marry a *house*!" she cried.

"But then ten thousand acres is vastly better than four? Especially when you don't own the four?"

"I wouldn't marry the acres!"

"So it's marriage you're set on?" His dark head came up and he sighed. "And here I'd hoped that by proving myself a better lover I'd have made you forget all that—once you'd had time to think about it." His knee probed impudently between her legs and she kicked at him.

"Of course it didn't make me forget anything!" she cried.

"Too bad," he sighed. "I fear I must try again. Obviously I didn't make a sufficient impression on you the first time. Bear with me while I try to do better."

Dorinda opened her pretty mouth to call him all manner of names—and found his warm mouth closing over her opened lips, his warm tongue probing. She made a strangled sound in her throat and tried to move her head, to push him away, but it was fruitless. He held her immobilized and stroked her body and clasped her against him—and the hot blood in her that was so easily aroused, the very tinder of her nature, worked against her. He was despicable, she told herself, he was a charlatan, a highwayman, a rover,—and worst of all he had deceived her! With Jeddie! He was everything she detested in a man! But his body was a wonderful magnet that drew her to him irresistibly, held her to him irrevocably, his maleness was tantalizing and inescapable. With a sob of fury she relaxed beneath this sweet assault and heard him chuckle as he let go of her wrists. Treacherously her arms stole around his neck in a dizzy wave of desire that—against her will—seemed to overwhelm her. She felt his thick dark hair brush over her face like fire, she smelled the faint expensive scent of fine Virginia tobacco that emanated from his coat— and her stomach gave a violent lurch as his knuckles slid across it as he tore open his trousers.

A moment later her skirts were impetuously dragged upward and his maleness entered her, pressed against her all too willing quivering flesh. She gave a little moan and moved sinuously beneath him, savoring to the full the ecstasy that he brought her.

"Dorinda, Dorinda," she heard him murmur into the perfumed wealth of her bright hair, *Let me take care of you. . . ."* A wholly unreasonable suggestion for how could a wanted highwayman, harried from place to place, take care of anyone? Indeed he'd be lucky if he could take care of himself and keep a rope from round his neck! But Dorinda was caught up by the magic and his words, however ridiculous they might seem later, had now a golden urgency that shimmered in her ears, intimate, unreal, important. And then the world drifted away and all she heard was their own ragged breathing and a kind of glorious inner singing that seemed to come from somewhere deep inside her, a marvelous angel chorus that was wild and high and sweet and sang of all the wonders she had found in these strong arms that held her.

Her eyes were closed, she had long since ceased to fight him, indeed she was helping him, moving as he moved, swaying as he swayed, arching her lithe young body toward him eagerly, surging toward a magnificent destiny that lured her onward and upward. Her whole body seemed to become one with his, united, her desire so deep it was almost physical pain until in a last esctatic moment she seemed to burst through into brilliant sunlight and know for a single blinding moment what heaven was all about.

How long it was before her lashes fluttered open, she did not know. Still aglow, she stole a guilty look at Tarn out of the corner of her eye. He was lying quietly beside her, his arms behind his head, gazing at the ceiling. His expression was tranquil and he seemed quite unaware of his surroundings, but he noticed instantly that flicker of her lashes and said without looking at her, "For a moment there, I thought you'd gone to sleep. I hope this time was better for you. After all, one has to be careful with a virgin. Mustn't hurt her too much. But today is different. Today you can begin to enjoy your newfound freedom."

Enjoy her newfound freedom! When he had seized her and actually flung her to the bed! Dorinda had a wild desire to strike him, no matter how much she had enjoyed the encounter!

"I am leaving," she told him in a shaking voice and made to rise.

"Oh, don't go yet," he said lazily, turning on his side and throwing an arm across her naked stomach. "We can do it all again. Who knows, we might even improve on it?"

It made her furious that even now she should tremble beneath his touch. She struck his arm away, sat up and smoothed down her tangerine skirts.

"I detest you!" She gave him a level look.

"Because I'm not a gentleman?" he asked curiously. "Or because I made you want me?"

"Oh-h-h!" She jumped up, furiously adjusting her clothes.

"Well, you *did* enjoy it," he pointed out. "The finer points of feminine feelings may sometimes escape me, but your enjoyment was glaringly apparent!"

Dorinda's face was red as fire for the barb had struck home.

"Dorinda," he murmured. "Don't go back to Haverleigh."

She gave him a bitter look as she managed to get the

last of her hooks fastened. "I'll go where I like! And I'll marry who I like! And if you try to stand in my way—!"

Some of the glow went out of his gray eyes, leaving them suddenly empty. "Oh, I won't stand in your way." His voice sounded flat. He watched as with shaking hands she tried to comb her hair back into a semblance of its former elegance. "So you're going to accept Ramsay's proposal after all?"

She turned as if stung. "How do you know he asked me?"

"You forget," he pointed out, "that I was hidden in the bushes nearby when he asked you."

Her color deepened. "Then why ask?" she demanded bitterly.

"I had wondered," he murmured, "if aught that had happened since might have changed your mind?"

Her chin elevated. "If you think I would marry a highwayman—!"

"Oh, 'tis more than evident that you would not," he said hastily. "You have in mind to marry the saintly Mr. Ramsay of the ten thousand acres."

She gave him a look and he sighed.

"Dorinda," he said frankly. "I am sorry that I have thwarted your attempt to reach Ramsay's bed a virgin bride. But there is naught now that can be done about it."

She lifted her chin again. "No matter," she said crushingly. "I have told him that I have been married before, that I am a widow. I had meant to tell him the truth but now I will stick to that story and explain that while the marriage wasn't consummated *after*, it was consummated *before*."

A shadow of laughter passed behind his eyes. "Yes, you *would* think of that," he murmured.

"You need not look so superior! I have also told him that I am not the true heiress to Merryvale and he wants me anyway!"

"Is he really willing to forgo Merryvale?" Tarn wondered, half to himself. It came to him stabbingly that perhaps he had been wrong about one thing—it was entirely possible that Bainter Ramsay loved Dorinda. As he himself did.

"And what do you have to say to that?" she taunted.

"It leaves me speechless," he replied, his urbanity asserting itself again. "And what course does the devious Mr. Ramsay advise you to take?"

"He urges me to accept the inheritance and sell the property to him—for something less than it is worth— and so be free of it. He will take me away when we are married. We will tour abroad."

His dark brows had drawn together as she spoke. "Dorinda," he said quickly. "Do not go back there!"

Her cold look told him she would go where she pleased.

"Tell me," he asked in a suddenly interested voice. "If you were to learn that the saintly Mr. Ramsay is as great a rogue as I, what then?"

"He is not." Crushingly.

"But if he were?" he insisted.

She gave him a wooden look.

"There is, of course, a way to find out," he mused. He shot a wicked glance at her. "You could confide in him that you have found me out, that I am The Blade—and see what happens then?"

A gasp escaped her lips. This impudent rogue was actually suggesting that she expose him to Bainter! She stood speechless as he got up and prowled to the window.

"Why would you want me to do that?" she asked at last.

"So that you may know the truth about your intended bridegroom." He turned to smile at her. "If Bainter is all you believe him to be, he will at once denounce me and strive to see me hanged. If he is what I believe him to be, he will take some other tack." His gray eyes narrowed. "Do you have the courage to do it?" he demanded. "To tell him and see what happens?"

"Of course I have the courage to do it!" she cried, enraged.

"Then your opportunity is upon you," he told her genially. "For I just saw Bainter striding into the inn."

Dorinda flung down the comb she had picked up from his table and jammed on her hat.

"There is of course still time for that glass of wine I promised you," he pointed out.

She tossed her head with a ripple of plumes and made for the door. At the door she paused and flung back five words—venomously: "I hope they hang you!"

His laughter followed her as she went slamming out. Its echo seemed to follow her down the hall, down the stairs, into the common room below. *Would he always follow her?* she asked herself wildly. *Would she always see him, hear him, where he was not? On far away streets, in other arms, would he follow her still?*

When the stars fall down and the sun turns dark
And even the winds are still,
When the blast we see is eternity,
I will love you still!

PART FOUR

The Unmasking

The White Hart
WILLIAMSBURG, VIRGINIA
Summer 1717

Chapter 34

By the time Dorinda walked down the front stairs of
the White Hart she had recovered her poise—at least
outwardly. Inside she was still seething with a variety of
emotions. When she reached the foot of the stairs she
saw Bainter Ramsay approaching her and all at once
she came to a decision.

He looked surprised to see her and came forward,
from a table in the far corner where he had been
sitting with another gentleman, to take her hand.
"Dorinda, about last night—let me explain."

"There is no need for explanations," she said crisply.

"I think there is."

He looked different, she thought, standing there. His
eyes were a trifle bloodshot, for he had been up all
night, and there was the strong smell of alcohol on his
breath as he leant toward her, but it was something
else. The glow was gone. Departed forever. He seemed
to her suddenly a very ordinary figure, somewhat
overdressed in lemon satin with all those green rosettes
on this burning hot day.

She cast a look about her; there was nobody near.

"Very well," she sighed. "If explanations are needed, let us have them."

"First, what are you doing here?"

"I came downriver to find you," she said, thinking it a reasonable enough explanation.

"How did you get here?"

"I ordered out your barge," she said.

He gave her an astonished look. "And where are the oarsmen?" He glanced around him as if expecting to see them.

"I left them at the Red Fox Tavern. I do not know how you got here, but you will have your own barge to take you upriver."

"Providential," he murmured ironically. "Well, since you are here, come and sit down. You look as if you could use something cool to drink." He turned to an aproned girl of about fifteen just then passing by carrying a brace of tankards. "Some cider for the lady, Nan." And led Dorinda to the table he had just vacated, a table in a corner a little apart from the rest of the noisy room, where a heavyset gentleman in green wearing a voluminous bag wig, who had been peering gloomily into his empty tankard as they approached, rose quickly and studied her through a glass.

Dorinda's heart seemed to come to a full stop.

Before her, staring at her through that eyeglass, was John Blore's nephew Jack, the man at whom she had wrathfully thrown hot wax one cold day in Philadelphia, and who had departed taking with him most of the family plate.

There was no escape.

"Mistress Merryvale," said Bainter formally, "this is John Blore."

"D'ye mean *this* is the heiress?" Blore gasped, dropping his glass.

"Yes." Bainter gave him an irritated look. "Keep your voice down, Jack. One would think you had never seen a lady before!"

"I have seen *this* lady before," said Jack Blore promptly. "She worked in my uncle's chandler's shop in Philadelphia."

Both men were staring at her, but a kind of composure had settled over Dorinda. The worst had happened and in a way she was glad of it. She could be open and aboveboard at last—no matter what lay ahead. And she hardly thought that Jack Blore would have had contact with Ada; from what she knew of him, he had not been merely exiled like John and Elissa but cut off entirely by a family that worshiped only success and could not accept a failure.

"The chandler's shop girl!" chuckled Blore.

His contemptuous tone nettled Dorinda. "At least," she said clearly, "I did not steal the family silver."

Jack Blore looked ready to strike her.

"Jack!" came Bainter's low warning and Jack settled back muttering, "So *this* is your heiress!"

"Heiress no longer," said Dorinda. "I plan to disavow the inheritance."

"What?" cried both men in unison.

Dorinda was glad they were too far away from the rest of the company for them to hear what was being said at their table.

"I am tired of sailing under false colors," said Dorinda wearily. "I am Dorinda Meredith and you should remember me, Bainter. Here outside this very inn you once stepped on my kirtle and tore it. Upstairs in this very inn you tried to rape me. That was three years ago. No doubt you find me greatly changed."

Bainter was looking at her with a fascination she would once have found highly flattering, but now no longer interested her. "You have taken me in again," he breathed. "I knew that you looked slightly familiar but—" he struck his thigh—"the chambermaid from the inn here!"

She nodded and instead of feeling unhappy about

having her shabby past brought to light, she suddenly felt free and able to captain her own ship. "The same."

Her mind was already flying ahead, making plans. She would bring Jeddie downriver, set her free. Free to go back to Tarn Jenner, who would no doubt welcome her with open arms. The thought hurt but she must face it—unless she chose to live in an eternal triangle, which she did not propose to do! Mistress Riddle would be kind to Lady Soft Paws. As for herself she would take her golden guineas and buy passage far far away. Far enough away that she would not hear about it and weep when a certain famous highwayman dangled from a hempen rope.... And when she could, she would make restitution. The money could be sent anonymously to George Peabody. He would take care of it.

"But what's this about giving up the inheritance?" asked Bainter. "Surely the one has nothing to do with the other?"

"I will never understand you," she sighed. "You cannot wish to marry me knowing that—"

"Of course I do," he cut in. "What were you doing upstairs just now?"

"Looking for you," she lied easily, for not for worlds would she have told him that she was with Tarn Jenner, any more than she would have followed Tarn's advice and told him she had found The Blade! "I meant to ask one of the chambermaids if you were here."

To Dorinda's relief, he accepted that explanation— the real one would have stunned him.

"Bainter," she said. "I thank you for your offer, but I cannot marry you."

Jack Blore grinned. "And 'twas for this slippery wench you put me off!" he jibed. "Ye'd have done better to have stuck with me!"

"Shut up, Jack," said Bainter, and turned his frown on Dorinda. "What do you mean, you can't marry me?"

"Yes," echoed Jack belligerently, not heeding Bainter's admonition. "Why can't you marry him?"

"Jack," said Dorinda, who was finding his intervention a trifle tedious. "This is between Mr. Ramsay and myself."

"Indeed it is not," said Blore hotly. "'Tis between the three of us, for I was to share half and half after out of pocket expenses on the sale of Merryvale Manor!"

Dorinda gave him a blank look. What on earth was Jack talking about?

"Jack," grated Bainter. "I told you to *shut up*."

"No, keep talking," said Dorinda. "I would like to know just what interest you have in Merryvale Manor."

The man in the bag wig leant forward and stuck his bearded jaw almost into her face. "The same interest as you have, mistress chandler's girl! I was set to be the 'heir' before you dropped into the scene and claimed it!"

"You mean you—?" Dorinda was thunderstruck. "And you knew about this, Bainter?"

"Knew?" sneered Blore. "Ramsay arranged it, he did. Just like all the others!"

Dorinda's stricken eyes flew to Bainter's face. He was looking as if he'd like to kill Blore. "Jack doesn't say it very well," he said coolly. "But that's about it."

"'Tis a profitable business our Mr. Ramsay has here, is it not?" Blore lifted his tankard, remembered it was empty, and banged it upon the table for more. Several people at other tables turned to look askance at him, and the aproned girl started toward them.

Dorinda sat speechless.

"Jack, if you want to get drunk, this is not the time," said Bainter, and waved the girl away.

"Are you saying—" Dorinda found her voice and it had a slight quaver in it—"that you *arrange* for heirs to receive inheritances they're not entitled to?"

Jack Blore hooted. "That's not all he does!" he said unpleasantly. "He arranges for those without known heirs to die suddenly so the 'heirs' he picks can inherit!"

Dorinda felt cold all over. It seemed insane that they

should be sitting here, discussing almost conversationally, what surely must be the wickedest plot in all Virginia. *If you were to learn that the saintly Mr. Ramsay is as great a rogue as I, what then?* Tarn Jenner had asked. And now she had learned that he was a far greater rogue!

"I will not be returning to Haverleigh," she said, and made to rise.

Instantly her elbow was caught in a fierce grip and she was yanked back down. "Stay there," growled Bainter.

"I will remind you," she said furiously, "that we are in a public place, and what is more, a public place where I am known and respected! You will let me go. At once!"

Bainter leaned forward until his whiskey laden breath was hot upon her face. His voice was barely a whisper but its menace pierced through to her soul. "That knob you feel against your thigh and which you probably presume to be the head of my cane is actually a pistol held in the hand of Jack Blore here."

Dorinda, who had been too excited to notice the pressure of it before, cast a frightened look down. The skirt of Blore's coat was spread out, touching her own tangerine skirt, but there was an unpleasant bulge there that *could* be a pistol.

She would have edged away but Bainter said, "If you do not do everything I tell you in the next few minutes, you will lie dead on the floor and whatever you may have to say will be of no importance any longer."

"You wouldn't!" she gasped. But she knew that he would. Anyone who arranged for people to die suddenly so he could inherit their money would not stick at one more killing! "You'd be hanged for my murder!" she cried.

"It would be a nasty accident," he told her grimly. "Blore would have pinched you, you would have struck him beneath the table and accidentally caused the gun to fire!"

She fell silent, hardly daring to breathe.

"You and I are going to get up now," Bainter told

her. "You will take my arm and we will stroll through the door. You may nod to your friends but you will not stop to talk; you will keep smiling and you will keep going. Blore will stroll along behind with his coat thrown over his arm—natural enough in this heat—and his pistol will be pointed directly at your back. I will keep you positioned so that at all times you will present a perfect target. If you value your life, Dorinda, you will do as I say. *Now rise.*"

Feeling as if this couldn't be happening to her, Dorinda got up and so did Bainter. She stepped forward and took his arm and he crushed it to his side so tightly that she could not possibly have freed herself.

A lady at a nearby table nodded affably. Dorinda nodded back.

I am being escorted at gunpoint from a public inn out into a public street! she thought, her amazement being equalled only by her terror.

"You are doing very well," Bainter murmured. "You have only to make it to my carriage in the innyard."

"And then where do we go?" she asked through stiff lips.

"Upriver to Haverleigh naturally," he said in an off-hand voice. "Where did you expect?"

Behind her she could hear Jack Blore's boots, pacing them. She wondered if upstairs Tarn Jenner was watching.

He was. It was with a sick feeling of loss that he watched Dorinda strolling away from the inn pressed close against Bainter Ramsay. His lean face was haggard as he watched her go, swaying along gracefully beside his rival. It cut him to the heart to see Bainter boost her up into a carriage. Frustration overcame him. He should have killed the fellow! With a sudden violent gesture he turned and swept his writing table clean. The boxlike slant-topped writing desk careened to the floor, parchment and quills were scattered, and his inkstand crashed against the wall. The black liquid oozed down the white plaster. He would have to pay to have the room repainted, he supposed dully, but whatever the cost it would be as nothing compared to what the sight of the woman he loved leaving with Bainter had cost him.

Dorinda had made her choice. She had chosen Ramsay....

For a grief-stricken moment his big head dropped into his hands.

How could she do it? he asked himself.

He would have been astonished could he have heard their conversation as they crossed the courtyard.

Once outside the inn, Dorinda steadied her voice enough to say, "Why don't you let me go now? You must realize that I could gain nothing by exposing you? I would only expose myself. All I want is to escape from Williamsburg!"

From behind them Jack Blore heard that. "Don't listen to her," he advised. "Wenches are always treacherous."

"Jack, you talk too much," said Bainter wearily. "No, Dorinda, I will not let you go. Our fortunes are linked now, for better or worse."

Dorinda did not like that connotation. It had a marriageable sound to it. "You surely wouldn't want to marry me now!" she said faintly. "Now that you know what a horror I have of you?"

His laugh was flint hard. "I'm not at all concerned with your feelings," he said. "But you will keep quiet as we drive or I will break your arm. This is a hired carriage and the driver is unknown to me. Jack," he flung over his shoulder. "Go down to the Red Fox and round up our oarsmen. You can catch up to us if you hurry."

Jack left them and Dorinda would have broken away from him at the carriage save that he twisted her arm with such force that she gasped with pain, fearing it would break. Up front the stolid driver took no notice.

In silence they reached the barge and Dorinda, still feeling that this was all a bad dream from which she must soon wake, climbed in. She was seated between Bainter and Jack Blore.

"You can talk now, Jack," said Bainter. "These lads are all in my employ and they know what's about."

Dorinda gave Bainter a horrified look. "*All* your servants are in this with you?" she cried.

"Not all." He frowned at her. "Just the lads here—and Clem."

She was amazed that he would tell her that. It showed how confident he was.

"Shut the wench up," said Blore rudely. "We need to talk about what's to be done now."

"I'm thinking of that," said Bainter. "First of all, there's no chance of your taking Dorinda's place as the Merryvale heir, if that's what's going through your mind."

"I admit it was," said Blore sullenly.

"It won't wash. One unknown heir turning up, then diappearing and another taking her place. There'd be an investigation, we'd be caught up."

Blore's jaw was thrust out. He looked about to argue the point.

"You should have stayed in Philadelphia until I sent for you, Jack," burst out Bainter. "I sent you money to outfit yourself like a gentleman and told you to wait. Why the devil couldn't you do it? Instead of showing up here and sending me a message in the middle of the night?"

"I told you I'd diced me a game or two and I'd run out of money," said Jack belligerently. He was growing red in the face. "And had not this wench showed up to gum things up, my timing would have been fine!"

"Then *you* were going to be the Merryvale heir?" demanded Dorinda, fascinated.

"Of course I was!" roared Jack. "Are you going to shut her up or shall I?"

"Let her talk," said Bainter thoughtfully. "I like the fact that she's cool in an emergency. You should have seen her, Jack. She hoodwinked all of us." He turned to her. "We could still do all those things I described to you, visit the capitals of the world."

"Thank you," said Dorinda coldly, "but I have other plans."

Jack laughed. "Did you hear that? The wench has other plans! I'd give her a taste of my knuckles if it were me!"

"Well, it isn't you," snarled Bainter. "And how would I explain her bruises? Now shut up, both of you, and let me think!"

By the time they reached Haverleigh, Bainter seemed to have come to a decision. As the barge was tied up at the pier, he turned to Jack Blore. "That wench walking down the lawn toward us is named Jeddie. I'll distract her while you take Dorinda to the house. He'll still have a gun on you, Dorinda, so do just as he says. If you meet a talkative old lady, Jack, tell her I've some news for her from Williamsburg and I'm waiting for her outside—that'll rid ye of her."

Bitterly watching an unsuspecting Jeddie chatting with Bainter up ahead, Dorinda found herself marched across the lawn. "Easy now, wench," Jack was muttering. "If I have to shoot you, I will and the law won't catch up with me near so fast here as it would in Williamsburg."

That was true, thought Dorinda miserably. *They* were safer here, but *she* was in more danger.

Jack looked up appreciatively as they reached the wide front steps. "Fine house, ain't it?" he said.

"Yes," said Dorinda in a strangled voice. *And Merryvale was fine too, and somehow these men meant to have it!* She had tried to catch Jeddie's eye, but Jeddie had been entirely preoccupied with Bainter. Now as they entered the house and Jack Blore whistled at the size of the thirty-foot-square room in which he found himself, she kept hoping Mistress Riddle would show up and create a diversion—perhaps an opportunity for her to run, to elude Jack Blore in a house that was strange to him.

She might even be able to make her way out through the ground floor and escape into the woods!

But Mistress Riddle, always so obtrusive, was nowhere in sight and she did not come out even though Dorinda raised her voice quite loudly in answer to some question of Jack's.

"Lead the way to your room," he growled, and Dorinda, feeling helpless, did so.

He shoved her inside, latched the door behind him and looked around him. "Live well for a chandler's shop girl, don't ye, wench?" he laughed. "Ye're a fool for not going along with us!"

"What makes you think Bainter will keep you around now?" she asked, hoping to stir up trouble that she could somehow turn to her advantage. "I would think you'd be a liability to him!"

Jack frowned darkly at her. "Watch your mouth, wench!"

Bravely she pursued that line. "You've been seen around Williamsburg—and with him. He can't use you as an 'heir' now. What use are you to him?"

"We can do it again somewhere else," he said sulkily. "Carolina maybe. Or anywhere the picking is good." He was looking at her slyly. "Ye're a likely wench," he muttered. "No wonder Ramsay—"

He was never to finish that remark. There was a rap at the door and Bainter's voice said, "Let me in."

Jack opened the door and Bainter came through it. He leaned over and muttered to Jack and Jack nodded and went out. Bainter turned to Dorinda. He looked, she thought bitterly, quite handsome. Plainly disaster became him.

"You can't keep me locked up in here, Bainter," she told him stubbornly. "People will wonder what's happened to me! The estate isn't probated yet. George Peabody will come looking for me to sign things. People will come to call. The Riddles will be curious if I don't show up for meals."

"I realize that." He looked pleased with himself and his amber eyes sparkled. "In a way, I'm glad you brought things to a head, Dorinda. I've been stagnating here." He paused as, in the distance, they heard the Riddles' voices. Dorinda's heart leaped and then she felt a bitter disappointment as those voices drifted away. "It's been an easy life, being a Virginia planter," he told her, "and in a way I'll miss it, but as Jack pointed out before you came downstairs and found us at the White Hart, the world is wide and every day Williamsburg grows less safe for me."

"What do you intend for me?" she asked bluntly.

"We are leaving here," he told her. "Tonight. We'll go downriver by barge and take the *Green Heron* to Barbados. The *Heron*'s captain is a friend of mine. He'll marry us on shipboard. Shipboard marriages are valid."

"And if I refuse?"

A mirthless smile passed across his handsome features and was gone. "The marriage will be recorded anyway. Your permission will not be required. I would prefer to take you to Barbados alive but if you give me too much trouble I will throw you overboard in the dark of night and the captain will enter in his ship's log that you suffered a sudden fainting fit and fell overboard and sank like a stone. Later if I find it is safe to do so, I will return and see if I cannot claim your inheritance by reason of the marriage."

He had thought of everything. It took her breath.

And now she had seen at last the depths of that dark side of him that lingered just below the surface. Not instability as she had at first believed, but a kind of singleness of purpose pursued to the point of madness. Bainter had decided he wanted wealth and gold in Virginia—Bainter would have it so. His methods were unimportant to him, and he was entirely callous with regard to who got hurt.

"What happened to her?" she whispered. "To that woman you married? The one who left you?"

His face for a moment was not a pretty sight. All semblance of humanity seemed to leave it. She had never seen a countenance so malignant. "Ah, you mean Denise? She thought to elude me, did Denise. She ran away with a wandering musician. I followed her and strangled them both. With these hands." He held them out for her inspection and Dorinda shuddered.

"But how could you do that?" she cried, revolted. "You loved her. Something in your voice when you spoke of her told me that."

"Yes, I loved her." He was suddenly melancholy, and the human mask fell down over his face again, making him seem vulnerable and alone. "I loved her and she defied me. She said she would not murder the old gentleman for his gold, she would run away first. I did not believe her. I thought she returned my love!"

Dorinda stared at him with the fascination of pure horror. Here indeed was a twisted mind. No wonder the planters shunned him! They sensed in him something evil, some wrongness that their sisters and daughters, beguiled by Bainter's undeniably handsome face, his wealth, his grace upon the dance floor, tended to overlook.

"And you killed her *for that*?" she breathed.

"What choice had I?" He shrugged. "She would eventually have gone to the authorities, she would have denounced me. I have had bad luck with women. They seem to fall in with my plans—and then abruptly they pull away."

And no wonder, considering the horrible things you plan! she thought.

"And what of me?" she asked with a bold lift of her chin. "What is my fate to be if I do marry you?"

He gave her a suddenly appreciative look. "I like your spirit," he admitted. "I liked it that day at the inn when I would have shared my bath with you and you fought me."

"If you liked my spirit so much," she said in a shaky voice, "you should have taken my part when Buxton's wife dragged me off to beat me!"

"Why?" he asked coolly. "You were claiming I'd tried to rape you! Faith, a bound girl in your position should have considered my attentions a compliment!"

Dorinda yearned to rake her fingernails across his insolent face. "And now that I am no longer a bound girl?"

"Yes, that is the problem. In some mysterious way you have acquired beauty—and apparently breeding. You would be mistaken for a lady anywhere. You could be useful to me," he admitted frankly. "You could walk beside me. When we are finished here—and of course it must all end soon, there are too many estates turning up with no heirs anyone has seen before. We can come back from Barbados of course if there is no great outcry here in the meantime and you can lay claim to Merryvale then. But after Riddlewood, we will have to take our leave." He sounded regretful.

"After Riddlewood?" gasped Dorinda. He was smiling at her, that fleeting transient smile that never quite reached his eyes. "Oh, no," she whispered. "It was *you* who set the fire! *You* who tried to kill them! Oh, *why*, Bainter? Why? They never harmed you, they have never harmed anybody!"

The remnants of that smile left his lips altogether. "But they have no children, no heirs of whom anyone knows, and they have a fine estate. After they are gone, an heir will turn up. He will inherit, the estate will be sold to me for a fraction of its worth, I will in turn sell it for a good price, just as I will sell Haverleigh and Merryvale—and I will show Virginia my heels! If you are sensible, you will go with me."

"You cannot do it," moaned Dorinda. "You cannot!"

Abruptly his countenance changed. It was a devil's

face she was looking into now—that face his young wife
Denise must have glimpsed just before she died. "I do
not ask that you assist me," he rasped. "Only that you
do not stand in my way! The Riddles will soon be
asleep. They are even now drinking the drugged wine
that I have prepared. Jeddie is serving it to them."

"Jeddie!"

"Oh, she does not know it is drugged," he smiled.
"But she is serving it all the same—to both the Riddles
and to Jack Blore." Her expression seemed to amuse
him. "Be not so tender-hearted. I assure you they will
all sleep through the whole thing."

"What—whole thing?"

"The fire," he said calmly. "It is a pity to sacrifice so
fine a building as this one for it would bring a good
price, even without its ten thousand acres. But once I
have stowed you safely in the barge—willing or unwilling, it makes no difference to me—I will slip back and
set the place alight. I will set it carefully and it will
smoulder for a while—had it not been for that sudden
cloudburst, Riddlewood would have burnt and the Riddles with it!" His voice grew pettish. "And I would not
have to go through all this again!"

"Oh, you can't do it, Bainter," she moaned. "*You
can't.*"

He ignored that. "We will be too far downriver to see
the glow when finally it bursts into full-fledged flames.
But the bedroom doors will be locked, the servants—if
they wake up in time—will be sleepy and disorganized,
there will be no one to lead them. We will have reached
Williamsburg, we will have sailed on the *Green Heron*
which weighs anchor at dawn—before it is known in the
town that upriver Haverleigh is burning." He gave her
a sunny smile. "A wife cannot testify against her husband."

"And Jeddie?" she asked through stiff lips. Even if
Jeddie was having an affair with Tarn, she still did not
want to see her burn!

He shrugged. "I told Clem to see that she drank a glass of the wine."

And Jeddie loved wine, she would not refuse it!

Dorinda stared at him with loathing. His callousness amazed her. But the steady logic of his reasoning left her feeling cold, as if icy winds blew inexorably upon her, winds that drove her endlessly forward, that would shape her destiny.

Standing there watching him, a terrible sense of hopelessness overcame Dorinda. He would have her, this terrible single-minded man without mercy, without human feeling, without honor or decency or pity. He would have her and she would be forever lost.

"No wonder you drink," she murmured. "Terrible things must float up in your memory, things that don't bear looking upon."

"Enough of that," he said roughly. "I don't need instruction from some wandering wench who somehow learned to pass herself off as a lady. I am offering you a fine life, Dorinda. We will have wealth—and we will get more." She shuddered inwardly at the way they would get more. "Your beauty will tempt men. You can lure rich men, highly placed men. They are subject to blackmail, you can learn things about them—and you will tell me and I will act upon that knowledge. Oh, I see us as a great success!" He was warming to his subject and that transient gypsylike smile was again on his lips. He stopped suddenly. "I will leave you now. I have much to do, papers to assemble, plate to pack."

Yes, thought Dorinda bitterly. *It would take him a while to strip Haverleigh of its portable treasure. And then he would get on with it—murder, arson, treachery to his accomplice, and God knew what deviltry with her!*

At the door he paused. "It will not take me long," he said as if reading her thoughts. "And there will be time before we leave. Time to enjoy ahead of time the fruits of our wedding night. Wear something attractive, Dorinda. A string of beads will be enough." His laugh jarred her. "I would be glad to tear off your clothes but there really won't be time for it." His tawny eyes glittered. "Clem will be guarding this door and he has orders to strike you senseless if you scream. It might anger me enough that I would leave you here to burn with the rest. How would you like that, Dorinda, to wake up with flames all about you and no escape? Think on it—and then take off your clothes and welcome me!"

He was gone.

Shakily Dorinda went to the window and stared out. She would have risked jumping out, even from this height, but she could see the lounging figure of the oarsman below.

The window was being guarded too.

She went back and sat down upon the bed, twisting her hands together. It was too late to warn the Riddles, even if they heard her screams and comprehended them, for they were already drugged. Jack Blore might have aided her had he known what Bainter planned for him, but he was drugged too.

She stared vacantly at the wall, trying to think, to plan. There was no hope at all. . . . Bainter was a monster, but he was an efficient monster. And up to now his plans had worked.

But she would not take off her clothes! She would not submit! She would fight him for every stitch, come what may!

Chapter 35

As the time fled by, Dorinda, alone and hopeless, made her peace with God and formed the only plan she could. It was not much of a plan true, but it was the best she could come up with. She would hit Bainter over the head when he came through that door, she would try to dart past him and make her escape.

It would fail of course, but she had to try it.

If she survived that attempt and was forcibly escorted down to Williamsburg anyway, she did not intend to board the *Green Heron* willingly. They would have to drag her aboard, kicking and screaming. One good solid blow would render her senseless, of course, and Bainter was a man who would not hesitate to deliver that blow, so she could be carried aboard unconscious....

No, she would somehow manage to alert the people around her. She would leap from the carriage. What matter if she broke her leg? She would scream to high heaven, she would cry out what was happening, how the Riddles and Jeddie were being burned in their beds!

She would be throttled before she could get out the first bleat, she told herself gloomily. Those big hands of

Bainter's that had squeezed the life out of his young wife, Denise, would be clutched around her throat before she hit the ground!

Still, she would try it.

And if all was lost and she was carried aboard unconscious, she would not live to be his plaything. He would not have to throw her overboard. She would throw herself over.

Now that she had reached that conclusion and realized that however it ended, she was unlikely to survive it, she felt calm again. Ready to try it.

But in the short time that was left to her, she wanted to remember those brief golden moments she had known in Tarn Jenner's arms. For now that he was lost to her, she realized how very much she loved him. Her fury at him had been great because her love for him was great.

Now that she would never see him again, she was fiercely glad that she had not denounced him to Bainter as The Blade—as Tarn had so impudently suggested. Bainter might have found a way to use that knowledge, to make himself a hero in the eyes of the planters by bringing down a daring highwayman who had even dared to rob the governor! At least she would face her own death without the painful thought that she had caused Tarn to be hanged! *That* would not be added to her shame!

The time ticked on, and Dorinda relived every achingly beautiful moment she had known with him last night and today. She had become a woman too late, it seemed. She had turned away from the one man she could have loved forever.

Footsteps sounded outside the door. Dorinda, her shoes already kicked off for soundlessness, picked up the heavy candlestick she had selected and ran to the door. She raised the candlestick and waited tensely.

"You can take in the wine, Clem," came Bainter's voice on the other side of that door. "And the tray with our dinner. Then go down and help with loading the barge. I won't be needing you."

Two of them! Dorinda had not counted on them both coming in. She hesitated, trying to calculate whether the odds might not be better later. *No,* some inner voice screamed at her. *Bainter would come in expecting trouble from her. He would be wary. The thing must be done now!*

Clem opened the door. With his other hand he balanced a tray on which reposed a wine bottle, two glasses, two pewter trenchers piled with food, napkins and cutlery, over which he was slightly bent, as if tallying up the silver to see if he had brought enough spoons.

Dorinda, flattened against the wall, moved more swiftly than she ever had in her life. She brought the heavy candlestick down with crushing force upon the back of Clem's neck and he fell forward like a rock, landing upon the tray as wine bottle and glasses and trenchers crashed to the floor.

Dorinda did not pause to look at the havoc she had created. Even as Bainter leaped forward with a yell he met the candlestick swinging again—but this time with less force, for Dorinda had not had time to throw her body into a really good swing. Nevertheless the candlestick caught his shoulder and as he staggered back from the blow, Dorinda fled by him.

"The front door! Guard the front door and the back stairs!" he bellowed and she could hear running feet.

There was only one alternative left and Dorinda took it. Her flying feet carried her up into the big attic. Once there she almost tripped over the cat and thrust her out of harm's way. But as she did so, her gaze fell on the soft bit of blanket that she had brought up to make a bed for Lady Soft Paws. It was crumpled up and bore the round imprint of a cat's body—and since Lady Soft Paws was shedding liberally in the summer heat, its woolly surface was a mass of fur.

And Bainter always sneezed wretchedly when he came into contact with cat fur!

Dorinda snatched up the blanket and turned back to the head of the attic stair that Bainter was even now thundering up. As he reached the head of the stair and paused, peering into the darkness, she let him have the blanket full in the face, so that if fell like a curtain over his head and wrapped around it.

He fell back cursing and fighting the blanket—and in that moment she had hoped to dash by him and somehow make it downstairs and perhaps leap out an unguarded window and—if she survived the fall unhurt—make for the woods.

But it was not to be. Although she tried to dodge around him, his arms flailed out and she leaped back—for she dared not let those strong hands seize her. And then he had torn the blanket from his head and tossed it aside. He gave a tremendous sneeze and teetered on the top step. For a glorious moment she thought he was going to fall backwards down the stairs but he did not. Instead he kept his footing and sneezed again.

His eyes would be accustomed to this inky darkness now. He would sense a shape moving nearby. There was no passing him now.

Dorinda turned away, leaving him blocking the stairway, exploding with great convulsive sneezes that seemed to shake the heavy floorboards. On silent feet she melted into the maze of rooms that lay ahead. If only she could lure him forward and then double back!

But Bainter had thought of that too. She could hear him slamming doors and latching them and her flesh crawled. Bainter had stalked women before—and found them!

Gradually she realized she was being forced forward, herded as it were, toward the only way left to her—the way up to the rooftop promenade.

On silent stockinged feet she made the journey and found herself atop mighty Haverleigh beneath a night sky lit with stars. A cool breeze played over her hot skin. She had sought for a weapon in the attic and found none. Now she wished with all her heart that she had not dropped the candlestick as she had rushed by Bainter downstairs.

Below her Bainter would be methodically searching the attic. And below her too was something else. She could see the landing clearly from here. She could see two barges full of men gliding up to that landing where Bainter's barge was being loaded. She heard a shout from below. Bainter, closeted in the attic rooms with the doors closed, probably could not hear it.

Men were pouring over the lawns now.

"Up here!" she screamed. "Bainter has drugged the Riddles and Jeddie! He's going to burn the house!"

"Where is he?" roared a voice she recognized with dazed relief as Tarn's.

"In the attic. He's cut me off from escape!" And then because she was afraid he'd be too late: "He's been latching all the attic doors behind him—you can't reach me before he does!"

There was a muttered consultation. Then two men ran back to one of the barges. Fighting was erupting down there. She could hear pistols discharge, see a group of men sweep around to the front while another ran around the back. But her attention was concentrated on the man who was running up the lawn toward her, carrying a coil of rope.

"Stand clear!" he sang out and sent the rope, with a hook on it, sailing through the night air.

Dorinda crouched back. She heard the hook strike the bricks, saw it glance along the railing—and leaped out and caught it, made it secure.

"Good girl!" cried Tarn and began swarming up the rope hand over hand.

In silent terror, Dorinda waited for him. Which would get there first, Bainter or Tarn? For she had no doubt what would happen if Bainter reached her first! Silently she prayed Tarn would hurry, for his life hung on his speed as well as hers—if Bainter arrived before he did, he would cut that rope and Tarn would fall to his death.

Leaning out, she saw that Tarn was having trouble with the overhang, but now he was over it and scrambling up the slanted roof toward the railing where she waited. Even as he vaulted over the railing, Bainter appeared at the other end, coming up out of the attic.

That he already knew what was happening below, Dorinda could see on his pale murderous face. And that he intended to make her pay for it was also stamped on that face. He looked demonic.

"Dorinda," he said calmly. And raised a pistol.

There was a rasp of steel beside her and Tarn Jenner leaped forward and thrust her behind him. Even as he did that his arm went up and a long blade sang through the evening air.

Dorinda, who had thought to make her last stand here, who in the last event had planned to throw herself over the roofs to her death, watched in a kind of terrible slow motion as the blade flashed through the air and buried itself deep in Bainter Ramsay's lemon satin chest.

His pistol went off—but at a rakish angle. Sight of that long blade winging toward him had spoiled his aim and the bullet flashed outward toward the stars. She watched him crumple, clawing at air.

"Are there more of them behind him?" asked Tarn tersely and Dorinda shook her head.

Her eyes were glorious. "Oh, Tarn, I haven't betrayed you," she cried eagerly. "No one here knows that you're The Blade! Oh, Tarn, he was going to kill them all—the Riddles, Jeddie, even Blore. He was going to burn down Haverleigh! And he was bent on dragging me along with him. He said if I refused to marry him on shipboard he'd throw me overboard!" She fell against him, weak with relief.

His strong arms went round her, steadying her, and the hard face that looked down upon her golden head, silvered now by starlight, softened.

"I thought I was too late," he murmured, and his voice was husky. "It drove me mad to see you leave with him—so willingly, I thought!"

"His friend Jack had a pistol pointed at me beneath his coat," she choked. "I was hoping you'd see us from the window."

"I did, but I thought you'd gone with him of your own free will."

"It's terrible what Bainter's been doing," she said, looking up at him anxiously. "He tried to murder the Riddles—it was he who set their house on fire, he told me about it calmly in the common room at the White Hart! And he's been killing people and sending in 'heirs' to inherit their property—"

"I know all about it," he soothed. "And the governor knows too. Those are his men that swarmed out of the barges."

"The governor?" she faltered. "I don't understand. What have you, a highwayman, to do with the governor?"

He smiled grimly. "I am no more a highwayman than that fallen fellow over there is Bainter Ramsay. When I told you I was The Blade, I did it intending that you should tell Bainter. There was a chance that he would go to the authorities and the whole thing would have to come out, but there was also a chance that he would seek me out as a fellow lawbreaker and enlist my aid—then I would be able to learn his game more quickly."

"You really thought I would tell him?" She looked hurt.

"I did not know what to think. You seemed to favor him over me."

"I never did," she sighed.

His arm tightened about her. "When it seemed you were keeping my secret, I realized that either you were not in the plot with him after all or that you cared for me. In either event I meant to protect you, so I sought out the governor and we hastened upriver."

There beneath the stars explanations and kisses flew back and forth:

About Jeddie and the gold button: "I really thought you were carrying on with Jeddie," she whispered shamefaced.

He laughed and ruffled her hair with gentle fingers. "Jeddie's a fine girl," he allowed. "But not for me. I've found my wench!"

About Jack Blore: "I got wind that there was this fellow up in Philadelphia who was somehow mixed up with Bainter—name of John Blore. I tracked him down, even saw him at a distance, but when his wife told me he was dead, I came back to Williamsburg."

"That was his uncle," said Dorinda. "My employer."

"Then when he showed up in Williamsburg and sent a message upriver, I followed the messenger to Haverleigh and reached the garden ahead of him, meaning to circle round. It was then I heard Bainter tell you he'd join you in your room."

"I was trying to force you from my mind," she admitted, unable to face him. "It wouldn't have worked!"

He laughed again for there was joy in him tonight—and relief. "All's well that ends well, lass!" He kissed her embarrassment away.

About the Blade: "Twas the governor's idea I should pose as a highwayman. But all the 'highway robberies' were faked. The governor's gold and trinkets are safe, the horses I'm supposed to have lifted are safely stabled at an upriver plantation."

She gazed at him in wonder. "Then who are you?"

"Haven't you guessed, lass? I'm not Tarn Jenner—I'm Tarn Ramsay, the real Bainter Ramsay's younger brother. I'd gone off to the East Indies to get a cargo of spices and when neither the ship nor I returned, I was presumed dead. Meantime my uncle here in Virginia died leaving everything to Bainter. Bainter came over to take charge. My ship had been wrecked in a storm. I found myself lost on an island and it was years before I could make my way back." His face was grim. "In the meantime, the real Bainter Ramsay never reached these shores. He had sailed aboard the *Green Heron* and he never arrived—a blackguard named Simon Crowe took his place and breezed into Williamsburg, claiming to be Bainter Ramsay."

Dorinda's gaze fled to that fallen lemon satin figure that lay so still with Tarn's blade standing straight up from his chest. *Not Bainter Ramsay—Simon Crowe.*

"It was the *Green Heron* we were to have sailed upon," she told Tarn bitterly, and recounted all that Bainter had said.

"The captain of the *Green Heron* has already been seized," he told her surprisingly.

Below them men were being rounded up, shots were still being fired here and there but there were fewer of them.

"I think we'd best go down now," he said. "I see the governor waving at us."

Down they went, stepping past Bainter's prostrate form, although Tarn did pause to withdraw his blade and to wipe it carefully across Bainter's lemon satin coat before he sheathed it again. Dorinda shuddered as she went past.

The handsome governor, his hair more silver than ever in the starlight, greeted them warmly.

"It was more than I should have asked of you, Ramsay," he said, clapping Tarn on the shoulder. "But when ye came to me with clear proof that the fellow we knew as 'Bainter Ramsay' was an imposter, I thought of all those other heirs who'd appeared out of nowhere—regular plague of them. I knew we'd never be able to untangle the plot without help—and we're all most grateful to you."

"You should be grateful to Mistress Meredith as well," said Tarn coolly. "She risked her life pretending—

at my suggestion—to be the heiress to Merryvale Manor, and so trip the fellow up."

Dorinda gasped. By that single statement Tarn had managed to cover her tracks. And no matter what Jack Blore said when he woke up, no one would believe him against the new and rightful owner of Haverleigh Plantation!

"All Virginia is grateful to you, Mistress Meredith," said the governor with a low bow. "We are not insensible of the risks you took. Tarn here told me as we came upriver that you have but waited to cry the banns until this matter concerning Haverleigh could be cleared up. I look forward to entertaining you both for dinner tomorrow night. And it is my sincerest wish that you will allow me—since Tarn tells me your own people are all dead—to act as your father in this matter. I would like to hold the wedding ceremony and reception at the Governor's Palace and personally give the bride away!"

Tarn was smiling at her. Lovingly. The governor was beaming. Dorinda smiled happily back at them both through her tears. She knew she didn't deserve it—but oh, she was glad it was happening!

"And I always thought Cupid was young," she murmured dizzily.

The governor laughed. "She has a wit, has your lady." He slapped Tarn heartily on the shoulder once again. "Until tomorrow night," he said. "Till then I'll leave you two young lovebirds to yourselves. Or are you coming downriver with us?"

"No," smiled Tarn. "I think I'll just stay with my holdings tonight and count myself lucky."

"Lucky indeed," commented the governor dryly, giving the beautiful girl beside Tarn a last look. "Well, this crew of mine will soon take themselves off, dragging their prisoners with them and we'll hang Simon Crowe's body in Williamsburg as a warning to others who'd flout Virginia law!"

They were soon gone, even the doctor who had

pronounced the Riddles and Jeddie sleeping soundly but safely. Jack Blore, of course, had been carried away trussed up like a Thanksgiving turkey, snoring loudly. Only a handful of frightened chambermaids were left and they were clustered together, worried about what would happen to them.

Dorinda spoke to them kindly, telling them their jobs were safe, that Jeddie—as housekeeper now—would be surpervising them and to bring their problems to her when she woke up.

"'Tis amazing," Tarn quirked a dark eyebrow at her, "how fast one learns to take over a large household. I'd have sworn just now, listening to you, that you'd been at it all your life!"

Dorinda laughed. "It will be a nice change!"

"A change you deserve, Dorinda." He drew her to him and together they walked up the wide outside stairway and through the big front door into the house that was now theirs. "You won't entirely lose Merryvale, you know," he told her. "I've arranged for my step-grandmother to buy it. She's coming to America and she wants a place of her own."

"I know I'm going to like her," said Dorinda.

"Indeed you will," he assured her.

They had reached the big square paneled central room on the main floor and Tarn was walking sure-footedly toward the bedroom he and Dorinda had occupied—could it be only the night before?

At the door to that bedchamber she hesitated. "Are you sure you want to sleep here?" she asked. "The room's full of broken glass where I struck down Clem and Bainter in my mad dash to the attic."

"Then I think we'll occupy the master's bedroom instead," he said, turning toward the east wing, "although," he sighed, "that room does hold sweet memories for me!"

"For me as well." Dorinda smiled.

They found the master's bedroom stripped of all

those expensive items Bainter—no, they must get used to calling him Simon Crowe now—had taken away: the silver candlesticks, the imported coverlet embroidered in gold and silver thread, the list went on and on. "All of it packed on board the Haverleigh barge," Tarn told her. " 'Twill be unloaded tomorrow. The governor's lending us some of his servants to supplement ours."

Dorinda gave him a blissful look. The single candle Tarn had lit made long shadows across the big room. "We don't need light." She leaned over and blew it out. "We didn't need light to know last night that we loved each other and we don't need light now."

"Dorinda," said Tarn huskily, pulling her to him. "Where you go, you light the night with your own glow."

"Liar!" she laughed. "Suppose it had been not me but somebody else in that room?"

"I'd have known," he said, working eagerly in the darkness at the hooks that held her tangerine bodice in place. "I'd have known the silkiness of your skin, the lemony scent of your hair."

But I did not know, she thought. *Or perhaps in my heart I did. Perhaps I knew and did not care.*

"Oh, Tarn," she whispered. "I never knew what it was to love—really to love, before you took me in your arms."

"Arms from which you'll not escape," he murmured lazily, moving toward the big bed, on which they'd just thrown lavender-scented sheets.

She drifted along with him, blown on air. Her heart was light and all the terrible events of the night seemed gossamer and gone. Here at last was her lover and she could claim him proudly before all the world.

"I would have gone with you, you know," she whispered. "Even if you had been The Blade."

He fitted her slender body the better to his and the touch of his fingers was roving fire. "And I came upriver determined to claim you had got into this thing at my instigation—even if Crowe and all of them claimed you as their accomplice!"

Tarn loved her, he had come upriver to save her. Her world was complete.

The wheel had gone full circle. From the ashes, Dorinda had risen. Adversity had formed her, a cruel world had shaped her. But love had found her at last and that love had transformed her. *She would be the best wife a man ever had,* she told herself, and lost herself in the arms of her lover.

The night sounds swirled around them. From the river came the croaking of frogs. Somewhere a screech owl loosed its thin plaintive cry upon the night wind. Haverleigh was safe and Haverleigh was home—and always would be.

That night, to the lovers who had lived and loved so dangerously, came all the sweet delights ever claimed by a man and a maid. Tomorrow they would dine in state with the governor, tomorrow they would plan with him a lavish wedding, tomorrow....But for tonight their naked caressing bodies would speak those golden thoughts of love too sweet, too passionate for words to express. Tonight belonged to them, this first wonderful night of so many golden nights to come.

Tonight they would spend together on a lavender-scented bed lit by starlight, and the fires within them would burn brighter than the stars. Tonight, tonight... and all the nights to come.

> *From out the cruel past they have won through,*
> *Their love has brought them through it, bright and new,*
> *To glory 'neath the azure summer skies*
> *And read their future in each other's eyes!*

She chose a man to ride beside and though she'd chosen
    wrong,
She stayed beside him till the end, courageous all along.
When all was lost, she paid the cost with all that she held dear,
But sometimes Fate rewards the brave—for Fate has brought
    her here!

EPILOGUE

But Fate, which guides us all, had one more strange turn to take.

A year had passed.

After a glittering wedding in the Governor's Palace, with everyone who counted in Virginia in attendance, Tarn and Dorinda had returned to Haverleigh Plantation where Tarn promptly set about making it the most prosperous plantation on the river. It was no secret that they were terribly in love. They attended balls and danced together with their eyes locked, smiling into each other's faces. They had private jokes, they were seen holding hands on Duke of Gloucester Street! And he—a notorious rake, for hadn't he even passed himself off as a highwayman for a time?—rarely went out, preferring the delights of his home and his beautiful bride. It was scandalous, people said, for a couple to be so devoted a whole year after marriage and soon to be rocking a cradle!

But the young couple who had just sauntered through the rose garden now neatly trimmed and abloom with flowers cared not what was said about them. Now they seated themselves in the summerhouse that Tarn had had built for Dorinda on the wide front lawns sloping down to the river and began to play with Lady Soft Paws and her four fluffy kittens.

"Do you know, these kittens are all tabbies and we've not got a tom on the place who's a tabby," said Tarn critically.

Dorinda laughed. "I had thought she was going to be faithful to that big golden tom Mistress Riddle gave us, but apparently she regards taking a mate as license to roam!"

"She is not alone in that belief," murmured Tarn, cocking an eyebrow at her. "Consider Lucy Claridge—she is after the governor now!"

"Oh, come now, I *like* Lucy Claridge! And besides, her husband is always gone and never takes her with him, and when he is home he's too busy with business affairs to bother with her! What kind of a marriage is that?"

"Obviously not the kind for you!" He tousled her golden hair and she pulled away happily.

"Don't muss it!" she cried, striking playfully at his hand. "I spent half the morning combing it." She changed the subject. "Jeddie was thrilled to be attending the governor's ball last week."

"Well, as the wife of Williamsburg's leading attorney, George Peabody, Junior, she could expect to attend," Tarn said reasonably.

"Well, Jeddie shall certainly be invited to every party *I* give," said Dorinda energetically. "Until that crochety old man, her father-in-law, finally accepts her!"

"He will. Give him time. In the meantime they're enjoying living in rented quarters." His keen glance swept the river and he rose to his feet. "Well, well, I see Elsinore has arrived."

"Already?" Dorinda jumped up and peered toward the river. Around her the land was in bloom and bees hummed through the warm scented summer air. Down at the river landing she could see a long boat just tying up at the dock and from it a woman in rich dark red silks was waving her hand to Tarn. "But we didn't expect her till next month!" She lifted her skirts and started down the lawn.

"Elsinore is always surprising," laughed Tarn, striding along beside her, "You'll see! I suppose she got tired of closing up the houses in England and decided to come on over to view Merryvale which she's owned for six months now!"

"She looks...familiar somehow," murmured Dorinda, eyeing the slender figure just alighting from the boat.

"Yes, doesn't she?" He smiled. "That's because you look so much like her. She's a bit older, of course. But what a beauty she must have been in her day!"

They had reached the boat landing now and the lovely woman who hugged Tarn and clasped Dorinda around the shoulders had only a touch of silver in her flame-colord locks. Her smiling face seemed to have an eternal youth and her gray eyes sparkled like a girl's as she said vivaciously, "So you are the pretty child who has taken my favorite grandson away from me?"

"No," demurred Dorinda, dimpling for she felt an unaccountable warmth toward this strange lady in the lovely clothes. "I think instead you have gained a granddaughter."

A warmer light appeared in the gray eyes. "I had hoped you would say that. But you must not call me 'grandmama'—nobody does for I am much too young for that. You may consider it scandalous but I wish to be called by the name Nick gave me—Elsinore."

"How did he happen to call you that?" she asked as Tarn whispered, "I'll leave you two alone to get to know each other," and strode away, leaving the two women to walk back to the summerhouse.

"It was a name he liked. I have no real name, you see. I do not know what my real name is—and dare say I never will. When Nick found me in the forest of Versailles I could not remember my name, so he called me Elsinore. I have no people, no childhood. I was born in my teens." She gave a little laugh. And at Dorinda's puzzled expression, she explained, "I must have been struck down for I came to on a smuggler's ship bound for France with a dying man too badly injured to speak beside me. It was thought my head injury came from my scalp being creased by a bullet, and so it was assumed I was one of the many who were then fleeing the Battle of Sedgemoor. But I had arrived with gold and two horses and it seemed I had traded these for passage on a ship whose captain cared not what cargo he carried so long as it was profitable." She sighed. "And fortunate for me it was that he felt so."

They had reached the summerhouse now and Dorinda had bent down to pick up one of Lady Soft Paws' kittens and exhibit it to this striking newcomer, but now she straightened up as she felt for a moment her baby stirring inside her. She put a hand to her stomach instinctively. She told herself it was that slight gentle motion of what well might be a fifth Dorinda that made what Tarn's stepgrandmother was saying seem suddenly so important to her.

"Did you never learn who the man with you was?" she asked.

The lady with flame hair shot with silver shook her head. "He was handsome and young, and I wept when they put him over the side—for he was buried at sea somewhere in the English Channel. There was an old gentleman who had also bought passage on the smuggler's ship—and he too was grievously injured. He had staggered to the cove, I was told later, not expected to live. But he had gold in his shoes and with it he hired a coach and took us both to Paris and I tended him there till he died."

"But I thought Tarn's grandfather—?"

"Oh, that came later. I met Nick in the forest of Versailles the day after the old gentleman died. We fell in love and he married me. We were in desperate circumstances for we had almost no money. And," she added, sighing, "I had no ancestry. I was not a virgin. Indeed—" she glanced at Dorinda's stomach gaining bulk with her advancing pregnancy—"I knew that I must at some time have borne a child because the nipples of my breasts had turned a dark rose. But Nick took me on faith and we lived precariously until the luck of the dice changed, James was deposed, William of Orange came to England—and we came back to Nick's family estates in England and suddenly I was a Countess! From nothing, we suddenly had everything!"

She paused, for the young woman who sat across from her in the white slatted summerhouse was looking at her very strangely.

"Were you wearing a red silk dress when you reached the ship?" Dorinda demanded. "And had you been riding a bay horse? And was the man with you tall and slender with curly saffron hair?"

The gray eyes across from Dorinda's were blank with astonishment.

"Yes. But how could you know those things? I have not told them to you."

"No," murmured Dorinda. "You did not have to. So *that* is why you never came to Banbury Fair to claim my mother!"

The fine brows opposite her elevated. "To claim— what are you saying, child?"

"I am saying—" Dorinda found herself staring spellbound into the eyes of a woman who with slight alterations could have been herself at her age. She who had passed herself off as the Countess of Ravensay knew she was looking into the face of the real Countess of Ravensay—lost lovely Rinda! "I am saying that I know all about you—who you were, what you did. Oh, Elsinore, you're Rinda—you're my very own grandmother!" She hurled herself into the surprised newcomer's arms. "How wonderful to find you at last!" She hugged the older woman and thought that somewhere where the Great Decisions of the world were made, mighty forces must have been set in motion to arrange this meeting, for here they were after all these years united at last!

There was so much to tell, so much to share that the whole of the afternoon was spent in reminiscing. And Rinda listened raptly to all that was said.

The years had softened her flame-red hair and touched it with silver. But the gray eyes that dared the world were just as bright, the reckless smile as startling as ever.

Rinda had loved the wrong man, had chosen the wrong path and near died for her reckless gallantry. But Fate must have looked down and shed a tear for her and spared her the tragic ending toward which the course of her life had sped like an arrow. Even as her fainting fingers had relaxed their grip on the dying Rory, a kindly providence had sealed off her past and given her, at the height of her youth and beauty, a second chance at happiness.

It had cost her her child, of course. But now—although, smiling at her newfound granddaughter, she did not realize it—her long ago whispered words to the child she had held so briefly in her arms were coming true: *Someday I will hold your daughter in my arms and all of this will have been only a bad dream.*

Only a dream drifting away in the smoke.... A dream long gone and forgotten save by the girl whose blue-green eyes were glowing and bright with tears.

The stories they told each other consumed half the night, for Rinda, who had found a better man and loved him and been lucky after all, was eager to hear about that tragic youthful past from which the veil had so suddenly been ripped away.

And those revelations that came to her that first night on the James would ever make this brave New World that she had found seem to her a magic world and tint her days here with a glory others might never see.

Governor Newbold discovered her of course—and set himself to have her, just as he collected rare gems and beautiful furniture from abroad, to crown his collection. For a while Rinda put him off, but finally she accepted the handsome governor and moved into the Governor's Palace.

For all the scandalous life she had led, no one would have dared to cast aspersions on Dorinda now, even had they dared to before, for not only was she defended by a mighty blade in the form of her handsome husband, the wealthy owner of Haverleigh Plantation, but she was also claimed by the governor's titled lady as her granddaughter!

"We are a very reliable family," Tarn had told Dorinda with a grin on the day of Rinda's arrival, throwing a possessive arm around her shoulders. "The men are attracted to the same sort of woman! And I have me no doubt that if you bear me a son—" he passed a hand lightly over her near-to-bursting bodice—"he will search the world over until he finds himself such a one as you and as my stepgrandmother here!"

"Nonsense," sniffed the lady with hair of silver and flame. "There *are* no others like us, there could never be! Unless of course Dorinda here bears us a Dorinda the Fifth!" And with those words the governor's lady, brave beautiful Rinda who had ridden into hell to save her man and carried him, desperately hurt, away with her to safety, threw her own arm possessively about the fourth Dorinda.

The child when it came, all agreed, was a marvel. And why should she not be? For little Dorinda the

Fifth, born with a silver spoon at Haverleigh and spending nearly half her time in the Governor's Palace, might grow up—Fate being the fickle creature she is—to inherit from her forebears neither goods nor coin, but they would have given her great gifts all the same: She had the glorious face of the London chambermaid who had married an earl, the wicked wit of Lady Polly, the green-gold eyes of Rory the dreamer who had dreamed mad dreams and lost, she had her mother's sunlit hair and the reckless gallantry of Rinda who had ridden into hell for her lover and borne him away with her.

All agreed she was a most fortunate child, for she would inherit not only Haverleigh Plantation and Merryvale, but estates in far off England as well.

"They say children most oft resemble their grandparents—I wonder if she will be like me," murmured Rinda, looking down as she had once long ago at a rainy crossroads, into a small sweet face.

The child gave her back an enigmatic baby smile that charmed all the world.

Rinda kissed her. "Be lucky, be happy," she murmured as a kind of blessing. For surely such a one as this, like Tarn's lovely Dorinda, was born to love—and never born to lose!

> *See we now a golden glow*
> *Winging where the winged things go,*
> *Love enchanted, winning through,*
> *And now a toast—from me to you!*